ALSO BY ROBERT COHEN

The Varieties of Romantic Experience: Stories
Inspired Sleep
The Here and Now
The Organ Builder

AMATEUR BARBARIANS

A NOVEL

ROBERT COHEN

SCRIBNER

New York London Toronto Sydney

SCRIBNER

A Division of Simon & Schuster, Inc.
1230 Avenue of the Americas
New York, NY 10020

First Scribner hardcover edition July 2009

SCRIBNER and design are registered trademarks of The Gale Group, Inc.,
used under license by Simon & Schuster, Inc., the publisher of this work.

For information about special discounts for bulk purchases,
please contact Simon & Schuster Special Sales at 1-866-506-1949
or business@simonandschuster.com.

The Simon & Schuster Speakers Bureau can bring authors to your live event. For more
information or to book an event contact the Simon & Schuster Speakers Bureau
at 1-866-248-3049 or visit our website at www.simonspeakers.com.

Manufactured in the United States of America

1   3   5   7   9   10   8   6   4   2

Library of Congress Control Number: 2009012256

ISBN: 978-0-7432-3036-0
ISBN: 978-1-4391-6511-9 (ebook)

The author wishes to thank the John Simon Guggenheim Memorial Foundation
for their generous support.

Portions of this novel appeared, often in very different form,
in *Virginia Quarterly Review*, *Cincinnati Review*, and *Literary Imagination*.

For Gary Sperling

Let a man go to the bottom of what he *is,* and believe in that.

D. H. LAWRENCE

AMATEUR
BARBARIANS

1

Down Time

Teddy Hastings hopped down from his treadmill after burning off the usual impressive quotas of time, mass, and distance, and reached for his bottle of purified water. If there was one thing he was good at it was running in place. Outside, the woods were dark along Montcalm Road. Sleet, like an animal scrabbling for entry, tapped against the panes.

The water he drained in one gulp. It did not appease his thirst.

To stretch out his tendons he leaned hard against the wall with both hands splayed before him, like a man holding back— or welcoming—a flood. His biceps bulged, his triceps trembled. He was a big, keg-chested man with a long list of aggrievements; even on a good day it took forever to get loose. And this was not a good day. His torso felt dense, congested; his hamstrings were knotted tight. Somewhere in the meat of his abdomen, beneath the pale, softening bulge, a cramp had clenched up like a fist. Older people, Teddy knew, were susceptible to such things, to intermittent attacks of localized pain, and though he didn't like to think of himself as an older person, maybe now that time had come. Fortunately he didn't mind a little pain now and then. In fact he welcomed it, as an employee welcomes a performance review, or a home team welcomes a formidable adversary: because without it nothing would be tested or advanced.

This was why he'd converted the basement that summer, after

his dreary little tussle with the authorities. Why he'd taken up the hammer and power saw, plastered and sanded and paneled the walls, tacked down the carpet, plexiglassed the windows and bolstered the frames. At his age you required some insulation in your life; you couldn't just lie down in the basement and freeze.

Above him the house lay quiet, submissive. He could feel its weight poised atop his shoulders. Yet another dumbbell to lift.

Dutifully, as if in obeisance to some cranky, intemperate god who oversaw his labors, Teddy sank to his knees and began to push himself up by the fingertips, thirty-five times. Then onto his back for thirty-five crunches. Then thirty of each, then twenty-five, then twenty, and so on, descending by increments of five toward zero's rest. It was a simple, satisfying routine, one he'd brought home from his brief incarceration in the Carthage County lockup that summer (along with an orphaned Koran, a whopping case of shingles, and the cell phone numbers of various felons, minor miscreants, and illegal aliens) and now practiced daily on the floor like a penitent. That was how you toned the self, Teddy thought: through torment. You set goals and standards you failed to meet, and you refused to forgive yourself for failing; that was one way you knew you were alive. He imagined there must be other, less arduous ways to know you were alive, ways forgotten or as yet unrevealed. But in the absence of those he'd keep crunching.

A few weeks before, in an effort to enliven the dismal ambience of the basement, he'd taped an enormous nine-color world map, property of the Carthage Union School District, across the corrugated grid of the ceiling. Now with every sit-up he watched the map approach, fall away, then approach again, as if the world from which he'd retreated were exacting revenge, teasing him with immanence, looming into view, then fading, like a pop-up ad on a computer screen. The map itself had seen better days. Its glossy sheen was fading, its arctic circle receding; the blue line of its equator quaked and bulged. Still, it gave him pleasure just to look at the thing, to scan the hot zones, the tropical canopy, the jumbled geometries of the borders, the progression of rolling, mellifluous names. Guyana, Nigeria, Ethiopia, Malaysia. He lay on his back, crunching his way toward them like a galley slave. Somehow he never managed to arrive. His capillaries were popping, his lungs wheezed like an accordion. With two shaking fingers he took his pulse. The skin over his wrist, thick as it was, failed to muffle that monotonous riot, that thunder inside.

The windows were slick with night's black glaze. There was no looking out. But say you looked *in,* Teddy thought. Say you happened by, an exile from sleep, walking your dog in the predawn gloom, and stopped to peer in through the lighted window. What would you see? *A red-faced, wild-haired person heaving for breath on an all-weather carpet, holding his own hand.* Fortunately Teddy Hastings was not outside. He was inside, generating steam and heat, stoking the engines. At his age a man shifts his focus, from the romance of building to the hard facts of maintaining. The building has all been done. Even if the nails are bent or mutilated and nothing is quite level or plumb or square. The building has been done; no room for more unless you tear something down. And he had no desire to tear things down. The hard thing was to keep them aloft. The tearing down came anyway; no need to contribute to *that.* Yet in the end one always did, it seemed.

Outside an engine was idling, some night taxi bound for the airport, waiting for a passenger to emerge from his big house on Montcalm Road. But no: it was only the high school kid who delivered the paper. Teddy listened for the dolorous *thunk* it made, then the tumbling fall down the steps.

Six fifteen. And so the day arrives, swollen with ads, coiled in its plastic bag.

He had nowhere to go. He was officially on leave from the middle school this year, half-pay. He had never taken a leave before, had never wanted one particularly, and now he was beginning to understand why. He wasn't good at it. Because a man can't live in an open field: he needs landmarks, contours, walls and roofs and floors. Once he'd stopped working, the days had become wayward and saggy, out of sync, a chain slipped free of its gears. A rift yawned open between theory and practice, between the capacity for action and its execution. There are people who prefer not to be left to their own devices, people whose own devices have grown rusty and unserviceable from lack of use, and Teddy supposed that was the lesson plan this year: he was one of these people and not the other kind. The knowledge was painful but intriguing. It gave his days the character of a search. Restless, he wandered the empty house, drifting from room to room like a detective making notes for an unsolicited investigation. In the mornings he drank his black, bitter coffee—Danielle had sent the beans all the way from Africa—listened to the radio, swept the wood floors like a charwoman even if no dirt was visible. His lunch he ate at the computer, playing solitaire, smearing the keyboard with oily fingers, splattering the screen with soup. He had never been much of a computer person before but he was becoming one now. He enjoyed solitaire but lacked the patience, and also the motive, to win. Winning ended the game, sent the kings bounding merrily away, and sealed up the window. It was losing that kept you going. It was losing that made you focus, that lured you back in with the promise of a new deal, an unplayed hand . . .

And so the hours passed. He could not remember feeling like this before, so indolent, so jittery, all bottled up like a soda. In the afternoons he'd sit at the old attention-starved Baldwin upright they'd bought years ago, when the girls could still be bullied into lessons, playing the same pieces at approximately the same tempo and level of competence he'd been playing since he was twelve. His Satie meandered, his Bach was a hash; his Chopin lurched and stuttered like a neurotic schoolboy. His heart it so happened was full of musical feelings; there was barely room in that clenched, spasmodic organ for the music and his feelings both. But his ear was bad, his dynamics were stiff, he lacked control and modulation, and he'd never learned to improvise. And now it was too late. He was fifty-two years old. Fifty-*three.* How much change was still possible? At this point he felt condemned to go on repeating the old mistakes, the unlearned lessons, forever, like a player piano scrolling methodically through its uninspired repertoire.

A jet rumbled overhead, going somewhere else. Above him the house slept on, making its night noises: its ticking clocks and groaning shutters, its whistling pipes, its four dormant stories. Sometimes, coming home late from a meeting, Teddy would marvel at the sight of it, vast and chambered, lit up in the darkness like a ship. Whether he was captain or passenger of that ship he no longer knew. More and more he felt like a stowaway.

No man becomes a prophet who was not first a shepherd.

The words were in his head when he'd awoken that morning, marooned in darkness, his body furled up like a flag. It was something he'd read in jail, a line of graffiti scratched into the wall over his cot. Jail, he'd been told, made poets of some men and criminals of others. He wondered what it had made him.

Beside him Gail stirred and sighed, her features wistful in dreams. Her body was a safe harbor just out of reach. He'd have liked to steer into it, take refuge there in her long, sleep-softened neck, the musky warmth, like risen bread, that emanated from her hair . . . but no: at the last moment she shifted her weight, and the mattress sank under her hip, leaving Teddy stranded alone on the far side of the bed. The cold side.

How long he'd lain there unmoving, wrapped in the straitjacket of his own arms, he didn't know. He'd refused to look at the clock. The red glow of its digits was an annoyance. So was the rank, fitful snoring of Bruno at the foot of the bed. Soon the old dog would be sleeping for good, he thought. Wasn't that a terrible thing? Hot mist rose in Teddy's eyes. His nerves felt nibbled down to the cobs. His feet dangled over the edge of the bed, seeking purchase in the invisible. (Older people, he'd read, had trouble sleeping too.) The stubbled topography of the ceiling was like a tote board of his discontents. His job was no longer his job exactly. His friends were no longer his friends exactly. His wife had retreated into her own busy sphere of influence and seemed no longer quite his wife exactly. His daughters, Mimi and Danielle, had abandoned the father-ship altogether—Danny adrift in the third world; Mimi at sea in her own house, eddying listlessly in circles. He groaned. The night seemed boundless, vast, a wilderness he'd never be permitted to leave. For him, as for Bruno, life had narrowed to a waiting game. What was left to happen? *Only the one great thing . . .*

He thought of Philip, in his own hard bed underground. His brother's death from melanoma the year before was like an explosion in space: stunning, weightless, invisible. Poor Philly, he thought, I'll never see him again. And yet in truth he saw Philip all the time. Whenever he closed his eyes, there was Philip's face, that pale bubble, floating untethered across the insides of his lids. Every night he loomed a little closer. Yes, it was almost oppressive at this point, almost tedious, how often he saw Philip. Time to close the door, he thought, on the whole death-of-Philip business. A year in any culture was long enough for mourning. And yet the door was such a warped, flimsy thing; it opened and opened but never closed. What kind of door was that?

It was only October but the leaves were down, the brook behind the house had grown its first skin of ice. Frost scarred the windows. Old apples, pulpy and bruised, lay strewn around the orchards like the aftermath of some stormy debauch. Gail kicked at him under the covers. No one wanted him to sleep.

Finally, as if conceding the battle to a superior force, he'd clicked on the bed lamp and reached for his book.

As a young man Teddy had no time for reading. Books were for the Philips, the moody, passive people who liked to sit alone in a room all day doing nothing. Teddy preferred the active life. No doubt Philip would have preferred the active life too, but he'd never quite mastered it, had been too haughty, too shy, too laid-back, too something. Now of course Philip was dead—*really* alone in a room, *really* doing nothing—and seeing as how he could no longer do much reading at this point, Teddy felt compelled to do it for him.

He was halfway through Thesiger's *Danakil Diary.* It was his sort of book: outward-bound, exploratory. He liked material of an extreme nature. The radical solitude of the desert, the dank resistance of the jungle, the flare and assault of tropical heat. Already that year he'd sailed up the Gambia with Mungo Park, floated down the Nile with James Bruce, crossed the Horn with Richard Burton, galloped the Levant with T. E. Lawrence. Now he'd set out again, with the cool, unflappable Thesiger, through the Abyssinian lowlands and into the Danakil Depression, the harsh, primordial emptiness of Afar.

The harder the way, the more worthwhile the journey: that was the idea.

He felt, like a programmer scanning a hard drive, on the trail of an encoded truth. It had something to do with going far out of your way toward an unknown end, then coming back. Vanishing into a distant, uncharted landscape, half-mad with fatigue, navigating by dead reckoning, starving yourself down to sinew and bone, then returning from the brink of extinction to tell your tale and claim what was yours. That it had become so much easier to imagine the vanishing than the return was, Teddy supposed, a troubling sign, but then he'd never been blessed with much in the way of imagination. He put his trust in firsthand experience, trial by fire. Hence his love for the explorers—the cranks, the misfits, the egotists, the desert solitaries, the hardship freaks. He toted them home from the library in a leather rucksack he'd once intended for his own travels, for smelly, balled-up socks and filthy boxers washed out in some remote youth-hostel sink. So far all it had carried was paper: essays, lesson plans, budgetary requisitions. But that could still change.

As for the books, he piled them up on his nightstand like a miser's currency, breathing their dusts and molds, the powders that escaped from their bindings. Their proximity was both goad and consolation. He felt their judgments bearing down on him as he slept, exonerating him from some crimes and indicting him for others. His job, he thought, was to determine which was which. It was the only job he still had.

Off in the foothills coyotes yipped and snarled, chasing prey.

Gail turned onto her side, hogging the covers, indeed the whole bed, as usual. Of course it was her bed—he'd made it for her as a wedding gift, wrestled it from the trunk of a bur oak he'd toppled with a power saw in the backyard.

"Mother of god," Gail had groaned when he'd presented the bed, "so that's what you've been up to out in the garage. And here I thought you were already tired of me."

"I'll show you how tired I am. Get in."

"The wood's still warm." She blushed prettily in her sleeveless nightgown. They'd been married by then for two years, but so what? The wooing of Gail was an ongoing process. Her childhood had been shorn away early. Her old man's dairy farm had slipped through his fingers; her mom, helpless, abstracted, would put daisies in Gail's lunchbox but forget the food. Teddy's job was to make up for their inattentions. He didn't mind. In his own eyes he'd got lucky; he didn't mind dealing with the infrastructural stuff—the lubing, oiling, and filtering; the ticket-buying and table-reserving; the playdate-arranging and calendar-keeping. These he made his province, while Gail staked out the unassigned territory upstairs. The inner moods, the private fears. So be it. He would deal with the externals. Doing things, fixing things. Making things.

"I hope it's sturdier than it looks." She flopped down onto the varnished platform, waving her limbs like a starfish; she was five foot eight but the bed seemed to swallow her. "What is it, a king or a queen?"

"What difference does it make?"

"If we want to buy a mattress and sheets, we have to know the size."

"Let's call it a king."

"Really? To me it feels more like a queen."

"Fine," he said, "call it a queen." But it wasn't that either. The planks of untreated oak, left too long in the dank garage, had warped over time, thereby throwing off his measurements, altering angles that had possibly, he conceded, been drawn a bit too hastily to begin with; and so the platform had turned out to be not exactly a king and not exactly a queen, but some odd transgendered size of its own. Gail for her part wasn't listening. Already she'd commenced the long glide toward sleep, her soft arms folded like wings, her white legs with their dark, cilialike hairs tucked in behind her rump, cushioning her fall. Teddy stood there watching over her, flushed with tenderness and pride. Okay, it wasn't perfect, but he had built her this enormous, solid, unclassifiable thing with his own hands. And it would last. He came from strong New Hampshire stock, from hale, red-faced men with roping arteries who worked outdoors all winter in the construction trades; for all his mistakes the workmanship was sound. Even now, a quarter century later, he was impressed by how well the bed had contained them, and how long.

Still, there were nights he lay in that bed, tracing a finger over the spines of the books on the nightstand as one might a lover who has turned her back, and wonder about the cost of that containment. Where was the book with *his* name on the binding? Some report was expected of him, of his life on this earth; but where and how to begin, and to whom he should submit this report, and in what format and what length and what language, he didn't know. His adulthood had thus far yielded few adventures. Marriage, children, ten years teaching math at the local middle school and another fourteen trying, as principal, to elevate it from a third-rate institution to a second-rate one. Make a book out of that! He'd never been to the Horn of Africa. Never wandered the deserts or savannas, never lunched on gazelle meat and camel piss under the acacia trees. He'd never even completed his application to the Peace Corps, though it had arrived the week he graduated college, the product of a sudden access of enthusiasm at an informational meeting in the student union. What had held him back? Why had he let that first restless storm pass, and why had it never returned? In the end it had been *Philip* who'd gone off after college, *Philip* who'd flamed out, somewhere in the jungles of Sierra Leone, of the very Peace Corps Teddy had wanted to flame into, *Philip* who'd then gone backpacking across Europe for two or three stoned, meandering years before finally settling, more by accident than design, into grad school in psychology at BU. Well, that was Philip's way. The roundabout way. The passive way. The feckless way. All those incompletes, those borrowed tuitions, those pliant, tragic-looking girlfriends, those abysmal studio apartments in the Combat Zone and the far ungentrified reaches of Jamaica Plain. Meanwhile Teddy the Elder, Teddy the Constant, Teddy the Builder, had stayed put in Carthage to—do what? Attain a secondary credential in mathematics? Buy and fix up this old house? Sit on town council, umpire Little League games at the recreation park, dig up stones in the yard on weekends and compile them into walls? Spend half his life reading about things he'd never do, and the other half doing things he'd never read about? Why? He was not the dead person, lying in a hole in the dirt. He could climb out whenever he liked. He was healthy and strong and cunning as an animal. He'd made principal at thirty-nine, the second youngest in the state. He'd put money away in tech stocks at just the right time. He could go, if he chose, anywhere in the world.

He'd gone somewhere, all right. He'd gone down to the basement. He'd eased from the covers, pulled on his sweats, grabbed his running shoes in one hand and his T-shirt with the other, and slipped out the door like a thief. Gail didn't stir. She was a long, luxurious sleeper; her face, hazy and white, floated in the dark like a lunar nimbus. Envy of her oblivion, and maybe fear of it, sent him off to the basement, through the door, down the twelve wooden steps—he knew each one's whiny, croaking country song by heart—and around the washer and dryer to the back room, where he flicked on the wan, solitary bulb that illumined his little gym.

True, the carpet was ragged, the walls smelled of mildew, and the windows were festooned with enormous drooping cobwebs to which insect husks clung upside down, trembling from invisible drafts. He should have swept them away a long time ago. But if his time in jail had taught Teddy anything, it was that freedom comes in paradoxical forms. One man's arbor was another man's cage.

He stepped on the treadmill and, with the usual mixed feelings of boredom and relief, began to run. The second hand on his watch progressed in jerks. The house was quiet and tense, like the skin of a drum. Hot air swelled his temples; old fillings and tarnished crowns rattled in his jaw. He felt like a zeppelin taking leave of its moorings. The ropes that bound him were brittle and frayed; someday soon he'd snap free. No doubt this was obvious to everyone, Teddy thought, not just the people he knew and loved but other people he didn't know, didn't love, and who did not in all likelihood love him. People such as Judge Tierney, and Zoe Bender, and his many enemies on the school board. Together they had not so much permitted him to take a year's leave—his existing contract was ambiguous on the subject—as insisted in the end that he take it. *For the best good of all concerned.* An admirable phrase, Teddy thought. He'd have liked to know how to distinguish between the best good and all the lesser kinds.

Meanwhile he kept running. It was important to make the most of it, this down time, this underground hour in his underground lair. Because it would not last forever. Soon he'd have to engineer a return. Ascend the stairs, take his place at the family table, and pretend, as all dreamers do, that he wasn't dreaming, that sleep was wakefulness and wakefulness sleep.

But say it *didn't* end, Teddy thought. Say he remained down here, amid the cobwebs and the radon, the dull, gurgling pipes. Say the family man removed himself from the family. Let the noisy model trains of domestic life sit idle, unattended. Lost the check register. Forgot how to separate the whites from the darks. Ignored the crumbly masonry poking through the plaster; the water stains spreading like rain clouds across the perforated ceiling; the recalcitrant furnace; the leaky sump pump; the asbestos sifting from the pipe joints like so much rancid flour. But then ignoring such things wasn't his strength. No wonder he was all in knots. Gail was right: he could let nothing go.

"Look at your hands," she'd told him that morning. "They're all knuckles and fists like a boxer. At night you grind your teeth so loud I hear it in my sleep."

"I've always ground my teeth at night. My old man did too. It's a genetic legacy."

"And then there's that other thing people do at night," she said. "I've almost forgotten what it's called."

Teddy stared at the kitchen window, awash in his own reflection. They were doing the dishes at the time. Her remark hung like steam in the air above the sink. "I thought we agreed," he said. "A transitional period, we decided to call it."

"Not to be a stickler or anything, but when I hear the words *transitional period,* I think of something that ends sooner or later."

"That's my point."

"Sometimes they end badly though, Bear. That's all I'm saying."

He nodded. His breath was short. It was as if he were back downstairs in his little gym, loading one more weight on the bar. Truth too was an exercise, he thought.

"Look," he said, "the cardinals are gone."

"Don't take it personally. They vanish around this time every year. Sunnier climes." She sipped her tea, eyeing him over the steam, then set it in the sink and reached for her yoga bag, a flame-colored thing bedecked with dragons. "What are you doing later? Any plans?"

"None."

She frowned, displeased but unsurprised. It was the expression she fell into every morning, it seemed, when Mimi came down, wearing the sort of thing Mimi wore. "Come with me to class," she said. "It'll do you good. Cleanse the mind."

Teddy nodded and paced, hot-eyed, like a caged panther. He didn't want to cleanse his mind. He preferred it in its natural state: messy, congested. How galling it was to be observed from a wary distance and found guilty of hunger by the very beings he looked to for nourishment. "Maybe next time," he said.

"Suit yourself."

He watched her bustle down the foyer and out the door, the iron knocker bouncing crazily in her wake, like the hand of an unseen visitor. But no one was there. She was always heading off these days, always leaving home early and arriving late. At dinner she'd condescend to sit for half an hour at the table with an expression of preoccupied forbearance, glancing over the mail as she picked at one of his overspiced, labor-intensive meals. Then out the door again: a meeting, a yoga class, a book group, a friend. On weekends she'd pop out of bed, wriggle into one of her sports bras, and go off biking or swimming or running along the side of the road in her orange vest. As if leisure too were an extreme sport. Her limbs had grown sleek and hard. Even their lovemaking of late, on those occasions love was still made, seemed only another workout, a cardiovascular shortcut on the long road to sleep. What was happening to them? It had something to do with time, Teddy thought, time and space: the shrinkage of one and the expansion of the other. Something to do with all these leave-takings and disappearances, with empty rooms, silent phones. If only he didn't hate yoga so much! But the one class he'd attended had not gone well. It was held in the basement of the Unitarian church, the same dingy, blue-carpeted space to which he used to drag his daughters to Sunday school against *their* wills. Now he too submitted to the larger, impersonal force. Women in leotards were poised on their mats, practicing their breathing. Teddy tried his best to attain the positions, the trembling Triangle, the ungainly Warrior, the flaccid Bow from which no arrow would ever be launched, and then those postures that came naturally it seemed to animals alone—the Lion, the Cobra, the Camel, the Upward Facing Dog, the Downward Facing Dog. But he could not hold still. He was left feeling very downward and doglike indeed, and hardly inclined to attend another yoga class should Gail ever happen to invite him again, which now of course she never would.

Earlier that week they'd gone out for his birthday to the Carthage Inn, the place one went for these things. Helplessly Teddy had looked over the menu. It was the same as last time. Nonetheless he'd managed over the course of the evening to consume a salad, a cup of gluey bisque, two sesame rolls, a humongous, fat-marbled shank of lamb, the mashed potatoes and asparagus it came with, and about nine-tenths of the crème brûlée he and Gail had agreed to split in half. His lone act of restraint came at the end, with the pale, bluish nonfat milk he poured stingily into his coffee like a rhetorical gesture. The rest he'd devoured like an animal—sopping up the juices, sucking greedily on the shank bone, furrowing out the marrow with his tongue—while Gail grazed numbly at the top leaves of her spinach salad, then consigned the rest to sleep moldering in the Dumpster. What waste. Maybe if they lived in the city there would be more to do at night and less need to indulge in these enormous, sedentary dinners that dulled the senses. But Gail's law practice was here in Carthage, and she was happy here, or if not happy then at least more or less content with her present level of not-happiness, as opposed to the potential not-happiness of moving somewhere else, which he did not think they ever would. They'd talked about moving for years but had in fact gone nowhere. Arguably the talk itself had become a form of movement, Teddy thought, or else a substitute for it, providing just enough current to keep the raft of the possible afloat. It was hard to know.

And now it was too late. He was fifty-two. Fifty-*three*. The raft had become rickety, precarious; they'd flirted with the possible too long; their credibility was gone. At some point you have to stop thinking about moving, Teddy thought, sliding his gold card out of his wallet, and just live where you are. You ate your meal and drank your wine and tried to wring some enjoyment out of it before the bill came.

"Shoot," Gail said on their way to the car, "I meant to put it on my card."

"It's a joint account. What difference does it make?"

"It makes a difference to me. I wanted to be the one taking you out for a change."

"It doesn't matter," he said.

But in fact it did seem to matter, on some level, and his insistence that it didn't made it matter more, not less. And now, down in the basement, running on his treadmill, he regretted his half of that conversation, and his half of the meal too, which had been more like four-fifths. The lamb was still with him. He could feel it, the carbs and proteins, the sugars and fats, settling sluggishly, like ocean sediment, in the linings of his heart. He'd be working it off for days. Both of his daughters were vegetarians; he was beginning to understand why.

He decided to keep running for another few miles and then see how he felt. The phrase came to him often these days: *see how he felt.* Right now as it happened he felt more or less okay, but he would take care of that.

He programmed the treadmill to its maximum verticality, so that for all intents and purposes he was running straight uphill, climbing a slope he couldn't see toward a summit he couldn't reach. His heart, that petulant child, pounded sullenly at his eardrums. The lungs in his chest rattled like toys. This inner hullabaloo, though alarming, was also the source of a tenuous satisfaction. He had after all bought this machine of his own free will, submitted himself voluntarily to its tedious and complicated punishments. And for what? Good health. The two words were conjoined in his mind like an arranged marriage—sturdy, dutiful, surprisingly effective. Good health, Teddy knew, was an absolute good. Not many things were. He knew this because he'd recently been forced to confront its evil twin, bad health—an incredibly clarifying experience he was eager not to repeat.

Well, he thought, get used to it. From here on life was a numbers game, an actuarial box score. Weight, body fat, heart rate, cholesterol, PSA. Fortunately he had a gift for numbers. But of course there were limits to what the numbers could tell you. Look at Philip: his numbers had been okay too. So had Don Blackburn's, and look at him: a stroke like a bolt from the blue.

Of course in Don's case factors of nature and nurture had to be considered. The man was fifty pounds overweight and did not own so much as a pair of sneakers. Clearly he'd made few of the compromises with age that Teddy himself had made. Don was still a smoker, a drinker, a gorger, a glutton. On bad days he'd blow through his classroom like a nor'easter, bushy-browed, all hot wind and pendulous rumbling, clogging up the aisles with his great mounded belly, his arms tossing around like tree limbs, squalls of saliva issuing from the corners of his mouth. That was what happened to English teachers. They grew indulgent as they aged, arch and capricious and mean. Don had long since lost interest in his lesson plans. He'd stand at the board making jokes the kids didn't understand, improvising fey little couplets of dactylic verse—

Silly Miss Peters has forgotten her binder
If only Miss Cobden had thought to remind her.

He might have been auditioning for one of those fat, burdened fools—Falstaff, Lear, Willy Loman—he was always requisitioning buses and handing out permission slips to take his students to see. Don too was a mess. His face a checkerboard of distress, at once pallid and overripe; his eyes like dry wells sunk deep in his cheeks. He had never seemed all that healthy in the best of times, and it had not been the best of times for Don Blackburn, not in a long while. Now he was into the other times, the worst of times. Now you could feel the furnace of his loneliness roaring in his belly, steaming up the storm windows, pouring through the vents.

Think in terms of forgiving me everything, Don would say in his cups. *God knows I do.*

And Teddy had. Selflessly and tolerantly he'd endured Don's eruptions over the years—the drunken phone calls, the retributive rants, the mawkish apologies—not because selfless, tolerant endurance of other people's moods was one of Teddy's specialties, though it was; not because he and Don were vaguely related by marriage, though they were; not because they'd successfully worked together at the middle school for twenty years now, though they had; or because, like most people, Teddy found both instruction and entertainment in other people's tragedies, though he did—no, he endured them because he genuinely *liked* Don, and feared him, and pitied him, and felt vaguely protective of him, and, though he did not like to dwell on this, vaguely guilty toward him as well. Three years before, after a successful production of *Guys and Dolls,* he'd walked petite, unsmiling Vera Blackburn out to her car and wound up kissing her smack on the mouth. Right there in the parking lot, under the fizzy halo of the sodium lights! Christ alone knew why; he'd only intended to buss her on the cheek. But Vera was so short, and Teddy was so tall, and his big, lumbering weight kept moving downward as if of its own volition, the white lines of the parking grid blurring at his feet, and suddenly Vera's fine dark hair was slipping its braid, her split ends whisking like feathers against his cheek, and it was as if they'd begun to sleepwalk their way through some strange, weightless twilight where everything was permissible and nothing quite mattered. Or was it vice versa? Of course the kiss itself lasted only a moment. And if later Teddy came to regret that kiss for ethical reasons almost as much as he'd enjoyed it at the time for aesthetic ones, on balance he was grateful for it, for the wealth of that deposit in his memory, and for the warm, tangeriney taste of Vera's lips, which remained with him as he sailed home that night in his purring Accord. All the lights were with him. Signs bowed in the wind; mica chips glittered in the sidewalks; the shops and their awnings fell away behind him, folding up like stage flats. As if this social world with its painted signs were only another amateurish set, waiting to be struck. When he got home that night he drank a little bourbon and let Bruno out to do his business, to approach and avoid the invisible fence that ringed the yard; and then he turned off the porch light, put his glass in the sink, and went upstairs to have his way with his own lawful sleeping wife. And that was that. Not long after, Vera Blackburn moved to San Francisco and opened a maternity boutique, ripping a small tear in the social fabric through which the weather poured in on them all.

It was the sort of bad luck Don was famous for. People said you made your own luck and Teddy supposed that was true up to a point—it was why he ran on the treadmill like this every morning—but the point was not as flexible as it used to be. Nothing was, it seemed, when you were fifty-two. Fifty-*three*.

His heart thudded against his ribs. His right knee was showing signs of meniscus fatigue. He felt a surge in the current, a kind of electrical empathy, as if he and the treadmill were old running partners huffing their way home, and not a man alone in an insulated basement with $700 worth of sporting equipment. He gripped the handles hard, holding on. Goddamnit, here was a position he *could* hold: not stillness, but motion; not tranquillity, but noisy, pounding labor. Blind persistence. Putting one foot in front of the other, again and again, while the rubberized mat unfurled beneath him like the flattest, most unvarying of rivers. This he could do. Never mind his recent trials, both medical and legal. Never mind the school board. Never mind that Gail had failed to present him with a birthday present at dinner, and that there was no present from his daughters either, or for that matter no card. So what? He was a grown man, not a greedy and dependent child, mooning after the attention of his loved ones, but a vigorous, determined adult of fifty-two. Fifty-*three* . . .

Finally he'd had enough and flicked off the machine. His towel smelled salty and rank; his shirt clung to his ribs like a second skin. He left it there, rolled up on his chest, like an animal skin half-molted. Water rushed through the pipes overhead. Mimi taking her shower. By the time she was finished the hot water would be depleted, the mirror lost in steam, the bar of Lifebuoy slim as a wafer. What an uphill battle it was, getting yourself clean.

Now he heard Gail's footsteps in the kitchen. The dull whine of the coffee grinder, the ticking of Bruno's paws across the floor. Mimi would be down in a few minutes, wet-haired and irritable, unhappy with her clothes. Gail, looking up from one or another domestic task she seemed increasingly ambivalent about performing, would make a motherly, affectionate joke—or a not-so-motherly, not-so-affectionate joke—after which with astonishing but not unprecedented suddenness Mimi would wind up in tears. There would be slammed drawers, and operatic threats and complaints, and inevitably a portion of breakfast would succumb to gravity and find its way to the floor, where bony old Bruno would trot over to lick it up. That was how it would go. The dog's presence at their feet, his goofy and enduring goodness, would allow for a truce. Then the room would grow still. Then after a while the stillness itself would become a problem, as stillness does. Dad's absence would be remarked upon by both parties, if not resented, if not singled out for blame for pretty much everything that was wrong. Such were the statistical probabilities of the morning. The coffee, the newspaper, the fruit shakes, the fights, the dog, the blame, the toast. The rituals of a household patiently assembling itself. Making its own luck.

Ten more sit-ups, Teddy thought. Because of the lamb.

2

The Very Exquisite Melancholy
of Acting Vice Principal Pierce

The very exquisite melancholy of Acting Vice Principal Pierce was a sight to behold. He was tall and skinny, fair-haired, with a loose, bent-shouldered gait. His smile for all its brightness was easily erased; it slipped off his mouth like a glove. He had no wife. No wife and no children. If you ran into him at the supermarket after school, you'd catch him floating thoughtfully down the immaculate aisles, pushing a cart with almost nothing inside it. Chicken breasts, lettuce, yogurt, and wine. He drove an old, long-finned Dodge with New York plates and a snaking crack in the side window—the scar, it was rumored, of some errant gunshot back in the city. A jealous husband? A drug deal gone bad? Nobody knew. The car's shocks, as if bending to the weight of the driver's secrets, sagged and sighed.

"Hey, Mr. Pierce."

"Hey, how you doin', Mr. P."

"Hey."

Still, Oren Pierce was that rare thing: a vice principal who wasn't an asshole. He was boyish, congenial, good-looking, and all in all, rather easy to avoid. He was rarely to be found in his office. He rarely yelled. He rarely indulged in pointless power plays or random disciplinary actions. When he encountered students in the hallways he rarely asked to see their bathroom passes, and when he did and found them wanting he rarely gave out detentions. He had only been promoted, if a promotion it was, a few months before; he was still finding his way. Every afternoon he stalked the labyrinthine corridors with his clip-on walkie-talkie, a minotaur in black denim, lingering attentively at the doorways of the classrooms, the teachers' lounge, the computer lab, the gleaming gym with its dangling, clustered ropes. His face loomed against the windows, as if looking for something—a way out, a way in, it wasn't clear. Meanwhile he circled the peripheries.

"Hey, Mr. P, I think they're looking for you down at the office."

Oren nodded. The school, or half the school anyway, had been left in his care, a challenge to which he had no choice but rise. Apparently Teddy Hastings had tapped him for the vice principal job last summer, and then gone off on his abrupt sabbatical—gone off, it was said, like a wayward rocket, in a wobbly, flaming spiral—leaving no instructions or navigational instruments behind. Even now, the fallout of Hastings's departure had not yet settled into clarity. The budget, half a dozen curricular issues, and at least one knotty tenure case were still unresolved, and now of course there was the Blackburn fiasco, all of which required some rigorous vetting from Oren and his fellow vice principal, Zoe Bender, with whom he shared power.

It was hardly a fair arrangement. Zoe, with her eighteen years of distinguished service, her hard-won doctorate in moral development, her handsome Eileen Fisher ensembles and officious pageboy haircut, had both the will and the tools to be acting principal; moreover, she had the experience, having stepped into Teddy Hastings's shoes many times in the past, even on some occasions when his feet were still in them. Zoe was a skilled administrator, it must be said. On In Service days she brought in big, flaky homemade pies and left them on the table in the teachers' lounge with a note ("ENJOY!") she never signed, though no one failed to recognize the handwriting. The secretaries adored her. Parents sought her out at concerts. Her office was full of tributes, framed photos, memory books. Why hadn't she been named acting principal? Only a flagrant act of perversity, of reckless, heedless passive-aggression—all qualities for which Teddy Hastings was famous—would seek to deprive her of the title and salary that were rightfully hers. But then Zoe Bender was something of an expert in the field of deprivation. She had made her mark in that area, it was said, a long time before.

As for Oren, he'd made a mark, or a smudge anyway, in a number of areas. That was the problem. His childhood had been a shower of gold. Doting parents, Quaker day schools, piano, chess, a tasteful but lucrative bar mitzvah, summer camps of every kind . . . no comforts were denied him, no deep wounds were lodged. In high school he'd been popular and canny, high-achieving; the girls had favored him with their blessings, his garage band was the best in town. Flying off to college, shooting down the runway in that big, gleaming jet, sunlight sparking giddily off the wings, his eyes had grown moist from the sheer dazzle of his future. But somehow when he got to Stanford, he never quite managed to land. For years he'd skidded from department to department, adding and dropping courses, trying on majors in the same inquisitive and fastidious manner he tried on clothes. Nothing fit. For years he'd been told he was a cool, gifted, creative person. But gifted how? Creative in what way? In his poetry workshop, he specialized in white space. In the painting studio, the old masters he sought to emulate turned their backs on him. He could stretch out a canvas perfectly well; what he could not do was fill one. All through his youth he'd understood, with precocious solemnity, that somewhere just out of view, in the banquet room of his future, an extraordinary meal was being prepared for him alone. Now came the hard part: narrowing his appetites to a single dish. After so much promise, no one actuality proved enough; too much of the world's plenitude was missing. And so he wound up like a lot of his classmates, loitering in cafés, reading poetry and art criticism of a theoretical nature and writing notes in his journal even he couldn't bring himself to reread.

He was good at smoking hash, actually. He was pretty god-damn masterful at that.

The drugs he'd done along the way, that was small, ephemeral stuff mostly, gone up in smoke. His dreams by now had calci-fied; the fine point of his will had frayed. The hash, looking back, had been a holding action, a way of stopping time while the equity of his potential gathered interest. But there was no stopping time. It went ahead and did its thing, whether you were with it or not.

"Hey, Mr. Pierce."

"Hey, how you doin', Mr. Pierce."

For years now he'd been wandering through the desert of his unformed intentions—though he preferred to see it as a quest—following lines in the sand from one hopeful and shimmering vision to the next. Always beginning, then ending, then begin-ning again, a motion in search of a motive, a train in search of a track. Even after his father had died, and his mother began to fail; even after his first love had broken his heart, and he'd ret-ributed for it with his second; even after his various graduate studies in law and film and rabbinical school and social work had come to nought; even after his friends, one by one, had jumped ship, swum to the comforts of shore, and begun to take root in the quotidian terra firma—which always looked like quicksand to him—he'd drifted on, until finally, after a decade of disap-pointment, of keeping all options open not closed ("You like to look over people's shoulders," Sabine told him once, "especially your own"), he'd arrived here, at river's end, where there were practically no options whatsoever.

Well, he supposed it was progress of a sort. The end of his beginnings, his false starts and hopeful embarkations. He had been a luftmensch, an aspirant, too long. Time to burrow in and build himself a life from the ground up.

"Wassup, Mr. Pierce."

These days he defined himself more by what he wasn't than by what he was. He was not a lawyer. Neither was he an artist, a rabbi, an independent filmmaker, a psychiatric social worker. These were his lost boys, the shadow selves he'd failed to become along the way. But perhaps that was being too harsh on himself, Oren thought. Perhaps he'd actually succeeded—succeeded in avoiding these false selves, thereby maintaining his freedom to become the formidable and significant person he was even now in the process of becoming.

"Hey, Mr. Pierce, can I get a late pass?"

"I think Ms. Bender's looking for you, Mr. Pierce."

Whom did they see when they saw him? Someone too different to learn from, or too similar? The mirror still offered, floating in the amber of his irises, the fossilized particles of his youth. Traces of it too were in his excitable cheeks, his high, avid brow, his golden dome of corkscrewed curls. But there were hints of maturity—or was it dissipation?—as well. His face had grown longer. The first white hairs, unnaturally elongated and smooth, had begun to insinuate themselves at his temples. He was no longer the youngest person in the room. He'd turned the corner somehow since his arrival in Carthage. Or perhaps the arrival itself had changed him. He remembered winding around the traffic rotary that cold October evening—broke, gaunt, pleasantly strung out on speed, peering through a windshield fogged with his own breath, looking for the unmarked road that might lead him to Sabine's house, to which of course he had no directions. People in shapeless sweaters stared at him blankly from the crosswalks. What, were you supposed to stop for pedestrians up here, when there were so few of them, and they were dressed so badly? Huddled over the dashboard in his black leather coat, wild-haired and bug-eyed, Oren must have looked like some anarchist or refugee, an outlaw in midflight. And in a sense he was. In flight from a life far too flight-heavy already, and hence in flight on some level from flight itself.

Ah, the frequent flier, his father used to greet him, half admiringly, half not, on the occasional stopover in South Jersey. *How's the air up there anyway?*

Well, now he knew. They both did. The air was thin; it would not sustain weight. Which was why no sooner did he alight in a new city—Seattle, Paris, Prague, Ann Arbor—than he began plotting his departure for the next. And now he'd left New York, which he'd supposed the final stop, in flight from all the venues in which he'd whittled away the last golden shavings of his youth: Columbia Law School (two years), NYU film school (eight months), Hebrew Union College (three months), and the CUNY program in social welfare studies (six months); from all of which he had, depending on whom you asked, either not chosen to graduate (his view) or chosen not to graduate (his therapist's) or made no choice regarding graduation whatsoever (everyone else's). In flight as well from Sabine, and his mother, and from a dozen other once amiable relationships that had ossified or attenuated or somehow gone wrong. In flight from his many haunts and habits, the bars and coffee shops, the movie houses, the hot-dog-and-papaya joints, the washed-out light at Julian's, the narrow underground aisles of the Strand, the spindly, yellow-skinned rotisserie chickens he'd buy at the Korean grocers and pick the wings off with his fingers. Yes, he'd given them all up. To succeed in life, his therapist liked to say, one had to make choices, to say yes to some things and say no to others. That was how the maturity business operated. And everyone agreed Oren needed maturing. Even the people he did not write checks to for $105 an hour agreed on this point.

"Dude, I fell asleep. I forgot it was even *on.*"

The first no was to his therapist. This to show them both he was serious. The second no was to the city itself. The third, renouncing all options to his rent-controlled studio in Alphabet City, was the most fateful no of all. He'd hesitated, down at the Carthage post office, before dropping his notarized letter through the OUT OF TOWN slot. It seemed an irretrievable message. And so it was. Even now he still dreamed of that apartment in all its shitty, claustrophobic glory, the blue-veined bathtub in the kitchen, the galaxy of cracks on the ceiling, the parched aspiring tendrils of the coleus plants, all those webby, intricate designs that had held him in place for five years. Who was living there now? It didn't matter: Oren Pierce was not. That bridge was a cinder. He had a new place now. A new life. New goals.

He'd learned a few things about goal-making since moving to Carthage, had found a strategy of sorts laid out in the administrator's handbook in his office. First you identified your particular need areas, then you reconfigured your systems and procedures to achieve them. The goals had to adhere to certain requirements. They had to be Specific, Measurable, Attainable, Results-oriented, and Time-bound. SMART goals.

"Hey, Mr. P."

"Hey, Mr. Pierce."

"Wassup, Mr. Pierce."

If on close analysis the choice of Carthage was not strictly, or even *loosely,* his own—he'd chosen it because Sabine had scored a job there, and he was in reckless, abject pursuit of her at the time—then he would refrain from close analysis, from any analysis at all. The facts on the ground were simple. He was here. And here he would stay. Because you had to be *some*where, apparently. And if you were going to be somewhere, you couldn't ask for a more congenial, low-impact environment than Carthage, with its cornfields and dairy farms and craft collectives, its postcardlike downtown in which one could buy, if one chose, something like eight different varieties of maple syrup. True, Oren didn't care for maple syrup, or any of the breakfast foods that went with it, pancakes and waffles and so on. But he liked the *idea* of maple syrup, of having a cabinet at home—of having a *home* at home—with maple syrup and all that other heavy, bland American stuff on the shelves, a place where you could either make pancakes and waffles or not, according to your personal preference, as the light streamed through the windows and the birds twittered musically in the trees. And that was what Carthage offered. A healthy grounding in the essentials. Weather, shelter, good light, local foods. A town free of urban pressures and noise, urban intrusions.

So free in fact was his new home of urban pressures and noise and intrusions that it struck Oren on first glance as incredibly boring and unreal, an impression his second and third glances did little to change. The trouble with Carthage, he thought, was that it resembled not so much an actual town as a movie location, a movie about a small, boring, unreal town like Carthage. Oren had worked on such a movie, as it happened, two years back, a dismal independent called *The Unknowables,* directed by his friend Roger Barstow from NYU. Roger was one of those fiery, long-maned, take-no-prisoners young-Turk types, as Roger himself would cheerfully tell you. What he wasn't was a director. Among the crew the film was dubbed *The Unwatchables.* It had some minor success on the film festival circuit, played the Thirteenth Street Quad for a week, then went straight to the back of the video stores. Oren logged no little time in the back of video stores these days himself. Such was the social life of a single man stranded in the provinces.

True, looking back, the decision to follow Sabine up here to Carthage—moody, unreliable Sabine—was itself rather dismal and independent, given Oren's antipathy for small, boring, unreal towns, and also his academic status at the time, a mere three credits short of taking his master's from CUNY, and also of course his romantic status: that Sabine had, to be ruthlessly linear about the chronology, already broken up with him two months before.

"There's this dependency issue," she'd announced the day the job came through, toweling dry her hair after a shower. "Like part of me wants to stay with you and part of me doesn't, and I can't figure out which part is the good, admirable part and which part is the bad, cowardly part."

Oren had stood there nodding both yes and no without ever quite being aware he was nodding at all. Meanwhile he couldn't help but notice that the kimono she'd put on—a glittery purple silk, frantic with doves—was his least favorite article of her clothing, hanging as it did in a weirdly unflattering way, and clashing as it did with her wide hazel eyes, and coming as it did from her previous lover, Jonno, a mixed-media artist who lived next to the matzo factory on Rivington Street. "I vote you stay," he'd said. "That would get my vote."

"I don't know what I'd do if I stayed. I mean, for a living. I've got no gigs lined up for fall."

"What about the New School? They love you there."

"Night courses for lawyers, dilettantes, and lost souls? I've done that, thank you. They pay about, what, a month and a half's rent?"

"Look, I understand," he'd said, putting aside for the moment that they had *met* at one of those night courses for lawyers, dilettantes, and lost souls. And a truly inspiring class it had been too. He'd hated to drop it; though he had, of course, halfway through the semester, not because he was sleeping with the dark, gangly, underfed-looking instructor—that came later—but to better concentrate on finishing up his law courses and beginning what were conceivably in retrospect his somewhat dilettantish film studies at NYU. He was a big one for higher education, all right. "You're overqualified for that, I agree. But there'll be other jobs. Real jobs. In the city."

"I'm not qualified for other jobs. I'm barely qualified for this replacement thing. You know how tight the job market is here. Even Jonno says—"

"Wait, even Jonno says what?"

"Nothing."

"Even Jonno says what?"

"Nothing, okay? Nothing."

"I don't understand how Jonno even *talks*. How can he talk if you don't see him anymore? There's a philosophical level on which I'm pretty sure that can't take place."

"There are other levels too," Sabine said mildly.

"What does that mean?"

"It means we can't all be as philosophical as you are. You have to start somewhere, that's the reality. You can't go from being a part-time flunky to a tenured professor at Yale. There are stages in between."

"Wait, since when do you want to be a tenured professor at Yale?"

"Look, I'm sick of flinching every time the Visa bill comes, okay? I'm not like you, Oren. All this freelancing and insecurity . . . it's not a game for me. I was *born* insecure, okay? I can't do it anymore. I need health benefits. And don't tell me it won't help to apply for jobs and grants on a nice piece of stationery with the Carthage College logo. Don't tell me that won't help."

It was, of course, eminently and practically true: it would help. So persuasive was she on this subject that Oren, by nature something of a dreamer, turned practical himself. That is, he begged. He was thirty years old, and Sabine had been his fourth and most serious romance; how many was a man given that he should surrender now without a battle? No, a fossil fuel like love, quarried from whatever deep, turbulent, and mysterious inner source, was not endlessly renewable: you had to fight to keep it. You had to tough it out, put some troops on the ground, conduct a Gulf War of your own. So Oren drew himself up to his full height and flung wide his arms, as if to show off a fresh new pair of invisible stigmata, and began to repeat more or less every argument his therapist had advanced so expensively over the past two years—about getting on with things, about the slow, winding road to maturity and growth, and the need to take shelter there with another person, and the hard, persistent labor required to build and maintain that shelter, and so on and so forth. Sabine frowned as he spoke. Her expression, which he tried not to observe too closely, was affectionate but distant, even nostalgic, as if she were already on the Hudson train headed north, time's black wheels pounding away, flattening all that was present into the past. So he talked faster.

"Wait," she said, when he was through. "Are you, like, proposing? Is that what's going on here?"

"Am I like proposing what?"

"Because you make it all sound so joyless. And if you're talking about the whole marriage-and-children thing here, if that's what this is about . . ." She paused. "Is that what this is about? Honestly, with you it's hard to tell sometimes."

It hadn't occurred to Oren that he was proposing marriage and children, exactly, but now that the idea had been introduced, it seemed possible he was. What was that line from Kafka he'd copied down so assiduously in his college journal? *There are questions we would never get over if we were not delivered from them by the operations of nature.* He remembered puzzling over the words in his dorm room, sensing in them, at nineteen, some obscure, only vaguely proximate application to his life. Meanwhile his girlfriend at the time, Ravenna Fox, had just gone off to Capitola with Steve Auerbach, her TA in Marxist Theory, a class she'd only taken in the first place because Oren had bullied her into "joining the struggle." Ten minutes in he was tired of the struggle and ready to shop around for another course. But not Ravenna. Not the Emma Goldman of Woodland Hills. "I thought you were so *committed,*" she whispered hotly. In her voice he'd heard a new, merciless sibilance, the hiss of a deflating tire. So long, see you later. Why were women always taking him up with so much fervor, Oren wondered, and then leaving him with so little? Where were the operations of nature that could deliver him from *that*?

Anyway he doubted Kafka could provide much help in these matters. That doomed, dreamy bachelor, what questions was he talking about anyway? Marriage, or death? Did he—did anyone—even know the difference?

"Listen," he said now, "here's the thing—"

"Just answer the question, please."

"I'm trying to, Sabine."

"Well, stop trying."

"That's what I'm *trying* to do, I'm *trying* to stop trying."

She stared at him, or rather through him, watching the tinny, creaking gerbil wheel turn and turn in his head, the poor animal, for all his exertions, never quite reaching a destination.

"Okay, well, look, what if I was? Do you even *want* the whole marriage-and-children thing?"

And now despite herself Sabine's eyes went moist, the dewy green in them ascendant, the hard, nutlike brown crumbling away. She was not so tough as she thought. Who was? At that moment she looked rather frail and drawn, hollow-socketed, chewing on her plump lower lip as was her habit in moments of intensity, whether shuddering in sexual transport or lost in skeptical deliberations. Regretfully, this appeared to be the latter. He watched her recede into herself, her gaze wandering, her arms crossed over her chest like a shield, weighing the package of her doubts at that moment—her parcels of romantic melancholy, her freight of fear regarding aloneness—against a lifetime of disappointments and betrayals. Her parents had met in a deportation camp; her mother had died when she was six. What could he possibly add to the stores of her knowledge when it came to getting on with things?

"Let's wait and see," she'd finally announced, in a tone he recognized from a thousand previous deferrals. "You've got your orals to concentrate on anyway. Let's just wait and see."

So that's what they did. They waited and saw. He waited while Sabine packed up her studio and shipped it north via UPS; he waited while she stalked lower Broadway in search of a down coat and some good thick leather boots; and while she handed the keys to her apartment and her still-valid Metrocard to a twenty-one-year-old Cooper Union student who could not believe her luck; and then, when no time was left for waiting any longer, no time for waiting at all, he saw her go. As she broke their embrace and elbowed open the door of his car, she sobbed, and her eyes filmed over. He saw that too, and God help him, took comfort from it, even as he acknowledged to himself that Sabine cried easily and often, at both life and the movies—sometimes at TV commercials—and so her sobbing now, in what was beginning to feel like a very bad movie indeed, or a hideously extended advertisement for Zoloft or Wellbutrin or Maker's Mark premium whiskey (he imagined the bottle he'd buy, the pleasure it would give him to violate its waxy, blood-red seal), did not seem as meaningful as it might have, nor prevent her from waving for a redcap and vanishing a moment later, swallowed up by the dragon's mouth of Penn Station, the breath of which was flavored as always with a rich, sulfurous scent of hell.

The truth is he was glad she'd gone. He was. Among all the other liberating new developments her absence made possible, he was now free to go ahead and fail his orals in peace. He didn't even try to pass; he merely stared at the feet of the committee members, the droopy socks, the sensible thick-soled shoes, waiting for them to take as much pity on him as he was taking on himself, to release him from the company of high-achieving academics and send him on his way. Surely they recognized a fuckup when they saw one; the condition, especially in grad school, was hardly rare. But no, there was the theater of communal disappointment to be performed first, the leave of absence to be nominally requested and then nominally granted, before he was let out to trudge back across town, under the throbbing gaze of a motionless sun, in search of the by-now-highly-mandatory bottle of Maker's Mark.

Along the way he brooded and sulked. As brooding and sulking was going to be his new vocation for a while, it seemed best to go ahead and get started. Shirtless drunks nodded gravely from the doorway, welcoming him to his new, losing team. The streets, having baked on high all morning, gave off a yeasty summer aroma of old trash, crystallized urine, and scorched turds. The sidewalks were strewn with remaindered books and old LPs and other discarded objects of obsession. He tried to collect a coherent impression of himself from the shards of reflection he glimpsed in other people's sunglasses. The pieces did not come together. His life was a two-legged table with nothing on it. He should never have let her go. He should never have proposed marriage. He should never have waited so long to propose marriage. He should never have moved to New York, or Prague, or Seattle, or Paris. He decided to go on walking and cataloging all the things he should never have done in his life but did anyway, then all the things he should have done in his life and failed to do anyway, until he came to the river. Then, what the hell, maybe he'd throw himself in.

The dust of demolition, sickly and gray, rose from the piers. A few ships were going out but none, Oren could not help but notice, were in any sense coming in. He stood at the rail and looked across the river at the dull geometries of New Jersey. The squat refinery domes and low, hazy cliffs, the tall, spindly condo towers advertising expensive vacancies. Yep: still there.

It seemed more or less redundant to kill himself. So he turned around and trudged home.

A train screamed underground, rattling the grates, belching heat. A limo swished past, carrying off his reflection in the black windows. He watched it sail up the Avenue of the Americas and out of sight.

In Washington Square the dealers with their fine radar approached him hopefully, but he waved them away. He had plenty of drugs at home, and that was fortunate; he had every intention of taking them all.

At the corner of St. Mark's he stopped to buy a soda and drank it down fast, watching people younger than himself go in and out of the tattoo parlor. It was the same cramped and grungy little establishment he'd been walking by twice a day for years, without ever being remotely tempted to go in. He wasn't tempted to go in now either. What was the point? He hated tattoos, hated needles, hated pains and punctures of all kinds. So no, he wasn't even tempted to go in.

That he went in anyway, and his motives for doing so, and the actual story of what transpired in that place over the next forty-five minutes . . . this would come to be shelved, in the branch library of Oren's memory, among the mysteries. All he knew was that when he reemerged, he felt like another person, a person perspiring heavily, a person with dilated pupils and a lighter wallet. As for his left wrist, it appeared to have fallen victim to some nasty, barbarous accident. It quivered down there at the end of his arm, encircled by a lurid tangle of what might have been thorns. The ink was still wet, but then why shouldn't it be? An enormous quantity of blood was mixed in.

Great, he thought: another biblical injunction bites the dust. How many were left to break?

For the next few weeks he lay low, virtually underground in fact, spending long days and nights on the sofa, waiting for the pulpy bruises in his wrist and his heart to recede. Sitting there in his Jockey shorts before the overtaxed air conditioner, watching the dust motes, briefly distinct in the failing light, take the last slow turns of their weary arabesques—his eyes, like his manhood, reddened and chafed, drooped sulkily at half-mast—he tried his best to lose himself in the usual self-pitying diversions, namely smoking pot, drinking whiskey, and watching tragic, meandering movies. It was a kind of depressive trifecta. The nice thing about smoking pot and drinking whiskey and watching tragic, meandering movies, Oren decided, was how well they got along together, how amiably they made room for each other on misery's moldering sofa. It was like being on the receiving end of a really good blow job, say, while also listening to jazz, and also watching a ball game you sort of but didn't particularly care about—and most ball games fell into this category for Oren—in the background. Each strand of the helix enriched your appreciation of the others; moreover, and here was the really crucial point, none of them demanded much from you, or for that matter anything at all, in the way of decisive action. You didn't even have to stand up. Simple reception was enough.

Yes, looking back, he had been on the receiving end of some

really good blow jobs in his life, Oren reflected warmly, and some really good whiskey, and some really good pot, and some really good movies and ball games, and that was important to keep in mind, all the modest but palpable pleasures he'd been granted in the past, distant though they might feel to him now . . . but perhaps in retrospect there had been something a bit passive and unhealthy about them, he thought, something he should consider changing radically about himself, provided of course that change did not preclude any future reception of jazz or whiskey or blow jobs or ball games or movies or pot.

The movie-ish thing to do, obviously, was to go up to Carthage and win the girl back. On the other hand, the reality-ish thing to do was to remain where he was, hanging out in his apartment feeling sorry for himself. The consensus among his friends was that any plans of action he concocted vis-à-vis winning back Sabine would come off as transparently foolish and pathetic, and perhaps legally actionable, in execution. To say nothing of how humiliated he would be if she refused him. Not that there was any shortage of humiliation now.

When she finally called, however, on a wan, cool night in September, her voice on the phone fairly pulsed with sadness. He could feel the effort it cost her, holding back. The quivering pizzicato of the heart's taut strings. Why? He had known she would call. Of course she would call. The lines of possibility could not avoid each other forever—they yearned like all things to converge, to be located, to bend and fold.

"I'm thinking I might come see you sometime," he said, laying down his cards, such as they were, right away. "That is if you're up for it."

He had ample time, in the lengthy and demoralizing silence that followed, to count all the qualifiers in this proposal. Sabine appeared to be counting them too.

"Here's the deal," he announced. "If you don't tell me no, I'm going to go ahead and take that for a yes."

"And if I tell you no?"

"It'll depend on how you say it. I'll have to decide then."

"You're always deciding then," Sabine observed mildly. "Always then, and never now."

"That's not a bad thing. That's actually a good thing. It comes from a very prudent and reasonable aversion to making mistakes." By way of illustration he held up his wrist, brandishing the dark tattoo, a mistake if there ever was one. But of course Sabine could not see his wrist.

"Not making mistakes," she said, "can be a mistake too."

"That's an interesting theory. Can I just say this though? I have no idea what it means."

"I know you don't." She sighed. "It *is* amazingly beautiful up here," she conceded airily, apropos of nothing.

"I know. I was there once, remember? That pretentious little gem I shot with Roger?"

"Roger?" His life and that of his friends, it was fading, fading, from her mind.

"I'm coming up there," he'd said. "I really am."

"How'd the orals go? You never told me."

"They went."

"Oh, well, I've never been able to see you as a therapist. Is that a bad thing to say? I mean, you've got good intentions, don't get me wrong. But you're not all that much of a listener, and you're not much into supporting other people, either."

"Well, neither are you."

"Exactly. Don't you think one of us should be better at it, if we're ever going to be together?"

"If?"

Oren reminded himself that *if* was just a word, and a short word at that; it was important not to make too much of it. No sooner did he get off the phone, however, than he proceeded to make too much of it. He clutched it to his chest, petted and pampered it like a kitten. True, it was a tiny thing, but how much purring, hopeful vitality rested on its paws. How that lean, vulnerable *i* and that sturdy, overhanging *f,* just by getting

37

into bed together, generated a home for themselves at the center of a *life.*

And that was enough, in the end. That one word. That was all it took to cut him loose, propel him off all the sofas he'd been occupying in recent weeks—his therapist's, his friend Sandy's, his own—sublet his apartment, say his good-byes, and soar up the Thruway to Carthage.

Carthage was of course a very pretty New England college town as pretty New England college towns go. Not that Oren had much experience with pretty New England college towns, or for that matter had ever wanted to have it. He'd never fantasized about moving to a pretty New England college town the way he had about such cities as Paris or Prague or Seattle or New York— fantasies that actually *moving* to those cities, living in them awhile, then ditching them for the next, had left oddly unaffected. But that was the point. This tendency of his to yo-yo from one place to another, his gaze forever trolling backward, through nostalgia's beaded curtain, to yet another place he'd just left . . . this failure to live completely in the present, or even *partly* in the present, was the very thing he must change about himself from this moment forward. And he would. Time to stop running around the globe, he thought, chasing a whisper he no longer heard. You'd have thought the only intensity in life came from pursuit, from the space between what was desired and what was attained. And what had he attained at this point? He'd attained nothing.

No, he was through with all that. Through with frequent flying, with romantic fantasies; those fickle gig-lights had lit his runway too long. Time to shut them off. And he would. Just as soon as he'd pulled off this one last flight. One final, fantastical flight, then he'd hang up his wings for good.

It didn't hurt that the rents upstate, after all these years in thronged, fantastical cities, were something of a revelation. Funky old Victorian houses, Sabine had told him, could be rented for a song, and that was an attraction, even if in the end she hadn't rented a funky old Victorian, but a rather prosaic ground-floor flat in the town's one successful subdivision. Anyway, so what? He'd done just what he said: gone up and won Sabine back. It hadn't been so difficult. Shorn of her friends, burdened with academic duties, tumid with nostalgia for the city and what she'd taken to calling "the person formerly known as myself," the poor thing looked, when she opened the door to claim him, as delicate and unguarded as a child. Her nose was swollen red; her front teeth, sallow and uneven, sought purchase on the slope of her lower lip. She stared at him dully, wordlessly. He could hear her breathing, or trying not to breathe, through her mouth. In her eyes the white jelly trembled. He saw hunger there, and perplexity, and something very like amnesia.

"Honey," he'd cooed, "I'm home."

She'd already taken a short step back, into the shadow of her rented hallway. "I've got a cold," she said, putting up her hands like a traffic cop. "Better not get too close."

"Okay." He nodded, all smiles. Admittedly on the list of reunion fantasies he'd compiled in his head on the Thruway, not getting too close ranked low. Still, it was higher than some of the others, like being screamed at or laughed at or finding her in bed with some thick-limbed, ponytailed country person who worked with his hands. "How about inside the house, though, instead of outside. Is that too close?"

"We'll see."

He dropped his duffel bag inside the door and followed her into the foyer, glancing around to see what Sabine had made of the Oren-free life. Not much, from the look of things. The walls were bare, and there was little furniture to speak of, let alone sit on. Indeed, the inside of the house did not seem noticeably more comfortable than the outside.

"All right then," he said, in the high-pitched, unattractive new voice he'd worked up specially, it seemed, for this occasion, "what now?"

"You don't know?"

"Not really, no."

"Look, you're the one who drove up here," she said, wiping her nose with a crumpled paper towel. "I'm figuring you must have some plan."

"That *was* the plan. The driving up. Honestly, that was as far as it went."

"Well, no one ever said you weren't honest."

"I mean, it's not like I had it all worked out in my head, like you'd just open the door and we'd jump into each other's arms and it would all be that simple."

"I'm glad to hear it," she said. "Because that would *really* scare me."

With that she lapsed into thoughtful, conflicted silence, staring down at the fuzzy pink slippers she wore, more or less ironically, in cold weather. Oren was determined to bide his time, to respect her mood for as long as he could and meanwhile to think of something winning and persuasive to say that might liberate them from the drafty silence of the foyer. But he'd just driven two hundred miles without stopping, and a dark, cumulous headache had heaved into view, obscuring for the moment whatever that winning and persuasive thing might be. "A beer might hit the spot though."

"Sorry," she said, "I'm on the wagon."

"That's okay. I've been drinking alone for a while now. I'm getting used to it."

"What I mean is, there's no alcohol in the house. Not a drop."

"I'll settle for coffee then."

"Actually I've gone off that too."

"No problem. It's just that I've been on the road all day and there's this little invisible jackhammer pounding on my eyeballs all of a sudden from behind."

"How about some tea? I've got this great rose-hips tea from the co-op here. Totally organic. You should try it, you'll love it."

"I probably would, if I didn't hate tea so much. Remember?"

"It's really good with honey," she went on blithely. What had they done to her up here? It was as if her brain matter, which was totally organic too, had begun to biodegrade. "They sell this fabulous honey at the farmers' market. It's made out of lavender."

"Wow, that does sound fabulous."

"Good old Oren. The commissar of sardonic remarks. It's not my fault that you're always so unhappy, you know."

Actually, he thought, it is. Anyway he was only teasing. "I was only teasing," he said. "Lighten up."

"I have lightened up. You wouldn't believe how much lightening up I've done lately. Ever since I left—"

"Left me, you mean."

"I was going to say New York."

"But you didn't mean New York. You meant me."

"You don't know what I meant, Oren. How could you? You barely know what *you* mean half the time."

"Admit it. You meant me."

"Fine. You win, okay? I meant you. Does that make you feel better?"

"You bet." Indeed it did; it felt so good to be arguing with Sabine again, engaged in their old combat, that he almost felt he *had* won something. But what had he won? Bile in his throat. Congestion in his heart. Pain in his head. "Listen, I don't suppose you've got any fabulous organic aspirin lying around?"

"No. Honestly, Oren, all this heaviness and fucking around we specialize in, don't you see? It wears down the system. I'm thirty-one years old: I don't have *time* to fuck around. From now on I just want to live close to the ground and do my work."

"How do you live close to the ground, anyway? I've always wondered. What, you get down on all fours?"

She shook her head with what appeared to be genuine sorrow. "And here I was feeling almost happy to see you again."

"Maybe if we sat down with a couple of really strong alcoholic drinks, we could recapture that feeling."

"I told you, I'm off all that stuff. No booze, no drugs, no caffeine, no sugar, no meat, no cheese. You'd be amazed how much energy it gives you, letting it all go."

"It's funny, but it's never given me energy to let things go. If anything it takes it away."

"Maybe you've been letting go of the wrong things," she said.

"What about the furniture? Did you let all that go too?"

"Most of it." She yawned contentedly. "Remember that ratty old plaid sleeper-sofa I inherited from my uncle? I thought, get real, do I actually want to keep sitting on this for another ten years? So I left it out on the lawn the day I moved in. The next day it was gone. Like a bad dream."

"Sometimes even ugly sofas come in handy though. Like when you're really whipped, say, and you need to sit down."

"I may get another one eventually. I'll have to see."

"I don't suppose there's any chance you could get one tonight?"

"Not likely," she said. "C'mon, stop being so crabby. I'll give you the ten-cent tour."

He allowed himself to be led, like any polite acquaintance, through the bare wood foyer to the back of the house. There wasn't a lot to see and he was in no mood to look. But Sabine seemed delighted. "Don't you love it? It's so clean and impersonal; it's like living in a motel. You have no idea how good it feels, coming back here at the end of a long, hard day."

"Yeah." Her enthusiasm for this pared-down life of hers was no longer getting on his nerves; it was jumping on them with both feet.

"Don't get me wrong, I still have my down moods, like anyone else. But it's like there are more hours in the day now. It's liberating. Nobody calls to have coffee or lunch or drops by unannounced to ask for favors. Nobody criticizes me to make himself feel better, or tries to undermine me by making snide remarks, or rolls his eyes when I express perfectly valid sentiments . . ."

Too late, Oren tried to rearrange his features into some approximation of a smile. Who could argue with liberation? It was only the thought of whom she had been liberated from that defeated him. He looked around the kitchen hopelessly. The linoleum was monstrous, and the cabinets were tilted at warped, perilous angles, like a German expressionist film. "I wouldn't mind lying down," he said. "I'm beat."

"Whoops." She winced. "I don't have a spare bed either. We'll have to think about how to do this."

"Sure," he said. "We'll give it some thought."

"Just to warn you, I've been wheezing and hacking a lot at night. It's this damned cold. Or it may be allergies. I've got this tight-ass dean who's always on my case. You wouldn't believe the stress I'm under. I'm not such pleasant company lately, is what I'm trying to say."

"I'm not such pleasant company lately either, believe me."

"Why not?"

"You know why not."

She regarded him for a moment through the narrow gray-green area between her lids. "So, when were you going to tell me about that little eyesore on your wrist?"

"I had the feeling you weren't going to like it much."

"Poor Oren." She frowned, touching the tattoo lightly with her index finger, as if wary of being impaled on its spikes. They would never get married to each other; he was certain of that now. "You didn't go to those butchers on St. Mark's, did you?"

"Now she tells me."

"And you're usually so cautious and uptight about your body. Repressed, even."

"Apparently I've made some progress in that area. I believe I'm what they call in the trade a real weeper."

She shook her head. "God, I can't believe you're here. It's hard for me to digest."

"Me too."

"I'd hate to think this is just about not wanting to be alone. I really would."

"What do you mean, *just?*"

"Come on, Oren. To drive all this way and spring this big surprise . . . it's one thing if you really miss *me*. But what if this whole thing's just because you feel all needy and horny and lost in your life?"

"What do you mean, *just?*" he said.

Nonetheless they did, later that night, enjoy a raucous and productive bout of sexual congress on the cold floor of Sabine's bedroom. This was followed by a lively bipartisan caucus the next morning, before she pedaled off to class on her bike, and then a slower, more deliberate and contentious assembly upon her return. Sabine's soft cry into the seam of the futon—half-surrender, half-misgiving—at 4:16 that afternoon marked the high point of their second term together, give or take. After that it was strictly a lame-duck session. They cooked, they cleaned, they went to crafts fairs and yard sales, attended lectures and movies, had dinner with Sabine's new colleagues and then came home to gossip about them, like any young academic couple. But then in the mornings they'd avoid each other's eyes in the bathroom mirror, the unpacked bags below the sockets, the forking red lines of antagonism that shot out from the pupils like lightning bolts. They were ex-ex-lovers: a double negative. Nothing had been settled; they were only waiting and seeing all over again, listening for some second shoe poised overhead to drop. If she could keep her job another year; if he could *find* a job; if they got along; if the graft of their transplanted affair would take, and grow . . .

But if nothing was settled, they told themselves, then everything was still in the air, still possible, within reach. And indeed, everything was. Including the very worst things.

The low point of their second term together was this: one frigid December weekend, Sabine took the train down to the city alone to consult with her allergist, then returned on Sunday evening to announce that though her allergist had gone home with the flu, which was the bad news, a tenure-track job had opened up at Wesleyan effective immediately—Jonno, remember Jonno? He'd been generous enough to recommend her for it—and her dean here, who'd actually turned out to not be such a tight-ass after all, had agreed to let her out of her present contract with a minimum of fuss, and to hire a friend she'd worked with at the New School to replace her. And wasn't that amazing? Now everything was decided, everything was clear. Sabine would pack up her things at once—it wouldn't take long—move back to the city, and commute to Wesleyan from there. And that was the good news. That was the big break. That was the new plan. The new plan was already in motion, executing itself and everything else in its path: that was what new plans did. Out with the old and in with the new. Yes, that was the good news, all right, and the low point, and the big break, and the new plan, and the second shoe, and the end, the end at last, of waiting and seeing.

The next move, in Oren's view, was a no-brainer: return to the city and lick his wounds. How could he stay in Carthage? What would he do up here, and why would he bother to do it, and with whom? No, it was time to admit defeat, time to crawl back to Alphabet City and relearn the basics, the remedial stuff, the ABCs.

And yet, as the days passed in their weightless, uneventful fashion, an odd thing happened, or rather didn't happen: he stayed right where he was. He'd already spent most of the previous summer licking his wounds down in the city—there was only so clean wounds, it occurred to him, could *get*. Besides, he sort of wanted to stay. This came as something of a surprise to him, and something of a disappointment as well. In town, the people continued to nod at him tolerantly as he slouched past, delivering unto him their stoic, good-fences-make-good-neighbors expressions, and he liked that. He liked these dispensations of casual goodwill, liked the way no one ever stopped to ask him what he did or had he seen that review in the *Times* or what did he think of that screening at the Angelika or that new Alsatian bistro in Red Hook, and all for the simple and miraculous reason that no one cared. Why should they? He was a flatlander, a visitor, a vacant circle on the census. Even he was tempted to overlook himself. *He had no reason to be here, yet here he was.* Striding down the sidewalk, he'd repeat the line to himself like a mantra, not in complaint but in progressive stages of wonder and defiance. *No reason to be here, yet here he was! Here he was!*

And then his savings began to run out, and with them went some of that wonder and defiance, until at last he was forced to dust off one of his old résumés (there were a number of versions to choose from) and find himself a job. Okay, it wasn't a particularly interesting job—filling in for a pregnant social studies teacher at the local middle school—but that was okay, he'd been interesting for years, he almost preferred to do something steady and boring and prosaic at this point, something mindless.

Not that he'd put it in quite those words of course, interviewing in the principal's office. What he'd said was "I've been on the student side of the desk for a long time. I've had some excellent teachers along the way. Now I'd like to try to give something back."

"A noble sentiment," the principal, Teddy Hastings, said mildly, taking a quick look at his vita. "Like what for instance?"

"Whatever I have, I guess."

"Ah." Hastings fixed him with a penetrating stare. He was a broad, thorny, agitated-looking person. His eyebrows were wild. Hairs flew out like notes from the whirled horns of his ears. His cheeks were pitted and flushed; his nose a bright pink bulb in the middle of his face. His forearms were huge slabs of meat, knotty with veins. They strained against the buttons on his shirtsleeves. Fortunately Oren was here for a job interview and not a wrestling match. The guy would break him in two. "Well, I hope you've got a lot then."

"I hope so too."

Hastings's tie, a hideous, mustard-colored thing, dangled

askew as he flipped through the pages of Oren's vita, the length and vagueness of which document appeared to perplex him. A thick shock of hair, gingery white, plunged over the frames of his glasses. He brushed it away reflexively, like a horse swishing off flies.

Oren looked around the office. The ceiling was discolored; the windows were frosted shut. BUILDING A FOUNDATION FOR EXCELLENCE, the school's motto, was emblazoned on butcher paper on the wall. And yet nothing about Teddy Hastings's office—the dented file cabinets, the congested in-box and out-box, the anarchic stacks of memos and letters shucking off the oppressions of their paperweights, the wayward constellations of stains, doodles, and coffee rings on the blotter, whimsically connected by fountain pen, the cheap bookshelves with their faded veneers, bowing under the weight of all those instructor's manuals, state licensing handbooks, and yellowed, inked-up standards like *The Scarlet Letter, Huckleberry Finn,* and *Call of the Wild*—suggested the construction was complete. Off to one side of the desk sat the constituents of the principal's lunch: a pint of milk, a tuna sandwich, a navel orange in a resealable Baggie, and a roll of Tums.

"Well."

Hastings took out a handkerchief and blew his high, beaky nose like a trumpet. Oren fidgeted. A few minutes before, sauntering through the glass doors, webbed with shatterproof wire, and signing in with a flourish at the front desk, he'd have sworn he was the star of this particular movie. But now he wasn't so sure. He smoothed the front of his shirt, which he'd neglected to iron properly that morning, and sat up straight, waiting for the lines on Hastings's forehead, dipping and merging like indices on a chart, to come to a rest.

"Christ," the principal said at last, "you can't tell much, can you, reading these things." His molars, grinding like pistons, gnawed away at a Tums, or perhaps the inside of his cheek. "You could be overqualified, you could be underqualified. For all I know you could be just right. I've given up predicting."

But isn't that your job? Oren wanted to say.

"Just talk to me about this, in your own words." Hastings leaned back in his executive chair, his fingers steepled on his chest, his ankles scissored up on his desk, not so much casually as belligerently, as if daring Oren to peek below the cuffs of his slacks, at the rounded calves with their dense, springy fur. "I'm curious. Why would a young man like you wind up here?"

Oren thought for a moment. "I suppose he'd wind up here for pretty much the same reasons I did."

The principal smiled, or at least his mouth did; his eyes remained steady. On the ledge behind the desk an antique globe tilted sidelong on its axis, its outer regions blurry with dust.

"Okay, look," he said, "I realize my vita isn't the most conventional document—"

"Oh, people always think their vitas are unconventional. And yet so few really are." Hastings yawned good-naturedly. "Though yours is more eclectic, shall we say, than most. It reminds me of a tapas bar I ate at once."

Despite himself Oren was encouraged by this. At least the man knew what a tapas bar was.

"On the other hand, you're young, right? What are you, twenty-eight?"

"Thirty-one."

"Okay, that's young too. It makes sense to take your time, explore your options. Why get trapped in one place prematurely if you can help it?"

"I've been fortunate, it's true. I've had a lot of opportunities, and not too many responsibilities weighing me down. So I've been able to experiment a bit. Take my time."

"It's good to experiment, up to a point. It's how we learn." The bullish intensity of Hastings's stare, an effect of either the lenses he wore or some turbocharged antidepressant, was disconcerting. "You'll find that our students here, they're experimenting too. Trying things out. It's what makes them so challenging to work with."

"Yes, I've always heard that about junior high."

"We call it middle school now."

"Middle school. I'll have to remember that."

"Of course when people say *challenging,*" Hastings observed neutrally, "they don't generally mean 'challenging.' They mean 'horrible,' don't they?"

Oren allowed, with the merest shrug of his shoulders, that perhaps this was generally so.

"Well, it's true," the principal said, "they *can* be horrible. But then so can we, right? The kids mirror back to us our own failings. Take all these terrific new shortcuts we've developed. Standards testing, bloc scheduling, Web-based research. They'll be around for a while and then along will come something newer still. The kids aren't stupid. They see what's going on. Their teachers are way overloaded—they can't fit everything in and also teach critical thinking and writing and also deal with all the state-mandated testing. It's easier to go through the motions. Pass out the old worksheets and get by. No wonder they're so bored. I'd be bored too. Wouldn't you?"

Oren nodded yes, then shook his head no. Having never once been sent to the principal's office as a student, it seemed a regressive development to find himself sitting in one now. On the other hand he hadn't eaten since breakfast and was enduring the latest in a series of migraine headaches, so it might have been that.

"It's not the kids who flatten out," Hastings went on, "it's us. We're lazy, set in our ways, we've stuck with burnout teachers it's impossible to get rid of, and the kids all know it. But they're not as jaded as they want to be; you can still do good work with them if you try." Thoughtfully he examined the orange on his desk, turning it this way and that, as if plotting an incision. "Every brain goes through two major growth spurts, according to the research. One as a baby, the other in middle school. So naturally they're confused at this age. They should be. Their frontal cortexes are going berserk. It's a jungle in there, see? All those half-formed cells, fighting it out for survival. The ones that get stimulated and fed—they grow and prosper. The rest dry up and die. It's a Darwinian process and it never ends. Ever been to a jungle, Oren?"

"No."

"I only ask because of that tattoo on your wrist. What do they call those, tribals, right?"

"I'm not sure what they're called."

"I see them on the kids these days. The design if I'm not mistaken comes from Borneo."

"Does it?" He'd meant to keep his damn wrist covered. But what difference did it make? The world will always unmask your mistakes.

"My daughter tells me these things. They're popular down at the high school, she says, particularly among the basketball players. I assume that's why you got one, because of basketball?"

"No." Now that the salad days of brain growth were officially behind him, there was no reason not to go on and admit, "Actually I'm not sure why. It was just this weird thing I did."

"I only ask because we've got this Wednesday-night pickup game at the municipal center. It's not too bad, if you don't mind playing with a bunch of old hackers. Come on out sometime. We could use a little height."

"That's a nice offer. But I'm afraid I haven't played ball in years."

"Come anyway. Get the blood flowing. Mix it up a little. If you could have, you'd have gone to Borneo, right? That's what you wanted—something new. Something really rough and different. The tattoo was just a shortcut, am I right?"

Oren shrugged. He was beginning to feel he *had* gone to Borneo. Hastings's office felt airless, impenetrable, crowded with knickknacks and orphaned texts and globby misshapen art projects. He no longer cared, if he ever had, whether he got the job or not. Why go back to square one, to the raw Crayola primitivism of childhood?

"Anyway give it some thought," Hastings said briskly, looking at his watch. "The basketball I mean. But the job too. It may not be what you're looking for. I know you've done some TAing, but believe me you'll find this more rigorous. You've got the federal assessment tests to teach to. The state mandates. The parents' expectations. And then of course there's the kids. The thing with the kids is to stay honest. Otherwise they'll shred you to pieces. Don't sell them short. They're still highly adaptable. Whatever they learn at this point, the connections they make— some of those are going to last forever."

"Great," Oren said. "I'm all for adaptability."

"I know." Hastings had begun to tear the skin off the orange in his hand, digging into the flesh with his thick fingers. Juice spritzed in the air. "I can see that from your vita."

Oren flushed. "I don't regret any of those fields I studied. It's just, I'm tired of working on an abstract plane. I want to do something actual for a change. Get down in the trenches."

"Of course the actual can get old."

"I realize that. But so can the other."

Hastings nodded. Suddenly he looked rather glum behind his corrective lenses, as men his age do, Oren thought, when considering how old things get. "Want some of this orange? It's tasty."

"No thanks."

Hastings frowned; apparently this was the wrong answer. In fact the orange did look tasty. Why was Oren withholding himself? He watched the man wolf it down, then toss the rind in the trash. "It's funny, you don't seem like the kind of guy who'd go out and get a tattoo for no reason. It raises the issue of stability."

"Look, if you're worried that I won't stick around, let me assure you: I'm fully prepared to sign a contract for as long as you say. A year. Two years, if you prefer."

"The board will insist on one. For protection."

"I don't need protection."

"Not yours," Hastings said. "Ours. According to Janis Lee, the teacher you'll be replacing, she's coming back next year, baby or no baby. Though I wouldn't be surprised if she didn't. Babies change things, don't they?"

"I wouldn't know."

"Well believe me, they do. Babies, wives, houses. The whole catastrophe, as they say."

Oren laughed. "A little catastrophe," he said, "might be good for some people."

"Maybe so. Anyway listen, bottom line?" Hastings pushed back his chair. "I'd like to say we'll think about your application and get back to you, but frankly we're in real need here, so if you want the job, it's yours."

"Great." In a small way Oren felt disappointed: he'd been hoping for greater resistance, the friction of a formidable challenge. But perhaps that would come later.

"You'll be a long-term sub to start. The certification requirements you'll have to deal with over the summer. There are special arrangements we can make. You'll have some pretty boring dues to pay next year, frankly. That is, if you're still here."

"I've got no other plans."

"Plans change. Take a day or two to think it over. I'll hunt up a copy of this year's curriculum. It won't be hard: it's pretty much the same as last year's. You'll find your worksheets and benchmark goals laid out for you there. A man of your potential should have no problem following along."

Oren nodded. Was he being teased? "I'll do my best."

"And if the actual turns out not to be your speed? What then?"

"I'll adjust my speed," he said.

Not twenty-four hours later, Oren was offered a much better job at the state Historical Society, with a higher salary, greater freedom, and more flexible hours. He turned it down at once. The last thing he wanted was more free and flexible hours. He'd had too many free hours already and spent them too meagerly, too wastefully, too unwisely, too unwell. His faith in freedom was broken; he wanted to be bound by other people's schedules, live the unfree inflexible life, like everyone else. So he said no to the better job, and yes to the duller one, because that, he seemed to recall, was how you went about the maturity business, by saying no to some things and yes to others. The greater the refusal, the fuller the reward. To say no was the key. To say no, and go on saying it, until yes sprang open like a magic door, like a lover's thighs, a parting sea . . .

Nowadays he had it pretty much perfected. Now he awoke each morning in a bed with no partner, in a house with no character, read a paper with no news, consumed a glass of juice with no pulp and a bowl of yogurt with no fat, kissed no one goodbye, spent his mornings addressing students with no interest in a subject with no parameters and for which in any case he had no training, and his afternoons wandering the hallways with no particular purpose, making no plans, no decisions, no mistakes, all in the service of fulfilling his duties as an acting assistant principal in a middle school with no principal.

"Hey, how you doin', Mr. Pierce."

"Hey, Mr. Pierce, they're looking for you in the office."

Strange: for all his expeditions over the years, his peripatetic yo-yoing across the country, Oren had never actually landed in *America* before, never docked, unloaded, and established a colony in the heartland. And now here he was. Enfolded by forests and mountains, in a town with eight churches, one movie theater, four restaurants, one supermarket, and two state-run liquor stores. So much for creature comforts. And yet comfort-seeking creatures flocked up here regardless, to stay at the inns and watch the leaves fall and browse for antiques. And *dis*comfort-seeking creatures too, hikers, hunters, skiers, fly-fishers, kayakers, people practiced in the arts of outdoor extremity, who put on cumbersome clothes and endured painful trials of endurance so as to remember—or was it forget?—what it felt like to be fully alive.

Oren had spent that first year in Carthage wandering up and

down the same five blocks on Main Street, his brain burbling like a fountain with the novelty of it all. Here he was, he'd think, going to the quaint little store, where the pies and the fudge were made in back and the bell over the screen door jingled when he walked in. Here he was driving right up to the quaint little post office to mail a letter, parking in a space with no meter, standing in no line. Here he was depositing his monthly check at the quaint little bank, where the teller, with her teased blond hair and woolly sweater, greeted him by name, as if just by opening an account he'd become personally endeared to her. Here he was, venturing out into the bug-infested woods, cycling on the nonexistent shoulders of winding, treacherous country roads, diving into the bone-cold, shadow-drenched, seemingly bottomless old marble quarry, and then coming home at the end of the day to gaze dreamily at the sunset from an actual Adirondack chair on an actual wraparound porch with a view of, unless he was mistaken, the actual Adirondacks, drinking a glass of dark, sediment-heavy local beer and feeling, if not inner peace, some of the precarious calm of a truce. Around him the creatures were tuning up their instruments. The mournful coo of doves in the driveway, the demented warbling of blackbirds in the locust trees, the phlegmatic bellows of the cows, shackled and stoic in their decrepit stalls, from the dairy farm across the road . . . what a ruckus the world made! You'd think all that noise must have meant something. But what?

True, there were no museums, the restaurants were awful, the movies crap, the bookstore a joke, and the local gene pool, in its doughy, homogenous whiteness, a less than inviting place to swim. But though he regretted the losses he did not regret them entirely. Losses after all were what he'd stayed for. Losses were what he'd hoped to gain.

It was difficult to admit, even to himself, how relieved he was to have slipped free of the city's net. All his life he'd been learning the best things; how good it felt, how weirdly necessary, to learn the other ones. To drink bad coffee, eat abysmal food, see terrible mainstream movies, hear vile, tinny, amateurish music . . . unshackled at last from the surface discriminations, that tyrannical train of knowingness and connoisseurship he'd been riding for years, mistaking scenery for experience along the way. Now other forms of transport would have to be found. Other scenery. Other experience.

"Hey, Mr. Pierce."

"Hey, Mr. Pierce."

His dreams that first year were a frolic through space. They vaulted up from his austere little futon, profuse, fantastic. In his loneliness and displacement he'd felt like a jailhouse philosopher gazing up at the stars. They'd been there all along, of course, but he hadn't seen them—the city's brightness had lain over them like a veil. You had to turn off the power to get a clear view. It was the absence of light, not the presence, that stirred his imagination. The vacancy that must be filled up from the bottom, in a new way.

And then in time the dullness set in. The team meetings. The parent conferences. The "conversations" over lunch in the teachers' lounge, in which he pretended to care who won the seventh-grade basketball game or who had seen what television show the night before. Soon he was no longer quite so enlivened by his new circumstances. For one thing they were no longer new. No longer could it be said that he was in flight from a previous life. From now on he was in flight not from, but to. But to what? And on what wings?

"Dude, my locker won't open."

"I'm like so dead."

"Me too."

Onward he went, down the hallway, past the faculty lounge, the special ed room, the band room. In the language lab kids were hunched in their cubicles, stiffly parroting back the blockish, unwieldy expressions. *Il est quatre heures et demi.* Everywhere he looked he saw the child he had been. The curse of the profession: you were forever being reminded of how for all your travels you had only made a circle.

Like most young men he had sought to build from his yearnings a great tower. But the babble of competing voices in his head had halted construction. Too many days and nights had sifted through his fingers. Unrecoverable.

"*Hola,* Mr. Pierce."

"*Bonjour,* Mr. Pierce."

"*Guten Tag,* Mr. P."

The girls in home ec were baking lemon scones. The smell of rising sugars had taken over the hallway, infiltrated the rooms.

Of course without Sabine he was lonely up here, massively and spectacularly lonely: he'd be the first to concede that. His prospects were limited. Unmarried women his age were few. There weren't many unmarried men his age either. When old friends visited from the city, he'd enjoy a brief boost, but by Sunday some of the novelty would fade, and they'd pack up their strollers and skis and whatever maple products and artisanal cheese they'd bought to boost the local economy and head for the Thruway. *Beautiful place you've got here,* they'd say. *You're lucky you found it.* And yet he sensed their impatience to get out of here already, away from beauty's thin consolations and into something more vital, more dense.

Poor Oren, he imagined them saying to each other on the drive home. *He should get a dog. He's got the space.*

Somehow I can't see Oren with a dog.

We couldn't see him moving way up here either, but he did, didn't he?

For no good reason.

No good reason.

No good reason.

"Ah, just the man I'm looking for."

He'd been standing at the school's back door, gazing out at a sky stretched thin, at a lawn bleached stiff. Already the kids wore ski coats in the morning to wait for the bus, breathing clouds of hoarfrost in the spectral light. Men were stalking the foothills for deer. The woods were full of bleeding creatures caught in unseen traps. You took your life in your hands, Oren thought, just going out.

He turned to face Zoe Bender, bearing down on him in her black knee-length toreador pants and her sensible flat shoes.

"You weren't trying to sneak out the back door, were you, Mr. Pierce? The bell hasn't rung."

"Just checking to see if it's locked."

"Is it?"

"Yes."

"What a relief. Of course," she said, "that door's been locked since 1987. But it never hurts to check."

He smiled. Being as he was more than a little afraid of Zoe Bender had never prevented him from enjoying her company. "Sometimes things come unstuck," he said. "You never know."

"Listen, I need to run over to the hospital. I left a note on your desk."

"Don?"

"Mmm. He may've taken a turn for the worse."

Don Blackburn's now infamous stroke had come midway through his eighth-period Language Arts class. By the time Oren arrived, the children had been hustled out. The overhead projector was on, but the stencil had slipped off; a vacant square of light beamed wanly over the blackboard. Don lay on the floor beside the AV cart. The chalk was still in his hand. His mouth was disarranged but his eyes were calm. He appeared to be waiting for something good to happen. Surely this wasn't it.

"Poor guy," Oren said. "To go down like that. Out of the blue."

"Oh, he's had high blood pressure for years," Zoe said, with the sort of casual good sense that made people think her harsh. "You could see it in his face."

Oren nodded. He'd been looking in Don Blackburn's face off and on for a couple of years now and had failed to see anything.

Its color he'd mistaken for health, its swollen capillaries for pleasure, high spirits.

"I better run," she said, "Gail's alone over there. Can you cover that curriculum meeting after school? It shouldn't go on too long."

Gail? The town was full of people he should have been able to recognize by now and yet rarely did. His attentions had been fixed on himself. He was aware that this was not a good thing, but he was aware of it only vaguely, as he was aware at night of the cold massing at the window. It did not disturb his sleep.

"Go," he said. But by then of course she already had.

3

Wine and Spirits

True, for a while there after Philip died he'd had a pretty rough time. But no life unravels from a single thread. Disaster is always a preexisting condition, a metastasized truth. So it would be wrong to blame Philip for the intrusion of the irrational in his affairs, and for all of what followed, a series of events with no beginning or end.

If he had to pick a middle, however, he supposed he'd choose that night of the Dunns' dinner party, back on Memorial Day weekend.

As usual, he'd stopped off at Cork & Bottle to pick up some wine. Teddy had no particular interest in wine as a subject area, though he enjoyed drinking it of course; nonetheless his approach that evening, running his gaze across the sturdy, square-shouldered Bordeaux, the sloping chardonnays, the various Malbecs and pinots and Syrahs, could only be described as scholarly. He squinted over the labels, reading the fine print, parsing out pedigrees and percentages, getting a feel for the *terroir.* Every bottle seemed its own glass house, a private world of hidden lights, secret fermentations. He could almost hear the earth that had yielded the grapes calling to him through the glass, begging to be released, sprung from its cork.

He was in need of some release himself. All week he'd been up late, losing arguments with various people who irritated him.

First the school board over budget and curricular issues, then his daughter Mimi over dress codes and curfews. This itself was annoying; he was accustomed to getting his way. To sit at the head of a long table, putting forth an agenda, conducting, over baked goods and coffee, a brisk, constructive dialogue—this was Teddy's forte. But lately something had gone awry. Some sag or softness had crept into the hard core of his will. The briskness, the dialogue, and the constructive vibe were gone. He tried to compensate for this by talking way too loud and far too much, but of course that only made things worse. "You've gone out of your tree," Mimi had told him, storming away. "You're losing it completely."

"I hate that expression. *Losing it.* What does it even mean?"

"Forget it. Go away."

The slamming of a teenager's door in a parent's face, though often intended as a provocation, is invariably experienced by that parent as something of a relief. In this case it excused him from the chore of entering Mimi's bedroom to hash things out and seek closure and resolution, as Gail and most of the mothers he knew surely would have. Instead he'd done the fatherly thing, what his own father had done in such moments, and his father's father before him—gone downstairs, turned on the TV, and zoned out. Better that than to listen to any more angry and resentful comments from the women in his life. There were too many angry women in his life, and not enough angry men. With the exception he supposed of himself.

Anyway Mimi was wrong: he wasn't losing it. If anything he was gaining. Gaining weight, accumulating burdens, amassing a hard, briny crust of disinterest over whatever pearls of longing and fear lay cradled inside him. Sometimes when the house grew quiet, and a calm had settled over the domestic battlefields, Teddy would lay down his arms and shields and pick up the remote, flipping to one of the high, distant channels—79, 83, 97—beyond the cable's reach, his head lolling against the cushions like a man swathed in steaming towels, waiting to be shaved clean. And any calls from upstairs or below, any signal wriggling toward him through the waves of tumultuous static, he failed to register or acknowledge. As people do, he imagined, when they've zoned out a little too far for a little too long.

In the end of course he'd chosen the wine the same way he always did: more or less at random and for all the wrong reasons. He liked the label, the logo, the stately antique font. He liked that it was in French, a language he did not speak well, though he often found himself employing it anyway. And then there was the price. Teddy didn't like to think of himself as the sort of man who chose his purchases based on money alone—though he was exactly that sort of man—but the price in this case ($12) appealed at once to his vanity, his thrift, and his sense of modesty. He took the bottle to the register and paid for it in cash. The clerk handed him his change. There was not so much of it as he'd hoped. Then he crumpled the receipt in his pocket and made for the car, where the engine was still running, his wife still leaning against the side window where he'd left her, eyes open but abstracted, her thoughts picking their way fastidiously through some dewy inner forest.

After all his deliberations they were now running late. They drove in silence to the Dunns', listening to the throb and purr of the engine shuddering beneath the hood. They could just as easily have been talking, but they weren't. Teddy had been married long enough to realize that sometimes not talking signified a problem and sometimes it signified more or less the opposite and sometimes it signified nothing much at all. So much depended upon context. A word at breakfast, a missed opportunity in the bedroom, the tenor of a dinnertime sigh.

"How you doing over there?"

She didn't answer. He looked at her, this person beside him, with real wonder and apprehension. Her black hair, threaded with gray, her white neck, her serious mouth, the elliptical blue smudge of her eyes, the milky veil of powder that clung to her cheek. Her long, inward-tapering fingers. Who was she? How *was* she doing? When he put on a piece of music, she invariably asked him to change it. When he cooked a special dinner or recounted some small triumph at work, her appreciation was mild, fleeting. It seemed they had wandered into yet another anteroom in the big house of marriage, a room with faded rugs and unpolished furniture and low-wattage lights. In the middle of sex they'd long for sleep, in the middle of sleep they'd long for sex, and so it came to pass they generally managed not enough of either, but simply—though it did not *feel* simple—lay stranded between, in the purgatorial half-light, while the second hand of the clock, feverishly amplified by silence, ticked and twitched. Sometimes you just had to muddle through on trust. Trust that your marriage was greater than the sum of its parts. Trust that even if you *were* only half-attentive toward each other—even if you held hands less often than you used to, kissed less soulfully than you used to; even if the only new thing about your bodies at this point was how not-new they were; even if the marriage, after twenty-two years, stubbornly refused to stabilize, refused to hold still and refused to change, even if it corseted and withheld as often as it gave and accommodated; even if it never got any easier, only harder, and then harder still—trust that this was what you'd signed up for, more or less. The epic struggle of two lives forced into one.

And theirs was a *good* marriage, Teddy thought. A busy, sexually ongoing affair, with interludes of comfort and laughter that eased the nerves and cajoled the heart to unclench its bloody fist. He didn't even want to think about what a bad marriage was like. Though he often did, of course. Bad marriages were something of a growth industry among his friends. Bad marriages had too *many* interludes of comfort, and of the wrong kind. Comfort became a mistress, an object of guilt and pleasure, a silken, cooing presence who understood how hard you worked, how oppressed you were by the needs of others. And then in time the guilt faded, and there was only the comfort, and the necessity for more of it, for a larger and better appointed comfort zone in which to lounge around by yourself. And your spouse was only a shadow, a dark mirror in another part of the house. And the good marriage was no longer a good marriage. Yes, Teddy had seen it happen. He'd seen it happen to a number of his friends.

"You were out in the yard today," Gail said. "I can always tell. You get all flushed and healthy and purposeful-looking when you work outside."

"Do I?"

"Mmm."

But it hadn't happened to them. He had not abandoned Gail: he loved her more intemperately, depended on her more absolutely than ever. He had wanted a strong-willed woman and he had got one. If she had turned out a bit *too* strong-willed, and if it was on some level baffling and depleting to be married to her all the time, that was hardly Gail's fault; no doubt it was baffling and depleting to be married to *anyone* all the time. That was only the B side of the record. The A side, the money side, was this: this feeling right now, this bottomless proximity, like a reservoir that never emptied, only filled.

His marriage was the triumph of his life. To have already done it, chosen and been chosen, to have made that profound, implausible compact, and out of what? Ephemeral longings, scraps of loneliness and lust, a catalog of insecurities as long as one's arm, and a piece of embossed paper from the state licensing authorities. Miraculous.

"I got a lot done out there."

"Of course you did," she said. "You work yourself like a pack-horse. You're so impatient to get it all done, you wind up going twice as fast as you should."

Then he remembered his irritation that morning when he'd discovered that the work gloves were missing, and the garden hose, hopelessly tangled, was unscrewed at the source, and the hedge clippers were rusty from being left out in the rain. People were often careless about things they didn't care about. And Gail was careless about a lot of things, most of which Teddy *did* care about, and arguably too much. But to bring out his ledger of petty complaints now would invite an argument, so he kept them to himself, the way people do in good marriages, and for all he knew in bad marriages too.

"I picked up a bottle of Grenache," he informed her modestly. "Some new hybrid. Anyway it was on sale."

"You don't need to justify getting a nice wine. It's what people do."

"I know."

"Do you?" Her tone in all fairness was not so much argumentative as absent, preoccupied. She was in one of her lonely planet moods for which he could find no index. "Forgive me. I'm feeling punky tonight. I don't know why."

"Maybe we should have stayed home."

"Interesting how you always say that the very minute before we arrive."

"It's because I always mean it, I guess."

"At home with me and the girls, you're restless and bored, you resist going out, but then if someone—i.e., me—forces you out, you wind up enjoying yourself way more than I do. No offense but it's a little maddening, frankly."

"And here I am thinking it's quirky and endearing."

"I know you do, Bear."

"I mean," he said, "thinking *you* think it's quirky and endearing."

The silence that followed this exchange, like that which preceded it, might have been either charged with meaning or devoid of it—or neither, or both—but there was no time to investigate it now, they were already pulling up to the Dunns' front yard, already at the door, already saying hello, already exchanging pleasantries in the language of that foreign country they still visited occasionally, where other people lived.

*   *   *

Immediately upon entering the house he all but *threw* the bottle of wine at his hostess, Fiona Dunn. Fiona, without bothering to peek inside the bag, handed it off to her husband, Alex, who coolly inspected the label with his usual air of half-concealed superiority and then whisked it off to the kitchen. Where, Teddy reflected dolefully, it would go the way of all wines, sitting around for months in the company of other bottles, probably better ones, brought by other friends, probably better ones, from previous dinner parties that would probably turn out to be better ones too.

In Fiji—where had he read this?—when a warrior comes to your hut for dinner, he brings a fresh corpse along. *It's what people do.* But then Teddy Hastings was no one's idea of a warrior.

Another thing people do, he thought, is attend dinner parties on Saturday evenings when they'd prefer to stay home and watch the basketball play-offs on their enormous flat-screen televisions. Teddy as a rule hated dinner parties. He hated small talk; hated listening to stories about other people's children; hated eating and drinking to excess around other people's tables; hated above all knowing that despite these aversions he'd inevitably wind up doing these things anyway, and enjoying them more than he should. Already tonight he'd knocked down a glass and a half of wine, several generous handfuls of pistachios, and a dozen olives, and they'd only been here ten minutes. You'd have thought he'd starved himself all day when in fact he'd had a late and enormous lunch.

To restrain his rogue appetites he thrust one hand deep into the pocket of his slacks. There it had to content itself fingering his keys and jiggling his change and, just incidentally, brushing up against his penis, which, summoned by friction, began to lift its stupid head, and rise.

A boner! At his age! He didn't know whether to be appalled or relieved.

He waited for someone to notice, to call attention to the bulge in his pants, the swollen contours of his shame. But no one was even looking his way. The house was full of people whom on some level to which Teddy did not quite have access at the moment he recognized to be his dearest friends. And yet they all steered clear. Who wouldn't? For months he'd been like this, moody and erratic, susceptible to sudden panics. Aside from Gail and his daughters, one of whom was in a foreign country and the other might as well have been, and three or four people at school— Carol, his secretary; Jeff Mazza in PE; Renee Daley—he tolerated no one. For a while he'd had hopes for that new hire, Pierce, in the friendship department, had gone so far as to recruit him for the Wild Bunch, his weekly basketball game, but after a few months of intermittent attendance the guy had stopped coming altogether. Unreliable. Anyway he wasn't much of a ballplayer, Pierce. He ran the floor well but he lacked aggressiveness; he never went all out, never drove to the hole or took a charge. Teddy knew the type. Philip too used to hang at the top of the key, biding his time, avoiding contact with the big studs in the paint. Mama's boys. He knew what they were like. That pampered, ironical look. That indolent slouch. That sly, grudging aura of not-yet. That was what came of being the favorite, the darling, the bright, skinny, good-looking one who waits for a clear shot . . .

Yet here was the injustice: Somehow, when he was with such people, Teddy's own best qualities—his force and vigor in the paint, his ability to *do* things and not just think about them, to fix a car, lay a floor, patch a wall—seemed trivial and commonplace even to him. Why? Especially when neither Philip nor, he was willing to bet, Oren Pierce had ever owned so much as a working wrench?

How easy it was, to step back and view this entire evening at the Dunns' through Philip's end of the telescope. In their ordered happiness Philip would find only smugness; in their warmth and vitality he'd see sublimation; in the subjects they spoke of he'd home in on the vanity and the materialism but miss the implied depths, the worries and sorrows that shadowed the words. It was unfair of course, it was ungenerous and reductive, but then there was no arguing with Philip. Philip was dead. Philip was gone.

Philip was exempt; he floated like a thought bubble over the comic strip of the days.

"What's the matter with you tonight?" Gail asked. "You've hardly said hello to anyone."

"Well, no one's said hello to me."

"What are you, four?"

"Actually I was looking for that bottle of wine we brought. Have you seen it? I was hoping for a taste before it disappeared."

She put a hand on his arm. "Maybe you should ease up in the wine-tasting department. Pace yourself."

"I am pacing myself."

"I realize that," she said. "That's what worries me."

Across the street, dogs were barking behind invisible fences. Fringes of twilight hung on the trees. The Bonavidas were pruning their rosebushes, the leaves so green you could not see the thorns. The apple trees were in blossom; brown wasps, sun-dazed, bonged against the screens. Women whisking bare-armed down the sidewalks, the blooms on their cheeks like the flush of love. The sway of their soft, fruit-colored dresses—plum, gooseberry, peach—turned on a sprinkler in Teddy's chest, sent forth a spray of liquid melancholy that was indistinguishable from happiness.

Why ease up, he thought, when easing up was not in his nature? He too had spent the day outdoors, astride his roaring Toro like a general. He'd buzzed down the weeds, pulverized the stalks, decapitated the dandelions. Gail had no idea. Gail was a liberal pacifist; if it were up to her, they'd all just have their way out there, the slugs and the bugs, the deer and woodchucks and rabbits, nibbling down the produce and bounding off to the woods to excrete it. But the garden was no place for pacifism. In the garden it was death first, and then the new life. You had to be a bit of a fascist, had to be vigilant and aggressive: wage war, declare martial law, ban free assembly, deploy chemical weapons, put up fences along the border, and deport the intruders—whatever short-term damage you might cause (he thought of all the harmless spruces he'd dug up, mistaking them for sumacs) along the way. Because nature was capricious; what it gave one day it took back the next. And Teddy should know. Already he'd landed his occupying force. He'd turned over the earth, ripped out the weeds, and flung away the stones. He'd heaped on the manure in huge loamy clods. True, the seeds he'd laid down did not conform exactly to their lines, you could glimpse the occasional veer and swoop. But so what? Soon the first crops would come up regardless—lettuces, herbs, heirloom tomatoes—in the same casual and miraculous way they always did. The Early Girls. To see their green shoots poking greedily, irresistibly through the earth's crust gave him an unnameable pleasure. He felt like a force of nature. A man who plunged his thick, hairy arms into the soil and brought forth the goods.

The stereo was playing old favorites. Talking Heads. The Stones.

"Nobody's eating," he heard Alex complain, across the room.

He turned. His wife was gone. Beside him, in the gurgling depths of the Dunns' aquarium, a solitary fish bumped blindly along the glass, waving his gaudy rainbow-colored fins. Some life, Teddy thought. Swimming circles through your own feces. He himself had always been partial to the bottom dwellers, the pale, bulbous types, the corys and caddises, who didn't mind a little darkness, who carried their houses on their backs to protect them from predators. You couldn't evict a caddis from his house. No way. You had to swallow them both whole.

"I love this cheese," Fiona said. "It's made from sheep's milk. And these spelt crackers. Try some."

Rising on tiptoe, she laid the cracker on his tongue like a Communion wafer. You had to hand it to Fiona: the cheese was superb. So were the olives: puckered, herb-coated, bitter and dark as tea. And the prosciutto shaved so thin it was almost translucent. It would have been easy to make fun of her—Philip would have—but Fiona was so stylish and smart, so immune on so many levels to the criticism of mere mortals (her waist, after three children, still slim as a teenager's), all he could do was admire her. And maybe every so often, right now for instance, fantasize idly about sleeping with her. Even as he acknowledged to himself that she and Alex made a winning pair. They were good at giving parties, at the soft arts of hospitality, the food, the music, the flicker and glow. True, Alex had failed to get tenure at Columbia, the great wound of his life. But at Carthage College he had the whole package: easy schedule, summers and sabbaticals, a wood-floored Victorian with a wraparound porch. And if, like Alex, you rarely *used* that porch, if you instead made something of a fetish of *shooting down to the city* as often as possible, and referred to your colleagues as *criminally dull,* and to your neighbors as *those weird thick-necked people on the other side of the yard,* and to that big house you'd bought and furnished so admirably as *the velvet coop . . .* well, this too seemed part of the package.

Meanwhile in Teddy's view it was a hell of a nice house. The living room with its Tunisian rugs and leather reading chairs seemed more ample and artfully arranged, more lived in, than his. Something about other people's living rooms reminded you how little time you spent in your own. But maybe that was the point of living rooms, he thought: to remind you to live.

Around him his friends spoke of the usual subjects, their children's lives, their parents' deaths. You couldn't blame them. It was an in-between phase.

Of course if Philip were here, Teddy knew what he would say. To Philip, the shining Steinway, the plummy Bokhara, the Mexican weavings, the Balinese puppets, the aboriginal masks, all the primitive tchotchkes brought home from summer travels, would reek of desperation and entitlement, the death throes of a second-rate empire. Hoarding of objects, Philip would say: a classic symptom of depression. Expecting the world to surrender its goods and lie belly-up at your feet like a dog—this was not just arrogance, Philip would say, but pathology. Yes, Philip would say that too. Even the music they were playing would be suspect to Philip. It was one thing, he'd say, to listen to these songs back when they were written; but an entirely other thing now, decades later, the warps, hisses, and cracks of the original vinyl stamped flat by the digital heel, processed and perfected into a small, shining disc. The problem with people like Philip was that they said way too much and did way too little. They were watchers, commentators; they couldn't just relax and enjoy nice stuff for its own sake.

Not that Teddy was so relaxed either, mind you. He was still holding the olive pits in his hand. A bowl should have been set out, but there was no bowl. But there should have been. But there wasn't. Suddenly he was furious. It had to do with the taste of the olives, and the feel of the cold pits in his hand.

"Looking for someone?"

Will Dennis, another member of the Wild Bunch, was examining him thoughtfully, trailing two fingers through his formidable mustache. He was a tall, high-domed pediatrician who worked half days in good weather and spent the other half out on his boat, roaring across the lake. He was going to talk sports, Teddy thought. It was one of their few subjects in common. "How's the thumb? Still jammed?"

"Always."

"Someday it'll heal, you know. Then you'll need a new excuse for that set shot of yours."

"One of these days," Teddy said, "I'll try a new sport. Racquetball maybe."

"What's the point, Ted? You'll wind up playing at the same level eventually. We all do."

Christ, he was surrounded by cynics.

"You should wipe your face, Will. The gazelle's out in the garden. Time to go hunting."

"Say what?"

"It's how the bedouins talk. It means you've got crumbs in your beard. Or mustache in this case."

"Thanks for the tip." Will dabbed his upper lip with a napkin and inspected the results impassively. "And how do the bedouins say people who aren't bedouins shouldn't try to talk like they are?"

"Actually I don't think they have a phrase for that."

"Too bad." Will smiled amiably. On the court too he was unflappable, a solid ball-handler and rebounder, a deadly shot from beyond the arc. Teddy was more of an up-and-downer, a player of droughts and streaks, erratic moves. Of course at their age the goal was just to fling yourself around and sweat out the toxins for a couple of hours without winding up in the hospital, ensnared by rubber tubes. Still, all things being equal, he'd have preferred to be calm and steady on the court, like Will, who wore his two first names easily, like an entitlement to boyishness. "I'm fine by the way, thank you for asking."

Teddy nodded. "Work going well?"

"Booming. Just the asthma and allergy cases alone. It's the environment."

"Yeah, all that filth."

"On the contrary," Will said, "all that cleanliness. All that good plumbing and sanitation and hypoallergenic soap. It's killing us. Immunologically speaking, we've cleaned up the environment way too well. We'd be better off out in the wild, living like barbarians. Out there with the mold and the germs and the animal feces. Our native state."

"Come check out Mimi's room sometime. It might change your mind."

"People don't realize. The body *needs* mess. That's how it keeps itself strong. Otherwise you get all these systemic overreactions to piddly little irritants like pollen. Speaking of which, what's the word from Danny?"

"She's fine." Teddy jiggled the olive pits in his palm, like dice. "Touring around Asia at the moment. She'll be home soon. She has that summer internship, you know, down in the city."

"That'll be nice for you. To have her back."

"Yeah."

Danielle had gone over to China on her junior year abroad. They'd expected her back in April, but she'd changed her return ticket, had needed, she said, a little more time over there to unwind. Unwinding appeared to agree with Danielle—one more Eastern discipline, like tae kwon do or meditation, to be practiced and mastered with her usual bravura intensity. But fine. The girl worked hard; she'd earned some time off. She was a type A, like him; it was her style, her fate, to throw herself into things. This the same plump, curly-haired girl who read *Mr. Popper's Penguins* at age four, who starred in *South Pacific* at age twelve, who brought the house down singing Billie Holiday at the ninth-grade cabaret. "God Bless the Child." So what if "unwinding," from what little information he'd wormed out of Gail, appeared to consist of hanging out on some beach called Haad Yuan, drinking and tanning and sleeping with pretty much any able-bodied boy who flip-flopped past regardless of nationality or religion? That was the energy of globalism: everyone smushed together in the same tent. Haad Yuan! What did it mean—mean about *him*—that he envied her as much as he did? What did it mean that he'd spend half an hour in his office poring over his antique globe, his finger tracing the extremities of the Pacific Rim, trying to locate the source of those two magic words he could not even pronounce?

Teddy too had had his wild times back in college—well, a couple of wild times anyway—but now those times were behind him, back in their day. Now he was that familiar, uninspired thing: a middle-aged man. His eyes in cold weather turned brittle and dry. The hair was vanishing from his calves; dark moles, bumpy and irregular, were spreading across his back. He felt weirdly hardened in some places and tender in others. He'd sleep badly, awake to small confusions of time and space, and stumble into the bathroom to piss, only to find his father's face, pouchy and peevish, glaring back at him in the mirror above the sink. The house needed paint. The cows stood frozen in the fields. Soon they would all sit down to dinner, he and his friends, and enjoy an evening of small, modest rewards. A good meal in your belly. A new joke. The name of a reliable handyman. Somewhere out there, in the gathering dark, he had two comely daughters—lean, long-necked, soft-armed—and just across the room, a beautiful and intelligent wife. A wife with tact and heart and strong values, who read substantial books and made note of their friends' birthdays in her crowded organizer, and whose busy schedule did not prevent her from undertaking pro bono work on behalf of the local Bosnian and Sudanese refugees, and the Mexican campesinos tucked illegally away on dairy farms, and the Jamaican pickers shipped in to work the orchards, and all the other needy, powerless people who'd arrived in their narrow green valley in recent years like messengers from that distant world beyond the mountains; a wife who after all this asked no greater reward for herself than to begin her day by climbing atop her husband and, in the throes of pleasure, arching her back like a pole dancer. Was this not a good enough life? Nice food, comfortable chairs, a snoring dog at the foot of the bed. Fresh flowers laid out in spacious rooms. The level blue heat of marital sex. Around him good friends talking about their children and houses, books they had and hadn't read, and while maybe nothing so brilliant or memorable was being said there would be occasional winning, perceptive remarks, and these were important to register, the smarts and goodwill of unexceptional people living as fully and honorably as their circumstances allowed, cooking meals, making plans, attending meetings, paying taxes, and continuing to love each other despite the fact that *soon enough they'd all be dead.*

"Are you still out here hogging the olives?" Fiona said, lifting her eyebrows. "Come, you beast. It's time for dinner."

Teddy watched them move away into the other room. No one waited for him. Why should they? He was not a child, even if he'd begun to feel like one, and, okay, to act like one too. He stood brooding by the unlit fireplace. Photos of the Dunns' handsome, soccer-playing children, whom he'd always liked, were displayed along the mantel. Danielle had never liked the Dunn kids; she had run with a different crowd. Athletics were not her thing. Not Mimi's either. He could compile a long list of things that were not his daughters' things, and an alarmingly short list of things that were their things. As a rule they'd always tended toward evasiveness on the whole thing question. But then so did he, he supposed. So did their mother. It was what made them tolerant and forgiving of each other. Even if it also made them the opposite of tolerant, the opposite of forgiving.

Suddenly tears were in his eyes. He felt stretched out and brittle, an elastic band that'd lost its shape. Lately it seemed no matter how sunny and serpentine the course of his thoughts, this was where they wound up. This finish line. This shuttered terminal.

Get a grip, he thought. Just because you're dying doesn't mean nothing matters; it means everything does. But he felt as if under a beam; he could not pull away.

They'd stuck Philip in the ground the last day of September. A cold clear morning, the leaves tipped with frost. Teddy had clutched his daughters' hands, watching the jets crisscross over Logan, their vapor trails hanging up there, puffy and white, like a frayed net. "In the midst of life we are in death," the minister had intoned. What the hell, the guy had done his best. Teddy knew what it was like, having to speak on landmark occasions, to preside over the crowd, dress up little threadbare platitudes in togas and garlands. So he admired the minister's professionalism, plugging away at the absolutes while the wind threw around everyone's hair and the stiff dewy grass, recently cut, adhered to their dress shoes, on a day better suited to football or hockey than to the burial of a forty-four-year-old clinical psychologist from Wayland, Massachusetts.

Then of course the others began to step forward to do *their* best. Philip's best friend from college. Philip's mentor from grad school. Philip's neighbor, tennis partner, supervisor, his former patients and protégés . . . all came up to deliver their own special tributes and anecdotes. Teddy's face stiffened like a mask. It seemed the final indignity in a long line of indignities: even now, with the last hour up, the last client gone through the door, poor Philip had to lie there and listen while the parade of moist-eyed narcissists droned on. Now *they* had the answers, and *he* was the one lying down and taking it. The shrink being shrunk. The cool, tough-minded ironist, sentimentalized to mush.

Oh, if only he'd had an ax! He'd have hacked open that pine box, thrown the corpse over his shoulder, and run. But he had no ax. Nothing to smash, nothing to smash with.

"And now perhaps Philip's brother would like to say a few final words?"

Teddy looked around expectantly, waiting like everyone else for the brother in question to step forward. But no one moved.

"Houston," Danielle whispered, "we have a problem."

His mind was an unmarked blackboard; there was no chalk. Worms were writhing in the dirt at his feet. Everything he had was going to be taken from him, he thought.

"Classic," Mimi hissed. "Absolutely classic."

Gail squeezed his hand. Jets roared across the vast, pitiless sky.

"There are of course feelings that resist expression," the minister acknowledged, "just as there are moments in our lives when it does us good to try. For the sake of our loved ones perhaps. If not for ourselves."

"Hear that?" Mimi whispered. "He's talking about you."

"Hush." Gail squeezed his hand.

He did love his wife. He did love his wife so.

"Nothing?" The minister's voice, beneath the FM glaze, took on a cloying pitch. He was pretty pushy for an Episcopalian. "Nothing at all?"

Teddy studied the ground bitterly, waiting to be released. The wind tunneled in his ears. *Nothing's something too,* he thought. He had a terrible impulse to look at his watch. Christ he hated Boston traffic. Hated the whole city—the lousy parking, the overpriced food, the squares that weren't square, all those think tanks and tech labs tucked away smugly on their symmetrical campuses like an alternate universe for PhDs. He remembered his last trip, back in May, stewing in ball-game gridlock on a Sunday afternoon, trying to drive Philip to the cancer center at Dana-Farber. The stuff was in his bones by then. There was only one other patient, a skinny young woman in a flowered scarf, taking chemo in a reclining chair. Her eyes were closed. He'd never seen such stillness, such aloneness. He'd vowed to himself never to forget that young woman, her lunar pallor in that windowless room. But of course he had. He'd forgotten and forgotten and forgotten. He had no idea now if she was alive or dead.

"Well then." The minister beamed decisively, as if in some way relieved. "May God bless you all."

And that was that. The crane whirred and clanked, lowering the coffin by incremental jerks into the hole in the earth. His wife and daughters wept. Big cars swished down the silent lanes. Teddy stood gaping like a child at the excavated space. Only at the last instant, when the box was about to touch bottom, did he turn away.

He went and wandered out among the enormous elms, their dry leaves dropping over him one by one. What was there to say? A man wakes up one day with a spot on his knee, a lesion roughly the size of a penny; a year later he's gone. No amount of Gemzar or Navilbene could deter the cells from growing; no amount of Dilaudid or morphine could relieve the pain. It was tragic of course, but such tragedies were common, inescapable, the rules of a club so inclusive it was hardly a club. And now he had joined this nonclub, or rather Philip had. Teddy remained outside with the others, behind the velvet ropes, gawking and complaining. To what end? One might as well complain about the falling leaves, and the frosted ground, and the snow that would inevitably follow.

No, complaining did no good. Better to shut up and *do* things. Better to live in the present and speak with your body, as the animals do. The Hastings men were good at that. Even Philip, the brainy one, the sensitive, psychological one—okay, maybe he wasn't much of a doer, but he had never been a complainer either. Until the end. At the end, he'd complained plenty.

And Teddy? The best you could say was that he was in a period of flux, oscillating between action and complaint. Not that anyone these days seemed eager to say the best of him.

For a while there after the funeral he'd consorted with grief like an alcoholic friend. There were dark, sloppy nights in underground rooms. There were bitter memories and dismal confessions and awkward meandering interludes of silence. But in the end grief had proved a disappointing companion. In the end grief had little to say that was new or interesting, and what it did say was numbingly repetitive, self-absorbed. Grief just sat there, sodden and grieving, taking up space. Teddy was glad to be rid of it.

True, he still cried a lot for no reason, and behaved erratically with friends. True, the human touch still eluded him. But he knew it would return soon, whether he wanted it to or not. Meanwhile Philip had left behind, back in Wayland, a six-year-old daughter, a ten-year-old son, and a forty-year-old widow, Sonya, who also cried a lot presumably, though on their own time. On the phone with Uncle Teddy they were perky and forbearing, as if sparing him their sadness, or hoarding it to themselves. Come to think of it, the only time he'd seen the little girl, Olivia, let fly with tears was at the catered lunch after the funeral, when she'd lost her favorite doll.

"Oh, I'm sure she's not really lost," he'd said, sitting in her father's chair, across from her father's wife, with a tiny plate of salmon on his lap from which he was laboriously picking the bones. "She'll turn up, you'll see. Know how I know?"

Grudgingly, the girl shook her head.

"It so happens I got a letter from her just the other day. What did you say her name was again?"

"Marguerite."

"That's what I thought. Yes, it was from her all right. Marguerite. She wrote to say that she was on vacation somewhere really nice, but planned to come home very soon."

"Show me," Olivia demanded unpleasantly. Her default mode, like her mother's, was hardness, assertion. No doubt this would prove useful in the days ahead. "I want to see."

"I'd love to show you, cookie. If I only had it with me."

"Where is it?"

"Why, it's on my desk back home, of course, with all my other important letters. Tell you what." He ignored the disapproving looks he was getting from Sonya, who'd never been one for fantastical thinking. "I'm going home tomorrow. How about if I forward the letter to you when I get back? Would that be okay?"

The tight line of the girl's mouth appeared to weaken. "I don't think dolls even *write* letters," she said.

"Sure they do." Had he ever sent that letter? he wondered now. He'd been preoccupied at the time with his own grief and his own children and had failed to stay as close to Philip's as he'd intended. Still, it wasn't too late. *Dear Olivia,* he'd write the girl later, when he got home, *I'm so sorry if my little vacation made you sad. I didn't mean to go away for so long. But I'll let you in on a little secret: sometimes even a doll gets tired of living in the same house all the time. The truth is, Olivia, even plastic people get worn-out sometimes, and feel the need for a break. But let's talk about all this when we're together again. Which I hope will be very soon . . .*

"I'm coming," he announced, to whoever might still be looking for him.

Making his way through the kitchen, he found the Dunns' cat, a pendulous tabby, squinting up at him through vertical pupils from his seat by the cellar door. Teddy was not a cat person per se—given a choice, he preferred engagement and affection from the animal world; for silent self-sufficiency and languid indifference he had his daughters, he had his wife—but the wine he'd drunk and the imminence of food made him tender, expansive. He ran his palm over the fur, the scruffy neck, the bony brow, the moist rubbery seam on one ear, the scar of an old wound. The cat rose to his touch, arching and shuddering with a deep, languid pleasure, purring like a generator fed by some delirious current. Then, almost as an afterthought, the malicious little fucker reared around and bit him.

True, it wasn't a proper bite, in that the skin, as Gail would point out later, wasn't punctured. There was no blood and no pain. Only a vague, dreamy numbness, a sensation of distance. He recalled Livingstone's account of being mauled by a lion: *Like a patient watching his own surgery under chloroform.* Not that this puny creature bore even the most vestigial and attenuated resemblance to a lion.

Still, all through dinner and dessert, his arm retained the impression of the animal's fangs. Teddy waved it around, brandishing the marks like a license.

"Wait, do cats even have fangs?" Will asked. "I thought they were teeth."

"Only until they sink into your skin. Then they become fangs."

"How strange," Fiona Dunn said. "He's never done that before." Her tone was musing, almost suspicious. Fiona was Gail's partner, a specialist in property and divorce, sinewy and brittle and shrewd. Like all lawyers she was inclined to seek out precedents. "I can't think of a single time."

"Well, great," Teddy said, "now that will be easy."

"There's not even any blood," Gail observed. She sounded almost disappointed.

"I doubt poor old Rex is capable of drawing blood," Alex said. "He's, what, fifteen years old? He can hardly get down the stairs."

"I've got news for you," Teddy said. "Old Rex is healthier than you think. He's got the jaws of a lion."

"I think you've made your point," Gail said.

"Poor baby." Fiona held up the wine bottle. "Will this help?"

"God, yes." The problem with other people's pain, Teddy reflected wistfully, was that it was fundamentally boring, like other people's dreams. There was no way to convey it that would make it feel real. "Pour away. Is that the wine I brought?"

"I have no idea. Was yours red or white?"

"Never mind."

"I can't drink red wine," Carol Dennis put in. "It gives me headaches."

"Me too," Gail said.

"We have to finish this bottle," said Alex. "It's no good having leftover wine. The damn cork never goes back in."

"That's why I like screwtops," Will said.

"Oh, you're hopeless," Carol said in an odd, high-pitched voice. "You haven't the *mistiest* notion of civilization."

"That's from this old movie we just saw," Will explained. "What was the name of that thing, hon?"

"Search me."

"This big industrialist, he retires early and goes off to Europe. But his wife keeps stepping out on him with younger men . . ."

"Dodsworth," Alex said, between yawns.

Will glared at him.

"C'mon, it's a classic."

Teddy pushed back his chair. *"Now* where are you going?" Gail asked.

"Be right back."

She nodded, unsurprised. He was known for his turbulent stomach.

Going through the kitchen, he saw all the corn husks, the squeezed-out limes, the congealing oil rings and moldering cheese. It was an occasion for wonder, how so few people, in the satisfaction of such prosaic appetites, could leave so much detritus behind.

And lo, in the Dunns' burgundy-colored bathroom, the intrepid explorer was rewarded for going forth. For there, in a brief but thorough survey of the medicine cabinet, he discovered the bottle of Percocet left over from Alex's hernia operation the previous March.

He swallowed two pills down dry, then sat on the toilet leafing through magazines, waiting for something good to happen. It took a while. The scent of potpourri, of stiffened petals and spiced herbs, filled the room. Down the hall he could hear Gail's low, confiding voice, ". . . the eternal husband. Every night in bed. You wouldn't believe how good it is . . ."

Sometimes his love for his wife and the need to distance himself from the sound of her voice occupied roughly the same space in Teddy's chest. He was not, he knew, the eternal husband; it was the name of a book by Dostoyevsky. With books as with legal cases, Gail preferred the strays. The minor ones, the difficult ones, the foreigners, the underdogs, the overlooked. Between her books and his you could hardly move around the bedroom at this point. But then books and marriages were well suited to each other, Teddy thought. Both were middle-class adventures: they conspired to keep you at home, sitting still, being good. Meanwhile the mind went sneaking off under cover of darkness, traveling the world, kissing strangers in parking lots, suffering torments and temptations no one could see.

It was what Philip used to call an unfunny paradox. After two decades as a therapist in Boston, Philip knew a lot about paradox. But Philip was dead. That was a paradox too.

Meanwhile Teddy could still hear her voice, that distant, cellolike murmur, going on about that goddamned book. No one interrupted her. Why would they? She was known as a woman of mercurial enthusiasms; it was part of her charm. The way her face in company opened suddenly like a flower, inviting you to gaze, just for a moment, at the pollinated brightness inside. Men were always trying to figure her out, wondering if she were brilliant in a way they failed to apprehend. True, she was no longer beautiful: her ankles were thick, her breasts had fallen, her round expressive face gone webby with lines. But she had a loveliness, an aura, sidelong and intermittent, like the thrum of a hummingbird; it brushed against you and was gone. Teddy liked to think of her as the kind of woman other men went home and thought about while they lay with their wives. Even he thought about her that way sometimes, a woman he'd spied across the room at a party, all slender and bright. Did everyone think such thoughts about his spouse? Or was it only people like him thinking them about people like her, people who seem always to be thinking about something else?

"I've always preferred the friend of the family," Alex was saying.

"Who wouldn't?" Fiona said.

The weight of the cell phone in Teddy's pocket was like a stone. He took it out and frowned at the blank window. It was like trying to read a broken compass.

He wished his daughters were around. For each other, if not for him. They were sisters; no matter how old they grew or how badly they got along or how widely they traveled, a few slimy fragments of the original eggshell would cling to their backs. You carried them with you, the whole cast of characters. And yourself too, he thought. Yourself too.

Personally he'd have liked to be free of him by now, that fat, angry kid who still shadowed his days, bouncing tennis balls off the ceilings, grabbing the biggest brownies on the plate, pitching fits over slights. Impossible to satisfy that kid. Always wanting and demanding. Forever getting banished from the dinner table, sent upstairs to sulk like Achilles amid the disorder of his room. *Crybaby,* the old man would yell after him, *what are you even* crying *about, crybaby? What now? Do you even know?*

At least Philip, like Jacob to his blundering Esau, had learned to avoid trouble, to be subtle and contained. While Teddy got sent home from school for talking back to teachers, and thrown out of the Indian Guides for errant marksmanship with arrows, and grounded for lighting up Marlboros in the basement, Philip went on quietly earning A's, leading his Cub Scout troop to distinction, playing first trumpet in the marching band, and smoking good Colombian grass all through high school in his immaculate bedroom. Yes, Philip had learned to fly under the radar. Teddy had taken longer to wise up.

Sometimes he wondered if he'd wised up too well. The crybaby had been banished from the table for good. But who was left? He felt his adult will, his rage for order and peace, hardening around him, constricting his bones like a cast.

"You think you're unique?" Philip would taunt—a real Hastings tradition, taunting the firstborn—when he aired such complaints. "You think you of all people should be spared the terrible fate?"

"Of getting old you mean?"

"Of becoming yourself. Your one and only self."

"See, that's the thing, Philip. One's not enough."

"Good. Glad to hear it. 'Cause it's people like you who keep me in business. Thousands of dollars in my pocket every month because one's not enough, Philip, I want to be more fulfilled, Philip. It never ends," he said. "The single ones want a spouse. The childless ones want kids. The ones with kids are so overinvolved they've forgotten how to be adults. Somewhere between the nursery and sickroom they got themselves lost. Now they want to know why. They want more meaning. More direction."

"So what do you tell them?"

"I tell them to get loster."

"What kind of a shrink are you? People come to you because they're in pain, and here you're telling them to go off and make things worse."

"Exactly," Philip said. "Not that I'm anyone to talk. My idea of a big adventure these days is to take off in the middle of the day and go see a matinee down at Coolidge Corner. Some long, depressing, highbrow stuff in Danish or Farsi. I like to sit in the back row and fantasize how maybe that mysterious young

Japanese woman across the aisle will come put her tongue in my mouth."

"Jesus, Philip." Of course the Carthage Twin did not play afternoon movies in any language. "I don't have time for that shit."

"So come up with something better. You're more resourceful than I am anyway. Your problem is you don't know it. Somehow you've decided I'm the existentialist and you're the nice selfless responsible citizen. That's what's killing you."

"But it's true. You *are* selfish. I *am* more responsible."

"No offense, Ted, but I liked you better when you were running around the woods like an Indian shooting off those plastic arrows of yours. You used to beat me up for snoring at night, remember? Of course it was you that snored, but that's okay, I didn't mind. At least it was the real, genuine, aggressive you. Now you're Mr. Goody Good, Mr. School Principal, Mr. Town Selectman, and what do you do? You beat yourself up. You call that progress? You think it makes dear old mom and dad, down in their graves, approve of you now? I bet you don't even jerk off anymore, do you?"

"That's a bet you'd lose, Bro."

"Yeah, but how guilty do you feel after?"

Now, whether as a tribute to his late brother or as an insult to himself, or because he could think of no better way to pass so much time slumped on the toilet, Teddy went ahead and jerked off—a desultory little self-encounter that took all of two minutes and ended unsatisfactorily. He stood, hollow and light-headed, and zipped up his pants. The water in the toilet was pink for some reason. Away it went. Away the pale, gluey semen, spiraling and formless; he washed his hands of it completely. Back in the dining room, voices were rising in laughter. How long had he been gone? He turned off the light and followed the sound down the corridor to its source. It was like following a rope out of a cave.

"It's this Israeli boy," Gail was saying when he got back to the table. "Gabi. He just got out of the army. He's on his way to Africa, she says."

"Who?" Teddy asked.

"Nobody." A membrane flicked over her eyes like a curtain. "Someone you don't know."

"Speaking of Africa," Alex said, "I hear the Lions Club's going this summer. There's an article in the *Courier.* They're going to build a school."

"A worthy endeavor," Fiona said drily.

"Don't you find it offensive," said Carol, "the way we talk about Africa like it's all one place? It's got like forty different countries in it."

"Fifty-six," Fiona said. "Jeremy did a report."

"Wait, the Lions?" Will said. "Are those the guys with the party hats who drive those wacky little cars in parades?"

"Those are the Shriners," Fiona said. "And they're called fezzes."

"Maybe I should volunteer," Teddy said. "I could use a new project."

"You've already built a school," Gail reminded him. "You've been building that school for twenty-five years."

"This would be literally though. Hammers and bricks. Rebar."

"I don't see the difference," she said.

"My sister went to Guatemala last year," Carol said, "with this Habitat group from Oregon? They built a whole house."

"Don't forget that environmental studies person she met down there," Will said. "Ethan something."

"I told you, they didn't have sex. They just fell asleep in the same bed."

"Uh-huh."

"I've always dreamed of sleeping with an environmental studies person." Alex was playing with a bit of candle wax, rubbing it into a ball. "Out under the canopy, with all the flora and the fauna."

Fiona smiled coolly, flexing a bone in her wrist.

"It's funny," Carol said, "the trip only lasted a week. But she talks about it like it was the most intense experience she ever had. She almost didn't come back, she said."

"That's not funny," her husband said, "it's sad. One week in the third world, she hammers some nails in a board, sleeps with a man she doesn't know, and that's how she makes a difference?"

"You're right," Carol said. "Absolutely. It's a lot better sitting around watching old movies on TV."

"Why didn't she stay?" Teddy asked.

"There was a sale at Filene's!" Will cried. "What do you mean, why didn't she stay? This is her *sister* we're talking about. The woman lives on sushi and lattes. She's got a four-hundred-thousand-dollar house in Portland with radiant heating and cathedral ceilings. Also, I might add, a husband and two kids. How long do you think she'd last down there on her own, going off to the outhouse after another meal of plantains and curried goat?"

"So I take it you're not signing up for this Africa thing then," Alex said.

"Sue me. I'm a nonconformist. You all go ahead. I'll tend the home fires."

"I don't know," said Carol vaguely, stubbornly. For all her mildness of manner, you could see how she could wear a man out. "There was something in her face when she got off the plane. I don't know what to call it. She hardly knew who I was."

Teddy looked up from his plate. "I'm trying to remember the last time I had an intense experience."

"How about sex with your wife," Gail suggested. "Or doesn't that one time count?"

She was regarding him as she had in the car, from the cool, shadowed side of her lonely planet. He could hardly bear the weight of her appraisal. He thought of what he'd seen in the bathroom just now when he had stood up from the toilet—

what his body was doing to itself—and a knot of bile formed in his throat. His eyes filled with tears again. *Crybaby!*

He drained what was left of his wine—quite a lot actually—and set down his glass, which rang unpleasantly against the plate. He glanced down to discover he'd broken the stem in two.

"Jesus," he said. "How do you like that."

"Oh," Fiona said, "they were cheap glasses anyway. Now I've got an excuse to replace them."

"So I've done you a favor then? Is that what you're saying?" Dregs of sediment and cork were lodged in his teeth. "You're happy I broke it?"

"You're shouting," Gail said quietly. "You're now officially shouting at our dearest friends, who are trying to make allowances."

"Allowances? Allowances for what?"

"Just stop, okay?"

"Fine. I'll stop. Okay? I'm stopping."

"How you like those Sox this year?" Alex piped in. "Are they something or what?"

"The thing is, though, Gail," Teddy said, "I don't really feel like stopping. I'm tired of stopping. Stopping is something I'm good at."

"Not right now you're not."

"True, but in general. In general, all in all, I'm a pretty good stopper. Pretty controlled, pretty restrained. But here's the thing. What if a guy gets *too* restrained? What if he gets so restrained, he can't even remember what he's restraining *from*? What happens then?"

Gail sighed. "You know what happens then, Pooh Bear. He says good night and goes home to bed, and then the next day he makes an appointment with a licensed therapist."

"Take your pal Dostoyevsky," he went on airily, and with a peculiar exaltation; if he'd had another wineglass in his hand he'd have broken that too. "Not a hell of a lot of restraint there.

Of course he had his reasons, didn't he? They say his old man was murdered by his own peasants. Strangled. Isn't that right, Alex? Tell her. You're the humanist."

"Actually I think they crushed his testicles."

"Good story," Fiona said. "Any others you boys want to share over dessert?"

"The point is," Teddy said, "you can't deny your own nature. Even if your own nature is terribly flawed. Even if it's ugly or annoying or hurtful to others."

"How about all three?"

"In Africa they let the big cats roar. Here we cage them up in the house. No wonder they want to bite us."

"Again with the cat?" Alex lifted his eyebrows. "I thought he didn't even break the skin."

"There are cuts you don't see. By the way, Alex, you've got a hell of a living room in there, have I ever told you that? Nice stuff. I like nice stuff."

"I know you do, Ted."

"You should see my TV at home. Thirty-two inches. Flat-screen. Hi-def. Five-comb filter for clarity of image. You talk about your resolution. Six ninety-nine plus tax. I went to Best Buy."

"Sounds like money well spent." Alex glanced over at Gail; his expression didn't change. "There's no shame in treating yourself to something nice, Ted. You've worked hard for a long time."

"Who's to say?" Teddy gestured expansively toward the windows, slung with lace, and the dark trees beyond them, growing taller and wilder as the season progressed. "The bedouins have a proverb: whatever we don't need is an encumbrance."

"Oh boy," Will said, "here we go again. Across the desert sands."

"The sedentary species, they don't hold up, do they, Alex? You've read the history. It's the movers that survive. The nomads, the bush people. The skinny guys who travel light and sing their way across the desert. The fat guys who sit around waiting for the next world? They all wind up buried in sand."

"It's late," Gail said. "Hey, big cat, what do you say? Let's call it a night."

"Fine. I'll just use the bathroom."

"Again?"

"Last time."

His second trip to the bathroom that evening, though shorter than the first, proved eventful in its way. Coming out, after drying his hands on the little towels and checking his fly, he overheard Gail say, ". . . even Bruno keeps his distance."

"Really?"

"I guess animals sense these things."

"Wives too," he heard Fiona murmur, in her insinuating purr.

"Tell me," Gail said on the way home.

"I'm fine."

"No you're not." She adjusted the vent, trying to coax out a little heat. "You skipped right over fine. You went straight from being weird and quiet to completely wigging out. Was it that business with the cat? I took it too far, didn't I? I must have been mad at you for some reason."

"Don't give it a thought," he said. "I had a perfectly good time."

"Did you?"

"No."

"I didn't either." She sighed. "I don't know what it was. I kept going on about that stupid novel, and everyone just kept sitting there staring at me, and I kept thinking about how hard I was working to sound interesting, and how they were all probably thinking, 'My God, look at her, she's put on all that weight.' And Fiona overcooked the fish, as usual. What a shame, that beautiful creature, grilled to death, and no pleasure in eating it at all."

"You had a lot of wine," Teddy observed mildly. "We all did. Anyway I'm the one who broke the glass."

"You should have broken them all. It turned out to be the highlight of the evening."

"Next time I will."

The wine, the semen, the blood he'd glimpsed swirling darkly in the bowl—all the evening's currents swam together in his mind. But he wouldn't say anything to Gail. There were doers and complainers. He knew on which team a man should play.

"That wine you bought, with the red label? Did you ever get to try it?"

"No. Did you?"

She nodded. "Oh, it was wonderful. You did a wonderful, wonderful job. Sometimes, you know, Bear, I think you're a better man than you even know. You know?"

He nodded. Gail was a cheap date; two glasses of wine and her syntax left the building. And yet he *did* know what she meant. He felt a luminous alertness, like the flash of a scoreboard in the late innings of a game. Somehow he had squeezed out a victory. He'd done away with that tiresome rival, her husband. Smashed him like a glass. And now they were making their escape from the wreckage, so something new could begin.

He looked out at the dark houses along the road, night's black curtain suspended overhead. If only they could continue on this way, and not pull up into the same old driveway, get into the same old bed. He remembered that night in the parking lot with Vera Blackburn, his sense, driving home, that his neighbors were looking down at him from their illuminated windows not with rancor but approval. As if *they'd* been the ones making him do it. As if, after two hours in a hot auditorium, they'd all been expelled out into the darkness with the same secret disturbance of the nerves, the same need to keep the show going, the wild tropical night with its lovable rogues and gamblers, its errant missionaries. *I can never fit the cork back in the damned bottle . . .*

"I'm on my period," Gail said, "but I'm thinking I'd like to have a little fun when we get home. What say you to that?"

"I'd like to have a little fun too."

"A little good clean perimenopausal fun at the Hastings establishment."

"Sure," he said. "We'll go with the flow."

She gave a low, voluptuous laugh. Like all women, she was accustomed to flux, to sudden eruptions and cessations, the pull of unseen tides. For men it was different. The sight of one's own blood, for example, in the toilet bowl, the crimson drops unfurling like jellyfish when they hit the water—at such times a certain terror prevailed.

"Did you know Mimi's been going out with Jeremy Dunn? They've been seeing each other for weeks."

"Christ. I had no idea."

"I just found out myself," she said. "Fiona let it slip in the kitchen. He swore her to secrecy."

"She'll get bored with him. She always does."

"Jeremy's a little prince. They've spoiled him terribly. I can't see it lasting. But it might." Gail looked out the window. "Does your arm still hurt?"

"Not so much."

"I shouldn't have teased you. I know you have a low threshold."

"Forget it," he said. "I hardly feel a thing."

4

Pinch Hitter

When he arrived at the hospital, Oren had to stop, roll down the window, satisfy the curiosity of the uniformed attendant, and wait for the meter to cough out its slim, time-stamped ticket before the long arm of the gate clicked and rose, permitting him entry. You'd have thought he was trying to get into some exclusive nightclub, not a dumpy sixty-five-bed hospital on the edge of a cornfield. Only a sick person would actually want to visit such a place. And Oren wasn't sick. He was only a visitor, a man who came and went.

If he was somewhat better prepared today for the latter than the former, that was hardly his fault. He'd been ensconced in the teachers' lounge, grading an atrocious set of pop quizzes, when Zoe Bender had cornered him. That administrators' conference down in Hamilton; she'd mentioned it the other day, remember? Of course she knew he had far too much on his plate already. But if he could just step in for a couple of days on some odds and ends, and if he wasn't too busy, if he could find a way to get down to the hospital later and see Don . . .

Oren as it happened wasn't busy at all; his plate was so clean he could see his own reflection in it. But he liked it that way, liked being a member of the clean-plate club. He liked going home after school, sitting on the porch with a mug of coffee, listening to music and watching the birds zigzag overhead in their giddy, intricate migrations. So he hesitated. Around him bells were ringing, kids sidling down the hallways in slow, undulating globs, like the insides of a lava lamp. The jocks and their entourages. The student-government types. The math geeks, the science whizzes, the song-and-dance crowd. Girls dallied by their lockers, waging their coltish campaigns, their sly insurgencies. The younger girls, he knew, were fond of him, his teasing half-smiles, his black jeans and yanked-down ties, his blond, unruly hair. It was the older ones, the ones already as tall as their mothers, who unsettled him. He watched them in the morning out in the traffic circle, stepping free from their parents' cars, their faces changing, blinking shut, like a membrane in a lizard's eye. Terrifying. But that was the price you paid, consorting with the young. This exposure to their moods. This susceptibility.

His experience over the years had not so much shorn him of his innocence as revealed it to him. He wondered if he'd ever outgrow it.

"Of course I'll step in," he said. "Whatever you need."

And so he'd done the necessary thing, had gathered up the flag of duty and trudged forward. How hard could it be? He'd shoot over to the hospital, drop off Don's mail and paycheck, a couple of magazines, a bundle of get-well cards from his students, then he'd pay his respects and go. True, he did not know Don well enough to *have* much respect, and this was something Oren might have regretted in a general way if he hadn't in a specific way congratulated himself for it. Because what little he did know about Don Blackburn—his loudness, his rudeness, his egotism, his closetful of frumpy vests and supersize corduroys and bizarre, sour-smelling hats, his twee Anglophilia, all those silly little songs he liked to hum in the teachers' lounge from the Gilbert and Sullivan catalog—he didn't like. Don was a know-it-all, a burnt-out case, a glutton who, having feasted too long on the same limited menu, fancied himself a connoisseur. He had a certain way of occupying space, of making his presence felt. He'd hold court in his own designated corner of the lounge, his teeth rutty and dark, his beard a museum of bygone snacks.

Whatever detergent, if any, Don used on his clothes, and whatever deodorant, if any, Don used on his armpits, were clearly the cheapest and most astringent on the market. So there he'd sit, sipping his specially ordered Chinese teas, wolfing his specially ordered Scottish shortbread, and chortling over the letters column in his specially ordered copy of the *TLS,* from which he'd read aloud at tiresome length until the bell rang to signal the end of lunch. All of which would have been forgivable, in Oren's view, had Don in any sense been welcoming or helpful to the new acting vice principal, or had even showed any sign of noticing there *was* a new acting vice principal. But he hadn't.

Of course to be fair, Don Blackburn had been teaching in the North Wing of the middle school since the Carter administration; he'd seen more than his share of intent young vice principals come and go. His sheer longevity, saying the same things about the same books to children forever arrested at the same freakish, bifurcated stage of development, was, Oren reflected, both admirable and sad. Apparently as a young man he'd published a couple of stories in a literary magazine; there was talk of an unfinished novel. Maybe that was the root of Don's problem. Writer's block. To know the words were inside you but not be able to access them—that would be a drag, all right.

Did you have to be a writer to suffer writer's block? Lately Oren thought he might be coming down with a case of it himself.

Now he put the car in reverse and began to back his way into a parking space. It was a habit of his, backing in; you could read something into that, he supposed, as Sabine had, something that reflected badly upon his character; but the truth was his father had taught him this method of parking, and he'd loved his father and admired his driving, as he'd admired a lot of things about him—his mordant, affectionate wit, his skill with power tools, his crisp way of folding the *Times*—though of course he'd never told him so, had he? Not even at the end, when he'd intended to tell him everything. But he hadn't. He'd been living in Prague when he got the call. In the time it took to change planes at Heathrow and land at JFK and take a cab up the Van Wyck, onto the FDR, and across Ninety-sixth Street to Mount Sinai, he'd lost his chance. When he arrived at the room, he found the bed inhabited by another man, attended by another man's son. Another question elided by the operations of nature. They were beginning to really pile up.

Now, to console himself for being an orphan and a bad son and a mediocre schoolteacher and a lot of other things he wasn't too proud of, Oren reached into the glove compartment for one of the joints he'd confiscated at the October school dance and held in reserve for a time he recognized to have now arrived. He lit up and took a couple of quick, furtive hits. The smoke trickled through his lungs, creamy and cool, seeking its own merry little pathways to his head. Though as a rule, in keeping with his policy of disciplined repudiation, Oren said no to recreational drug use these days, he tried not to be dogmatic about it; every so often, as if to demonstrate to some dim, censorious inner bureaucrat that he was above any foolish consistency in these matters, he'd say yes. Was the opposite of foolish consistency foolish *in*consistency, or was it a wiser, more discriminating consistency? As he pondered the matter in the driver's seat, the smoke weaving a fine blue scarf around his neck, the answer escaped him. For that matter so did the question.

How long had he been sitting here, anyway? According to his watch his visit to see Don at the hospital was already one-third over, and he hadn't even got out of the car yet. What had he been so worried about? The world was a placid, benevolent place, and everything that attached to it was splendid. The sky was clear. Sunlight bounced harmlessly against the windshield and shattered into brilliant sparkly bits. Soon of course it would be time to go do something else, like getting out of the car, for instance, and carrying on with his visit, or else maybe taking a nap. But no, he'd reserve napping for later. Because that was the whole point of visiting the hospital: to put his own needs aside and perform an act of charitable good works for others. Which so far as he understood these things entailed doing more or less the opposite of whatever one really wanted to do instead. If he could just remember what that was . . .

He dreamed, as he often did when stoned, of popcorn, then opened his eyes to find acorns bouncing off the hood of the car. Or was that a dream too? His mouth was dry. A fine constellation of ashes had settled over his coat sleeves, like fallout from some unseen eruption.

A siren keened around the corner, ululating madly. He wondered where the fire was.

Time to get going, he thought.

He eased himself out of the car, slammed the door behind him, and made his way across the parking lot, shielding the sun from his eyes with the flat of his hand. The afternoon sunlight was blinding; it skittered across the hospital windows in dazzling coronas. Next time he'd be sure to bring shades.

There was no way, nor should there have been, to look upon Don Blackburn in his present state and not be moved. His face was blotched, bulbous, weirdly scrambled; his lips were purple and swollen, bunched up like grapes; his tongue lolled thickly from one side of his mouth. Beached against the pillows, clutching the blanket to his chest with clawed hands, he stared up at the ceiling through his one good eye with something like absolute comprehension of its function. His eyes in arrest looked as vacant as they were haunted, his skin as flushed as it was pale, his belly as bloated as it was emaciated. Hard to believe this shrunken wreck was the great and powerful Don, who strode honking down the corridors like an SUV.

Fortunately he was asleep at the moment. At least that was how he looked from the doorway, where Oren was still standing, clutching the lilac bouquet he'd bought downstairs at the gift shop for $12. Of his own money! When the tulips were only $8! Oh, selfless and charitable, that was Oren Pierce!

Downstairs, entering the lobby, he'd had an intuition of crossing a line in space on the far side of which everything would become unrecognizably strange. Now this seemed confirmed. Selflessly and charitably he stood there, willing Don's puffy, discolored eyelids—so laced with broken capillaries they were almost beautiful—not to open any farther, while the saline dripped down from its elevated bag, ticking away the seconds like an hourglass. How long was he expected to remain in the doorway with his cotton mouth and his twelve-buck bouquet before he could split? After all, Don Blackburn, whom he had come to console by his presence, was asleep, if not comatose, if not—it was beginning to seem perfectly plausible—dead. There was nothing to be done about that. Still, he should try to do *some*thing, Oren thought. The presence of two expectant-looking teenage girls, Don's children presumably, staring out at him from the jointed photo on the bedstand as if tracking his movements, or rather waiting to track them, left him that much more paralyzed and self-conscious. The older one was about twenty, dark and pretty, with a penetrating gaze and a plump little mouth that reminded him of Sabine.

Sabine! A lock in Oren's chest sprang open, and all the channels of his heart flooded at once.

He felt thoroughly and stupidly stoned. The framed posters on the walls of the room, bygone exhibitions in distant cities, aroused familiar feelings of roads not taken, opportunities missed. *No reason to be here, yet here he was.* It had begun to take on in his inner ear the cheerful, chiming inanity of a pop song.

Go, he thought. Go. A hospital was no place for idlers and dilettantes. What was wanted were brilliant, tireless experts, people who knew how to read X-rays, to make incisions, to draw and redraw lines of fate. Oren was only an errand boy, a courier between the adult world and the adolescent mind. That, plus overseeing the lunchroom, scheduling the athletic events, and chaperoning the monthly dances, where he went around breaking up grudge fights and sexual encounters and relieving industrious eighth-graders of their hard-earned Mexican dope. For 36K a year, plus benefits.

He should have gone for the tulips, he thought.

Fortunately to this point he'd been spared much in the way of hospital time himself. Or cheated of it. But perhaps both came to the same thing. In any event, it was, he knew, only a suspended sentence.

It was beginning to seem imperative to either leave or lie down. His mouth was parched, his head tinny and light, like a flyaway roof. Either he shouldn't have smoked that joint out in the car, or else he should have smoked two. The world, that fat drunk, teetered woozily on its axis. He hadn't slept well, not last night, not the night before. Come to think of it, he hadn't slept well in years, not since Sabine had broken their not-quite-engagement, leaving him to honor and comfort himself in sickness and in health. Which was this? He stood clutching his flowers, waiting for the man in the bed to either awaken or not awaken, conclusively. In an effort to speed things along he issued a brief, exploratory cough.

"Zat you?" someone demanded, not Don Blackburn but someone else, behind him and across the hall. "Junior, zat you out there?"

Oren didn't answer.

"Get over here, Junior, you piece of dirt. I got a message for you."

Oren looked down at the supine, motionless figure of Don Blackburn, who if bothered by the tone or volume of the voice gave no sign to betray it. Then he eased across the corridor and poked his head into the room directionally opposite, hoping, as usual, to look and not be seen.

"You ain't Junior." A stout, white-haired man stared up from his bed through a pair of enormous spectacles. He fingered his sparse goatee. "Who might you be?"

"I came to see Mr. Blackburn."

"Who?"

"The man across the hall."

The patient's eyes narrowed behind his glasses; his gaze, as if under the spell of some vagrant hallucination, took off in a spiral around the room. "That fat guy, you mean?"

"Yes."

"He your father?"

"Actually I'm kind of his boss."

The man in the bed let out a hoot.

"Well, it's true." Oren felt not so much defensive on the subject as amazed himself. The world's skepticism and incredulity regarding his progress in life were no match for his own. "He's a teacher over at the middle school. I'm the vice principal."

"You don't look like no principal, son."

"Actually I'm the *acting vice* principal, technically speaking. It's complicated." Oren perched himself on the edge of the visitor's chair. "Basically I'm filling in."

"Sure, I got you." The patient gave a knowing little nod, as if he and complexity were on good terms. "You're the pinch hitter. The Gates Brown so to speak."

"I guess." Gates Brown? The name cast only a dim light through the fog. Some journeyman ballplayer. Oren had come to baseball, as he'd come to many of his adult interests, rather late, had picked it up by proximity from housemates in college. He didn't know a lot about it but he knew a little. He was like that with a lot of things. "I'll leave you alone now. You look like you could use some sleep."

The man in the bed regarded him warily; he appeared to have arrived at some firm and uncharitable conclusion.

"I'm waiting for Junior," he announced, and promptly fell asleep.

Oren may have dozed off a minute too, sunk in the wheezing vinyl of the visitor's chair, because when next he moved he startled himself. Outside the sun was sliding meekly toward the horizon. His eyes felt sandy and gelid, like crusted shellfish. A dull film of saliva clung to his teeth. He was pleased to see that the man on the bed was now snoring mildly through his nose, his hands drawn together on his chest like the lid of some poor knight's sarcophagus. Good, Oren thought, all the tired men are getting their rest.

He picked up his flowers and tiptoed back across the corridor. An orderly trudged past, pushing a cart with a wobbly wheel. He'd just slip into Don's room, leave the flowers he'd brought— the petals now hanging their heads in sorrow, or embarrassment—and run on home.

So intent was he on slipping unobtrusively into Don's room and slipping out again that he almost failed to register two critical pieces of new information. The first was that Don's bed was empty. Stripped of its linens, it stood exposed in the slanting light for the graceless, inhospitable mechanism it was.

The second bit of news had to do with the chair beside it, which was now occupied. A woman lay sideways against the cushions, her head sunk to one shoulder, her calves draped negligently over the chair arm, a legal pad cradled to her lap, blackened and busy with notes. She failed to move when Oren came in, or to register his presence in any way. Another slumber artist, he thought. He supposed she was Don's wife. But wait, Don was divorced. Still, she was wearing a ring; she had to be *somebody*'s wife. Her hands were long and veiny. Like the clothes she wore, and her turbulent, white-flecked hair, and the single row of pearls that hung from her neck, reflecting, at this moment, the violet onset of dusk, they seemed pretty well tended. Her feet were bare, the toes jumbled, heaped together. The inside of her leather briefcase, splayed open on the floor, was paisleyed with scars and bruises, the accordion folds tattered, the pens leaking ink, a pair of knitting needles entangled hopelessly in yarn. If the condition of her briefcase was in any way a mirror of her life (as Oren's, empty at the moment but for a cheese sandwich, an apple, sixty-two unpersuasive essays on the Battle of Gettysburg, and a bloated social studies textbook, probably was), then this was a life that required some attention, he thought.

"You must be the minister." Her eyes were open. Her mouth twisted to suppress a yawn.

"Sorry?"

"I'm Gail. The cousin. They said you were coming down today."

Oren stared at her. The minister. The cousin. The hospital was a busy place; you needed to speak in shorthand, definite articles. You had to know who you were. "I'm Oren."

"Oren who?"

"Oren Pierce. I'm at the middle school. I'm acting principal over there."

"Oh?" A shadow flitted across her eyes. He glanced down at her legal pad: the page was bordered with doodles. "I thought Zoe Bender was acting principal these days."

"We're sharing the job, actually."

"Since when?"

"Since the summer." Was it really such a Herculean task, being co–vice principal at a mediocre middle school, that no one should believe him capable? "Since the principal turned into some kind of wacko head case and wound up in the county jail, making a lot of extra work for the rest of us."

"Is that what happened to him?" She picked up one of her knitting needles and began to play with it. "I was wondering."

"Speaking of head cases, what about your cousin Don? What's up with him?"

"He has a blood clot in the left part of his brain."

"I meant, where is he now? Where did they take him?"

"Upstairs."

"Oh?" Oren wondered if she meant by the word some sort of euphemism.

"Mmm. Intensive care." She touched the point of the needle to her thigh and held it there, absently turning it back and forth. "He seems to have taken what they call a turn."

"I see."

"They want to monitor him more closely. He's not responding to treatment the way he should, in their opinion. The systolic pressure's off. I won't even pretend to know what that means. But apparently he's not in any immediate danger." She smiled false-brightly. "Famous last words."

"I see."

"You see." Her eyes skated over him vaguely from beneath their pale hoods. Something sullen in the lines of her mouth suggested to Oren the kind of teenager she'd once been—a very different kind, he reminded himself, than he'd once been—and kept him more conscious than he'd have liked of the needle in her hand. "Do you know Don very well?"

"Not really. We say hello in the hallways. He's an impressive guy though. All that energy. The kids really look up to him." Like any bad liar, he'd adopted a tone of vehement sincerity. "I mean, who wouldn't?"

"And you? Do they look up to you too?"

"I wouldn't know."

"You don't feel like you're making a difference? Fighting the good fight? Expanding young minds? Winning over young hearts?"

"I do okay." He had no idea why she was attacking him this way. To change the subject, he nodded to indicate the photos on Don's nightstand. "I didn't know he even had kids."

"He doesn't. They're mine."

"Yours?"

"When a man's ill, he gets lonely. I thought it would be nice for him to have some pictures around. Men like to look at pictures of pretty girls. It gives them a boost."

"I see."

"Why do you keep saying that? What could you possibly see?" She picked up her cell phone, frowning as she checked for messages. "Where is she, anyway? She was supposed to get a ride. It's not as if she's so busy with after-school activities these days."

He was damned if he was going to say "I see" again.

"And *him*—" She shook her head at the empty pillow, a boulder on the long trail of her preoccupations. "He's a child. He doesn't take care of himself. Never has. Vera said there'd be problems once he hit sixty, and she was right. What is it with men? Don't they believe there's such a thing as causes and effects?"

Oren smiled noncommittally. He'd have preferred to be included with the rest of his gender, but he wasn't going to make a lot of noise about it.

"Look," she said, "I don't want to be rude, but I'm a bit frazzled at the moment. Do you mind if I just ask what you're doing here? What you want?"

The question struck Oren as at once terribly simple and terribly complex. What *did* he want? He was tired and thirsty; his libido, after a brief flicker of wakefulness, had all but blown out. For some reason the only thing that came to mind at the moment, in the area of palpable desire, was the image of Teddy Hastings lounging in a hammock between tall trees, sipping a tall, cool ice-coffee drink, courtesy of the Carthage Union School District. Oren too hoped for a sabbatical someday. That fantasy got him through all the detentions, the parent conferences, the antidrug assemblies, the field trips, the Friday-night basketball games on cold, butt-flattening bleachers. And Vera—who was Vera? More shorthand. What he really needed, that is, what he actually *wanted* . . .

"I mean, this is strictly a formality, isn't it? You have to come visit sick teachers in the hospital. It's part of the job description, no? That's why you're here."

"You could say that, yes."

"Well, I've said it, so consider it done. You paid your little visit, now you can run on back to your little school, okay?"

"You sound a little angry."

"Do I? Heavens to betsy, I'll never forgive myself."

Okay, she didn't want him there, fine. He didn't want him there either. And Don Blackburn? Whatever Don's vote may have been was no longer relevant—he was upstairs, on a higher floor. So now Oren could go.

And yet, now that he'd been released from his errand at last, he found himself reluctant. It seemed important to mark his visit somehow, accomplish a little good. "Maybe there's some way I can help."

"That's a lovely offer. It is. But honestly? Unless you've got medical rehabilitation training, no."

"I meant, help you."

"Me?"

"I mean if you want to talk things out. I do have some train-ing, you know. I've got pretty close to a master's in counseling."

"Golly," she said brightly. "Pretty close to a master's. Wow."

"Okay, forget it. Just trying to help."

"No offense, Owen. But if you were me, would you talk to you?"

"It's Oren. And to answer your question, I guess it would depend on the circumstances."

"Circumstances," she sighed. "Okay, let's see. Circumstances. Try working for a firm that's barely solvent, in a town that's not too solvent either. Try coming home to a daughter who hates you, and a husband who's been publically humiliated and won't go out of the house. Try a cousin you're at least twice removed from who gets hit by a stroke. He's got an ex-wife who wants nothing to do with him and like no friends, so guess what, you're the one elected to keep him company. You want to know how many *New Yorker* stories I've read him this week? How many op-eds from the *Times*? But the doctors say it's important, the human voice. They need to hear it." She spread out her hands and examined them like a map: the veins' blue highways, the dry, knuckled mountains. "And then of course there's the usual fun stuff. The migraines, the disk problems, the pre-ulcerative colitis. The more hot flashes than a microwave. So what do you think, Mr. Pretty Close to a Master's. Given those circumstances, I mean. Would *you* talk to you?"

"Probably not."

"There you go."

Oren reflected on the photographs for a moment. "You're Ted Hastings's wife, aren't you?"

At approximately this point she began to laugh, if you could call it laughing, the pained grimace her mouth was making, the subtle spasmodic trembling of the shoulders. In an experimental way he touched her arm; he was more perplexed than relieved when she failed to shake it off. He stood as if in a swoon, wishing himself gone.

"You were almost right by the way. About that minister thing." He withdrew his hand. "I did go to seminary for a year. Rabbinical school."

"Wait, was that before the pretty close to a master's in counseling, or after?"

"Before. I realize it must sound quaint, in this day and age. You probably don't meet a lot of rabbis up here."

"Oh," she said, "I grew up Unitarian. I'm used to meeting rabbis."

"I see. I mean, of course. Anyway yeah, it seemed like a good idea at the time. Off the beaten track. Kind of interesting and scholarly."

"So why did you quit?"

"I quit because I didn't want to be a rabbi."

She frowned. "This is getting too deep for me, I'm afraid."

"I liked *studying* the stuff. Hanging out in the library, arguing over the nuances of some medieval commentary? That's fun. But come on, writing sermons? Raising money for some temple? Standing in front of a congregation, telling people how to live? No thanks."

Gail Hastings shook her head. "I don't see the point of all that study if it's not *for* something."

"Oh, it was for something. I'm confident of that." Oren looked out the window: the elongated shadows, the sun a pale, closing eye, colorless through the clouds. "But maybe I should leave you alone now."

"Yes," she said vaguely. Now she too seemed reluctant. She inclined her gaze to see him better. "Only tell me something first."

"What?"

"I don't know. You're the almost-rabbi. Whatever you've got."

"Well . . ." How do you like that? he thought. He was a man on a mission today after all. "There's always prayer."

She gave a depleted sigh.

"Hey, that's no small thing." He spoke in a loud voice; she seemed all of a sudden far away. "That's really quite a lot, if you can manage it."

"Can you?"

"No."

"Look," she said, "no offense, but most people I know, their lives are pretty chaotic. Do you really think following some outmoded commandments is the answer?"

"Chaos is the germ of life, according to the kabbalah. Even when there's chaos, there's an order below the surface. An egg, for instance, would be the chaos of the bird."

"We must have read different bibles," she said, pulling back her hair and compiling it into a loose knot. "I thought religion was about peace and love."

Her cell phone rang. She picked it up without changing her expression. "This better be good," she said.

"Okay, well." He made a show of patting down his pockets, hunting for his keys. "Nice meeting you," he mouthed, backing toward the door.

"Wait, hold on a sec." It wasn't clear if she was talking to him, or to whoever—this Vera person?—was on the other end of the phone. "I'm sorry. I didn't mean to bite your head off just now."

"Forget it."

"Down at the school. What you said before. Do they really think my husband's gone crazy?"

"Yeah."

"Too bad. Well, say hi to Zoe. Tell her to call me, okay?"

He closed the door behind him and made his way down the corridor to the elevator. He should have stood up for himself better, Oren thought, for the curiosities and hungers of his youth. But she was an angry person, anybody could see that.

The elevator was slow. By the time it came, a small group had gathered behind him: two residents, a nurse, and an orderly pushing a patient in a wheelchair. Only when they had all crowded in and were descending toward the lobby did he glance down to see who the patient was.

"Yo, Gates Brown, still here? Don't you got nowhere to be?"

Apparently his sleep had not done him much good. His eyes were sunken and moist, his arms like slackened ropes.

"I'm on my way out," Oren said. "And you? Are you being released?"

"Me? Nah. Down to the lab. Got to see a lady 'bout a test."

The elevator stopped. The doors shuddered open; Oren had to step aside to let people out. A gurney went by, IV bag swaying like a metronome. Just before the doors closed again a young man in a lab coat slipped in, sucking the tip of his pen as he studied a chart. Tests, and more tests. Oren stepped back to give him more room.

5

Aliens

It was Mimi's fault, of course, that business with the aliens, but then so many things were these days. She was the one who'd dragged her friends down to the lake, having heard about the eclipse on the public radio station that morning on her way to school. She was the one who'd told Jeremy at lunch and also mentioned it to Lisa, who must have said something to Yuko, who let slip to Marcus, who was hanging out after school with Kyle, who snuck out of his house around ten thirty and picked them up in the elementary-school parking lot in his mom's Cherokee—the front end of which he'd already dinged up considerably, thanks to this unfortunate habit Kyle had of driving under the influence of pretty much anything he could get his hands on.

Anyway there they were. The lake was deserted, the air chilly and moist. In the paltry moonlight, the ghosts of old enjoyments—the rusted skeleton of a swing set, the boarded-up cinderblock refreshment shack—stood silhouetted against the trees. They had the whole shore to themselves. They proceeded to their usual place, a grassy inlet with a pale fringe of sand where the toadstools and lake scum grew thick. The Black Lagoon, they called it. Then they spread out some blankets and lit up a bowl and hung out waiting for the eclipse.

Earth science not being among Mimi's better subjects, she'd been kind of vague on the details. She had no idea for example whether this particular eclipse was supposed to be lunar or solar, total or partial, brief or long-lasting. Nor did she care. Basically it was an excuse to hang out on the beach with her friends that night, scrunching her toes up and down in the cool weightless sand. Water slapped monotonously against the docks. Above them a thin layer of clouds had begun to curtain off the stars. Mimi shivered; for a second she was truly happy. Then Lisa said, "I'm bored."

"Me too," Kyle said. "Let's go."

"Be patient," Yuko said. "The light's about to change. Can't you feel it?"

"You can't feel something like that," Kyle said.

Yuko shrugged. "Maybe *you* can't." She was sophisticated, you could see it in her clothes, her hair, her grades, even the food her mother packed her for lunch, those compact little sushis. It all seemed fed by some underground source, some hidden spring. Japanese people were extrasensitive, Yuko said; it had to do with the wiring of their brains. No wonder the guys turned to check her out in the corridors as she walked past, ticking off her features like a résumé. Her straight black hair, her sad little eyes, her flawless skin, et cetera. Even Mimi stared at her sometimes, like in French class, where she sat two rows behind, wondering over Yuko's bare, unblemished shoulders, so slender, so pale, so incredibly smooth that even the knobs of her spine, as she wrote out her assignments in her tiny, meticulous script, hung low in her skin, invisible. Next to that tender and delicate assembly that was Yuko, she felt like some gross, clueless creature—a dog, not a cat, a clumsy white girl, out of place in her own skin.

"Wait, is that it?"

"Is what what? I don't see anything."

"*That.*"

If you could classify eclipses by gender, the way they did with hurricanes, then the one that night must surely have been male: it made a long, drawn-out production of arrival, peaked before they knew it, then slipped away like a thief. All they could see was a smear of half-light, vague and formless and runny, like eggs left on a breakfast plate.

"Wow, Mimi, thanks a lot," Lisa said, in case anyone had forgotten who was responsible. "I'm so glad I skipped rehearsal for that."

"Yeah right," Jeremy said, "she's the god of weather, she totally controls these things."

"I'm just saying, she made it out like some big deal, and it's not."

"Whoa now." Marcus was polishing his pampered skateboard. "Keep the peace. Make impermanence your friend."

"What does that even mean, Marcus?" Jeremy said. "I never know what that means, when you say shit like that."

"It's all about focus, man." Marcus bestowed upon them a smile of infinite tolerance. "Focus and detachment. Like the gatha says, in three hundred years, where will you be and where shall I be?"

"You'll be stoned, Marcus. As usual."

Marcus nodded amiably—the idea appeared to agree with him—and cradled his board in both arms. You could see the nicks and dents in the titanium bearings. Since his last trip to the emergency room, he'd been forced to cut back on the X-treme stuff, the ollies and Half Cabs and Gay Twists, and devote himself to the cultivation of transcendent consciousness instead. He still carried his board around with him though. It kept him centered. Seeds and stems could be seen sticking to the lacquer.

Marcus had showed Mimi a trick once—they were still going out at the time—called, fittingly enough, the Disaster. She'd spent the better part of an otherwise pleasant afternoon at the skate park watching him try to master the damn thing, his eyes all lit up as he shot down the ramp, a blue vein popping out from his forehead like a highway on a road atlas. Sometimes she envied guys their concentration. The way they wanted things so badly, the way they tunneled into that feeling and lost sight of all else. Even when they fell—and Marcus fell *a lot*—you could see they still thought they were flying.

"Yo, Lisa, about that play?" Kyle said. Lisa had won the lead role that spring in *The King and I* over about fifty other girls, something that in some circles, Mimi supposed, would have been considered an accomplishment. "I hate to tell you, but it's totally racist."

"You say that about everything, Kyle. You said it about *Hamlet* too, and everybody in it was white."

"Dude, I misspoke, all right? I didn't mean *Hamlet.* I meant the one with that big black dude who strangles his wife. *Macbeth.*"

"That's *Othello,* dickhead."

"My point is, like, here comes the great smart white lady to teach the ignorant natives how to do things? That's not cool. That's just perpetuating racial stereotypes."

"Well, you're perpetuating retarded stereotypes, so we're even."

"This is not focus and detachment, people," Marcus informed them. "In fact it's pretty much the opposite."

There was a pause. Everyone was thinking, what am I doing here? Why don't I find some new friends? Marcus, when he came back from Burning Man the previous summer, told Mimi how people there referred to their home life as "the default world." Mimi felt that way too. Except she had no other world to go to. She'd never been anywhere else. And if she didn't get her grades up and do something about her shitty SATs, she never would.

Right then Jeremy put his arm around her and tried to kiss her again. That did it.

"Don't," she said, a lot louder than she meant to. Then, because they were all looking at her now, she blurted out, "I think my dad's got cancer."

The problem with being shy, in Mimi's experience, was that whenever you finally *did* send up the occasional verbal flare, it

was always too bright, too loud, too sudden, too loopy; it mes-
merized for a second and then sputtered out. Really she hadn't
intended to say *any*thing; it was just one of those involuntary
reflexes, the random firing of some lonely twitching nerve in her
head. Anyway, the result was annoying. You'd have thought
that, given the general witlessness of the conversation, everyone
would be glad to have a new subject introduced, something serious to talk about for a change. But instead they looked repulsed.
At least Jeremy did, and he was the one closest to her, basically
about a tongue's length away in fact.

"Dude," Marcus said, having pondered the matter for a while.
"That's tragic."

"He went in for this biopsy last week. I don't think he's heard
yet. But he like shaved off all his hair already."

"I always liked Mr. H," Kyle said. "He was pretty cool for a
principal."

"He's not dead, dumbshit," Jeremy said. "People go in for
exploratory things all the time, and most of them turn out to be
nothing. Right, Mimi?"

Mimi nodded. In truth it hadn't occurred to her that most
things turned out to be nothing, though she herself might well
turn out to be nothing, she thought.

Yuko got up, brushed sand off her legs, and came over to
where Mimi was sitting. "Let's go in the lake. The water'll feel
nice. Maybe we'll see some ospreys."

"We'll come down in a minute," Jeremy said.

"I was talking to Mimi."

But Mimi just sat there, avoiding conflict as usual. The world
was full of personalities stronger than her own. She was tired of
grappling with them. "Maybe in a while," she said.

They built a fire out of driftwood, not so much for warmth as
for light, then Marcus lit another bowl and passed it around.
They sat taking hits and drinking beer and staring at the flames
with something like smugness, because they had achieved for
themselves some of what the sky had failed to provide them ear-

lier, that reversal of darkness. Everyone partook but Lisa. She was cutting back on weed, she said, to preserve her voice for the play.

"Well, that's one thing she's preserving anyway," Mimi murmured to Jeremy. It was beyond her that night to pass up an opportunity for meanness.

Jeremy laughed, nuzzling her ear with his soft, papery cheeks as he worked his fingers around the rim of her bikini bottom. It tickled, but she didn't want to discourage him. He was working so hard.

"I'm going to really miss you this summer," he told her for about the tenth time. "You know what I mean?"

She nodded. Then, having learned in geometry that the shortest distance between two points was a straight line, she added, "Me too."

"I never felt this way before. I mean about a girl."

"Mmm."

"I'll call you every day, from work. We'll have long talks."

"Mmm. Except it's hard at the pool. They don't like it."

"So we'll talk at night then."

"Mmm."

They watched Yuko wading in the lake, looking for some beautiful winged seabird that eluded her. Mimi wanted to go down and join her, but she knew if she did, Jeremy would tag along, and anyway the bugs were out, and the water was really cold, and she wasn't altogether clear, to be honest, what ospreys even *looked* like. Between the various opiates they'd consumed, and the fact that their parents had all gone to bed already and it was June and the school year was nearly over and none of the standardized tests they'd be taking in school the next day could possibly be either studied for or important, the consensus seemed to be that they had no reason to get up and do anything at all. So it became understood that they were just going to hang out there at the lake until morning, then grab some breakfast on the way to school. The sky was not exactly black and not exactly blue; it was, however, unpunctuated by light, as if someone had forgotten to throw the switch that turned on the stars. She leaned against Jeremy and closed her eyes. For a lacrosse player he had bony shoulders. But at least they were there.

"Uh-oh," Kyle announced. "Company."

Mimi opened her eyes. The aliens were coming out of the water one by one, staggering across the sand, chests heaving, like the last finishers in some ghostly marathon.

"Who are they?" she asked, yawning.

"Aliens. Space invaders."

"I told you," Marcus said, "didn't I? We're not alone in the universe. We have this huge circle of friends."

"Hide the stash, just in case."

A boat horn sounded in the distance, maybe coming toward them, maybe going away. The aliens huddled on the sand, rubbing their pale, sticklike arms together, shivering. Long ropes of algae coiled around their ankles. The moonlight was so strong you could practically count the bones in their rib cages.

"Spindly little things, aren't they?" Lisa got to her feet and began waving her arms. If the aliens noticed her, this loud, red-haired, big-chested person braying at them from the little cove behind the swing set, they gave no indication.

"Yo, Lisa, be nice," Marcus said. "We should befriend them. They've traveled all this way."

"Course with alien creatures," Kyle said, "you never know. They come on like E.T. and next thing it's war of the worlds."

"It's weird," Yuko said, staring at them thoughtfully, "but they kind of look Chinese."

"Get real," Kyle snorted. "There's no Chinese people in outer space."

"Maybe they're not from outer space. Maybe they're from, like, Canada."

"Make up your mind."

The visitors, wherever they were from, did not appear to be an attractive species. No doubt some life-forms in this universe looked good when they were naked and wet, though God knew Mimi wasn't one of them—not with those blotchy, jiggling flesh pods around her thighs, passed down so considerately by her father—and neither were these emaciated little creatures who'd washed up on the shore like so much cosmic refuse, and now stood tilting and teetering against each other in an effort to stay vertical, as if gravity were a test for which they'd neglected to study.

As if to illustrate this point, one of the aliens now dropped to his knees and began retching noiselessly on the sand.

"Great," Lisa said. "Just what we need around here. More puking."

"It's the atmosphere, man," Marcus said. "All those petrochemicals? I bet breathing that stuff for the first time really blows."

"Good," Kyle said. "Maybe they'll think twice, next time they go probing people's minds."

"Of course in your case that'll take what," Lisa said, "half a second?"

"Lisa's not interested in minds," Kyle said to everyone else. "She's hoping they'll probe, you know, that other thing."

"Har har."

"Maybe they lost their sun," Jeremy said. He was fitting a zoom onto the Nikon his parents had given him just for being, as they put it, himself. The photos he took would never come out—the light was too dim, he had no flash—but no way was Mimi going to say anything on that score. Jeremy's self-confidence was precious to her. It was like a lever she held in her hand; with the tiniest movement she could steer it up or down. "Like that movie last year, remember? That alien planet lost its sun, and everybody had to troop into the spaceship to go colonize some other galaxy."

"How do you lose a sun?" Kyle said. "Those things're fucking *huge*."

"All suns flame out eventually," Jeremy said. "Even the big ones. It's basic thermodynamics. They teach you that in AP."

And the voice of the Honor Roll was heard in the land.

"I got another theory," Marcus said. Palming the joint, he blew out two jets of smoke, one headed east and one headed west. Everyone had to wait for him to finish. It was a kind of quiet tyranny he exercised, keeping up his rep as the guy who laid down the big ideas. "They're here because they're here."

"Say what?"

"They're just here, man. There doesn't have to be a reason. They're just here."

Actually," Mimi said, "they're here because *we're* here."

Everyone turned and gave her an unfriendly glare. Jeremy, who'd gone back to what he'd been doing before the aliens arrived—feeling her up—abruptly pulled his hand away, as if this sudden tendency of his girlfriend to make dumb, confounding statements might be contagious. He was applying early admission to Brown next year; he had to be careful. Finally Lisa, with her usual zero tolerance for ambiguity, said, "And what the fuck does that mean, O wise one?"

"It means, if we weren't here, we wouldn't be seeing them, right? And if we didn't see them, then they wouldn't be here. At least not to us. It's like if an alien tree falls in the forest, and there's no one around to hear."

"Dude," Marcus said, nodding. Anything the vaguest bit Zen-like appealed to him. "That's cool."

"Wait," Kyle said. "Alien tree? What the fuck is that?"

Sometimes she felt like *she*'d lost her sun. First Danielle had abandoned her for college, then she'd gone off to backpack around Asia on her junior year abroad, and it was awful to be the one left behind, to have to take over the parental spotlight, a solo act, doing the whole song and dance yourself. All those tiresome how-was-your-day and have-you-done-your-homework and what-are-you-thinking-about-college questions, because the show must go on. If only she too could go to Asia. Danny would be happy to see her, she was sure of it. Every e-mail she'd sent—

not that there had been so many—bubbled over with how fabulous it was. *They have these great trance parties that go on all night to celebrate the full moon. It's really cool, Mims. Everyone comes out of their bungalows and starts dancing and doing E and there are flying fish that jump out of the water and these cool magic lanterns and people showing up from all over the world and even though some of them are creeps you want to avoid if you can (I could tell you stories, but I don't trust the um Great-And-Powerful-Ones not to get their hands on these emails somehow) and even though there are a lot of jellyfish around—and you have to watch out for those suckers, they're really pretty but when they get a hold of you, yow!—there are good people too, people into healing and massage, who really want to purify and get rid of all these western hangups we don't even realize we're weighed down by all the time. There's this really great energy all around, even though the electricity keeps going on and off like every five minutes. Whatever. Doesn't matter. The people are really nice too. They all call us* farenjis, *which means white person I guess. I don't think they mean it in a bad way though. Gabi says everyone needs a name for people who're different. It's human nature, Gabi says . . .*

Gabi was the new boyfriend, or maybe the old boyfriend, Mimi couldn't keep track anymore. There did seem to be a lot of action in the boyfriend department over there in Asia. *Asia.* Just saying the word, just whispering it to herself, made her feel calmer somehow, more together, like it opened a door to this really cool, quiet place where people lived in paper houses and walked around in black slippers and invested everything, even their baths, their meals, their sex, with this fabulous refinement and care. Lately she had this fantasy of setting out in a boat, just floating off, crossing all those tiny pencil lines of longitude and latitude you only see on maps, and then washing up on the beach one day like a message in a bottle, where some nice, calm Asian couple would happen along and take her home to their clean paper house on the side of a mountain. Why not? Her parents were so self-involved, they'd never miss her. Besides, American couples were always shooting off to Asia to adopt little girls; it was only fair to turn things around once in a while and give the Asians one of ours.

She looked over at Yuko, cooing quietly into her cell phone. Her boyfriend, Ivan, was in Guam, having graduated back in January and enlisted in the navy to protect them all from terrorism. It was a big responsibility and, according to Ivan, way less than fun. For one thing, he missed his little Yuko. He lamented loudly, loud enough for the news to travel nine thousand miles without the aid of phone wires, how much he missed her, and how often—like, say, every time he beat off, which from the sound of it was not exactly an infrequent pastime over there. Lisa, who'd gone out with Ivan before he'd started up with Yuko—Lisa had gone out with Marcus too, actually, before *he*'d started up with Yuko—couldn't take it; she began to dance around the fire in these weird little hula steps, tossing her red hair and her humongous freckled boobs, singing a tune Mimi recognized to be one of her featured numbers from the play at a volume Mimi recognized to be irritatingly loud. Showbiz was Lisa's default world, her own little Asia; it was the place she retreated to in times of stress.

Mimi was feeling no little stress herself these days. A stress that had really intensified the night before, when she strolled into the bathroom to find her father at the mirror with an electric razor, buzzing off his hair.

"So how do I look?" he'd asked, with a crooked grin that made him look truly awful, as a matter of fact.

"I don't know. Like a bald guy, I guess."

"I should have done this a long time ago," he said. "It feels good."

"You're going to clog up the drain."

"Disposal is an issue," he agreed. "It's harder than it looks. Anyway believe it or not, Sweetpea, I'm doing this for you."

"Well, don't." Her face was like a mask, her mouth a hard shell. "We didn't ask you to. It's not fair."

"Do you want to talk about fairness? Do you want to hear my views on the subject of fairness?"

"You don't even know it's cancer, Mom says. You're probably way overreacting."

"The trouble with people who underreact to things is they always think other people are overreacting. Where is your mom, anyway?"

"I think she went out for a bike ride or something. She had on her sports bra."

"Ah. Finished with your homework?"

"Sort of."

"You have to be prepared, Mimi. Life throws things your way, and they're not all pretty." Briskly he rubbed his head with a towel and inspected his scalp in the mirror. "See what I mean?"

"I just *said* I did my homework."

Actually what she was thinking was, he's enjoying this. He's been waiting for this.

"Don't be such a hard case, okay? You're the kid here, I'm the adult. It's not easy to find the right attitude. You think I'm not terrified? Of course I'm terrified. But I'm trying to keep my head straight, and to spare you the sight of your dear old dad falling apart."

"Good," she said. "So close the door."

There was a 10 p.m. curfew at the lake, according to the signs in the parking lot, but fortunately the cops were never around to enforce it. So until the aliens showed up, Mimi and her friends had the whole place to themselves. Which was a good thing too. Because it probably wasn't strictly legal to have that big fire going either, or to be smoking all that dope, or drinking all that beer Marcus had liberated from his dad's garage, or scarfing up all that Ritalin Lisa was passing around, because aside from her voice and chest that was kind of her other acknowledged talent area, pharmaceuticals . . . and God knew what Jeremy was doing to Mimi with his tongue, after she'd wriggled her bikini bottoms down over her hips—oh my, that hummingbird routine of his, that silent dip and flutter, that filthy raid . . . that *couldn't* have been legal. But maybe it was.

She cried when he stopped. She had no idea why. It was a confusing night.

"Tell me you love me," Jeremy said in his soulful, petulant voice. "Tell me."

But she was too busy crying. She'd been crying on and off for about three weeks at that point; she was getting reasonably good at it. That more often than not she had no clue what she was crying about did nothing to stop her from crying so much. If anything it made her cry more.

"Don't I make you feel good, Mimi?" Jeremy's long face looked washy in the moonlight, as if she were draining the life out of him. "Don't I make you feel good?"

The sand was digging into her butt at this point, leaving marks that would, she knew, lie engraved in her skin. Down the beach the fire was crackling, flinging sparks at the vacant places in the sky where stars should have been. The heads of their friends bobbed up and down.

"I wish I wasn't going in two weeks. Especially now, with your father and all."

"I know."

"The thing is, I don't even know if you'll miss me."

"I know."

"You know you'll miss me, you mean? Or you know that you won't?" He narrowed his eyes. "Are you fucking with my head here, Mimi? I don't know, it feels like you're fucking with my head."

"Shhh." She stroked the soft hairs on his rounded upper arm, trying to shut him up. He was a great guy in a lot of ways, and she sort of loved him better than any other boyfriend she'd ever had—all two of them—but he was starting to bring her down with these morose and needy moods of his, the way he kept bearing down on her, trying to read meanings into whatever she said or didn't say.

Mimi, Mimi, don't I feel good?

All she'd meant was that she knew he didn't know if she'd miss him or not. But he didn't understand. He was always after her to be more *expressive*. Apparently crying all the time didn't count as expressive enough in his book. She was failing him again. Ever since they'd downloaded their SAT scores, he'd been finding fault with her capacities for expression. The distance between them had been there all along, but he hadn't seen it, not until those numbers came back from Princeton, New Jersey. Now that he'd caught a glimpse of the hard facts, he knew he had a project on his hands. He knew that in a couple of years, thanks in no small part to those scores, he'd be off at Brown, or Penn, or Georgetown, where he'd really get going on his expressive life, and thanks to her own scores there was absolutely no chance at all that she'd be around to share it. In two weeks she'd be lifeguarding at the town pool, as she had the previous two summers, while Jeremy went off to New York to intern at his uncle's law office. He had uncles and cousins in all the best cities. Maybe that was what made him feel so self-important, so entitled, so certain—the world was spread open for him like a silken web: he was already at home in it. The only exception, apparently, the only holdout in the opening-up-to-Jeremy department, was her.

Me me, me me, don't I feel good?

His voice nagged in her mind as she dozed and dreamed. At one point she thought she heard, way out on the lake, a motor chugging, but then the sound went away. She decided it was just the engine of her own mind, laboring noisily as usual in the darkness, going nowhere fast.

"Ahem, people," Kyle said. "The Klingons are getting restless."

Mimi blinked open her eyes. The light was gray. Mist rose from the water. The sun peeked through the trees, bleaching out some things and darkening others. The shadows of the meters stretched over the parking lot. You had to pay, she thought, for every fucking thing.

Down the beach, the alien visitors were dressed now, their rafts collapsed behind them, flattened and faded like old gum. They wore cargo pants and sweat suits, baseball caps with folded visors. They tied up their sneakers, then straightened the sleeves of their ridiculous outfits.

"Someone should go talk to them," Mimi said. "Let them know we're friendly."

"A little close encounter," Marcus agreed.

"Hand my brain over to some alien in a jogging suit?" Kyle said. "No fucking way."

"Believe me," Lisa said, "no one will know the difference."

"I'll go," Mimi said.

"No you won't," Jeremy said.

"Why not?"

"Because I'm not letting you." To soften it, he added, "Not alone, anyway."

"I'll be fine."

"Well, you'll be even finer if I come too."

"No, Jeremy, I won't."

"Ouch," Lisa said, giggling. "Check it out. The mouse that roared."

Jeremy turned to Mimi with his big heavy lit-up eyes. "What is it with you, Mimi? Why are you always working so hard to pull away?"

"I'm just—" But it seemed impossible to explain to him, or even to herself, what she was just doing, even though she could see that it was of tremendous significance to him that she do just that. His eyes went small, his lips pursed, and that cute, hardworking facial muscle of his, the one that connected his fuzzy cheek to his bony jaw, clamped up tight. She pictured him two weeks from now, down in New York, shaving those fine, soft cheek hairs in the bathroom sink and staring into the mirror, as if demanding it to tell him how nice he looked, how good he made it feel.

Right now though he looked pretty tense. He kept digging divots in the sand with his feet. From the way he avoided her eyes, he seemed already afraid of what she might say. This was what Mimi didn't like about having a boyfriend. The way every move you made was seen as either good or bad, either brought you toward him or took you away, when often as not you intended neither one. Maybe if she'd been smarter, more expressive, she'd have found a way to make Jeremy understand what she meant and would not have had to endure all this self-absorbed confusion of his, and the pain that seemed to be waiting for him, like a boat just offshore, when that confusion passed.

Around then they heard the first sirens.

"Uh-oh," Marcus said. "The cavalry."

After that things unraveled very fast. Mimi sort of half-ran down to the lake, while the aliens scrambled to button their pants and gather up their stuff and get going already. No one saw her approach. The closer she came, the more she found herself agreeing with Yuko: underneath the baseball caps the aliens did look Chinese. In fact it began to seem possible, even probable, even, sad to say, incredibly freaking obvious, that they *were* Chinese.

"Whoa," she said, breathing hard. "You're Chinese."

The Chinese guys seemed almost as taken aback by this news as she was. Had they been floating out on the lake so long they no longer remembered who they were or where they were from?

"It's stupid, I know, but for a minute there we thought you might be extraterrestrials. You know, space creatures? But I guess not."

They continued to observe her inattentively at best, showing only the most minimal interest in this one-sided conversation. Clearly they did not speak her dense, stupid language. And to be fair, they probably had a lot of last-minute details on their minds. It must be a pretty complex operation, she imagined, sneaking into a new country. She remembered her immigration unit back in sixth grade, all the tired, poor, huddled masses, like her great-grandfather, who'd also snuck his way in, come to think of it, on a boat, with no money or family or possessions, trying to get out of some shithole village in Central Europe the name of which she could never remember, and would in any case never find, given that between one fascist dictator and another it had probably been obliterated three or four times by now. The old guy had died way before she was born. She knew him only from his picture at the top of the staircase, a fierce-looking gray-beard in a collarless smock who glared down at her, tracking her comings and goings. What did he think of his progeny now, she wondered, with her crying jags, her drug consumption and bitchy friends, her lousy SATs? Was it worth the trip?

"Hey, listen," she said, wanting to ease their passage some-how, "I just wanted to say, on behalf of me and my friends up there, welcome to the land of the free, et cetera."

No response. She watched her little welcome speech do a 747 over their heads.

"Of course it's kind of a shitty, boring place to live," she acknowledged, by way of full disclosure, "and the weather sucks. But most of us are friendly. And you've got the lake here and all, which is good for swimming and partying and stuff. Though I realize you probably aren't too interested in partying at the moment."

The aliens watched her like a television going in the back-ground, flickering away harmlessly, making noise. Fair enough. She watched herself too—grinning and babbling and flapping her arms like a puppet on a string. That seemed to be the thing to do at this moment to put the aliens at ease: show them how silly she was, how ungainly. Because silly and ungainly people, as everyone knew, were incapable of harm. And the aliens looked a bit nervous and defensive all of a sudden, as if even her pres-ence here talking to them was evidence somehow of a plan gone wrong. It happened sometimes, people getting busted and deported, hauled off in chains, and all because some plan or other had gone wrong. Because once you set off from home, crossed that border between the claustrophobic familiar and the infinite imagined, nothing ever seemed to go the way it should.

Anyway they did plenty of harm, silly and ungainly people. As a reminder of this you had only to listen: the sirens were getting closer.

"Hey look," she said, grabbing the nearest Chinese guy by the arm. "You better get out of here, I'm serious. Someone's coming."

He examined her hand on his arm with considerable hostility, until she removed it. "I not deaf," he said.

"Oh good, you speak English, I mean, what a break. It'll come in handy. 'Cause they're going to be looking for you, you know, and it'll make it easier to get away if you can actually speak the, I mean . . ."

She should have brought Jeremy with her; she was no good in these situations. Her father was good at them, her mother was good at them, Danielle was good at them, but something had gone wrong, some genetic mishap or botched inoculation, and now she'd never get into college, never travel, never get married, never be the one whom people listened to in an emergency. The Chinese guy must have sensed this, which was why he continued to look so hostile, she thought, as he tugged on his baseball cap and patted it down on top.

"My friends and I want to help. We saw you guys float in. You probably saw us too."

"We saw. You play in sand. But we very busy now."

He wore a wedding ring, she noticed, a silver band around the fourth finger. His eyes were red, his black hair matted and peppered with sand. She was tempted to ask him what his wife was doing at this moment, but it was none of her business.

"Hey, you guys hungry? We've got some Doritos and stuff back there . . . might help tide you over."

"No food!" he said. "No time!"

He was right about that: the sirens were everywhere now, as if the whole cosmos were on red alert. Boats were roaring across the lake, their headlights tunneling paths through the murk and mist, their hulls crashing up and down, not so much skimming the water as beating the hell out of it, churning up foam. Mimi stood tall, watching them approach with a kind of matadorial disdain. She understood now why she was there. She was not the helpless orphan on the beach; she was the mother who happened by. The protector.

"Come on." She grabbed the Chinese guy by the hand. "My friends and I will hide you."

"Friends?"

"It's cool. You can trust us, I promise."

He seemed to consider her offer. "You friends?"

"Yeah, we're friends."

But he didn't seem to believe her. His eyes went large and cartoon-round, fixing on some phantom panic-point over her shoulder. She turned to find Jeremy bearing down on them at full speed, the sand exploding up behind him in spasmodic bursts like the discharge of an automatic weapon.

"Me me! Me me! Me me!"

Between the red lights strafing the lakeshore and Jeremy charging down the beach in lacrosse-attack mode and the feds in blue windbreakers jumping awkwardly into the water, the little levee of calm Mimi had tried to erect was breached: the aliens took off in every direction and disappeared into the woods. The beach lay empty. Two INS boats circled in the shallows. Men were pointing flashlights, barking through bullhorns. Mimi stood alone, clutching herself for comfort, mindful even now of the extra layer of flab that adhered around her elbows.

Then Jeremy was beside her and, as if by some amazing good-boyfriend instinct, enfolding her in his strong, hairless arms. "It's cool, Mimi," he murmured, his lips warm against her neck. "Everything's cool."

She closed her eyes. It was one of those moments she knew she'd look back on someday with wonder and satisfaction. *This guy I went with junior year,* she'd tell the daughter she would probably come to think of it never have, *he just had this way of standing by me that was so unbelievably great.*

But Jeremy was not standing by her, actually: he was leading her away. Or not away exactly, but out, in the direction of the parking lot, where the patrol car was idling, and two guys in ugly blue blazers were talking through bullhorns, barking terse, crackling instructions. Hands up. Walk slow. Stay together. Get in.

"Wait," she said, "where are they taking us?"

"Not us," he said. "Them."

"But why?" Something about the way he said *them* really turned her off. "What did they do that was so bad?"

"Look," Jeremy said, in a tired, calm, exasperated voice that she found both scary and impressive, "these guys mean business, okay? Check out those boats. They've got infrared, heat sensors. These guys can track you down, Mimi, from the fillings in your teeth. This Homeland Security thing is no joke." .

"So what's a few Chinese guys more or less? It's not like they're terrorists. They'll probably just open a laundry or something."

Jeremy shook his head in that superior, condescending way of his. He was still red-cheeked from his psychotic charge down the beach, which made the wispy hairs where his beard would grow in someday, if he let it, that much more prominent. "It's the law. You can't just let everybody in. The whole system'll fall apart. It'll be like back to the Stone Age."

Good, she wanted to say.

But he was already trudging dutifully toward the parking lot, never turning, not even once, to see if she was still following him. Either he assumed she was, or he assumed just the opposite, or else he was no longer thinking of her at all. She could see the bulge in his shorts where he carried his cell phone. Had he been the one to call in the feds? She looked down at the sand, where the aliens had dropped their stuff—gum, cigarettes, photographs—when they ran away. There was an address book with a plastic cover. Packets of nuts and dried fruit. A damp Polaroid of a Chinese woman and a teenage girl. The girl was a lot prettier than she was, Mimi thought, more somber and substantial, more mature. And now that girl had lost her father to another country, which would make her even more somber and substantial and mature, to say nothing of totally miserable probably. And he hadn't even made it *in.* They'd put him away for a while, then send him back. And that too would be miserable for her, Mimi thought. Not just the wait, but the return.

"Come forward, please," a guy barked through one of the bullhorns. "We're asking that you please come forward at once."

A crew from the local TV station pulled into the lot. The back door slid open. Two guys came running out with a camera and a boom mike, both of which homed in on her at once, before she could turn away.

"What's that?" they called. "What's that in your hand?"

And that's how she looked that night, on the local news— alone, frozen in the light, dangling that soggy Polaroid in the air like a flag.

6

Sympathy for the Devil

Though God knew it wasn't something he'd have sought out for himself, spending July 4th weekend in the Carthage County lockup had to be ranked, on Teddy's rapidly growing list of traumatic experiences, somewhere in the middle. He'd almost have preferred it worse.

Down the hall, like a low-amperage current, flowed the melancholy Esperanto of his fellow inmates, swapping hardluck stories through the bars of their cells. Justice was not being served in the proper amounts to anyone: that was the consensus. Guilt, it seemed, had no place at the table. Innocence flourished underground, in the dankness and poor light, as mushrooms do: top-heavy, dubiously shaped.

Teddy for his part felt no guilt at all. Why should he? He was not the transgressor in the family. He was not the one who'd managed, in the course of a single night, to break half a dozen local, state, and federal laws. Oh, Mimi and her friends had stuck it to them all right. Stuck It to the Man. Teddy, having grown up in the golden age of Sticking It to the Man, might have been inclined that way himself, but after fourteen years as a principal—fourteen years of *being* the man—his allegiances had tilted and he no longer quite saw the appeal. Neither in his experience did most authority figures, especially the men. They didn't like being stuck to, and they had a number of cold, hard strategies for letting you know. Fortunately Mimi and her friends were middle-class children: to be insulated from cold, hard realities was their fate.

The Chinese aliens, being neither children nor middle-class, and having no mothers who were lawyers at their disposal, were another story. First they'd been forced to brave the terrors of a night journey through woods and water. Then when they arrived, they had to contend with that unholy welcome wagon, Mimi and her crew of feckless stoners. Then they'd been rounded up by the feds and tossed into some moldy, underfunded county jail in which to languish away the summer. And meanwhile all they wanted from this country was what Teddy and his neighbors already had: a house, a yard, a garden, a minivan with sliding doors in which to drive the kids to soccer. Soon of course everyone in China would have these things, but apparently these guys had not been willing to wait. Now they would be punished for that impatience. Now they'd *have* to wait, wait for all the legal-jurisdictional issues to be worked out, for the state and federal authorities to weigh in, for asylums to be granted or more likely denied. And all the while so far from their families.

Though conceivably, when you're stuck in jail with no prospect of asylum, a little distance from one's family was not a bad idea.

So it seemed to Teddy, and from the evidence to Gail as well, for she never did visit him in prison. He supposed she had her hands full, logging all those nonbillable hours on Mimi's behalf; probably no slots were left in her appointment book for that other pro bono project—that other rogue relative—her husband. Well, he wouldn't complain. He had his books for company: Burton, Thesiger, a life of Rimbaud. From these restless madmen he hoped to learn a little patience. God knew patience was a virtue at times like these.

Of course patience would have been a virtue in times just *before* these too. Say like in dealing with Mimi, whose own legal journey had proved highly taxing all around. Even after they'd gotten her released, after they'd taken the girl home and finished brow-beating her into sullen, slack-faced silence at the kitchen table, the smog of willful criminality still hung over the house.

"The legal charges aren't the issue," Gail had said later, grim-faced in bed. "Obviously they're only symptoms."

"Symptoms of what?"

"You tell me."

"I have no idea. I'm assuming you do, though, which is why you're so upset."

"I'm upset *because* you have no idea."

"Do you?"

She'd sighed, the sheets bunched against her chest, as if all questions engendered by Mimi at this point were too weighty and imponderable to answer. Teddy turned to the window. The bright bulb of the reading lamp blazed in the glass. Somewhere beyond it, in the dark woods, they'd lost sight of the girl. His fault too. Ever since that party at the Dunns' he'd been a sad case, stumbling blindly through the panic fields. Lab tests, biopsies, radiology reports: his head was crammed with numbers and probabilities; there was no free space. Darkness found him at his desk, revving up the search engines, graphing intricate night journeys of his own. No wonder Mimi had slipped between the cracks.

A dumb expression, Teddy thought. You don't slip between the cracks; you slip through them. He was beginning to feel a bit cracked these days himself. But enough. He resolved to stop coddling himself at once and start paying his daughter better attention from this moment forward.

And indeed, he did. So much better attention did Teddy pay her, and of such a charged and singular kind, that he wound up brushing against the law himself. Then the law, taking exception, brushed back. Which was how he came to spend the three-day holiday weekend here in the Carthage County lockup, with only old books for company.

The real prisons are the hospitals, and the real hospitals are the prisons. Teddy had found this out the hard way: by visiting both.

Naturally it had been something of a shock, the sight of his own blood parachuting into the depths of the Dunns' toilet. But he hadn't panicked. Teddy Hastings was a man with deep strategic reserves of denial and displacement, and he'd tapped these reserves at once. The whole ride home with Gail he hadn't said a word. The next day they'd gone boating on the lake with friends, and that had been pleasant; the day after that, he'd recaulked the shower; and after that he was busy at school. So it was not until the following Friday, after the last bell had rung and he'd gone into the administrator's bathroom, locked the door of the stall behind him, and found blood there too that the drill rigs of denial went quiet, the wells of repression ran dry.

Then he did panic. He panicked for real. His forehead went slick; his heart spun and creaked. He could hear, down the hall, the swoosh of the custodian's wax-and-buff machine making slow, somnolent circles of erasure, like some inexorable mechanism of fate. He held his breath, waiting for it to pass. When it did he felt better.

But later at home the panic returned. Then receded. Then returned. This went on for some days. Finally, when his body politic had grown too riotous and incendiary for sleep, when he was at his most wrought up, calmed down, done in, and worn-out, he'd called up the new internist in town, Scott Wainwright, and scheduled an appointment.

Wainwright was a crew-cut, no-nonsense young man with a swimmer's sloping shoulders and a thirty-inch waist. Teddy disliked him immediately. His office was cold but bright, still littered with *Field and Stream*s and *National Geographic*s addressed to his predecessor, kindly old Doc Englehorn, who'd retired to Arizona. Englehorn had been the soporific, sit-back-and-chat type. Wainwright was more hands-on. He nodded officiously while Teddy ran through the family history, connecting the black dots, rattling the old skeletons. Christ, there were a lot of them. His was the only one left with any flesh and blood in it. And now the blood was taking leave of him too.

Wainwright frowned, tapping his pen against the clipboard, not bothering to write much down. "I wouldn't worry," he said. "A little minor colonic bleeding. It's in no way unusual at your age."

Teddy nodded hopefully, though the last clause depressed him. He had arrived at the age where no calamities of the body were unusual.

"On the other hand," the doctor said, "it's not entirely common either. So we better go ahead and get started."

"Started on what?"

Wainwright looked appalled. "We have tests for these things, Mr. Hastings. Surely you've had a colonoscopy before."

"Actually I'd been meaning to get one. I was thinking maybe in a year or two. But I guess you're thinking earlier, huh?"

The doctor stared at him blandly.

"Okay fine," Teddy said. "Let the games begin."

The tests turned out to be exactly as he'd feared: multiple, invasive, painful, protracted. What got him through was the phrase Wainwright had employed, that bit about how a little colonic bleeding was not unusual. Teddy kept this in mind as he weathered the indignities in his blue clip-on smock. He gave away his blood, his urine, his stool, everything they wanted, and all the while he kept shuffling those words in his head like a pack of cards from which only winning hands could be dealt. He was still engaged in this merry mental blackjack when Wainwright called him into his office on a hot day in June and informed him rather casually of the three small, adenomatous polyps they'd found in the lining of his colon.

"How small is small?" Teddy asked.

"Minuscule. Less than a centimeter. I'm not concerned in the least."

"Why would you be? I'm the one with the tumors."

"They're polyps, Mr. Hastings. At your age, a few colorectal polyps of this nature are hardly unusual."

"Which is what you said about the bleeding."

"Come now, don't be frightened. In all likelihood they're benign. There's very little doubt in my mind. But we'll just send them to the lab and make sure. Should we call you when the results are in?"

"No."

"Sorry?"

"I mean I'd rather get it in person, if it's all the same to you."

Wainright frowned; clearly it wasn't all the same to him. "Okay. Go ahead and make an appointment."

About the next two weeks there was little to be said. He went about his business, at school and at home. His mind was an unpocked moon, bright but remote; no landing crafts of thought or expectancy adhered to its surface. In a sense he was happier than he'd been in some time. He could not have begun to say why.

Then he went in for his appointment.

The verdict, when it came, affected him strangely. He'd steeled himself for the other. It was difficult to reverse course, to *un*steel himself now. Other things that proved difficult at that moment: moving, breathing, speaking, and letting go of Gail's cool, familiar hand, which he clutched to his chest like a buoy as he blinked back hot tears. Benign, malignant—how easy it was, slumped in a chair in the waiting lounge, with the sun shooting at you like a ray gun through the floor-to-ceiling windows, to mistake one fraternal twin for the other. He gazed mistily around the room, that pastel purgatory with the all-weather carpet. He'd spent forty-five minutes here already. Forty-five minutes of colorless furniture, and odorless plants, and back issues of travel magazines advertising deals no longer available for hotels he couldn't afford. And the people too, the hunched and sickly, the elderly and infirm, settled deep in their chairs, staring glassily ahead. As if stupefied by waiting. Made sick by waiting. Teddy hoped his own face did not look like theirs, but he supposed in time it would. All he had to do was wait.

On the wall was a Kurdish poem, elegantly framed, courtesy of the state council for the arts. Dutifully he scanned the lines.

> *We should not blame the stones*
> *For their silence, their dignity.*
> *We should not blame the swift rivers*
> *For their impatience, their madness.*
> *We should not forget to console the mountain*
> *Which laments after a deserting cloud.*
> *We must learn to love the different hearts.*

The usual maddening bullshit, in short, funded by his own tax dollars. And yet he kind of liked that line about the rivers, about not blaming them for anything. This struck him as wise. He wondered if the Kurdish poet knew his work was being displayed in American hospitals, and whether he'd receive royalties for it, and what sort of life he lived over in Kurdistan or whatever it was now called. An embattled people, the Kurds. But then who wasn't? He liked the line about the mountain too.

He was sufficiently absorbed in the strange landscape of the poem that he almost failed to notice Scott Wainwright, a rather grim-faced young man even, Teddy imagined, under the most lighthearted circumstances, plodding down the corridor in his direction. His white coat, as it approached the double doors, was mirrored in the glass, so that for a moment it was unclear where doctor left off and patients began.

Then he pushed his way through.

"Mr. Hastings?"

Calmly Teddy rose from his chair. Now that the moment had arrived, the parade of apprehension in his chest—anxiety's rattling snares, fear's bellowing woodwinds—went mute. His mind was a blank field. He stood swaying in the doorway, heavy and dumb as an animal. His file was in the doctor's hands, already splayed open. There was writing on all the pages.

"Okay, so let's sit down, shall we?"

Teddy nodded. His limbs were frozen. He didn't move. Steam from some internal grate clouded his eyes. He was not a believer in God but it was in its way a religious instant. He felt himself under a beam of pure light. Someone had glimpsed the things inside him, taken their measure; his flawed body had been seen and understood. Now he would hear the report.

The doctor cleared his throat. There appeared to be some blockage.

And then after that Teddy must have checked out for a while, or rather in, for he now discovered himself to be the sole inhabitant of a quiet, tucked-away little hotel, which by virtue of his no longer being conscious (for abruptly, as if a plug had been pulled, all the blood had *whooshed* from his head) seemed his own natural home in which to lie around and rest for as long as he liked. His ears hummed a pleasant tune. He was aware of some guy in a uniform, a porter no doubt, calling out loudly for room service, but he hadn't ordered room service so he paid no attention. He was fine where he was. True, the room smelled a bit smoky, but he doubted the place was on fire. Next time he'd request a nonsmoking. He liked this place; he was comfortable here; he had no wish to leave. All he wanted was to go on lying where he was, watching the sunlight stream through the cracks in the blinds, the dust motes riding their fickle currents, the updrafts and downdrafts no one could see.

"For a second I thought you *had* died," Gail said, assessing him thoughtfully over the bloodied quarters of her grapefruit. "Lying on the floor in your smock that way, with your eyes all rolled up in your head. It was a pretty dramatic sight, let me tell you."

"Actually it was very peaceful," he said. "It just seemed, I don't know, the next thing."

"Peaceful for you maybe. The rest of us were frantic. Then the smelling salts didn't work and even that cool customer Wainwright got freaked. You didn't hear him bellowing at the nurses? Like it was *their* fault?"

"I didn't hear a thing."

"The luck of the oblivious." She probed the tip of her spoon experimentally into the pinkish pulp. "You know, we can joke about it now, but it wasn't funny. I thought you'd left the building. I said to myself, 'He's not coming back.'"

"Sorry if I scared you." It occurred to him however that he didn't *sound* sorry, he sounded weary and proud and a little bit exhilarated, as if he'd won something from her. He chewed his dry wheat toast, eyeing the marmalade jar with its shreds of jellied fruit, the stick of butter softening in its dish. The toast would taste better, he knew, if he covered it in these things. But he didn't want it to taste better; he wanted it to taste like what it was. "Anyway, no harm done. I'm back now."

"Are you?"

She made a soft clicking noise with her back teeth and examined him through narrowed lids, not so much thoughtfully as clinically. He knew more or less the picture he presented. The terry-cloth bathrobe with its frayed belt and broken loops. The plump white potato of his belly. The calico stubble in the hollows of his scalp, the jutting slopes of his cheeks. Even sitting up, he knew he looked vaguely like a slob in a Barcalounger, lying down. An invalid. A sicko.

Yet, as things had turned out, he *wasn't* sick. He did not feel like an invalid exactly; if anything he felt *more* valid. More alive.

"I have to go to work in a minute," Gail said. "You'll be okay here?"

"Of course."

"Well, okay. If you're sure."

A stark, lacerating thought bloomed in Teddy's mind like a cactus flower: Gail too had steeled herself for that other word. Prepared herself for the crisis of malignancy, for full-out assault, radioactive war. Those whispered phone calls, those late nights hunched over her computer, squinting through her reading glasses, browsing the Web for what-ifs . . . after so much work and so little consequence a certain letdown, he supposed, was only to be expected. After all, what was there to celebrate? A victory by default? The opponent had simply failed to appear. It was a forfeit, a nonevent, an apprehension of something large that's passed you by, like not getting hit by a truck.

Benign: 1. of a gentle disposition; 2. of a mild kind.

And was this how the years would now go? Dry crusts swathed in marmalade and butter. The soft mesh of routine. Everything mild and regular as the tick of a watch. And all the while waiting for the crisis that would shatter the glass, and arrest time for good. You spend half your life erecting a canopy over yourself, and the other half anticipating the brilliant jagged flash that splits it open, and lets the elements come raining in.

Outside, birds were lined up in the locust trees, singing the same old chirpy, unvarying songs. Shut the fuck up, he thought.

"I'm trying to decide what to make for dinner," Gail said. "Any ideas?"

"None."

"Fine," she sighed. "We'll improvise."

He looked at her, his wife, his partner, his running mate. The skin had loosened under her jaw; her hands were veiny and thin. How long did they have left? Nothing had changed. He was still healthy, still operating in a world of relative happinesses, relative disappointments, where people had breakfast with their spouses and discussed their affairs. All he had to do was get up, get dressed, and go to work like everyone else. And yet herein lay the problem. For better or okay, maybe for worse, he no longer *felt* like everyone else. The sight of his X-ray on the illuminated screen in Wainwright's office stayed with him, that dark sheet with its twiggy, outflung arms, the brittle cage of his ribs . . . like a snapshot of the inner man, the corpse you carried under your clothes. A stick figure! A cartoon! And so much empty space between the luminous bones! It was as if some benign nonfunctioning organ had died in the hospital and been scraped away, in order that another, more singular organ might live.

But live how? And want what?

He wished he were hungry, but he wasn't. He wished he were thirsty, but he wasn't. He wished he were horny, but he wasn't. He could feel his appetites flaking off one by one, like so much dead skin. Shaving his head had, he saw now, been only the first step. There would be others. The body lightening its load, stripping itself down, as if in preparation for a voyage. To make the new, you had to discard the old. Leave a little slag heap in back of the factory.

"So are you going to school today?" Gail had slung her bag over her shoulder and was checking her keys. "I'd imagine they miss you down there."

"Zoe is exceptionally capable."

"True. Of course, so are you."

"It's only been a few days. Give me some time to recover."

"To recover from not being sick, you mean? How does that work, exactly?"

"I'll tell you when I know."

"Fine. So you'll be here when Mimi gets home then. I mean, really here. Like, present. Like, back in the swing or whatever you want to call it."

"The swing?" Under the circumstances, it did not seem wise to confess to Gail how he'd spent the day before, how much solitaire he'd played, how much television he'd watched, how much empty space he'd surveyed through the window, how much coffee he'd made and consumed; how, lighting the stove in his terry-cloth robe and his fake-suede slippers, he'd idly toyed with the idea of holding the oven mitt over the jet's blue fluttering flame, wondering how long it would take to burn. A stupid, random impulse, it came and it went. He had not moved the oven mitt into the flame; he had not moved the oven mitt at all. Whether it was courage or cowardice that restrained him, Teddy didn't know. There was no way of knowing why one didn't do the things one didn't do. Just as there was no way of knowing why one did the things one *did* do, without going ahead and doing them. "But I never got out of it," he said.

Thank God it was June: the budget was already passed, the new curricula set, the school year, that bloated epic, already inscribed in the books. Teddy could stay home and recuperate for as long as he felt like. Let Zoe deal with the field trips, the band concerts and honors assemblies. She was better at such functions than he was anyway, as she often made a point of reminding him.

"Why not take graduation off too?" she'd said. "No need to rush back. We've got everything under control."

Normally Zoe's cool, authoritative tone, so effective with boys in detention, along with her cunning imperial use of the first-person plural, would have annoyed Teddy no end. In fact it annoyed him now. Nonetheless her proposal was tempting. How many years had it been since he'd last enjoyed a graduation? Since the solemnities of the event, the tearful parents, the earnest speeches, the piping choir, had roused any emotion from him at all?

"I may just do that," he said. "I've got some sick days stored up. If you're sure you're on top of it?"

"I'm on top," Zoe said.

"Gretchen can step in if necessary. Or Mary Anne. They've done it before."

"I know."

"Don't forget Pierce. He's single—he doesn't have to run home after school. Plus he's a fan favorite."

"Not with me," Zoe said. "There's something about that man. What is it? His eyes are all over the room."

"He's just a kid. Give him time. He hasn't settled in yet."

"I was a kid too when I started. Weren't you? But we weren't like that." Her voice had taken on the steely, imperative tone he dreaded. Like most number twos, Zoe was known for her hard work; it was part of her long-running advertisement for a school of her own. That this campaign seemed doomed to failure—that school boards preferred to hire principals who made their job look easy, not hard—was unfair of course, but unfair in a good way, for it kept Zoe around, working harder than everyone else.

"I've got another call. Take care of yourself, Teddy. Let me know if you need something."

Teddy was nothing if not open to instruction. Boy, did he take care of himself. And boy, did it agree with him, this pared-down, horizontal life. He had the house to himself. The phone rarely rang; when it did he didn't answer. He wore no watch, cooked no meals, took out no trash. Light poured through the curtains and pooled at his feet, dreamy and sluggish, like a golden benediction. He was on the other side now. One of those people who stay home in the middle of the day doing nothing, a master of that lost, esoteric art, sitting still. Robe drooping open, bare calves plunked on the hassock, he leaned back in his reclining chair like some contented provincial aristocrat, plucking grapes—black, seedless—from a ceramic bowl. Around him the house lay tranquil. The rocker sat at rest, the tulips held their petals. The mail and newspapers piled up on the sideboard, unread. Out on the streets, the postmen and cable guys and housepainters and lawn-maintenance people and the other day workers made their noisy, oblivious rounds. What a waste, Teddy thought. All that effort just to travel in circles.

In the bathroom he'd find Bruno curled in the tub, white flanks rippling liquidly in dreams. So this was how old dogs spent their day. He felt like a man with a secret, a second life. Wars and the suffering of innocents were in the news, but the news was far away, the news wasn't new the way *this* was new. This was a feeling he'd have liked to hold on to forever, as one wants to hold a fresh-plucked flower forever, knowing all the time it isn't possible, that soon enough the petals will dry and fade, crushed into powder by the weight of one's palm. And God knew his palms were weightier than most.

The thing about not-dying was this: in the end, it turned out to be, like flower-petal-holding, a lyric condition, transient and bright, a moment snatched from the jaws of eternity. You couldn't live that way forever, all lit up and indolent and marveling. Soon the old motors would begin to race. Soon the weight of gravity would come bearing down, the old habits begin to impose themselves, as habits do. But before that happened, before the slow, exquisite, otherworldly quality of those June days was gone and forgotten, Teddy took two preemptive measures: he ordered himself a treadmill and enrolled in a summer photography course at the college.

VA 103: Black and White Photography, with instructor M. McVay, met in Sunderland Hall, high on the western slope of College Hill. Sunderland, with its tortoiseshell façade of concrete, wood, and steel, had been designed to provoke—the shock of the new and all that—but now that it was no longer new, it stood revealed as the cheap, shabby construction it was. The gray pockmarked walls and industrial-looking floors put one more in mind of a bunker in which to sit out a bombing raid, Teddy decided, than a studio for the pursuit of fine arts. But when he paused to look over the bulletin boards, all littered with colorful flyers, and surveyed the summer internships, the cars and laptops and stereos for sale, the rides being offered to Montana and San Francisco and New Orleans, the seniors looking to share their off-campus houses with nonsmoking vegans and bisexuals, it all came back at once—the giddy socialist élan, the fuzzy vibe of shared intense experience that made every year in college seem as rich and eventful as five years outside it. He knew then it was the right decision, to return to school.

He'd always wanted to take a photography course, back in college. But math had been such a restrictive major; he was usually holed up in the library, or washing dishes in the dining hall, or peer tutoring in the Math Center, bulling his way through. Such were the joys. If he had it to do over again, he'd have bulled and holed up less and done more of that other stuff, the smoking and drinking and creative arts courses and so on. But he did not have it to do over again. Time's odometer moved in one direction only; it could not be rolled back.

He found the right room on the right floor and took a seat out of habit in the back row. Students were milling about, catching up on each other's summer achievements and dissipations.

"Dude, how was India?"

"Sweet. How was Peru?"

"Sick."

It was 7:08. No sign yet of Professor McVay. Teddy opened his rucksack and rummaged through its contents, the notebooks and pens, the rulers and erasers. He was both disappointed and relieved to see he was not the oldest person in the room. He counted three other people "from the community," as it was known on campus, though in this case, judging by their sweat-suits, it appeared to be the *retirement* community. The rest of course were college kids, Danielle's age. For a change Teddy was glad she wasn't around to get mad at him for encroaching on her space, as she used to back in high school when he'd linger in the kitchen on Saturday nights chatting up her friends, or, as Danielle put it, "bothering everyone." Yet in truth he could not have felt more harmless, more *benign,* than he did at this moment, holding his new Montblanc pen over the first unmarked page in his new Wilson Jones Nomad binder, as some skinny young thing with hennaed hair clunked up to the lectern in her clogs and peered out at them skeptically.

"VA 103?"

He looked at his watch: 7:16. He was about to lean over and ask the nearest student what time the class started when he realized what everybody else appeared to know. Class *had* started. Which made that lost waif at the lectern, the one who was now speaking to them in an irresolute, weirdly transatlantic voice, her sleeveless T-shirt dangling halfway to her knees, her long, wil-lowy neck bent like a pretzel from the weight of her head, adjunct instructor M. McVay, for whose services he'd just written the Carthage College registrar a $600 check.

"This is, as you've surely noted in the catalog, a beginning course in theory and practice. The lecture portion will emphasize historical trends, contemporary applications, and an appreciation of the art and craft. In the lab portion we'll concentrate on camera technique, film exposure and processing, darkroom techniques, lighting, and composition. Any questions so far?"

No one had any questions so far.

"I am, as you'll see, a great believer in asking questions. Making pictures is an interrogative experience. You don't make a picture from an answer; you make it from a question. When all your questions are answered, you're no longer an artist, are you? You're either a guru or a corpse. So you see, if you *do* have questions, any questions at all, I'd like you to just go ahead and ask them."

She hesitated, tidying her notes against the lectern with her long, tremulous fingers. Surely, Teddy thought, Professor M. McVay had not intended to come off quite so runic and kung fu–ish as she had. But this early in the hour, with the air conditioner humming senselessly in the window and the sinking light of a spectacular sunset slanting through the maples, the effect of her remarks was to shut down any prospect of inquiry at once. Nobody had questions, nobody had ever had questions, and moreover nobody would ever have questions: that was the basic state of things in VA 103.

"Well, down to business then. Please don't fail to correct me if I mispronounce your name."

She peered down at the computerized roll sheet through her blockish black-framed glasses, and proceeded to do just that. Of the thirteen names, she tunelessly butchered half of them, and nobody corrected her. She looked jumpy enough as it was. She had the posture of some oversize mantis, nervous and twiggy, sharp-jointed. Had she ever taught before? According to the catalog she was currently in residence at the

New School; but whether she taught there or studied there—or hung on the wall—wasn't clear. Her face was a kind of survey course all its own. Her skin had the milky-blue glow of a Vermeer. Her eyebrows had a Gothic arch; her cheekbones a modernist severity; her lips, a glossy, sullen impasto. Yet compared to Gail, she seemed, like most young women, somehow rather vain and shallow, unformed. Which did not prevent him from noting the steady undulations of her pelvic mound moving rhythmically against the lectern, or the bouncy musical way she walked over to the blackboard, her heels clicking on the linoleum, her bracelets jangling away like tambourines. She made a considerable racket all right, this tiny, anemic-looking person to whom he'd committed the next six weeks of his life.

She picked up the chalk and his heart gave a squeeze. Oh, he did love these first days of school—walking into a strange classroom, being handed a new set of tools, and getting down to work. Already the blackboard was filling up with perplexing new equations:

Art's one subject = the human clay.

Professor McVay turned to face the class. "Anyone want to hazard a guess about what this means?"

Apparently no one did want to hazard such a guess however.

"Well, I'll give you a hint. It's from W. H. Auden." She kept up her smile for as long as she could, but her gaze was directed downward, at the fluttering sheaves of her lecture notes. "The poet?"

All hope of pleasure now fled the room for good. It was fifteen minutes into the first class, the thermometer read eighty-five degrees, everyone with any money or sense was off in Europe or on the coast of Maine, and already the first deadly warning signs of pretension—quotes on the board, the invocation of poetry—were flashing yellow on the long road to nine thirty. Was there to be any actual *photography* component to this photography class?

"Now the task of the artist, if I'm reading Auden right, is to engage in dialogue with earthly forms. To keep our perceptions fresh. Be alert to what Cartier-Bresson calls 'the scars of the world.'" She took a sip from her paper cup. "But fresh perception is no easy task. We're bombarded with images every day. Think of it—every one of you has the technology at your disposal to make a movie, record a CD, post a blog, and take a picture of yourself with your cell phone and send it to the ends of the earth. Surely this is a good thing. But if everything's so accessible, what then has value? If images are just more cheap goods to produce and consume, why bother to perfect them? Why learn how to use a thirty-five-millimeter camera? Why master the rudiments of the darkroom? Why squirrel yourself away all night, breathing toxic chemicals and fussing over composition? What purpose does it serve? These are questions I hope we'll be addressing together in the weeks ahead. Now, if you'll all turn to the syllabus for a moment . . ."

But nobody had a syllabus, so the class came to another screeching halt while she passed copies around. The document ran to three pages, none of which were stapled to the others. Students were taking out their cell phones and staring frankly at the screens, as if willing some message of deliverance to appear.

"As you'll see, I've included the usual suspects. Warren's *Concise Guide,* Stahl's *What Is Photography?* Berger of course. Baudrillard. But I'd like to begin with a little volume by Rimbaud, *Illuminations.* Perhaps some of you have read it? Rimbaud was of course a highly visual poet from the first. But even after he grew bored with poetry and moved to Africa, he did not abandon art altogether. He worked hard at his photography. He had his mother send him the latest film and equipment from Paris, though eventually he grew bored with that too. Not the most emotionally stable person, our Monsieur Rimbaud. But then highly creative people are easily bored, aren't they?"

The fellow in the second row, the one who'd just got back from Peru, was an easily bored creative person himself—you could tell by the extravagant way he now leaned back and yawned. A girl beside him tittered. Meta McVay glanced up from her notes in distress, her long throat mottled, her eyes filmy behind her glasses. *My God,* Teddy thought, *she's never taught before.* The stuttering, overemphatic gestures, the extraneous digressions about this guy Rimbaud, the way she kept looking down at her note cards like a game-show host, shuffling them in search of an answer—he'd seen all these signs and symptoms before: the novice pedagogue in over her head. The father in him wanted to sling his big, protective arm around her white shoulders and sit her down. The lover in him, that rough beast, wanted to rise, shake out his woolly coat, saunter forward, and *lie* her down. And of course the school administrator in him, that cold clerk with his rolled-up sleeves, wanted to have her canned immediately. A teacher as poor as M. McVay wouldn't last a week at the Carthage Union Middle School. So naturally it followed that she'd been hired at Carthage College. That was the private-education racket for you: the more paid, the less received.

He stuck his hand in the air and waved it like a flag.

"Yes?" M. McVay groaned, truly apprehensive now.

"This is probably just me," Teddy said, "but I'm a total beginner here. I feel like it would help me to maybe get some of the basics first? Like what sort of equipment we need, and how we'll be evaluated, and all that?"

"Yes, I was going to come to that, once I laid out the, uh, groundwork as it were. But perhaps it *would* be better to start with the basics." She put down her notes. "Shall we just go ahead and start with the basics? Would that be okay for everyone?"

A few people nodded grudgingly. Already you could feel it, the change in pressure, the new beginning. Nobody appreciated how hard it was, Teddy thought, the teaching business. You couldn't just start in the air: you had to get purchase. Build a concrete foundation, then ascend from there.

He watched her now, crisply ticking off the requirements.

The books to be bought, the craft areas to be addressed. Filters and lenses. Dodging and burning. Light and shadow. At one point she paused, glancing up at Teddy with what might have been gratitude or deference or puzzlement, but he didn't linger on the implications. There wasn't time. He opened his Nomad binder, freed a clean white page from the steel-toothed clasps, and copied down the basics like everyone else.

The first assignment was the most basic one imaginable. The Visual Diary. A kind of meet and greet. "Get to know the camera," Meta McVay had said. "Carry it with you around the house. Just take pictures. You'll find that anything becomes interesting when you look at it long enough."

Teddy was eager to get started. He'd already ordered his equipment by Express Mail: a 35 mm Leica M6 range finder with a 50 mm lens. A Vivitar flash. Fifty rolls of Fuji Acros and Kodak Tri-X film. Enlarging paper, dodging wand, burning board. When they arrived, he carried the boxes down to the basement and set them on the ping-pong table he'd insisted on buying the girls for Christmas ten years ago, thinking they might enjoy the game as much as Philip and he had in their youth. But they hadn't. Now the net was down, the surface gouged and scarred, and the table's sole function was to provide storage and exhibit space for the Hastings Museum of Bygone Technologies—all the old printers, slide projectors, tape recorders, boom boxes, and VCRs bought over the years and then discarded in favor of the new. Well, maybe this one would break the string. Maybe this one would last.

Just tearing open the cardboard gave him pleasure. The cheerful snap of the bubbled plastic. The squeal of goods being extracted from their Styrofoam harnesses. The dehumidifier hummed and cackled, urging him on. Carefully he inspected each piece of equipment, admired its heft and shine. Then he reached for the operating manuals. Teddy had contempt for people who didn't read their operating manuals, people who, by choosing not to read manuals, were passively electing to be dependent upon people like him, people who *did* read manuals, to map out the circuitry of their lives. And he was surrounded by such people. Hence he was the one who'd set up Danielle's laptop, who'd programmed Mimi's MP3 player, who'd installed Gail's tax software on her hard drive. It was the price he paid for having that sort of mind. God help him, he liked taking things apart and then rebuilding from scratch. But at last there comes a time to put the manuals away, to stop reading and start doing. So he pushed all that crumpled packaging aside, picked up the camera—it was heavier than it looked—and tromped out into the startling daylight.

One nice thing about living in the country: all these picturesque landscapes were just lying around, waiting to be noticed. The yard, the garden, the woods, the snaking brook and muscular mountains and golden fields—it all came flooding through the lens, rushing and indiscriminate; he had only to stand there and catch it with the Leica like a bucket. He tried to do it as Meta McVay directed. Tried to see things *as if for the first time,* whatever that meant. Tried to *defamiliarize the environment,* whatever that meant, and to *decontextualize it,* whatever that meant. Tried to *reassemble it as a series of progressive visual relationships using memory and personal narrative,* whatever that meant. Above all, he tried *not to be overly self-conscious about being overly self-consciousness,* whatever that meant.

At moments, it was true, facility seemed within reach, the instrument in his hands felt light and responsive, and every click of the shutter was soft as a kiss. But there were other moments too, and a great many more of them, when nothing held still, when the light was all wrong, the Leica jerked in his hands, when every shutter speed was too fast or too slow, every detail gone smeary or marginal. At such times he felt like a drunk fumbling in the dark with his keys. He could not coax the doors open. Could not work his way past his own security system and step inside. He kept plugging away at his nature shots—the bloody sunsets, the spindly deer posed stoic in the fields, the frivolous finches lighting up the weigela bush like Christmas ornaments—with a sinking heart. He could no longer conceal, even from himself, his boredom with the whole nature-shot enterprise. What he prized about nature was its impersonality, its indifference to human will, human designs. Now he began to loathe it for the same reasons. He trudged back to the house, set down the Leica, unslung his brand-new $40 camera bag, and left it on a chair, bulging with chargers and adapters, and the long hard barrel of the telephoto, and ten film canisters all in a row, like the gun belt of a sleeping sheriff.

Then he took a hot, punishing shower and, wrapped in his terry-cloth robe, settled into the recliner, a king reclaiming his throne. The robe was still musty from his long convalescence. It was as if he'd never been away. As if it had all been one long sleep.

He woke to find the Leica entangled in its own straps, staring at him through its dark, unblinking eye. He could see his own reflection floating upside down in the lens, like an embryo, like an astronaut in a space capsule. Beside him, curled on the floor, Bruno snored and shuddered in a pool of light. His scraggly flanks were dotted with flies.

Sometimes, contemplating Bruno, a pressure would rise in Teddy's chest, a flutter and swell of the heart, like an intoxication with being.

Without thinking, he reached for the Leica.

Just one picture. The dog and the flies.

And that was how it started. Not an interesting portrait, not meaningful or suggestive, in no way well composed. Just bony old Bruno, dead to the world, and his hovering entourage of flies. A dumb thing to focus on, but so what? He'd already made up his mind to drop the course anyway. You had to learn such things when you were young, Teddy thought, the way you learned a foreign language. And he hadn't. Now it was too late. He would never learn to take good pictures. He didn't even *want* to take good pictures. So he forgot about taking good pictures and took bad ones instead, very bad pictures of nothing at all. No fields, no mountains, no sweeping vistas . . . just random, boring pictures of no interest to anyone. The meeting, say, in the depths of the fruit bowl, of kiwi and banana. Danielle's closet with its toppled pyramid of shoes. Mimi's frown in the mirror when she brushed out her hair. The webbed shadow of the hammock, arrested over the grass in late afternoon. He snapped away carelessly, wastefully, hopelessly. It didn't matter that the pictures were bad. No one would ever see them, these bad pictures; he had no intention of developing the film.

And here was the odd thing. Not until he'd given up taking good pictures entirely and begun to enjoy taking bad ones did the lens fill with life, and, if his instructor could be believed, some good pictures too.

"It's a start, perhaps," she said, looking over the contact sheets the second week of class. "There's the beginning of something honest in these last shots."

"You like the one with the dog?"

"I'm not much into dogs, I'm afraid. But what does interest me, Mr. Hastings, is the latent content here. The beginnings of a narrative strategy. I think I see what you're up to."

"You do?"

"Of course you risk trafficking in some historical clichés here. The empty rooms, the lost connections. The symmetries are perhaps too neat." She pivoted, holding the pictures up against the light. "But you give them your own spin, don't you? These ghost traces—they make us feel something quite terrible has happened in this house. And yet there's a sense of judgment being withheld. It's rather haunting I think."

"Haunting is good, right?"

"Here too. The way you pull back here to expose the clutter on the closet floor. Very nice. All those empty hangers. They're reminders, aren't they, of what isn't there. The authority figure. The legitimizing presence. The unifying principle."

"Yeah."

"Now here's a case where you do go over the line, I think. The crumbs on the tablecloth say it all—there's no need to hit us over the head with the melting butter and cracked plate too. And those dying flowers, they're far too elegiac. You're milking the pathos. Give the viewer some credit. We see what's gone wrong in this family. It's unmistakable."

He stared at her blankly. Nothing she was saying bore the remotest correspondence to his intentions, but then how could it? He'd *had* no intentions. The butter was melting because Mimi had forgotten as usual to put it back in the fridge. The plate was cracked because at this point in their communal life, *most* of their plates were cracked. And the flowers weren't dying; he'd only picked them that morning. Though now that she mentioned it, they did look droopy.

"I keep getting the light wrong," he complained. "I can't seem to adjust for shadow."

"You'll learn. It takes time."

"Listen, I'm past fifty. I don't *have* time."

"Then I'm afraid you'll have to find some," she said.

Still, at least he was trying. Which was more than he could say for the women in his life.

Mimi, grounded, had turned listless and silent, a renegade monk. All day she sat high in her lifeguard's chair at the town pool, long nose swathed in zinc, gazing down at her noisy fellow Carthaginians with a fine and distilled contempt. Then she'd drive home, eat three bites of dinner, and go sack out in the hammock for hours, whether from depression, surreptitious drug intake, or lack of nourishment it wasn't clear. When had they last shared an entire meal together? When had they last exchanged an entire sentence? As for Danielle, the fond firstborn, the academic all-star, she too, from the photos she'd e-mailed, was now an accomplished slacker, lying in a glassy stupor on some palm-studded beach in Thailand or Vietnam or someplace, in the arms of a dark, shirtless, rapacious-looking young man gone AWOL from the Israeli army, while the last deadlines for renewing her merit scholarship scattered in the wind like so much dandelion fluff.

And Gail? Instead of cutting back her summer hours as usual, she had at Mimi's urging (the negotiations had been strictly closed-door) taken on the Chinese-refugee case pro bono. As a result of which her hours at the office had not halved, but doubled. Mostly she skipped dinner altogether, proceeded directly from work to yoga or the fitness center before falling into bed at midnight with a groan. Teddy would lie there listening to the slow intake of her breath, waiting for her to ask him how his day was. If only she would ask him how his day was, he thought, then he'd gladly go ahead and ask her how *her* day was. But she wouldn't. Anyway he knew how her day was: tiring. But then so was his. When had their marriage turned into a competition, a race to exhaustion, a land rush to stake out the high ground of complaint? And why did he so seldom win?

Case in point: VA 103. Though nominally encouraging about his enrollment, and though technically solicitous of his progress, Gail was not yet entirely on board, it seemed, with the demands of the course.

"Are you still on that same assignment?" she asked one morning, her lips going tight as he raised the Leica. "I thought surely she'd have moved on by now."

"Sometimes moving on means staying put. Going, you know, deeper."

"Interesting. And you came by this idea how?"

He didn't answer. He was fixing her in the lens, adjusting the light meter for contrast.

"It intrigues me to hear you talk this way. It's like you've joined a cult."

"Just hold still."

Even when he did manage to bully or cajole her into posing, Gail would find a way to withhold herself, to elude the camera's grasp. She'd blanch under the lens's examination, or make tense, unflattering faces she claimed to be unaware of, or move abruptly at the last second, blurring the exposure. Mimi of course was even worse. She poked her head into the kitchen—her shoulders bare, her hair wet and dangly like a mop—saw the two of them sitting at the table like conspirators, noted the Leica in his hands, and swore. The next sound they heard was the bang of the screen.

"You're driving her crazy with that thing," Gail said. "She's at that awkward stage. She hates everything about the way she looks."

"I thought the *last* stage was that awkward stage. How many are there going to be?"

"I don't know. Every child's different. In her case it looks like a lot."

"Listen," he said, "this photo diary? It's a class assignment. If I don't finish it, I'm going to fail."

"I thought she didn't give grades, this Meta-person. I thought she said it should be pass/fail."

"It should be, she said. But it's not. Anyway I'm not doing this for grades." He'd let her strange construction—*this Meta-person*—pass, recognizing it for the casual sliver of bitchery it was. "Besides, look at the kid. She's never been more beautiful. All those hours at the pool, she's brown as a berry. You could eat her up."

"It's her thighs," Gail said. "They're too doughy, she says. She wants cosmetic surgery for her next birthday."

"First I've heard of it."

"Where have you been? She's been talking about this for months. Her thighs and her ass, her thighs and her ass."

"Why doesn't she exercise then? Why doesn't she cut back on the Doritos? Why does everything have to be a shortcut?"

"First of all, she happens to be built big, thanks to certain genetic indicators she gets from her father. Also, you really want to declare war on shortcuts? Keep in mind, toasters are shortcuts. Cars are shortcuts. Even cameras are shortcuts."

"I don't see what's so wrong with her ass," he muttered. "It's just like yours."

"Exactly."

"So then what's the problem?"

They regarded each other across the table, surprised. His question, for all its innocence, had struck a suggestive note. He reached a hand to her cheek, cupped it softly in his palm. Gail, dimpling prettily, hung her head. Her hair came down over her eyes. Her beaded necklace—black, putty-colored, ocher—uncoiled itself in increments like a slinky. "Ah," she said. "Now he's interested."

"I'm always interested. You know that."

She shook her handsome head. Her hair was still lushly dark, more black than white; her scalp shone like marble through the part. The lines on her face were barely perceptible. The age spots on her hands might have been freckles. Her breasts, just visible in outline, still formed their taut, shapely parabola.

The problem with marriage, Teddy thought, was that people stopped looking at each other as photographers do. Stopped seeing each other *as if for the first time.* Then every so often started again. Then stopped.

"Do I look like a mind reader, Teddy? Because I'm not. I just absolutely refuse to play that game."

"Okay."

"And I won't sit still all day and pose for you. I won't pretend to smile and I won't twist myself into positions to satisfy your curiosity. I've got things on my mind too, you know."

"I know, I know."

Actually he didn't know, had scarcely bothered to imagine what Gail might be thinking about these last weeks—he'd assumed that she'd been thinking about *him.* But probably she hadn't.

"I need you back, okay? I need you to put the camera down and get out of your bathrobe and start working and living like a human being again."

"Okay, fine. You've made your point."

"And while you're at it, you might trouble yourself to touch me once in a while in a way that isn't strictly accidental. Or has this Meta-person made you take some kind of purity oath too?"

"Shhh, okay, okay. Come here. Look, I'm putting it down, I've got the lens cap right here, I'm snapping it on."

"Too late. I've got to go. You'll have the monastery here all to yourself." She poured some coffee into her travel mug and added milk. "Disappointed?"

"What can I say, Gail? I'm just trying to keep up."

"Well, try harder." She tasted the coffee and grimaced. "Ugh. So bitter. What kind of beans are you using?"

"Ethiopian," he said. "Harar."

Pronouncing the name was like clearing his throat—harsh, spasmodic. He did so with particular relish. Rimbaud, he'd have gone on to tell her if she'd been even half-listening, had spent the last part of his life in Harar, trafficking in this very coffee. He'd done some research on the man at the college library. Another mad genius wandering in the desert. Another white guy on the lam, going native. Teddy was thinking of doing a paper on him for Meta McVay. Extra credit.

"It's supposed to be the best," he said. "Anyway it's fourteen bucks a pound."

"Tastes burnt." She poured her cup out in the sink.

"Are you kidding? This is from where coffee *started*. They've been growing coffee in Harar since the dawn of man."

"Gee, you'd think in all that time they'd figure out a way to make it not taste burnt."

"Try adding a little sugar."

"No thanks," she said. "And while we're on the subject, you may want to hold off on the sweets for a while yourself. You might even consider putting down the camera and trying out that pricey new treadmill you bought without consulting me."

"One step at a time. I need to finish the basement first."

"Is that what you call what you're doing down there?"

He watched her through the lens as she gathered up her wallet, her phone, her tissues and Tic Tacs and allergy pills, and stuck them deep in her purse. The neat snap her glasses made, when she folded them up, was like a meter ticking.

"Why not? What do you call it?"

"Honey," she said, "I can't tell what's being started anymore and what's being finished."

Later that afternoon, Mimi came home from the town pool, took a twenty-five-minute shower that exhausted the hot water, and wrapped in her leopard-spotted bath towel, padded out barefoot to the hammock. Teddy, weeding the garden in T-shirt and knee pads, looked up and waved. Mimi did not wave back. Maybe she hadn't seen him. Or maybe she was still mad about being grounded. Or maybe she'd committed other felonies that summer besides the ones he knew about and now felt guilty about those. Or maybe she was on her period, or hungover from staying up two and a half hours past her clearly stipulated curfew the night before with her obnoxious friend Lisa, or maybe she was just worn-out from a long, hot day of working for a living. A feeling Teddy of course knew well, as it was both different from and similar to being worn-out from a long day of *not* working for a living. Not working, and not much living either. Just taking his pictures, and weeding his garden, and waiting for that evening's class to start as the gnats inscribed their mad, scribbling calligraphy in the air around his head.

"Hey, Mims, check it out. You're going to like this."

Earlier, he'd set aside a snakeskin he'd found flattened in the grass, certain that for all her apathy she would find its freakish, morbid beauty thrilling. Now he stood dangling his prize. It swayed in the breeze like a hypnotist's watch.

"You wouldn't believe how light this thing is," he said. "You can see right through it!"

Even now, faded and crinkly and dry, the snakeskin still

retained its form and markings. Mimi's eyes however remained closed. The girl he used to have to *drag* out of science museums, the girl who could name every animal at the zoo and its country of origin, who'd tear the brown wrapper from the new *National Geographic* before she'd so much as wriggled out of her coat, was no longer interested in such things. She too had shed some skin along the way.

Reluctantly he laid down his find, set the sprinkler on low, gathered up his tools and the lettuce and chives he'd picked, and went into the house. The kitchen was cool and dark, a sanctum. He placed the lettuce leaves in the sink as an offering to his wife, a reminder that all evidence to the contrary, his powers of hunter-gathering were undiminished, washed the dirt off his hands, and leaned in for a drink. A water pitcher with an activated-carbon filter made of crushed coconut shells was in the refrigerator, but he preferred to drink straight from the tap. He wiped his mouth with the back of his hand and went to browse in the pantry. The shelves were crowded with things he had no desire to eat. He recalled what Meta McVay had said, how when everything is accessible nothing has value. Maybe she was right. Sometimes the very plenitude of the pantry seemed a disincentive to hunger. On the other hand, what did a woman like Meta McVay know about American life? She was a foreigner, she lived in Brooklyn. Probably she didn't *have* a pantry. Probably she lived on hummus and beer, like Danielle's roommates at NYU. That was how the starving-artist gig worked. You starved. You lived like an anorectic teenager with no family or responsibilities. No, he would never become an artist with a pantry like this. A house like this. He should have burned it down, the house and the pantry both, when he had the chance.

But of course if he had, then all these inconsequential little items in the pantry he so dearly loved—the corkboard full of old art projects and news clippings from the local paper; the pencil marks on the wall delineating the girls' inexorable growth; the screw-top mason jars full of homemade salsas and sauces and jams; the malted milk, the chocolate powder, the old honeys and syrups and granola bars—all that sweet stuff would be lost forever.

Down the street he could hear the McDurfee kids splashing in their backyard pool. Summer's day. What the hell, he'd whip up some milk shakes. Surely Mimi would wake up for that.

He unscrewed the lid of the malt jar. Only a tiny bit of powder lay scattered at the bottom, but the smell of it—dry and chalky, subtly sweet—flew up his nose like a drug. His head began to swell. The flywheel of memory whirled. Christ almighty, he was not a sentimental person, he did not want to live in the past. So why did the past insist on living in him?

He'd bought the malt powder for Philip's last visit, the previous June. The guy was down to ninety pounds by then. They'd sat out on the screened porch in the dusky half-light, in cool wicker chairs, listening to the crickets, the shrilly cries of the birds, while the fireflies did their on/off thing on the other side of the mesh. Gail and Sonya were at work in the kitchen, opening cabinets and slamming them shut. Then a clunky, chaotic roar. Milk shakes for Philip—the doctors had prescribed three a day—and margaritas for them. Live it up. Bruno whined and paced, unsettled by the noise of the blender. As if time itself were being pulverized, hammered senseless in the next room.

The only problem was, Philip couldn't handle three milk shakes a day. He couldn't handle two. He couldn't handle one. He lay wasted against his chair, slack-mouthed, eyes yellowed and smoky, his lap swathed in Gail's plushest fleece blanket. His pants hung loose. There wasn't much of him left. The flesh was fleeing his cheeks; the hollows of his face lay pooled in shadow. All that was human was receding. What remained was just this frail cage, this basket of bones.

"Want a sip of this?" he offered. "I'm full."

"No thanks. I'll just work on my margarita here. That one's all yours."

"All mine." Philip sighed. "I'm tired of milk shakes, frankly. Too much of a good thing. Even the kids are tired of them."

"Don't be ridiculous. No kid in America gets tired of milk shakes."

"Mine do. It's just one of many ways they're being warped by my experience."

"The kids are all right. Trust me."

"Sure, they're insulated by youth. They still live in the wonderful world of Disney. Dancing bears. Lovesick beasts. Singing lions." Philip's voice was flat, impersonal. The shake had left a mustache trace on his upper lip, a joker's leer. "This cancer business bores them. It taxes their imagination."

"Yeah, mine too." Teddy felt a hot pressure behind his eyes, inflating his head like a tire. "Christ, Philly, I don't know what to say. It's like this is the first real thing I've ever dealt with. I don't even know what the other stuff was about."

Philip smiled. His eyes had begun to close. Bruno, responding to some high, imperceptible signal, sat up and nuzzled the dying man's hand. "And people say you're superficial," he said.

"They do? Who?"

"Well, Mom and Dad for starters. And Sonya of course. And me. Pretty much everyone who knows you basically." Philip set down his milk shake; it sloshed onto the table. "Sorry. I can't drink this shit."

"Don't worry about it."

"No more milk shakes. That's my new policy."

"Fine."

"And no more casseroles either. We're up to five a week on the casseroles these days. Apparently no one down in Wayland's too concerned with the obesity crisis."

"You can't blame people for trying, Philly."

"I don't. I blame them for failing. The good thing is, I don't have to pretend to be nice anymore. No more niceness. I don't have the energy to make people feel better."

"You don't have to make me feel better," Teddy said.

"Are you kidding? You're the worst of them all. Get a load of yourself in the mirror sometime. That drippy, morose look. It's ghoulish. I liked it a lot better in the old days when *I* was the one feeling sorry for *you*."

"Why on earth would you feel sorry for me?"

Philip didn't answer. His bruised eyes were fixed on the glass. "Sure you don't want this?" For all his efforts, little had been drunk. "It's actually pretty good. Remind me to tell Gail. And believe me, when it comes to milk shakes, I know the difference."

"I believe you."

"Mom made good ones too, remember? She put in Ovaltine or something. She used to give me extra you know. Because I was so skinny."

"Yeah, you were a real runt. I was embarrassed to be seen with you, if you want to know the truth."

"I don't," Philip said. "I'm at the point where I prefer the other."

"Anyway you're wrong. Mom didn't give you extra just because you were skinny. She did it for spite. It was all about making me feel bad."

"Boo hoo, here we go. The *Real* Victim of the Family Award goes to—"

"It's true, Philly. You were always the good baby, remember? The one who never woke them up crying in the middle of the night. It was your report card they put on the refrigerator. Mine got stuck away in a drawer with the bills and the stamps."

"Nobody likes a whiner, Bro."

"You should have heard them. 'Ah, Philip,' they'd say, 'with his books and poems, his little pen-and-ink drawings in that spiral notebook of his. So soulful. So sensitive.' To *me* they'd say this! As if *I* should feel proud, having this sad-eyed god for a brother!"

"Not that you resented me for it or anything."

"You were the favorite, Philly, let's face it. You were the favorite and I was the fatty, the big crude oaf with hair on his back. End of story."

Philip fell silent, his brow furrowed like a walnut shell. He reached for one of his little morphine sticks and stuck it in his mouth. The pain-management people had given him a whole case. But it still wasn't enough; he chewed them up like lollipops. "Come to think of it, it wouldn't have killed you to lose a few pounds."

"Yeah, I carry too much weight around. I always have."

"It's not your fault. It's how you're built." Philip closed his eyes now for real, sucking away at the white stick, his face slack, cheeks concave in the dusk. What little color the day's light had lent them was gone. Who knew the loan would be recalled so soon? Saliva leaked from the corners of his mouth. The drug was working its way through his membranes. "Wait—" His eyes popped open again. "What were we talking about?"

"My girlish figure."

"No, we were talking about ends of stories."

"Oh, shut up, would you? No one's talking about ends of stories."

"Well, guess what," Philip said. "They better start."

And would it have killed him, Teddy thought now, to take a sip of that goddamn milk shake when it was offered, instead of leaving it on the table to go flat? But it was just one of many irretrievable mistakes.

For Mimi of course a milk shake would have no unpleasant associations: it would simply be a milk shake. A cold drink. A peace offering, a tension breaker, a little summer indulgence to remind her that her father, for all his brooding preoccupations, was still capable of boyish, impetuous fun. He dumped in the milk, the banana, and two scoops of ice cream. Then one more, because that was the sort of fun thing boyish impetuous people did. *Just blend and serve.* Across the street the McDurfee kids were playing Marco Polo. He heard their calls and taunts, their blind flailing lunges. A mean game, Teddy thought. And he should know: he'd been meaner at it than anyone, back in his own childhood pool, that flimsy oval of corrugated tin. The old man had bought it on sale, the same way he bought most things; any half-decent cannonball sent the water flooding over the side. For the death of the grass below Teddy would of course shoulder the blame. That was the drill, out there in the backyard. Philip shivering blue-lipped in an oversize towel; their mother facedown in the chaise, a Pall Mall smoldering in the ashtray, trailing wistful lines of smoke; Teddy getting his ass handed to him by the paterfamilias, who, still dressed for work, had not even opened his mail yet, while, on the domed grill, a flank steak soaked in its peppery marinade, waiting for the coals to turn white. Okay, you wouldn't have called it a happy childhood, but on balance? At least they *had* a pool. At least they *had* a grill. At least they *had* a steak, however impregnable beneath its black, bitter crust. Back then they didn't obsess over ultraviolet radiation or secondhand smoke or polycyclic hydrocarbons (though arguably these were the very agents of Philip's early death); they didn't run off every two minutes to check the e-mail or cell phone or PalmPilot (though arguably they'd have enjoyed being more connected to other people); they didn't fret about kids reading Doc Savage and James Bond instead of something heavy and difficult to enrich their SAT scores (though Mimi could have *used* some enrichment). No, they'd lie baking in the mortal heat of the sun, wreathed in coils of unfiltered smoke, listening to a ball game on the transistor radio and gazing up contentedly at the Chinese paper lanterns their parents had strung along the patio for a dinner party and then never taken down, the barberry hedges both wall and screen, both fruit and thorn. That was the summer. And nothing was demanded or expected of you but play and rest and the consumption of cold, fattening drinks. *Just blend and serve . . .*

True, the milk shakes looked, when he poured them out, now

somewhat cementlike, and some essential flavor seemed to be missing from the taste. But maybe some essential flavor was *always* missing, Teddy reasoned, when you tried to engineer a reality from an abstract impression, a vague residue of memory in your head. They were still pretty good milk shakes. He filled up two glasses, set them on a wicker tray, and shouldered open the back door to the patio.

Out in the flower garden Bruno was curled up in a hole he had dug for himself, his nose deep in his own ass.

"Hey, look what I made," he called to Mimi.

Mimi, her fair head lolling on one shoulder, moaned some low resistant threat in her sleep. Never mind that once upon a time *he*'d been the one in the hammock, and *she*'d been the one emerging enthusiastically from the house, begging him to attend to some whimsical concoction she'd whipped up with her mother to please him. Now she didn't move. He set the tray down beside the book she'd been either reading or pretending to read, splayed facedown on the grass. *Mr. Bridge.* Teddy frowned. Three long, demeaning phone calls to Rick Moyer, the snotty young principal at the high school, to get her into AP English, and here she was, seven pages into the first book on the summer reading list, and dead to the world. What was it composed of, this mystifying apathy and impassivity of hers? This ability to be proximate to things but not participate in them, to read books without ever quite turning their pages, to drive for hours without ever quite speaking to the driver or ever quite looking out the window, to love your parents without ever quite being affectionate to them or ever quite conceding their reality?

Her towel had fallen open just far enough to reveal the absence of a bathing suit underneath. This too annoyed him.

The sprinkler was twirling rings over the garden, *tsk-tsk*ing through its metal teeth.

It was not the nakedness per se. He and Gail had made a point of exposing the girls to a certain amount of casual, good-humored nudity around the house, in the hopes that they would grow up free of shame and embarrassment about the human body. Of course that was back when the girls, and also he and Gail, were younger. Lately he supposed there *was* something shameful and embarrassing about their bodies, or his anyway— Gail's was lean and sinewy as ever—which was why he rarely walked around naked anymore, and why he tried to avoid his own blobby, oversize image in the mirror these days as compulsively as once upon a time, when he was Mimi's age, he'd sought it out. True, she often began her days with a shower of invective toward her "mouse-nest hair," then feasted uncharitably over breakfast on the idiosyncrasies of her "fat, gross" body and her clothes that made her look like "a hideous troll," but he'd never believed she was serious. To him she was a marvel: beautiful, full-figured, ripe like a plum.

Nonetheless, his impulse to cover her with the towel was almost painful. He thought of all the leering boys in short pants riding by on mountain bikes. All the toxic spores and molds hitching rides on the afternoon breeze. All the potentially pre-cancerous freckles she'd inherited from Gail's side of the family on the pale, pinkening skin she'd inherited from his. Both sides had a history of cancer. You had to be wary of exposure. So he pulled one fringed side of the towel over her hip. Which made the other side, obeying the law of unintended consequences, slip that much farther off her thighs.

Mimi didn't stir. One eyelid fluttered like a hummingbird. The other remained in place. She breathed quietly through her mouth, her front teeth just visible through the part in her lips. Two years of braces, he thought, and still crooked.

Even the smallest things have something in them, Meta had said, *which remains unknown.*

He looked down at her feet. The toenails were painted a garish white; they curled into their sockets like a doll's. Her arches were high, the soles puckered and grooved. He could smell the hemp and coconut oils, the jojoba, the shea butter, all the creamy tropical potions she used on her legs. She would be seventeen, he remembered, in a few weeks. She'd forbidden them to throw a party. Not even so much as a cake.

Now, as if in accordance with this spirit of exclusion and defiance, she shifted her weight, effectively turning her back to her father. The gap in the towel widened. The slope of one budded breast could be seen, ascending into a terry-cloth cloud. Bees hummed in the grass. The locust trees were shedding bark. Dandelions lay spread over the lawn like a blanket of gold. Who was this lovely, distant stranger who'd wandered into his yard and fallen asleep in his hammock? He missed her intensely all of a sudden. Yet here she was in front of him. But the moment he reached for her, she'd disappear.

He thought, as he screwed on the zoom lens, of the slides Meta had shown in class. The seashells that looked like nudes. The nudes that looked like landscapes. The landscapes that looked like clouds. The clouds that looked like dunes. The dunes that looked like shells, and like nudes, and like clouds. The closer you looked, the more similar they all became. As if everything really was fashioned from the same clay.

But if Meta was right about some things, she was also wrong about others. Because the goal, in his view, was not to see things *as if for the first time.* It was to see as if for the *last* time. To capture the light of being in the shadow of its opposite. Touch the moment before it vanished. *Because* it would vanish. *Because* it would end.

He folded up his glasses, stuck them in his shirt, and eyed his daughter through the viewfinder. Her face, under the canopy of the willows, was soft, unguarded. Every subtle sway of the hammock sent it oscillating through zones of light and darkness, memory and invention.

The camera makes us a tourist in other people's reality.

By now he was used to the weight and feel of the equipment. The black strap like a ligament around his neck. The chassis bumping on his chest like a second heart. He watched the sun pour over the girl's shoulders, preserving them in amber. A filament of saliva dangled from her lip; it glistened in the light like a wire.

He lifted one trembling finger over the shutter, and waited.

What happened next did not lend itself so well to explication. This became all too clear in both the oral testimony he'd delivered in court and his mandated follow-up letter to Judge Tierney. There was no motive, no conscious decision, no reasoned analysis. He was merely responding as he'd been trained to a set of singular and specific visual indicators—the sun dipping in the west; the girl glowing with backlight; the undulant sag of the hammock; the willows nodding mournfully overhead, weeping their long-shadowed tears. His assignment for class, so far as he understood it, was to record what was around him. That was his homework. To locate the image and follow it where it led.

The proof that something was there and no longer is. Like a stain.

He fretted about the light of course: it kept veering toward overexposure. So he bracketed around the meter and adjusted the f-stop to ensure consistent depth of field. Then he circled in close, like a boy playing Indian, like a hunter sneaking up on his prey.

The first roll he focused on the lower extremities. The variegated ridge of the toes. The slung bows of the calves. The dimpled slopes of the knees. Then he went higher, toward the head.

To photograph an object, have it look like an object, but be more than an object.

The girl's face from this angle was moonlike in its serenity, with plains of light and crevices of shadow, tiny acne craters around the nose. From her open mouth, slack and dark like a cave, dangled one silken stalactite of drool. He shot an entire roll on that alone. Then he switched lenses and swooped in closer.

The privileged moment that passes with the ticking of a clock, never to be duplicated. So light, balance, expression must be seen—felt, as it were—in a flash.

Mimi didn't move. It was as if she were posing. As if they

were collaborating, playing a game of hide-and-seek. Her upper arms, sunk into the hammock's weave, had taken on its intricate inscription of diamond-shaped grooves. Like a creature caught in a spiderweb.

Teddy moved closer. The Leica was like an extension of him; all he had to do was point and shoot. He was so absorbed in his work, he nearly failed to see the broad, hunchbacked shadow, like a creature in a horror movie, loom up out of nowhere and interpose himself between the girl and the light.

He knew right away who it was. They'd logged some time together, the two of them, in this very yard. But by the time he'd lowered the camera, the creature was gone, vanished back into the woods.

Mimi had in a sense vanished by this point too. Strictly speaking she was no longer his daughter, the toddler he used to cajole from tears by dropping her from his shoulders and catching her (and what was it about falling from a height that made them laugh? A return to vestigial origins? To hairy, half-evolved primates swooping through the forest canopy?); no longer the impressionable eight-year-old with neatly combed bangs who'd drape herself across the window seat, bare toes idling in Bruno's golden fur, and read tales of beauties and beasts. No. She looked now, through the viewfinder's frame, more like some exotic wind-stripped artifact he'd stumbled upon in the desert—a statue, an icon, a hieroglyph—than a sixteen-year-old girl whose genetic code roughly mirrored his own. It was the teenage dream come true: she'd been transported to another planet where they were no longer obligated to irritate each other. If she woke right now, he thought, she wouldn't even see him. She'd see only the Leica's big glass eye, and herself encased and upended in the lens.

The sun was plunging in the trees, the sprinkler hissing over the sodden garden. Teddy circled the hammock like a thief. He heard a sickly crunch underfoot—his glasses. But there wasn't time; this golden light wouldn't last forever. Soon Mimi would wake up, and everything would change back to how it was. They would no longer be partners, innocents marooned in a lawless enchanted garden. Every unconscious flutter of her lids was an extension of his, every involuntary tremor of her skin a response to his, her mouth with its soft, flaking, corrugated lips lay on the far side of an invisible breathing tube that connected up with his, and through that tube the breath flowed back and forth, mingling with his; and so too the modulating breezes, and the conspiratorial light, and the dark perfume of the mulch, and the spindly branches of the locust trees, looming like under-takers, and the sprinkler *tsk*ing over the weed-strewn lawn, and the nodding daylilies, flaring like candles; and the tuneless fre-netic warble of the cicadas, and the distant bellow of the 5:10 train bearing machine parts down from Canada, like the half-heard bass note in a minor chord. The whole world had gone liq-uid and musical, exultant. Teddy wielded the Leica before him like a conductor's wand. *Just blend and serve . . .*

All of which was a difficult sensation to put into words, of course, let alone use as the basis of a legal defense when you're fighting two counts of child-endangerment charges from the Carthage County prosecutor. But for the moment all that hassle still lay ahead. For the moment he was content, ecstatic even, right here and right now, taking pictures of his daughter as she slept on in the hammock, dead to the world.

Then she jerked awake.

"Hey," he said.

"Hey." She stretched, her hands shooting skyward toward some cloudlike apparition she'd been tracking in her dreams. She looked down at her nakedness and frowned. "Where's Mom?" she asked, adjusting the towel.

"Work."

"Mmm. There's something new."

He wasn't up for another gripe session about Gail, though of course he preferred it to another gripe session about himself. "I was just shooting some pictures. The light's incredible right now."

"Oh yeah, how's that photography class going? I keep meaning to ask. You like it?"

"I like it a lot. Tuesday night was really interesting. Tonight should be good too."

"Mmm." He could see her deliberating over whether to end the conversation right here, or out of simple politeness—or boredom—continue. But he wouldn't push her. These soft moments were wispy, precarious; if you pressed too hard they collapsed. "So what do you guys talk about in there anyway?"

"Oh, you know, technical stuff mostly. Compositional stuff. Nothing too glamorous." He spoke slowly, matter-of-factly, not pushingly. "Meta keeps it pretty basic. She wants us to be birds, she says, not ornithologists."

"Wait, I don't get it, she wants you to be birds?"

"The idea is, find your moment, then act. Not get all muddled up thinking about it." A panel of black flies had convened around his milk shakes, dipping their antennae in the foam, buzzing out commentaries and critiques. "It's like when you go fishing, and there's this lag time between when you see the bobber go under and when you react? That's when things generally go wrong."

"Jeremy's into photography," Mimi informed him abruptly. She had her mother's gift for listening in a way that wasn't quite listening, but wasn't quite not-listening either. Or maybe it *was* quite not-listening. "He's like obsessed with it in fact."

"Jeremy Dunn?"

"His parents gave him this camera for Christmas. He says it cost five hundred dollars. They're going to build a darkroom for him down in the basement, while he's away this summer."

"It must be nice to have parents with a lot of disposable income," Teddy said.

"He's a pretty hopeless photographer though in my opinion. He's got like no eye at all." She looked at Teddy for a moment. "Where are your glasses? You look kind of mole-ish without them."

"They broke." Suddenly he understood where this conversation was leading. "Listen, Mimi, if you'd like us to seriously consider buying you a camera, we could talk about it. Maybe not such a nice one as Jeremy's, or even mine, but a good, sturdy starter's model? That we could swing. Naturally," he went on, "we'd have to work out who'd pay for all the film and development and stuff. But if you want us to seriously consider it—and by serious I mean not like the pony that time, or the electric-bass lessons, or the motorbike—it's certainly something we could talk about. That is if you're serious."

"No thanks."

"Why not?"

"I hate it when people take pictures all the time." She brushed away a fly. "It's a power trip. They're always hanging back, ordering people around. Like they're all separate and superior from everybody else."

"Listen," he said, exasperated, "*anything* you do seriously separates you from everybody else. Haven't you figured that out yet?"

Mimi, in a show of either refutation or agreement or something else altogether, let loose a yawn. Her listless, honeyed apathy set him pacing around the hammock again.

"Mimi, you're an intelligent girl. A talented and wonderful person . . ."

"So?"

"So remember eighth-grade biology? You've got your nekton and you've got your plankton. The nekton are the swimmers. The plankton are the drifters, the passive types, the jellyfish—"

"And in the end, they all get eaten by bigger fish anyway."

"I'm not talking about the end. I'm talking about the middle. That's when things go wrong, see. People go to sleep, Mimi; they just do. They start out like gangbusters but they fall back. They can't maintain the intensity. Can't take being separate, as you put it."

"And you can? What, you're some kind of role model now?

Who does most of the sleeping around here anyway? Who's spent the last three weeks shaving his head and not going to work and sneaking around the house taking pictures of Bruno?"

"I told you," he said calmly, "this photography thing, it's a process. A discipline. It's a whole new way of concentration."

She frowned. "You're starting to sound like my friend Marcus. He speaks fortune cookie too."

"Which one's Marcus? Is he the one with the dreads and tattoos and that little thimble of hair on his chin?"

"Um, Dad? Half the guys I know fit that description."

"Can I just say I find that disturbing?"

"Why? What's wrong with it? They want to be birds too. All guys do. Anyway when it comes to personal grooming you're no one to talk. Jesus, *look* at you." Her eyes, as she followed her own instruction, went small, glossy. "What is it with you, anyway? You were always the rock around here. Is this about Uncle Phil? That's what Mom's saying."

"How's that again?"

"Mom says we have to be extra nice to you, 'cause you're all guilty and fucked-up and maybe having some sort of break-down, she says."

"Listen, don't get me wrong, Mom's a very perceptive and intelligent woman. But in this case she happens to be just totally, totally full of shit."

"So we don't have to be nice to you, is what you're saying?"

"It's outrageous, the way people need to attach a label to things they don't understand. You start to feel like Gulliver in Lilliput."

"Where?"

"Forget it," he said. He brooded for a moment while she picked at her navel. "You know, I may have been wrong, but I thought I saw the Ogre pop in while you were sleeping. Speaking of giants."

Mimi rolled her eyes and glanced over her shoulder toward the house, a bit wearily, he thought. The Ogre was a rough beast who used to come visit sometimes, when the girls and their friends were small. But he had not been seen in these parts in some years.

"Well," he said, "enough about him. How about you, Sweetpea? How are you? I feel like ever since that little incident at the lake, I never see you anymore."

Her expression, registering the note of complaint in his voice, closed down like a shade. "I'm fine, Dad."

"I know you're fine. I'm not asking if you're fine. What I'm asking is, how are you doing underneath?"

"Underneath what?"

"C'mon, Mimi, you know what I mean. How are you feeling about things, about school, and your life, and the future, and do you basically feel good or are you all confused or depressed or what?"

"I'm fine."

"Because we all go through rough patches from time to time, let's face it. And you're probably missing your big sister too, I imagine, God knows Mom and I do. And I probably didn't help things with that whole cancer scare either."

"*You* were the one scared. We kept telling you it was nothing."

"Sometimes, kiddo, nothings can be somethings. Even when they're nothing. Maybe especially then. You'll understand that better when you're my age."

"No offense, Pops, but I doubt it."

He hated it when she called him Pops. Hated too the artichoke quality of their conversations, the effort of stripping away the tough, ironic armor, getting down to the hairy heart.

"I'm just saying," he just said, "I know there've been a lot of distractions lately, and maybe we're not quite as close right now as we usually are, which is something I feel bad about frankly. So if you'd like to maybe just, you know, talk about what's going on, like say that night at the lake and what you guys were doing out there, not just drug-wise but in general, though drug-wise too, I'd be really interested in hearing about that. Or say about

Jeremy and what's going on with your whole, you know, relationship. That would be okay too."

"I knew it. You and Mom. It's like all you can talk about, am I having sex with Jeremy or not."

"I didn't say anything about that, did I? Though of course it's a perfectly reasonable question for a parent t—"

"Jeremy's boring, okay? He's like you, always hovering over me, keeping track of my stuff, trying to figure me out. I'm not so complicated, okay? I'm not some brilliant exotic woman of mystery. I got like 520s on my SATs."

"We told you, you can take them again. Some people are better test takers than oth—"

"Danielle got 750s."

"Danielle has different academic strengths from you. We've discussed this, right? There are people who're more naturally oriented to analytic thinking, and others more naturally oriented to intuitiv—"

"I don't even care, okay? I wasn't even talking about that. You're the one so hung up on my scores. You and Jeremy. It's all you can talk about."

"I wouldn't say I was hung up, exactly—"

"Jeremy, he thinks he's cool, but he's not. He tries too hard. He's always burning me these CDs from his dad's collection and then getting mad if I don't play them. Like I give a shit about Sarah Vaughan or Chet Baker."

"Can I have them? I love those g—"

"It's like he has this picture of how his life is going to be, and it has to look just that way, and you either fit into that or you don't. It's really tiresome. And it's never about me, either, all this concern he's always expressing. It's about him. He just wants me to be happy so he can feel good about himself."

"So I take it then that you haven't yet gone ahead and actually had interco—"

"Jesus," she said, looking around wildly, "what's that smell? It's like, ugh, spoiled milk. Did you leave something out?"

*   *   *

Because he was still learning the photographic arts and lacked the time and expertise to set up a darkroom of his own, Teddy was forced to rely upon the town's only decent photo lab, Sudden Exposures, to get his film developed. Because he'd taken so many pictures so quickly and was worried about the light meter, the workings of which confounded him, he made a point of asking the clerk when he dropped off his armful of film canisters at 5:15 p.m. to push the film in development. Because the clerk, a weedy, sandy-haired boy of twenty, stared back at him sullenly as if he were on downers, which he probably was, and as if he'd had an unrewarding secondary-school experience, which he probably had, and held Teddy in his capacity as principal accountable for it, which he probably did—Teddy's entirely reasonable request may have come off sounding a bit strident, even harsh. In any case the boy, who appeared to have no idea what pushing the film even *meant,* stared at him resentfully, his hooded, lizardlike gaze all slitty and dark. "I'll tell Kevin about it," he mumbled, "when he gets back."

"Thanks. Will they be done by tonight though? I've got class in a couple of hours. What time do you guys close?"

"Just write your last name down on the slip." The clerk spoke with the low-grade apathy of a toll taker on the Thruway. "Kevin'll call you when they're ready."

"Later today, you mean? Because I'm anxious to get them back for tonight."

"Whenever they're done, Chief."

"I've got class at seven, see. So there's a certain amount of time pressure on these."

"Okay, Chief."

"Okay, great. So just to be clear. You'll write this down. You're going to make a point of asking Kevin, whoever the hell Kevin is, to push the film in development and have it ready before seven. Okay, Chief?"

The boy nodded, his mouth puckered with hate, as boys of

all ages do when you have just browbeaten them into submission.

On his way home, Teddy reviewed his conversation with Mimi about the importance of separating yourself from other people— even occasionally *hating* other people. Not your parents, of course, but *other* other people, people like the clerk at Sudden Exposures, for example, who were genuinely hateful. Because if you couldn't rouse yourself to hate hateful people, Teddy thought, whom would you ever rouse yourself to hate? And if you couldn't rouse yourself to hate, how would you ever rouse yourself to love?

Naturally when he arrived at the house he found it empty— Mimi off with friends, Gail nowhere in sight—so any further clarification he might offer on this or any subject was moot. That was one disappointment. A bachelor's dinner of eggs and toast: that was another. And when, promptly at 6:45, he stopped in at the photo lab on his way to class and the film wasn't ready either, that was a disappointment too. Or maybe it *was* ready. It was difficult to tell with the shutters drawn, the lights off, the doors bolted shut.

He read the hours posted on the window: 11–7:30. Apparently the clerk had mastered the art of hating other people too.

And so, without a single contact sheet to show for his labors, Teddy was forced to just *sit* there through the entire class, listening to Meta McVay answer the stupid, trivial questions of his classmates and make highly detailed critiques of everyone else's work but his. Even tiresome old Mrs. Landgren and her Polaroid butterflies—which, if he was honest with himself, were actually rather pretty—came in for praise. Meanwhile he sat glaring vengefully at the wall clock, whose hands for some reason had stopped moving.

The moment class was over, he marched directly to the lectern and blurted out an apology. "For what?" Meta McVay asked.

"For not being prepared tonight. I ran into some technical difficulties."

He went on to catalog at some length the precise nature of

those difficulties. Meta McVay nodded vaguely as he talked, her hands busy on her desk, compiling her notes into a stack, then shoveling them into her briefcase. Why wasn't she listening? The difficulty of executing one's intentions in a recalcitrant world: surely this was a subject that should engage her sympathies. To keep the conversation going, he offered to help her carry her slides and equipment out to her car. "That's very kind of you, thank you."

"Bah," Teddy said. *Bah* was not a word he'd ever before used—not a word, in fact, at all—but it would have to do. They went down the corridor, through the back door, and down the concrete ramp. In the moonlight, the arcing parabolas of the intracampus walking paths looked like silver filaments of a net, weaving the stone buildings together. He watched Meta search the parking lot for her car. "Do you have a long drive home?"

"Quite long, I'm afraid. I live in Brooklyn."

"Oh." He stumbled on the curb; the slides rattled in their plastic partitions.

"I drive up on Tuesdays and stay over two nights in a faculty apartment. Then on Thursdays I drive home."

"Well, anything beats being stuck in one place."

"Does it?" They were approaching her car now, an old Jetta with obscure stickers on the windshield. "I'm beginning to think there's a lot to be said for staying in one place."

"Don't be too sure. Me, I've lived here thirty-two years and counting," he informed her with a vehemence that surprised them both. "I came for college. After that I just stayed."

"I see." She rummaged in her pocket for her keys.

"I mean I had plans, believe me. Irons in the fire. I almost did that whole Rimbaud thing myself. I was going to head off to Africa, build a school maybe, help some poor kids. But you know how it is. Life gets its hands on you."

Meta nodded but said nothing. Still, he could see what she was thinking: it was there on her face.

"Oh, it's not *that* bad, I guess. Living up here. I mean sure, there's nothing to do, and the weather's terrible, and you have to find a way to get through winter and all. But at least there's no traffic. People are friendly. It's a nice place to raise kids. At least until they get to be teenagers. After that it's a nightmare of course, but by then it's too late, you're sort of comfortably stuck, for better and for worse. Hey—" Suddenly Meta McVay's features were all in commotion. "What's the matter?"

She shook her head, waving her hand before her face like a fan.

"I'm talking way too much, aren't I? I'm boring you with my whole life story, and here you're in a hurry to get on the road."

Meta was still shaking her head. Was she about to cry? Was she crying already? Why? He didn't even mean half of what he was saying. He was just talking, running off at the mouth, feeling both manic and sheepish—*Bah!* he thought, *Bah!*—the way people do taking leave of each other in parking lots. He remembered Vera Blackburn three years back. Another strange encounter with a moody, wayward woman. For a man who prided himself on his fidelity to his wife, Teddy seemed to be accumulating a lot of such moments.

"... but I *do* like it," Meta was stammering.

"What? Like what?"

"This little town of yours. It's ... it's rather like a dream, isn't it?" He examined her face for irony but found none. "Your quiet evenings. Your little shops. Everyone out on a warm night, buying those soft ice creams that come twirling out of that machine."

"Creemees."

"Creemees, yes. I love them. They're so, I don't know the word ..."

"Bland?"

"*Smooth.* I must've gained five pounds since I began teaching up here. And I'm usually very strict about these things. But I can't help it, I love them, and I feel better when I eat one, and what's wrong with that?"

"Nothing's wrong with that," Teddy said, though he wasn't

sure at this point what *that* even was. Meta McVay was beginning to irritate him a little, honestly, with this condescending fantasy of hers. What did she know of the rural life? She was only a commuter, a tourist. He should bring her down to the middle school sometime and open up the lockers. Let her see the knives, the pills, the little plastic Baggies full of dope. Maybe if she stopped commuting back and forth and actually lived in one place for a change, she would see that place more clearly. But no one saw things clearly, he thought. No one even wanted to.

"Sometimes I wonder if my own children will ever have this experience. This rustic simplicity. This coherence. Presuming I ever *have*—"

And now she went silent again, the lines of her face screwy and crosshatched, as she wrestled with what appeared to be a number of personal issues that were none of Teddy's business. He wouldn't have minded continuing this conversation some other time—over a beer, say, or a cup of coffee—though he was beginning to mind continuing it now. All he wanted was for her to find the right key and open up the trunk of her rusting dysfunctional-looking Jetta, so they could both get on home.

Still, he felt obligated out of courtesy to go ahead and offer to buy her a drink. It seemed under the circumstances the courtly, gentlemanly thing to do, provided of course she didn't take it the wrong way and make it seem the seedy, scumbaggy thing to do. Anyway he fully expected her to say no. She had a whole life down there in some hip and enviable quadrant of Brooklyn; why would she go out for drinks with a man who wore the wrong clothes and read the wrong books and could not even manage to bring in his lousy, overexposed contact sheets on time?

"How kind of you Mr. Hastings, thank you. Thank you very much."

"We could go down to the Lyons' Den," he heard himself proposing hopelessly. "You know that place over on Exchange Street? It's a little on the dingy side, but they've got some decent microbrews on tap."

"That sounds like just the thing, actually."

She was only demurring gracefully, of course, as a matter of form, just as he'd only offered the drink as a matter of form. And yet the thing about matters of form was they always seemed to morph sooner or later into matters of content. All at once Teddy *did* want a beer. In fact he wanted a pitcher. He wanted to take Meta McVay down to the Lyons' Den, order cold, frothing mugs of the darkest imaginable ale, and unburden himself of his every longing and fear, his every stifled roar—

". . . afraid I can't tonight, however," his instructor was mumbling, as she lifted open her trunk. "Must head back to the Thruway, the bane of my existence. I'm terribly grateful for the offer, though, Mr. Hastings."

"Teddy. Call me Teddy."

"And just for your general gallantry, both in class and outside it. You have no idea how helpful that's been."

"You're terribly welcome," Teddy said, settling the slide trays into the black cavity of the trunk, and slamming it shut.

He wound up going to the Lyons' Den anyway, all by himself. There he engaged in the usual barroom multitasking—drinking dark beer, watching a ball game, eating far too many stale, heart-shaped pretzels, and having a coarse and often borderline offensive conversation with Steve Lyons, the proprietor, about upcoming bond and budget issues for the fall. It was a dull way to pass what had promised to be an interesting evening. He stared at the stuffed jungle cat mounted over the bar. The great shaggy beast remained aloof, his gaze fixed on some long-dormant memory of prey. What had he been thinking, inviting a woman like Meta to a hole like this? She lived in Brooklyn. With a *partner.* Which meant, if Teddy understood the linguistics, she was either gay, or cohabiting with an attorney, or simply too urbane for such hackneyed and pedestrian labels as *boyfriend* or *husband.* Anyway he'd been to Brooklyn, four or five times, to visit Danielle. They always wound up in some pencil-thin bar with deplorable acoustics, where people in black clothes sat around drinking mojitos and eating tiny plates of marinated shellfish. Nothing like the Lyons' Den, its shag carpet like a terrarium for mold spores and dust mites, its pretzels that carbon-dated back to the previous century, its antique air conditioner clanking like a convict against its rickety, ill-fitting frame. The jukebox didn't work. The eggs on the counter were yellow. The restrooms were neither roomy nor restful. Thank God Meta had turned him down. Thank God Teddy had the place to himself, to do as he wished. And what he wished to do now was drink a whole lot of beer.

The first pint, though it went down with gratifying speed and efficiency, could hardly have been called satisfying. The same was true of the second. With the third he grew canny, nursing it along with miserly little sips for as long as he could, trying to make it last. But it didn't. So he ordered a fourth. Four pints was approximately one over his limit; nonetheless he drank it down with a minimum of fuss. Then he ordered another. Conceivably his sense of his own limits was wrong, Teddy thought, was outgrown and outdated. Conceivably he *had* no limits. It was something to think about as he ambled toward the men's room to take a leak.

Swaying at the urinal, under the penitential light of the overhead bulb, he let fly with a thick rope of piss. The very force of it cheered him. This was no leak; this was a torrent. First he carved his initials in the pale round icelike cake of soap; then he shattered the rest into pieces; then he hosed down the dregs of a cigarette butt; and still enough was left in reserve to splash back against the enamel and onto his trousers.

Well, such was life in the men's room: messy but vital. If a little indignity was the price one paid for vigor, then he was willing to pay it, he thought.

He zipped his trousers and began washing his hands in the dismal blue-veined sink. Glancing up, he had the bad luck to encounter his face in the mirror. His eyes were sunken and red;

his scalp gleamed wanly under its pale corona. Mimi was right: he should never have shaved his head, never exposed this bone-plated ugliness to the world. His ears, with no hair or sideburns to obscure them, were now revealed to be a pair of enormous winged creatures—half-angel, half-dragon—affixed like twin succubi to the sides of his skull. An invading army of rust-red stubble crept up his neck; another streaked raggedly across his cheeks; a third patchy, rearguard unit traversed his scalp. Taken together they occupied a territory that now ran the length and breadth of his head. He looked as if he'd lost a fight with an Etch A Sketch, as if his big, moony face had been doodled over with lead shavings by some hyperactive child. Whatever the relation between his prior self and this demented cartoon character he now glimpsed in the mirror was a riddle that would require, Teddy thought, a great many more microbrews to solve. So he returned to the bar to get started.

Back on his stool, he was treated to a number of Steve Lyons's voluble opinions on property taxes, and the need for fresh paving on Exchange Street, and the encroachments of chain restaurants just south of town, subjects that might, to be fair, have engaged Teddy in the past, even if in the present they failed to distract him from his own preoccupations, and from the acrid scent of his own urine rising off his trousers. He popped a Tums and crunched it between his molars. The chalky blandness coated his tongue like a salve. The exultation he'd felt that day, shooting those portraits of Mimi, had gone soggy and shapeless as the napkin under his glass. And it was his own fault. He was the one who'd pushed too hard about Jeremy Dunn. He was the one who'd lost his temper with the clerk at Sudden Exposures. He was the one who'd put a busy visiting lecturer in the awkward, compromising position of having to turn down a student's offer of a drink. He was the one who'd foolishly descended into the Lyons' Den, alone, among the boors and the stuffed cats, without an exit strategy, and had gorged himself on five, or wait, seven pints of beer. Somehow he'd allowed himself to become that man in the mirror, that bald, bloated fellow who needed his family to be extra sweet to him, instead of some leaner, finer, self-sufficient creature.

By the time he finally pulled into his own driveway, Teddy's bladder was so full and his level of self-discomfort so profound on so many levels both figurative and literal that he almost crashed into the black sedan someone had thoughtlessly left running there in the darkness. He swerved just in time, neatly avoiding the collision. But now, wait, here came the headlights of *another* car, bearing down fast from the other direction, and this time he wound up swerving not so neatly and plowed into something hard—the garage door—with a thud.

For a moment he sat there in the freakish darkness. The car roared in idle. His palms were clammy; his pulse skittered in his wrist. Through the ragged, Tennessee-shaped gouge he'd made in the door, he could see the old sleds and skates on which they skimmed through the winters, the mountain bikes, hanging upside down from ceiling hooks, they pedaled in fall and spring, the Toro mower he rode like a knight in summer. The only form of transport missing from the garage was his car. There wasn't room. Though now that he'd bashed in the door, there might be room for it after all.

As for whom the black mystery sedan purring in his driveway, its radio muttering peaceably, belonged to, and why on closer inspection it bore such an uncanny resemblance to a sheriff's cruiser, that was anyone's guess. And the second car he'd swerved away from? Gone. Fled the scene. Unless of course (the idea welled up in his belly like a sea monster) *his* was the second car. Which would mean the headlights bearing down on him had been his own low beams, reflected in the garage windows. Which would mean that homicidal maniac who'd just tried to run him over in his own driveway would only be the usual suspect: himself.

He turned off the engine and struggled out of the Accord, closing the door quietly behind him. The last thing he wanted was to wake everyone up.

Though from the lights on inside the house, and the sound of people talking in the foyer, and the hoarseness and volume of Bruno's barking, everyone appeared to be up already.

As he trudged up the steps, his head sloshed back and forth like a fish tank. The taste in his throat was like unslaked thirst. And yet he'd had a great deal to drink. How long had he been at the bar anyway? It felt like years. He thought of old Rip Van Winkle, another small-towner, returning home from his prolonged debauch to find that nothing was quite as he remembered. The porch light was not on. The door was not open. Bruno was not whining at the screen to greet him.

"Uh-oh," he heard someone—Mimi?—say. "Speak of the devil."

True, it was a very singular and memorable event, being arrested in one's own living room. Breathalyzed and handcuffed and read one's rights, then led down the front stoop like a yoked ox while one's wife and daughter trailed behind, their faces gone sallow with wonder, or pity, or fury, or relief.

"My God, Bear," Gail said, "what on earth did you *do?*"

"Nothing," he called over his shoulder. "Absolutely nothing. It's just some dumb mistake."

"What did he say?"

"He said he didn't freaking do anything," Mimi said.

"Watch your language, please."

"All I did was invite the young lady out for a drink. Did I touch her? Nooo. I did not. Nooo sirree."

"Would someone please tell me what he's saying?"

"I complained about my life, she complained about hers. Is that a crime? Not everything that goes on in a parking lot is a crime, you know."

"We're at .20 on the blood alcohol here," said Bruce Germaine, the sheriff. "For what that's worth."

"Is that so high? That's not so high."

"It's high enough. Along with the other."

"What other? You keep talking about an other."

"I've got to take him down to the station. We'll talk in the morning. You'll most likely be getting a call from Social Services tomorrow too."

"Why?"

"We'll talk in the morning."

Then Gail and Mimi disappeared from view, or rather stayed right where they were; it was Teddy who vanished, fell into the black hole of the police cruiser. It was no place to be. The backseat, though less than two years old—he remembered the budget initiative that made its purchase possible—was scarred and abused; it reeked of motor oil and old vomit. Wrappers for several weeks' worth of convenience-store snacks lay strewn on the floor like the detritus of a cheap picnic. Ruffles. Slim Jims. Peppermint Patties. Hard to take the authorities seriously when they insisted on eating such childish foods. He tried to roll down the window to get some fresh air. The handcuffs proved an impediment. He supposed that was their function.

Nonetheless under the circumstances he felt remarkably calm. Somehow it wasn't as surprising as he might have expected, to be arrested in the middle of the night for doing nothing wrong. Maybe doing nothing wrong was the crime, he thought.

Bruce Germaine opened the door and fell into the driver's seat with a grunt. "Well, some fun, huh Ted?"

"Yeah."

"I'm too old for this night work. I'm going to have to find me some new drugs."

"I hope you'll share them with me when you do."

"I believe you've had enough, friend." Germaine opened his logbook and began to write. He was a methodical writer. Though like most men his age Teddy maintained a vestigial loathing for police officers, those he knew personally, such as Bruce Germaine, he rather liked. The two of them had coached Little League together one year, had overachieved with a lousy squad. When he needed an officer to come down and address an assembly, or open a kid's locker, or file a report on a vandalized window,

Germaine often showed up himself, tall, amiable, and wide-bodied, patient in the face of complexities. It was easy to like him. He was a bass player, a scratch golfer, a sensei at the local dojo; his jazz quartet was one of the few in the state to feature a bona fide black person on bona fide vibes.

Now he chewed the eraser end of his pencil, as if racking his mind for the mot juste that would complete his lugubrious report. The radio gargled and spat. Lights had begun to come on in the neighbors' windows. The taciturn Harts, the elderly O'Learys, the riotous, pool-happy McDurfees . . . all these good law-abiding citizens had left their beds, roused by the commotion, and were moving back and forth attentively behind the curtains, like shadows on the wall of a cave.

"What say we get going, Bruce? We're kind of creating a spectacle here."

"What do you mean, *we?*"

"I'm trying to remember if I even voted for you last time."

"Not many did. Luckily I was unopposed. Now shut up for a second while I finish this."

What the hell, Teddy thought, let them gawk. New Englanders liked their public humiliations. All those stocks, pillories, and scaffolds, that hardware of punishment; it was cheap entertainment. He sat up tall in the seat, made his profile high and proud like an Indian nickel. Farewell, neighbors! Let them look upon his trials and learn what life was like out on the frontier. The sudden raids, the broken treaties. Being hunted down and persecuted for things you hadn't done. He sat there unmoving, his face a stoic mask, like a mannequin in a diorama. The last of a martyred species, frozen behind glass. Hail to the departing chief . . .

"*But what did you* do?" he heard Gail saying, back in the house. "*Would someone mind telling me what he* did?"

He was beginning to really sober up now. It seemed an unavoidable fate.

At last the sheriff put down his logbook and backed the car

down the driveway and out onto Montcalm Road. Teddy watched his house and those of his neighbors recede into darkness, their lit windows blown out one by one, like candles after a dinner party. He leaned back against his seat and closed his eyes. Voices puttered on the radio. The engine hummed a monotonous tune. It was nice to be the driven for the change and not the driver, to let go of the wheel and be taken somewhere new. He supposed they were passing the dairy farm now; he could hear the cows bellowing in their stalls. Smell them too. But that was how things were out in the country. You had to be willing to take the whole package: the smell of shit and the green things it fed.

"Let's get this straight up front, Ted," Germaine said, after they'd parked in the underground garage, wound their way through the labyrinthine corridors, and arrived at the center of the station house, at whatever the penal-system equivalent of a reception desk was called. "I'm figuring you're right, that this is all some stupid mix-up and a total waste of time. That's the assumption I'm operating on right now."

"Good. Me too."

"But I have to do this anyway, okay? So stand still. These cuffs can be tricky. It's harder than it looks in the movies. You'd be surprised."

"I'm already surprised."

"The DUI you'll have to deal with, naturally. Whatever happens with the other. I hope you realize that."

"Sure," Teddy said. "Of course you'll have to deal with some stuff too."

"Oh? Like what?"

"The lawsuit for starters. I'm married to an attorney, remember? We're going to sue you for false arrest. We'll bleed this town dry."

Big Bruce nodded pleasantly, though his eyes went hard. "Which is your right as a citizen, absolutely."

"Sheesh, hey Bruce, I'm only kidding. Let's not lose our sense of humor."

"You're right." The sheriff gave a wan smile. "Absolutely. You'll forgive me if I put my sense of humor aside and go ahead and book you now though."

"Sure. Book 'em, Danno. I bet you hear that a lot, huh Bruce?"

"Yeah. Now how about emptying those pockets."

"Sure." Teddy divested himself of his wallet, his change, his phone, his keys, his watch. He felt like a scuba diver getting ready for a plunge. The change and cough drops, the ATM and gas receipts, the torn-up grocery lists . . . the more personal items he pulled from his pants, the lighter and more buoyant he felt. "You know, I never did understand that expression. What book?"

"The law, I believe it's called."

"Never read it."

"Well, you may want to start," the sheriff said. " 'Cause you're coming up in front of Judge Tierney on Tuesday morning, and he's likely to have read it pretty closely."

"Tuesday! But it's only Thursday now. Can't I come up tomorrow?"

"The judge goes fishing on Fridays. He's got this little camp in Quebec. Also it's a holiday weekend."

"I can't spend four days in this dump. It's cruel and unusual."

"Oh, it's not so bad. You'll get used to it. We try to keep things spiffy if we can. Got a new thermal coffeepot in the kitchen? Keeps the stuff hot for hours. See that watercolor over there? The loons over the lake? My mom did that one at her care facility. What do you think?"

"I think they look like squirrels."

"I thought so too. Keep looking though. It gets better over time."

Something about the way that last phrase resounded in his head made Teddy apprehensive. "You know, Bruce, I'm trying to be a good sport and everything, but I'm starting to wonder why I'm here."

"Ah, the big existential questions. I was wondering when we'd get to those."

"Okay, I had a few beers, and I roughed up my garage a little. But isn't that between me and my insurance company? I've got comprehensive coverage."

"In my experience, there's no such thing as comprehensive coverage."

"Only what was your car doing in my driveway in the first place? That's where I'm foggy."

"I explained that to you back at the house," Germaine said. "Weren't you listening?"

"No."

"Usually it gets people's attention really focused, being put into handcuffs."

"I was under stress back at the house. Tell me again."

The sheriff explained one more time about the charges. It was a pretty astonishing story. When it was over, Teddy laughed. "C'mon, what's the big deal? So I got into a little tussle with that kid at the photo lab, and now he's getting even. It's not like I'm some criminal."

"Why would you feel like a criminal? Just because of the handcuffs, you mean, and the bars on the doors, and the fact that you're about to surrender all your valuables to our safekeeping?"

"You're taking this way too seriously." Teddy watched Germaine write out a receipt for the valuables in question. "How's the band by the way? Any good gigs? I love that word: *gigs*. But I hate jazz. No offense, it makes me want to scream."

"Yeah, I get that a lot. Now hold still. I'm going to pat you down."

But of course holding still was the problem. Teddy thought about this during the whole tedious and demeaning interlude of strip-searching, form-filing, mug shots, and fingerprint-taking that followed. He'd had enough of holding still. He'd never been good at it in the first place. And now he had to hold still some more, submit himself to these procedures, the ones written down in the book they'd thrown at him. The book would accompany him everywhere now, he thought. Its lines would be imprinted on his skin.

"Now the clothes."

"Christ," he said, "it's a regular police state down here." But he did as he was told. He kicked off his shoes, undid his trousers, wrestled free of his shirt. When one of the buttons popped off his sleeve, he watched it skitter across the floor and disappear. He understood the importance of not stooping over to retrieve things in a place like this. His leather belt, with its bulges and bruises, its misshaped holes, was next. As he released the clasp, he felt the last of his resistance go with it. His chinos collapsed as if from shame into a heap around his ankles.

He stood on the concrete floor in his boxers and his socks. His belly gleamed like glass. The hairs around his navel bristled. He told himself that he had finally arrived at the end of something. The end or the beginning. Either way, he was determined to hold nothing back from here.

As a new arrival, he was given his own holding cell—small but tidy, and discreetly set apart from the others—along with a set of name-brand toiletries, some clean bedding, and a foam pillow. The door slid closed behind him. He sat down on his cot to wait. Institutional confinement he could do, he thought. After all, he'd been confined to institutions for years. Painted cinder blocks, corrugated ceilings, hot-water pipes with fire-retardant wrappings. Even the meals he'd be served over the weekend— the chili, the hockey-puck chicken patties, the too sweet apple-sauce—were more or less the same as the middle school. As why shouldn't they be, both contracts having been won by the same supplier.

No, institutional confinement was nothing new. The question

was what you *made* of your confinement. Were you one of those men who, stuck in a cell, soared inwardly to freedom (he thought of the great prison diarists, the birdmen and madmen, the revolutionary thinkers), or one of the others (he thought of himself) who secretly *enjoyed* losing their freedom, who felt tyrannized by freedom, afflicted by its possibilities and temptations, and wished only to retreat behind solid walls?

It seemed the American condition: to be blessed with so much open space you experience it as vertigo. To hole up in your big house and shut the door.

Well, he was in the big house now.

At last the sheriff went home to *his* big house, and the jail grew quiet. The only sounds were those of Tahir, the trustee on night duty, at work in the narrow, windowless kitchen. He was fixing a sandwich for the new inmate. A few minutes passed, then it came sliding through a slot in the door, fat and salty-smelling on brown bread.

"Thanks," Teddy said. "Very considerate of you."

Receiving his food on a tray made him think of the old Eighth Avenue Automat where his father used to take them for lunch on their biannual trips to Manhattan to consult Dr. Schein, the specialist, about Philip's arches.

"Do you want milk with that? They bring the milk in fresh, you know, from the dairy in town. It's quite good."

"This'll do me fine."

Schein had lived way up on West End Avenue, in an overheated apartment choked with draperies and cushions and rugs, like a pasha's den. His wife, plumpish and rouged, gave the boys butterscotch candies and fondled their cheeks on the way out. All gone now, of course: the Automat, Schein, his poor childless wife, Teddy's parents, Philip . . . they'd all slid off the globe like seals off a rock. He was alone in an empty cell. He did not just *feel* as if he were alone in an empty cell. He actually was.

"It is our tradition," Tahir informed him. "Every new member of our community is to be greeted with a sandwich. Food for thought, quote unquote."

Teddy forced a smile. "Good one."

"One must make do in a pleasant fashion. It does no good to complain of adverse circumstances, do you agree? Things are what they are. We must emphasize the positive elements, take what is good. Sundays for example there are pancakes in the morning. Pancakes and bacon with your famous maple syrup." Tahir studied him through the bars, as if assessing his capacity for such enjoyments. He was a handsome, long-faced young man with a fanatical-looking buzz cut. "I give my bacon to the other guys. But you can have it if you would like."

"That's a nice offer, thanks. But I'm not allowed to eat it."

"You are a Jew?" Tahir's gaze narrowed.

"Actually it's a cholesterol thing. Doctor's orders. I've got to change my ways."

Tahir nodded. He seemed relieved. "So, well, this is very common I think. An obstruction in the walls of the heart. A result of excessive fatness and decadence in your society, do you agree?"

Teddy shrugged. He was no one to talk about excessive fatness. "Wait, how do you know they always serve pancakes on Sunday? How long have you been here anyway?"

"Let me see. Sunday will make"—Tahir's thick brows came together to consult on the math—"eleven fine pancake breakfasts I have enjoyed so far, quote unquote."

"Hell, but can they do that? Hold you here that long without a trial?"

"Apparently they are very busy, your authorities. Very busy and yet also quite remarkably inefficient. Though perhaps in your case it will be different."

"It's already different." Teddy chewed his sandwich thoughtfully. "What did you put on this chicken? It's really good."

"There is some turmeric, and cardamom also. A pinch."

"Pretty fancy spices for a jail-house kitchen."

"Sheriff Bruce has a liberal policy. I give him a list of what I require, he sends someone to get it."

"Well, you're an excellent cook, no kidding. You should open a restaurant."

"No kidding, I did. A very profitable establishment it was too. Back in Kabul, Crown of the Air. You know where is Kabul?"

"I read a book about it once," Teddy said. "It was written by a guy named Elphinstone."

"Yes, I know this book. Only there are two guys named Elphinstone in our proud history. One was indeed a distinguished writer. The other was an incompetent general who was massacred thankfully at the Battle of Kabul."

"It must have been the first one then."

"Yes." Tahir's face grew pouchy and reflective, the eyes sloping downward like commas. "They say you know that when Allah made the world he had left over a great pile of stones. With these stones he created my country. And then came the people to make things worse. And then came the invaders. And so on and so forth."

"So that's why you're here then? To get away from all that?"

"I am here? I am here because it is my nature to be trusting and optimistic. I am here because when my no-good brother by marriage writes to me from Toronto and says, 'Tahir, I have investors who wish to meet you,' I come. In Toronto it seems there are many homesick subcontinentals eager for good food. So we open a fine establishment near the hockey arena downtown. Nostalgia, you see? The *farengee* dreams all his life that he will come to the New World. But then he arrives, and so what is left to dream about? The old one. Kebabs, *buranee,* pilau. So we are very profitable. But then my brother by marriage goes off to Vancouver with a prostitute—excuse me, a nice young lady from Vietnam who he meets in a salon for nails. And after this we encounter labor difficulties. And this becomes all she wrote."

"Union problems, huh? I know about those, believe me."

"Not unions," Tahir said, *"cousins.* I am blessed with two

cousins in Toronto who come to work for me quote unquote. They are never on time but, okay, people have obligations to others. They steal meat from my walk-in but, okay, they have been poor, they are hungry. They abuse my customers but in fairness my customers some of them are quite abusive too. But then I catch these cousins in the bathroom doing all this coke up their noses on the dinner shift, so I fire their slovenly asses at once."

"Good for you."

"Yes, it felt good. But then they must have their revenge on me, so they whisper bad things to the health inspector, maybe one-half true, one-half false. So I get closed down. No more restaurant. I pray to Allah for guidance but he too has obligations to others it seems. But then one day a customer comes to see me, a very prosperous man. He says, 'Tahir, you are a fine cook, we will get you into the U.S., just three thousand dollars, I will arrange all the papers, we shall start again with a new establishment.' Sounds good, yes? Only at the border it seems my new papers are not so in order. And too I am Muslim, which supplies its own problems. They have their own little room at the border station, you know, just for talking to us. I assure you it is a dark one."

"Listen, my wife's a lawyer. Let me talk to her."

"Yes, yes. Certainly. I would be grateful." Tahir did not look grateful however. He looked reserved but polite, a little embarrassed at having shared his story with a stranger.

"It'll work out, you'll see. They can't keep you here too much longer. You're obviously a nice, decent, hardworking guy."

"Ah, but you seem this way too. And yet they say that you are terribly perverted and make pornographic pictures of little girls."

Teddy nodded wearily. He lapsed into silence, but not from offense. It had been a hell of a long day.

"Listen, thanks for the sandwich," he mumbled. "It hit the spot."

For a town as small and remote as Carthage, the jailhouse certainly offered an impressive display of diversity that weekend.

Aside from Tahir, the inmates included a Latvian cabdriver, two Jamaican fruit pickers, a Serbo-Croatian plumber, nine Taiwanese dishwashers-in-training—Mimi's friends from the lake—and a trio of Dominicans from Washington Heights caught speeding west on Route 17 with a trunkful of Chinese heroin. That was globalization for you: the whole border concept was coming apart, clunking toward obsolescence like a GM car. Imports kept zipping by, passing on the left. Barriers falling. You could hardly tell the native from the foreign.

Nonetheless, as the only white American in the place, and a local at that, Teddy's position was awkward. He might have been a consul in some distant beleaguered embassy. If he came on too friendly, he'd seem clueless or condescending; if he remained too aloof, he'd seem privileged and smug. Everyone knew the score. He was the one with diplomatic immunity; he was the one who could at any moment be airlifted free. And the helicopter only had room for one.

So he kept pretty much to himself. He met twice with Fiona Dunn, who had agreed to represent him in court, going over the particulars. No one else came to visit. Okay, fine. He tried to read, but the bad light, and the monotonous *beep-beep* of the Road Runner on the lounge TV defeated him. In the end, he gave himself over to simple tasks: eating, sleeping, crushing spiders against the wall with the heel of his shoe, and trying to avoid any provocative encounters that might lead to violence or male rape. Fortunately no one seemed much interested in him in that or any other way. It wasn't a sexual environment. And he towered above most of the other fellows. Indeed, viewed objectively, if anyone in the lockup looked capable of violence or male rape, it was Teddy himself.

And that was good. Wow, that helped a lot. Because once you wiped violence and male rape off the blackboard of potential outcomes, jail lost much of its shock value. Jail became just another waiting room, another sparsely appointed teachers' lounge, with the same stale air of boredom and retreat, the same acrid smells of cheap disinfectant and bad coffee left too long on the burner. Maybe this was where he belonged. For he too was waiting. Better to wait down here, among these troubled men, this melancholy tribe, than to go on living a solitary sentence on the outside.

Was this what Philip had discovered in those final weeks? The clarity of an absolute state, where everything has been taken from you? His brother had never lost his temper in the hospital, the way sick people do. Had never been mean or small. He'd just lain there listening to Dylan on his black boom box, eyes bright and keenly extruded, as if he could see it approaching: that clean hard floor, where all the cushions were gone. To be sprung from all the little traps and caught at last in the larger one. To finally touch bottom. To know for a change that the bottom was *there.*

Teddy got down on his knees. He'd heard some of the other guys doing exercises in their cells, as if in training for whatever would happen next. Now he would join them.

He forced himself through a brief, desultory set of push-ups. Christ but a body was a heavy thing to lift. Still, one had to carry the burden; he'd better get used to it. He was damned if he was going to sit around getting fat, passively bemoaning his fate. *Actively* bemoaning his fate was another story of course. Teddy was not the passive sort. He was the impulsive sort, the foolish sort, the blundering-coyote sort admittedly. But not passive. Even when he made a mistake—and he made a *lot* of mistakes— even when he went plunging over the cliff to the canyon's bottom, he kept getting up again, and resuming the chase.

And that was how he spent the rest of the weekend. Pushing himself up, letting himself down, sitting himself up, lying himself down, as if the body were some knotty, insoluble algebraic problem that had to be worked through anyway, had to be tested and tested and tested some more.

Afterward he'd lie breathing hard on his narrow cot, his nerves buzzing and humming like a train. True, the train had entered a long, dark tunnel. True, the tracks were rattling, the ties popping loose. True, life was a torment and a tease, a moronic chirping bird that would not stand still. But what could you do? It was the only program on.

At last Tuesday morning rolled around, and he was permitted to dress in his own clothes again, with his own wallet and keys and change, and proceed upstairs to the courthouse for arraignment. On the way out he waved a fond but sheepish good-bye to Tahir and the others. "See you soon," he said. But he did not really expect this to happen.

His case was second on the docket. A good omen. According to Fiona, the judge, Richard Tierney of the Eleventh District, was at his best in the mornings. Not that his best, she conceded, was so distinguishable from his worst.

"Now what fresh nonsense is this," the judge said in a voice like crushed stones. His robe was creased. His face had a yellow cast, like a night clerk in a failing hotel. The ruptured vessels in his nose were like scars from lost drinking wars, from his three failed bids for state Senate, from his spectacular follies in lakefront real estate. Every so often he'd pick up his gavel and swat petulantly at his block. He might have been a child hammering some errant nail.

"Your Honor," said the DA, Jerome Gash, "may we approach?"

Tierney nodded grudgingly from his elevated desk, which had cost the taxpayers of Carthage County $1,300, not including the chair. Jerry Gash sauntered forward in his blue suit, beaming and expectant, an altar boy with a receding hairline. Teddy knew Gash from that other court, their weekly basketball game at the municipal gym. He was plodding, unimaginative, and finicky about fouls. The two lawyers whispered for a while. The judge leaned toward them, his face stern but vacant; you could see in his eyes the boredom and deferral, the reluctance to contemplate any issue larger or more pressing than what to order for lunch. This was just a show they were putting on. A little burlesque. The legal issues had been worked out in advance. Already the lawyers were headed back to their respective tables, Fiona, smiling grimly, in her good mint-colored court clothes, giving him the nod. Everything was under control. Teddy had only to play his part, the role he and Fiona had rehearsed together in the lockup over the weekend. Plead nolo contendere on all charges. Participate—"*cooperatively* participate," Fiona emphasized—in a six-month Court Diversion Program. In exchange for which his record would officially be wiped clean, and he could get on with that prolonged and depleting exercise, his life.

"Here's the thing though, Fiona," he'd said during their strategy session the day before. "What if I don't *want* it wiped clean. What if I insist on keeping the record as dirty as possible?"

Fiona contemplated the sight of his big hand with its angry red hairs crumpling the sleeve of her rayon blouse. "I'd say you're off to a good start then."

"You don't think this deal's selling us a little short? You don't think I should maybe contest the charges, plead yeso contendere?"

"No."

"You don't think if I stood up for myself in there this would all be dismissed as a ridiculous farce?"

"With Dick Tierney in the chair? No."

"Listen, maybe winning or losing isn't what's important here. Maybe what's important is just making the point."

"Oh?" she said. "And what point is that?"

Teddy hesitated. Honestly, when you thought about it, there were so many points to be made. His innocence for one. The point that in a free democratic society no one should be bullied into subjugation by the arbitrary enforcement of an arbitrary law. The point that even if you *were* bullied into subjugation, you didn't have to go down quietly—you could go down noisily, like a freedom fighter, a revolutionary hacking out a path through the jungle hills.

All of which went on one side of the ledger. On the other side went the counterarguments as outlined by Fiona. The local press coverage, which would be embarrassing at best. The potential loss of his job, which would be messy and difficult at best. The costs involved in going to trial, which would be ruinous at best. Plus that other morbid and depressing little fact Fiona insisted on bringing up: that if they did go to trial, he was likely to lose.

"They were nude pictures, Teddy, of a sixteen-year-old girl. How's that going to look to a jury of your peers? This is New England we're talking about, a place with a proud tradition of repression and denial to uphold."

"First of all she wasn't nude, I told you that. She was wearing a towel, more or less."

"The pictures suggest less."

"Secondly, it'll look like what it was. A homework assignment. An exercise to get us comfortable with the camera. Get a feel for our, you know, material."

"You got a feel all right," Fiona said. "But whose material are we talking about, yours? Because I must tell you that in Jerry Gash's office, and the judge's too, they're inclined to be more protective of hers. They'll say you violated the privacy of that poor girl."

"Look, the only violation here is what happened to *my* privacy rights, thanks to some disturbed young punk who gets minimum wage for standing behind a counter being rude to people. If anyone's a victim here, it's me."

Fiona snorted cheerfully through her nose. He needn't have worried about inconveniencing his wife's partner by dragging her down to the jailhouse on a gorgeous July weekend; he was supplying her plenty of recreational amusement.

"If that damned photo clerk hadn't called the cops, the only ones who'd have seen those damned contact sheets would be the people it was intended for—me and my photography teacher. Who wouldn't be shocked, let me tell you. I mean, you should check out the slides she shows in class. You should see the nipples and pubic hair on view today in the great galleries of the world. Hooboy!"

"Thank you, Kenneth Clark, for the art lesson. I'm not a

Philistine, Teddy. I'd wager I know a lot more about the history of portraiture than you do."

"Good! Then back me up! Do your job! Tell the judge! And tell Jerry Gash to get his mind out of the gutter while you're at it, and stop worrying so much about other people's bodies. Sheesh, it's not my fault his wife's put on all that weight."

Fiona smiled wearily, with a mild inflection of disgust. Always a tactical error, he thought, making reference to the weight troubles of a middle-aged woman in the presence of another middle-aged woman. Their bodies, themselves. Besides, he was no one to talk. He'd put on a fair bit of weight himself.

"I'm telling you, Fiona, talk to my photography teacher. She'll explain the whole thing. It was a class assignment. Document the natural forms that surround you, she said. The substance and the, um, quintessence. Of natural forms! Which are already *there* all around us! Is it violating an ocean to take a picture of it? Is it violating a flower?"

"That depends on if the flower is under eighteen. And on the opinion of a court-appointed psychologist."

"Everyone's so protective of that girl now. Where was all this protection when she was off at the lake with your son doing god knows what? And why doesn't he call her anymore? You should see her mooning around at night. What, out of sight out of mind? Isn't that a violation too?"

Fiona's mouth went tight. "Please, don't make me regret my decision to represent you any more than I do. The conflict-of-interest pile is high enough already. The question is, how much of your time and savings are you willing to part with to fight this?"

"All of it," he cried. "What the hell, I'll take a second mortgage on the house. It's a principle worth defending."

"Amateur pornography? Endangering a minor?"

"Artistic freedom."

Fiona clicked shut her briefcase with a laugh. "No offense, Ted, but you're nobody's idea of an artist."

"Who's to say? Jerry Gash, that boob? The man can't read a simple give-and-go. He's been falling for the same pump fake for ten years now."

"Be that as it may, there's still the judge. Let me assure you, to him you're no artist in a beret—you're the guy who until recently has been officially responsible, in loco parentis, for three hundred sixty of our impressionable youth. What will they think when they see this on the police blotter in the *Carthage Courier?*"

"They wouldn't do that, would they? Put me in the paper?"

"Not if we can work this out before the arraignment and get you into the Court Diversion Program. You're a first-time offender. Show the right attitude, write a nice, remorseful essay, agree to do some volunteer community service like, I don't know, Meals-On-Wheels . . . you may have a shot."

"I wouldn't mind doing Meals-On-Wheels," Teddy said.

"That's just one possibility. It could turn out to be something else. Hospital work."

He closed his eyes. "Dear God."

"Maybe it won't be a hospital. The point is to get you into a diversion program and go on from there."

"And if I *don't* show remorse? If I wind up writing the essay I want to write, not the one they want me to write?"

"Then you go to trial, and probably lose. Then you've got Social Services to deal with, no job, no probation, and maybe a chunk of jail time up in Fair View added on. Who knows, you might like it there. They've got a nice library, you'd get a lot of reading done. And you'd be able to share your views with all the other nice, unremorseful guys in the sexual offenders program."

"Boy," he said, knotting his moist hands together. "They do put you in a corner."

"I'm afraid you put yourself into this one, old friend."

He bowed his head, as if from a blow. The idea that he had courted his own ruin, had desired it, wooed it, coveted it, seemed ludicrous. And yet here he was. "What did you mean before, *until recently?*"

"Let's talk about it after the arraignment."

"What, they're giving me the boot, is that it? Tossing me over the side?"

"The board, since you ask, has communicated a number of legitimate concerns. They've expressed a desire to meet and discuss these concerns with you in executive session. At your earliest convenience, is how they put it."

"How delicate they are, those cowardly pricks. They must be loving this. They've been after me for years."

"They've actually been very decent under the circumstances. They're aware that the difficulties of these past months, your brother's death, your little health scare and so on, may be contributing factors to any so-called erratic behavior you may be showing—"

"Erratic! Erratic to whom? Trust me, Fiona: when you carry a hammer, everything starts to look like a nail."

"On the other hand, there's the liability issue. So. The current thinking is, presuming all goes well with Judge Tierney, a year's leave at least. Personal time."

"A year!"

"That's not bad. It's a lot better than what they gave Bobby Murtaugh."

"That creep?" Murtaugh, a music teacher down in Wallingford, had been caught in the act with a second-chair violinist after the spring concert. A sophomore. "But there's no comparison."

"Believe me, if word gets out, there'll be comparisons." Fiona put away her notes. "Now, as to your salary. That may be iffy. But I think I can get you half. You'll need it too, to defray the mandatory counseling."

"They're stripping me blind, aren't they? It's one humiliation after the other."

"You're not helping your cause much. What's this business

about fingerprints? Your buddy Bruce Germaine says you got his deputy all worked up."

"All I said was, run over to the drugstore and get a new ink pad."

"They don't use ink anymore, Ted. It's a digital computer program now."

"Well, the digital program didn't *work*. According to the digital program, I barely *have* fingerprints. My right hand was borderline, and it couldn't even *read* the prints on my left. They said it happens sometimes with older people. The prints just dry up. *Older people.* Those wheezing, pathetic specimens . . ."

"I'm sure it was just a mechanical glitch."

"Have you any idea how awful it is, Fiona, to lose your fingerprints? I mean, all those neat, swervy little lines—where do they go?"

"Something tells me your lines were never so neat in the first place," she said. "Anyway, how about concentrating on your family for a change? The judge can still bar you from contact with Mimi, you know. You could wind up living down at the Sugar House Motel with the other degenerates."

"Hell, maybe I should. There's free cable."

"Tell that to your wife. Tell that to your daughter."

"They're not terribly interested in talking to me at the moment is my impression. How about you?"

"I'm not very interested in talking to you either," Fiona said. "But give them a chance. They're strong women. More unflappable than most. We both know they'll be there when you need them."

"As opposed to me you mean. I'm the flappable, one right? Maybe I should just flap off somewhere with these dirty old wings. What do you think? Everyone's life would be easier."

Fiona shrugged and gathered up her bag. He could see that she was genuinely weary of him now.

"And if I take a pass on the counseling and probation, what happens then? If I say took some sort of trip. They wouldn't chase me, would they? They wouldn't even care."

"Don't make becoming a fugitive from the law sound like a virtue. As an officer of the court, I'm obligated to enforce its decisions. As a friend, I'd remind you of your responsibilities to your family and your community."

He reached for her hand. "And as a *close* friend?"

Despite herself, she laughed. "We're not that sort of friends, darling. Not by a mile."

He nodded. She was right, they were not that sort of friends. Which was too bad: he could use one. A buddy, a fellow traveler. But it seemed the next step was his to take alone.

7

Midworld

Sometimes, in fact most of the time, in fact *all* of the time, it seemed to Oren that he'd watched far too many dramas in his life and acted in far too few; that for all the films he'd studied or worked on in his twenties, all the abstruse criticism and theory he'd committed to memory, he had learned nothing of practical value, nothing of *use,* and was now condemned to play out on an endless loop, in dreams and in life, the dreariest and least edifying of scripts. In the movie of his days, the production values were always low, the direction forever shapeless, the cast incessantly drifting off the set. Those rare moments of dramatic resolution came either prematurely or too late; and meanwhile the middle act, where all the narrative decisions hung precariously suspended, the middle act seemed to stretch on forever.

It was his own fault, of course, this mess and disorder: the price one paid for postponing the future too long. He'd been out of college for a decade now. So why was he still fucking around purposelessly like some outtake from *The Graduate*? And why drag Gail Hastings into it? To require her to inhabit Anne Bancroft's black fishnets was unfair to Gail, who for one thing did not even *wear* stockings, or skirts either, but preferred billowy black pants and nubby, rust-colored sweaters made of natural fibers. No, Gail was in no sense the seductress in this little flirtation of theirs, if you could even call it that, if anyone could be said to be seducing anyone else in a relationship that consisted of such depraved adventures as visiting a stroke victim in rehab, swimming laps in the Y's overheated pool, then occasionally going out for a cup of coffee afterward. Decaffeinated coffee no less.

"One of these nights," he mused, "we should think about getting a room."

"We have a room." She gestured around them, at the blank walls of the rehab unit. "This is our room."

"It's not ours. It belongs to him."

"It's ours if we're here long enough. Squatters' rights. I used to do my share of housing law, back in my idealistic youth."

"That's not the him I meant though," he said.

"I know what you meant. I know."

The second time they'd met had been the week before Thanksgiving—a month after Don Blackburn's stroke, and, possibly more to the point, four months since Gail's husband had somehow got himself incarcerated in the county jail. Now the leaves were down but the snow wasn't; the bleakness of the landscape lay fully exposed, bared and shivering as if from a virulent flu. Cornstalks hung broken in the fields. The sky was a civil war of blues and grays, ringed by tattered violet clouds that rose puffily from the hills like the discharge of cannons. When had the geese all fled? When had the grass stopped growing and started dying? Oren had lost track of the seasonal calendar, the little white squares that framed the days, the tidy processional rows that marched off the weeks, the big picture at the top that lent each month its own unique coloration. Without it he felt dazed, unaligned: the survivor of a battle he hadn't even known was taking place.

In the supermarket the shelves were ravaged. The canned pumpkin was gone, the cranberries depleted, the pyramids of clementines in ruins. The last unthawed turkeys, blockish and upended, lay strewn around the meat freezer, latticed in yellow string. Marked down. Not that Oren cared. He had no plans for the holiday—he'd only half-realized it was coming—and his habits of consumption tended toward the ascetic anyway. He was a bachelor; he was used to carrying meals home in one hand. When he went to the market, he would glance in other people's carts, noting with satisfaction all the bulky processed foods he himself had passed on and feeling, in the uncluttered velocity of his own cart as it zoomed over the polished floor, a testament to his best qualities, his leanness and stoicism, his great gift for doing without. Or was it his great curse? He could not make up his mind. He was a master of deferral, all right, an artist of abstention with a thirty-inch waist. But today he was hungry, and tired, and dreading the long holiday to come; today, the fact that he could see right through his few well-considered purchases to the bare metal grid at the bottom of his cart made him more aware than he liked of the holes that had opened up—or rather never been closed—between himself and his fellow beings. He had deferred too much, he thought, too much and too well. So he decided to get a turkey after all.

The one he chose for himself was a monster—the fattest, lumpiest, most steroidally freakish of the entire flock. He laid the bird gently in his cart like a prize. Then, because it looked a bit lonely down there amid the three little tubs of low-fat yogurt, and the tiny loaf of twelve-grain bread, and the small recyclable bag of organic produce, he began to throw in a lot of other stuff too, as he worked his way down the aisle, sweet potatoes and frozen green beans and canned pineapples and cranberry sauce and pale chemically enhanced coconut slivers, along with a liter of Australian Shiraz to wash it all down, along with yet another bottle of Maker's Mark to wash *that* down. Then he wheeled his cart proudly to the checkout, where he made his final impulse purchase of the day: one of those glossy food magazines they place in the racks by the registers as you line up with the other late shoppers, waiting to be scanned and released.

Paper or plastic, came the cashier's little song. It was a weekly test Oren always seemed to fail. "I don't care," he said.

"You have to choose." The cashier was not paid her lousy

minimum wage to go around deciding what materials other people's grocery bags should be made of. "It's up to you."

"Honest, it doesn't matter in the slightest."

He detected from her voice, however, as she swooshed his purchases across the scanner, a clear preference in the matter, so he went ahead and chose the bag the store, or at least the cashier, seemed to want him to choose, and as usual that choice—plastic—proved the wrong one. When he lifted it from his cart, it ripped neatly and noiselessly down the middle; the big bird thunked onto the car seat and came to rest on the floor.

He'd chosen plastic the last time, Oren remembered too.

At home, he extracted from the closet his largest cooking vessel (that is, *Sabine*'s largest cooking vessel, for she had left the bulk of her kitchen equipment, as she'd left so much else necessary for sustenance, behind) and as the magazine instructed, plunged the turkey breast-down in brine. The stuffing promised to be complicated so he got to work on that next. Never mind that he didn't *like* stuffing, any more than he liked pancakes and waffles; he'd been seized by a vision, back in the market, of a big, joyous, carb-loaded holiday meal, and stuffing was essential to this vision; without stuffing this meal of his would rest on a hollow foundation, as hollow as the cavity that yawned, loveless and dark, between the bird's thighs. So he rolled up his sleeves and set to work.

Clearly this was how you got through holidays like Thanksgiving, Oren thought, as a mature single person with no girlfriend: by solving arcane, demanding, self-created problems of no real significance. How you got through a *life*. And that was cool. That was fine. Because self-reliance was a time-honored New England trait, and for better or, okay, maybe for worse, he was a New Englander now, a can-do, hardscrabble Yankee, a rugged individualist who did not waffle over grocery bags or sit around whining about the difficulty of spending major holidays alone, but actually did something about it—like cooking his own huge, expensive, ridiculously labor-intensive meal.

The only problem was fitting the ingredients for this great feast into his dwarfish and unaccommodating refrigerator. Even after he'd covered the turkey in foil and jammed it onto the bottom shelf, the bird continued to offer resistance, as if some residual evasive instinct still lingered in its bones. Its legs jutted against the bars of the shelf above; its pimpled wings, bleeding at the joints, poked through the foil like an admonishment. But of whom? Not of him, Oren thought, but of the great fallen creature itself, its white, denuded obesity, its useless dreams of flight. Because in the end, what were wings for if not for flight?

It seemed an important question, one that reverberated at odd moments through the chambers of his head. And there were many such moments. Indeed, when it came to the design, production, and distribution of odd moments, no source was quite so hummingly efficient, in Oren's experience, as the middle school in which he worked and, it often seemed, lived, or failed to, Mondays through Fridays, seven thirty to four.

" 'He had contrived, or rather he had happened, to dissever himself from the world . . . to give up his place and privileges with living men, without being admitted among the dead . . .' " Looking up from the assigned text, the afternoon before his little shopping spree, Oren had confronted the students with his most receptive and unthreatening expression. "Who wants to tell us what *dissever* means?"

Hopelessly he waited to be delivered from the ensuing silence. But no deliverance was forthcoming. With Don Blackburn laid up in rehab indefinitely, and half a dozen teachers under the weather—and there was a lot of weather, God knew, to be under—and also, as Zoe pointedly reminded him, no Social Studies class of his own to teach after lunch, Oren had been the logical if not only choice to take over Don's eighth-period Language Arts class. And so he'd bowed to necessity once again. Already he'd bluffed his way through the proper use of quotation marks and some rudimentary state-mandated vocabulary lessons. Now they were into a new, more substantial and trouble-some unit on Classic American Authors.

That week they were discussing a story by Hawthorne, a writer Oren did not much care for and had read exactly zero books by since his freshman survey course in college. Fortunately most of the kids in eighth-period Language Arts hadn't read him either, or even, from their lofty, shellacked expressions, been seriously tempted. This appeared to be standard practice in Room 101N for dealing with such pedestrian matters as homework. Oren didn't blame them. For weeks, through no fault of their own, they'd been hostages to their teacher's illness, left to drift unmoored as a procession of surrogates sailed across the front of the room, slowing down but never stopping, never landing . . . now their loyalties had closed like a gate. Reading Hawthorne wasn't proving to be much help either, any more than Emerson and Thoreau the week before. Reading about transcendence didn't do it for these kids. They had, it seemed, transcended read-ing about transcendence. He didn't blame them for that either.

Still, he *did* blame them for some things—the unattractive, hectoring tone in his voice as he posed them questions, the tumid half-moons under his armpits as he waited for their answers, the odd quaalude-ish slowness of the clock overhead, its hands drooping listlessly at its sides, unable or unwilling to advance. Even under ideal circumstances the class would have been a trial. Right away he'd counted three basketball jocks, two clowns, four bright but docile underachievers, and three totally flatlined morons, and that was just among the boys. The girls and their subterranean sympathies were anybody's guess. They stared up at him now with a serene and pallid blankness. He might have been a crossword puzzle in a magazine to which none of their parents subscribed.

"Can someone just remind us what's happening in this story? So we're all on the same page, as it were?"

No one smiled at his lame little pun. Why should they? Still, it would have made for a nice change.

"Anyone at all?"

More silence. For lack of anything else to do, he squinted out the window, at a sky shorn of color and sunlight and all memory of birds. Where had they gone? He'd never given much thought to where birds went when they weren't flying. Probably very dull, conventional places where nothing was happening. But even birds couldn't fly around 24/7—they had to come down sometime. Even if that coming down felt more like a falling. A capitulation . . .

"Ooh. Ooh."

The trick, he supposed, if one was a bird, was to make oneself at home in both venues, in flight and at rest. That way you didn't miss the sky so much when you weren't in it. Didn't waste a lot of time staring out the window, wondering where to fly next . . .

"Ooh. Ooh. Ooh."

Funny, though, how the longer he stood there doing just that, the more the sky, like a bashful student under pressure of scrutiny, seemed to blur and recede, while his own face, flattened and pale, a bit googly around the eyes, superimposed itself over the glass like a palimpsest. And so we imprint ourselves upon their minds, Oren thought. Stubbornly. Provisionally. Ephemerally. And around that ephemera, the grid of student faces, five rows wide and five rows deep, like a net he'd fallen into, or that had fallen over him . . .

"Ooh. Oooh. Ooh."

He turned from the window and regarded them, his wards, his charges. The best if not only evidence of ongoing mental activity was the salty musk they gave off, like trapped fog, and the way their eyes, slitty and vacant, blinked away at intervals like cursors on a screen. This stultifying boredom, this waiting without knowing what it was they waited for, without knowing that they *were* waiting—was it infectious? Was this the very virus, the flaw in the software, that caused Don Blackburn's mainframe to crash? That wiped the drives clean, rendered the chat rooms inoperative? Already he could feel his own operating system, that patchwork assembly, begin to flicker and squawk . . .

"Ooh. Ooh. Ooh."

Jenny Saunders—a major suck-up whose father taught political science at the college, and whose mother had homeschooled
her through fifth grade, and whose desk, alas, sat right in front
of his, in the unavoidable center of the front row—was issuing
the breathless marsupial gasps she always made when she raised
her hand. For a change he was grateful to hear them.

"Jenny?"

"Okay, so, there's this guy, Wakefield—"

"Dude," Tucker Byrnes called out, "my uncle lives in Wakefield."

"That's *Waitsfield,* dumbass," said Taylor—or was it Tyler?—
Cook.

"Ahem," Jenny said, her cheeks mottling and measling from
this commotion she'd given rise to, "so there's this guy, Wakefield, and one day he like takes off on his family for no reason at
all and moves into this house down the street, though where he
gets the money for two houses nobody even talks about, and he
sort of stalks his family in this really creepy way because he's got
no job and nothing else to do, and he doesn't have to pay child
support because they all think he's dead. And then one day, it's
like twenty years later? It's pouring down rain and really really
cold, and all of a sudden, and this is kind of random too in my
opinion, and I showed it to my mom by the way and she agrees?
He just shows up at his old house out of the blue, like nothing
ever happened. And just when you'd think his wife's going to
finally really ream him out good, which he totally deserves in
my opinion, the whole thing just stops for no reason. The end."

"Thank you, Jenny. Good summary. So what do you make of it?"

"Me?"

"You. Or anyone. But sure, you."

"Well, to me," Jenny said, "honestly, it makes no sense. Why
would someone go to all that trouble just to move down the
street from his own house, when he's got this really nice family
that totally appreciates him? It's unrealistic."

"It's not supposed to be realistic," Tyler/Taylor explained pedantically. "It's a book."

"The guy's fucked-up," put in Colin Boudreau, an authority on such matters. "It's obvious. He doesn't know if he's coming or going."

"Dude, this story sucks."

"The last one sucked too."

"I didn't read the last one."

"What *was* the last one?"

"Let's settle down," Oren said, "and just pretend for the sake of argument that there may be something interesting going on here. Sophie? What do you think? Is there anything Hawthorne can teach us here?"

Sophie Fontana—whose parents had, Oren remembered too late, divorced the previous year, setting off a plunge in both grades and general deportment from which she had yet to right herself—gazed out the window at a pair of geriatric clouds, tattered and gray, lowering themselves onto the cold shoulder of the mountains. Sophie was a tall, semi-attractive girl with slumpy posture. He'd have liked to tell her to straighten her spine, that it would make all the difference, would show off her high intelligent forehead and her arresting blue eyes, but then he remembered his own posture was lousy much of the time when he was her age and he'd never appreciated being reminded of it, so why would she? He was about to give up and call on someone else when he heard Sophie murmuring quietly into her shirt.

"Sorry?"

"He's bored," she said. "He's bored with his life."

"Wait, he's bored with his wife?"

"His *life*."

"Ah," Oren said. "Very interesting." *Very interesting,* as a synonym for *not very interesting,* was Oren's reflexive response to pretty much any student contribution in class, however meager or unformed. But in this case he actually meant it. "Do you mean he *left* because he was bored, or he went *back* because he was bored, or what?"

But Sophie had now fulfilled her quota of interesting remarks for the day. She lifted her burdened shoulders imperceptibly, then dropped them again. It was less a shrug than a rhetorical gesture in the direction of a shrug, and not much of one at that.

"What does it say on page three?" Oren was now in rhetorical mode himself. " 'He was now in the meridian of his life' . . . *meridian* means 'high point,' right? He left his life at the high point."

"In Latin it means 'middle point,' " Jenny informed him promptly. "My mom and I looked it up."

"Right. 'Middle point.' " Was it a dismissible offense to strangle an eighth-grader? Or should he just go ahead and strangle himself? "The point is, the guy seems to be doing just fine, right? He's perfectly comfortable and happy and well-adjusted to his society. So why the sudden change then? Hawthorne never tells us. What do you think?"

Nobody appeared to think anything.

"Okay, maybe Sophie's right—he changes just to change. Maybe he's more bored than he knows. Maybe it gets to be a drag, being comfortable and happy and well-adjusted all the time. So he decides to conduct an experiment. Or maybe he doesn't decide, he just does it impulsively, not knowing why. But here's my question," Oren said. "Once Wakefield's already *left,* for whatever reason, done this very weird, mysterious thing—why does he decide, twenty years later, to suddenly go back?"

"He's retarded?" Colin said, offering his standard line of literary analysis. "He's a total dweeb?"

Oren hesitated. Was Colin some kind of savant in idiot's clothing? Because it struck him in that moment Wakefield *did* have a rather dweebish and retarded quality. And perhaps by extension Hawthorne did as well, conjuring this feckless being in the first place and loosing his metaphysical riddle upon the world. And perhaps this same quality be might further extended to include Oren himself, for mediating this unhappy transaction between the dead, misfit author and these living, well-adjusted sons of farmers and shopkeepers' daughters, plunging them headfirst into that troubled space between the lines and margins of the text in search of ontological meanings, on the assumption that mastering the dark, byzantine arts of hermeneutical inquiry would help them prosper in their later lives. Which judging by his own later life, Oren found ample reason to doubt. Hadn't they just read the previous week, in gassy old Emerson, that *the great gifts are not got by analysis . . . the mid-world is best?*

Still, they were here, for seventy-five minutes a day: they had to talk about *something.*

"So. What do the rest of you think?"

"Ooh. Oooh."

"Jenny?"

"Maybe he's mad."

"Okay, good. But why would he be mad?"

"I don't know."

"Well, what do you think, though?"

"Maybe 'cause his wife doesn't miss him more?"

"Interesting. And why do you think she doesn't miss him?"

"*I* don't know," Jenny pouted, like the spoiled little specimen she was. She'd misinterpreted his question: he wasn't asking her to speculate about Mrs. Wakefield's motives, he was asking what evidence could be quarried from the text in support of her argument. But he didn't bother to correct her. Her sense of entitlement was such that if she didn't get the right answer, she wanted it awarded to her anyway, by virtue of being first to claim it. In his irritation Oren decided to direct his question to someone else, anyone else—even Kyle Fuller, who wasn't listening as usual, preoccupied as he was by his ongoing project of defacing his desk—until Jenny surprised him by adding, "Maybe she never liked him so much in the first place?"

"Ah! Very good! You may just be right, Jenny, I think."

"Really?"

217

"Of course there's no way to know for sure. But Jenny here has raised an intriguing possibility. Think about it, people. What if Mrs. Wakefield really *wanted* her husband to leave?"

"I wasn't saying she—"

"Or, okay," he said quickly, "even if she didn't *want* him to go at first . . . what if, say, after he *does* leave, she sort of changes her mind? What if she discovers she's kind of *glad* to be rid of the guy, who maybe wasn't such a great guy in the first place? Hawthorne doesn't tell us much about their marriage either way. But marriages are complicated, right? It's hard to know what's going on from the outside."

The students—children, he reminded himself—nodded grudgingly, precocious in their skepticism regarding all things marital. As who wasn't, Oren thought.

"Could the whole thing boil down to the fact that Mrs. Wakefield gets *used* to her husband being gone? Adjusts to it emotionally I mean? Or at the very least logistically? Because people do adjust to new things, even bad things, don't they? I mean when they have to."

"*He* doesn't," Sophie pointed out, addressing her remark to the window.

"No, Wakefield doesn't," Oren agreed. "That's true. And you can't help wondering why not."

But apparently you could help wondering why not, as Sophie Fontana and the rest of her classmates were only too eager to demonstrate.

"What was that line from Emerson we read last week? 'Every ship is a romantic object, except the one we sail on' . . . ? Maybe for Wakefield the only time his life looks interesting, looks *real* even, is when he's standing outside it, looking in. What do you think, Kyle? Any ideas?"

Kyle Fuller ducked his round, vacant head, searching for an idea amid the blizzard of dandruff on the surface of his desk. Did Kyle's mother know they sold medicated shampoo over the counter these days? Oren would have to remember to say something, gently of course, inoffensively, at their next parent conference, presuming they showed up, which most parents didn't. And thank God for that. Because now that he'd taken on Don's class in addition to his own, bluffing and prevaricating his way through parent conferences, trying to keep them all straight in his mind, his students and their various needs and prospects and learning issues and so forth, wasn't easy. Still, Kyle Fuller stood out, especially with these sociopathological tendencies he was manifesting at this moment with real diligence and enthusiasm, hacking away at the much maligned surface of his desk with the metal backside of a pencil (the eraser nowhere in evidence), gouging some kind of deep, encoded logo or message that unfortunately—the students were looking up at Oren, expectant of release, the last minutes ticking off the clock—there wasn't time to read or deal with at the moment, other than to note the presence of a familiar and at the same time weirdly exotic-looking name:

Oren Pierce.

Strange: in the past weeks Kyle Fuller had shown few indications of literacy of any sort, fewer still of tolerating, or acknowledging, or even noticing Oren's presence. But then Oren remembered Teddy Hastings's little speech that day he was first hired, about the dynamics of early-adolescent brain development—the thirst, during these boom years of cerebral expansion, for raw materials and good scaffolding—and it struck him that even a limited and well-camouflaged young mind such as Kyle Fuller's must on some sub- or unconscious level be loitering around the academic construction site, waiting to be put to work. Perhaps Oren had tapped into that latency. Perhaps without realizing it he'd gained an acolyte, a protégé. Teaching kids was like that, an invisible process, a seeding ground for transference, like psychotherapy—and here was a subject Oren felt very qualified to talk about indeed—in its dependence upon trust. Trust was the key. From trust came security, from security came receptivity, from receptivity came knowledge, from knowledge came empathy, from empathy came depth of feeling and breadth of perception, and from depth of feeling and breadth of perception came identification with the longings and tribulations of other animate beings, of the whole history of other animate beings, since the first single-cell organism divided in two. That was the mechanism of enlightenment. The flowering, inexorable beauty of it. In the beginning was the word, and the word spread . . .

Whether the word had spread all the way to Kyle Fuller; whether he'd been levitated these past weeks, by the silver wand of Oren's pedagogical charisma, into some heady transcendent orbit he lacked the facility to describe; whether his apathy in class, his sullen jokes and rude monosyllabic grunts, were only a defensive screen for his fear, confusion, and excitement in the face of the unknown; whether, in his transferential haze, he'd lashed out indirectly by writing—okay, gouging—onto his desk the name of the awesome guide who'd led him into this bewildering new place . . . Oren didn't know. *Couldn't* know. And that was good. Because as long as he couldn't know, he too would have to depend on trust, would have to keep plugging away in earnest at this teaching thing until he figured it out. Because Kyle Fullers were everywhere: slugs, deadbeats, morons, mouthbreathers. Kids with minds like idling screens, waiting for someone to push the button that lights up their circuitry . . .

"Ooh. Ooh."

A couple of other words too, he noticed, were floating on Kyle's desk in a festive, inky cloud. Something about *socks* or *sacks* . . .

"Ooh. Ooh."

"Anyone other than Jenny?"

Out in the corridor, lockers were slamming. The basketball players, grinning and graceful, began to ease out of their chairs and gather up their backpacks. They let the jocks out early on game days, so they could head off to play. To compete.

Something about *cooks* or *cokes* . . .

"Well, okay, quickly then . . . and, Jenny, we'll resume with your comment first thing tomorrow . . . but for tonight, think about that passage I just read, and see if you can connect it to what's going on in the rest of the story. On the one hand Mrs. Wakefield thinks her husband's dead, so there's nothing more she can do about that. Which makes it easier for her, you might say. Still, on his side, he's *not* dead. On the other hand he's not quite alive anymore either. He's—"

The bell rang. Despite himself the sound still excited him.

"—between," he announced, though no one was left in the room to hear him.

As he approached the hospital, the light was waning over the foothills, the sky gone grapy and thin. The heater was on high. The roar it made was impressive, but the steering wheel remained icy, the breath continued to fly from his mouth in pale, scudding clouds.

It was visiting hour: the lot was full. Through the frost-embroidered windshield he spied the red flare of brake lights ahead. He clicked on his blinker and waited. The driver, and this annoyed him, was adjusting her makeup in the rearview mirror. While he waited for her to finish, he turned up the music on the car stereo—a new CD his friend Sandy Krause had burned for him, by a band he'd never heard of—and tapped out a bass line on the dashboard. If there was one thing from his former life Oren really missed, it was going out to hear new bands, new music. He liked not knowing where a song was going; not being able to anticipate, in the silence between verses, the makeup and tempo of the next. It was important to stay attuned to the new music, he thought. Once you let go it would never come back. And then in its absence something lazy and insidious would move in to fill the empty space, some soft, pendulous sag in the brain wires, some mental flabbiness and spread, which inevitably like all processes of incremental corruption led to a loss of the new and its replacement with the old. Oren feared that process and fought against it and complained about it, even as he recognized that with every passing year he was succumbing to its pull a little further.

Which may have informed his decision to yank out the CD right now—he did not care for this new band after all—and put in an older, more familiar one instead.

So intent was he at that moment on finding the right music to listen to that he almost failed to recognize, in the awkward do-si-do of parking, Gail Hastings backing out of the space he'd been waiting to back into.

As she passed, they exchanged a pair of silent, civil nods from behind their respective windshields—hers warily acknowledging; his reluctantly acknowledged—and that was fine, really. But after she'd gone, and the billowing clouds of her exhaust had dissipated into clarity, he discovered in letting it out that he'd unconsciously been holding his breath the whole time. Why? And why had he slumped so low in the seat, as if he were hiding? And why too, given that unlike his first trip to the hospital he'd smoked no marijuana this time and was hence enjoying none of its benefits, was his mouth so dry, his head so hazy?

He felt caught out, exposed. Just the casual flicker of her gaze had left a burn on his cheeks, a capillaried stencil of guilt and shame. Because this was not in fact his second obligatory trip to see Don Blackburn at the hospital. It was not his third either. Or his fourth. It was his fifth. And it was no longer obligatory, not in any sense that Oren—or, he supposed, anyone else—could even pretend to understand. Least of all Gail Hastings.

His second trip to the hospital had been the Wednesday after his first one. His third had been the Wednesday after that, and his fourth had been the Wednesday after that. And now here he was again, the Wednesday after *that,* and still sneaking his way through the corridors like a truant, still edging away from eye contact in the elevators, still no better able to articulate what had drawn him back to this place, why afterward he felt better about himself, and not, say, worse, as a result of having come, and why the emotions engendered by hanging out in a stroke victim's room—helplessness, sadness, clumsiness, boredom—were emotions he or anyone would seek to recapture. But recapture them he did. Every Wednesday afternoon, from approximately four fifteen to five, he squatted dutifully by Don Blackburn's bedside, saying nothing, while Don, red-faced and bug-eyed, stared vacantly at the wall, saying nothing back. It was madness. Perversity. It was as if he were operating under some weird, inexplicable compulsion every bit as meaningless as Wakefield's. Sunk like a bag of wet sand, week after week, into the same chair, running his eyes over the same generic get-well cards from school, the same blue plastic vases full of what appeared to be the same roses, lilies, tulips, and irises, with the same double-jointed head-and-shoulder shots of the Hastings girls, Mimi and Danielle, lined up politely on the bedstand like ministering angels, or fates.

Men like to look at pretty girls. It gives them a boost.

Every Wednesday afternoon, as if reporting for duty, Oren submitted himself to their knowing, mirrored inspection. Every Wednesday afternoon he'd sit waiting for the clock to release him. Every Wednesday afternoon, in a fugue of boredom and low blood sugar, he'd shock and appall himself by stealing another chocolate from the otherwise-unviolated sampler on the bedstand. The ethics of which were made somehow both better and worse by the fact that *he* was the one who'd bought and put them there in the first place, a sequel to the pricey bouquet he'd delivered earlier and then watched wither and die with astonishing speed. Hence he was not simply stealing candy from Don Blackburn: he was also stealing from himself.

How complicated and strange, all these forces that guided or bypassed or thwarted a man's will and conspired to strand him here, in a sick person's room, beside a sick person's bed, stealing that sick person's chocolates, then eating those chocolates in full view of the sick person himself. If only he could bring some clarity to that region of the brain where self-understanding takes shape! But it seemed his brain had no such region, only the hope of one, the stubborn enduring need of one, like the vestigial myth of a sunken continent.

Pensively he nibbled his (that is, Don's) chocolate, his teeth fighting for traction in the dense, clingy nougat, seeking a core that might for a change prove worthy of the effort to reach it. With every bite he sank deeper into his chair, feeling that much more the interloper, the trespasser, the voyeur. And at the same time that much less. His flesh had by this point molded itself so seamlessly into the contours of the visitor's chair he no longer felt like a visitor at all. He felt like a proprietor. The chair belonged to him, or he belonged to it; in any case the two of them belonged together. Such is the nature of repetition. Slowly, over the weeks, the strange becomes familiar, and the familiar becomes strange, then familiar, then strange again, until all such distinctions seem arbitrary, moot.

His body wanted him here in the hospital. He had no idea why. Perhaps his body was sick; perhaps it knew something the rest of him didn't. Every Wednesday afternoon, descending in the elevator to the ground-floor lobby, he'd utter the same silent vow not to return; but then the next Wednesday would roll around, and at the buzz of the eighth-period bell he'd rear his head like a docile dog and lope out to his car. He was no longer driving to the hospital—he was being *driven* to the hospital, or so it seemed, by the force of some unnameable necessity. Not an urgent necessity but a solid, boring, structural one, as a hinge is necessary for the swinging of a door, open and shut.

Two Wednesdays after they'd crossed paths in the parking lot, he arrived in Don's room to discover Gail Hastings occupying her old chair. He was reasonably certain she'd arranged it that way.

They nodded at each other like strangers, then sat awkwardly on opposite sides of the bed. A misting sleet glazed the windows. It was a few weeks before Christmas; the mournful drone of "The Little Drummer Boy" echoed down the corridor. Don, his condition stabilized but unpromising, lay sunk in a fogged-in, aphasic Santa Land all his own.

Finally Oren cleared his throat. "We've got to stop meeting like this."

Gail frowned. "And here I was hoping you'd find a way not to say that."

"Someone had to."

"Did they? Why?"

He shrugged. So far this was not going at all well. On the other hand, what *was* this anyway? What did he expect *this* to be?

"I realize," he said, "this must seem like pretty bizarre behavior to you. My being here. You'd be totally within your rights to be wondering why."

"But I'm not wondering why."

"Well, I sure as hell would. I'd be wondering why like crazy." He seemed incapable of lying to this woman for some reason. And he was good at lying to women; it was something of a trademark in fact. "I'd find it very strange and disturbing."

"Not to burst your bubble, rabbi, but I've got a lot on my plate at the moment. I wasn't thinking about you at all."

He nodded, stung.

"I'm assuming though, if you're here," she went on more kindly, "you must have your reasons. Vaguely spiritual reasons. I seem to remember that's your forte, isn't it? Spirituality? The relief of existential distress?"

"Okay, wait, isn't this where we left off last time?"

"Or maybe you were hoping to get another look at me, is that it? The poor disgraced wife in her time of need. Maybe you wanted to save me, hey?"

"Actually," he said, truly irritated now, "I'm just here to drop off some Christmas cards from the kids in Don's homeroom."

"Let me see."

Obediently he handed her a thick manila folder stuffed with cards and watched her leaf through them. "There's a nice one from Zoe in there too. She must have worked on it for days. And a jazzy seasonal number from the gals in the outer office."

"Nothing from you?" she said, glancing up from her reading.

"Me?" Reflexively he showed her his palms, then turned them over to admire their emptiness himself. "I'm just the mailman. Here to spread some holiday cheer."

"The lonesome courier."

"Something like that," he said. "Merry Christmas to you by the way."

"Thanks. Is it still Hanukkah, or is that over now? Should I wish you something for that?"

"Don't bother. My feeling is, people should enjoy the privileges of being in the oppressive hegemonic majority culture without having to apologize for it."

"I wasn't apologizing."

"Anyway I'm not particularly observant. It's not my mode."

"What is your mode, exactly?" She leveled her gaze at him across the bed. "I'm having trouble getting it straight."

"Right now I guess my mode is visiting sick people in the hospital, and not knowing why."

"Then maybe you're more observant than you think."

He gave this idea a moment's consideration. It seemed to him rather fanciful and charming.

"Don't get me wrong," she said, "I'm grateful to you for coming. I was grateful the first time too. I'm not too proud of how I treated you that day. You went out of your way for a man you hardly knew. That's more than most people do."

"I guess most people are pretty busy. You know, with their lives and all."

"I don't care about most people. I only care about the people I know. And for some reason they're always the ones who behave the worst."

"Well, now you know me too," he said.

She gave a little laugh. "You're pretty self-confident, aren't you, for a guy who has no idea what he's doing here."

"I didn't say I had no idea what I was doing. I said I had no idea why."

"I'm not sure I see the distinction. But whatever. I'll reserve judgment." She took a sip from her travel mug. He could tell from the arch of her neck that she was down to the dregs of whatever liquid was in there. "You're kind of a piece of work though, aren't you, Oren?"

"How so?"

"Well, on the one hand you like to make an impression. You come on like such a good boy, all nice and attentive. But there's this hovering, vampire thing going on too. I can't help but feel there's something you want, only I can't figure out what. I don't think *you* can figure out what."

"This you call reserving judgment?"

"I also think you were flirting with me a second ago and you didn't even mean it. I find that frankly disturbing."

"Would it be less disturbing if I did mean it?"

She frowned, picking at a nail on her left hand. She had that intelligent way of coping with hypothetical questions: by ignoring them.

"Maybe you're not used to people being attentive," he offered. "Maybe that's why you don't trust it."

"Well, and that's the other hand. Maybe you're right, and I'm just a cranky, dried-up old bag who wants to be left alone. There are worse things than being left alone, I'm beginning to think."

"Are there?" He tried to conceive of what these worse things might be. But obviously he was in a different phase of his life than she was. He supposed this had been evident to her from the first. "Anyway you're not so dried up."

She frowned and looked away. How stupid and transparent he was, what a vain, foolish, predictable person, imposing himself on this overburdened woman, when all she wanted was the thing he had too much of.

The silence between them having now conclusively been restored, she squeezed out some white hand lotion and rubbed it over her fingers. A boy trudged down the corridor, trailing an

IV stand with rattling wheels. The oncology unit was just down the hall.

"Okay then." He rose and reached for his peacoat. He'd bought it on Canal Street some years back, marveling at its heft when he'd tried it on, its substantiality. But it took forever to get the thing buttoned. Everything he did took much too long. He looked down at Don Blackburn's droopy, insensate form. He felt, as he always did visiting Don, a vague but powerful attraction, if not to Don then to the bed in which he lay.

"Boy," Gail Hastings said, watching him pull up his collar, "you do give up easily, don't you."

"Okay, I'm confused. I thought you *wanted* to be left alone."

She shrugged. "Well, are you going to keep coming back, or not? We should get that straight don't you think? Before you go running off?"

"I'm not running off. But sure. Fine."

"Who am I to discourage you from doing something nice, if that's what you want to do. Maybe you should stick around for a while, I'm thinking, until we figure it out."

"Fine."

"You're fine either way, aren't you?" She watched as he sat down again on the edge of the chair, his coat half-buttoned. "How refreshing, a man who likes being told what to do. You'll make a good second husband for somebody. Maybe not such a good first husband though."

"Yeah, so I've heard," he said. "Unfortunately, I was proposing to the person who said it at the time."

When she laughed, as she did now, the whole shape of her face changed, became more open and heart-shaped, more recklessly discomposed. "Poor baby. And that was when?"

"A couple years ago. Back in New York. New York was kind of Fiasco Central there for a while."

"And before New York?"

"How much time do you have? I'd need to draw you a whole map."

She laughed again. He was beginning almost to require this of her, this grudging bemusement. The effort it cost her felt like an accomplishment. "It must be great to live life so lightly. Go anywhere you want, whenever you want. Just pick a place and go."

"Yeah, it's a real riot." He ran a hand through his hair; was it less thick than he remembered? "And just for the record, I'm thirty-three."

"Really? I'd have said younger."

He tried, and failed, to receive this as a compliment.

"Hey, don't look so glum," she said. "At least you've been out there extending yourself. I find that appealing in a person. Just so long as they don't extend themselves, you know, too far."

He couldn't tell if she was playing with him, or flattering him, or whether she was thinking about him at all. The hand cream she'd rubbed on her fingers smelled milky and sweet. He could not recall the last time he'd noticed the smell of a woman's fingers. "And what about your husband?" he said abruptly. "Did he go too far?"

The window of her face went dark. "Ask him yourself," she said.

If he were still in therapy—and, boy, Oren was thinking, could he use some—he'd have been forced to confront the possibility that he'd invoked her husband on purpose. First to punish her for her interest in him, such as it was, and then to punish himself for his interest in her, such as *it* was. But his therapy days were over. His therapist was back on West Ninety-first Street, treating the next generation of overeducated neurotics, while Oren made his own way unguided through the wilds. Or was his own way making *him*? If so it was doing a deplorable job—he could tell from the firm, efficient way Gail now turned her back to him, to say nothing of her arms and legs and feet, and began reading the holiday cards aloud to Don, which Oren should by now have long done himself. Her voice was lucid, patient, and expressive: a mother's voice. The very mother, he reminded himself, of these two sly, watchful-looking girls in the doubled frame, whose eyes he felt upon him even now, waiting for him to slip up somehow, to pilfer one too many sweets.

Don for his part lay breathing noisily through his mouth. His face was red; his eyes raked the ceiling. The more Gail read, the more trapped and distraught he looked, like a toddler stuck too long in his crib.

"Why bother?" Oren said. "He isn't listening."

"He might be. He's not deaf, you know. They say most of his faculties are intact even now. He's still in there somewhere."

"If so, he's pretty well hidden."

"Give him time," she said. "Sometimes it takes a year, the doctor said. For all we know he could be on his way right now to a full recovery. Isn't that right, Don?"

Don blinked up at her helplessly.

"They'll be moving him to rehab later this week. It's an impressive facility. He'll get speech and movement therapy and a lot of other stuff too. One thing about our generation, we know how to mobilize our resources. We're not going gently into that good night, no sir."

"To have to start over again from scratch though," Oren said. "At his age."

"Oh, I imagine it's not so bad, starting over." She ran her palm over Don's limp white hair, smoothing it back from his forehead; she did so tenderly, and with cool insistence, as if channeling all her energies into dominion over this one narrow, lawless area. "You'd get the chance to relearn so many things you've taken for granted. How to walk, how to talk, how to eat . . . it's like being a baby again, I should think. Or *having* one. You get to rediscover the world."

"To me it sounds pretty tedious."

"Anyway there's no choice," she said. "So that's that."

That's that. He thought of all the caretaking that must go into being a mature woman, the sick children to be attended, the medicines and compresses to be administered, the worried phone calls to be made, the bowls of soup, the cups of tea. How sexist and unfair it was. Though the narcissist in him, which generally had the run of things, hoped for a grown daughter of his own someday to tend to him when he was old and failing, the moralist in him was outraged in advance on the poor girl's behalf.

Fortunately this daughter of his was, like so much of his life, still hypothetical. "So how can I help?"

"Help?" Gail looked amused.

"Why not? It's my job, you know. He's a member of the faculty. I'm not just being polite." Of course he *was* just being polite, but what the hell—that was what politeness was for. To make you seem better behaved than you were, on the chance that at some point it stopped being a pretense and became the truth. "Try me. Give me something to do."

"Well, if you really want to do something, just keep doing what you're doing. Come visit him in rehab. That *would* help. Even if he doesn't show it, the human contact does him good."

"It does me good too." Outside it had begun to snow, hard. The sight of it was satisfying somehow.

"And maybe bring more of those chocolates with you next time. They keep disappearing. The orderlies I guess. They're like pirates around here."

"Okay, I will."

"Also, and this may really be more than you want to take on, but sometime in the future I might ask you to stop by Don's house once or twice. There's not a lot to do. Take in the mail, water the plants, feed the cats and goldfish, that sort of thing. Shovel the walk. Zoe and I've been taking turns, but sometimes it gets away from us."

"Sure thing." Nothing could have come as less of a surprise than Don Blackburn having cats in his house. "Happy to do it."

"Don't be too quick to commit yourself. This might go on for several more weeks. Longer even."

"Honestly, committing myself too quickly has never been a problem." The snow was coming down in ropes, burying the grilles and hoods of the cars below. "How much longer though?"

"You tell me. There's a lot they don't understand about aphasia. I've done some reading, and I don't understand it either. It seems we all carry around this inner world and this outer world, and then something breaks, and they stop linking up."

"Story of my life."

She regarded him coldly. "It's so easy to be glib about other people's problems."

"Actually, if you want to know, I was being glib about my own."

"Ah, right, I forgot. Poor baby. How stressful it must be, so young and beautiful, with all this time on your hands you don't know what to do with."

"I think he's still waiting for you to finish." Oren nodded toward the get-well cards in her hands. Had she really said he was beautiful? "I left the best ones for last. Some of the girls in his homeroom went a little wild."

"I'll bet." She shuffled through the cards, her mouth turned down wryly at the corners. Oren was sufficiently proud of the effort that had gone into them—even if that effort wasn't voluntary, but a required project in Renee Daley's art class, which had devoted two periods to it—to overlook all the cross-outs and spelling mistakes. But was Gail? "I bet they like you over there, don't they? Girls that age, they go for the cool withholding types."

"I wouldn't know."

"You're Mr. Mellow, hey, Oren? Is that the secret of your popularity?"

"I'm not that popular. I just have one advantage over the others, that's all."

"What's that?"

"I don't care."

"Well, congratulations, Mr. Pierce. You've attained a state to which I aspire."

"Oh?"

"Nonattachment. You're traveling light. It's a rare thing.

Maybe I should stop going to yoga, and let you give me lessons in your kind of purity instead."

"Maybe you should," he said. "Maybe I will."

For Oren, after so many years as an underachiever, it was almost as gratifying as it was enervating to be called upon so often and so relentlessly as he was that winter. No longer did he meander his way through the long, aimless afternoons, peering listlessly in classroom windows, like a tourist in some placid landlocked country—Switzerland, say—with a favorable rate of exchange. Whatever principality he inhabited now was more like India, a messy, anarchic place full of traffic noise, bad smells, and strange gods, with a wobbly infrastructure and a maddening bureaucracy and an array of highly dubious and provisional public services. It was not the sort of place Oren would have chosen to visit at this particular moment in his life, but then he *had* no choice. With Ted Hastings gone, and Don Blackburn in rehab, and a virulent Asian-flu bug mowing down the other faculty; with the snow piling up in the parking lot, the ice glazing over the sidewalks, the mercury loitering in the teens, the buses lurching and sliding in the circular driveway, he couldn't just do what came naturally—that is, go home after school and leave Zoe Bender to deal with it all herself—even if everyone, Zoe included, might have preferred it that way; even if nothing made her happier than sitting alone at a desk deep into the night, sipping burnt coffee and nibbling on whatever strands of her hair had strayed, in the tumult of the day, from the strict confinement of their elasticized band. That was how Zoe got her kicks.

"Off somewhere interesting?" she'd call blithely from her office as Oren struggled into his coat.

"Nah. Just going home."

"Home." From the fond and reverent sigh that followed, she might have been Judy Garland in Oz. "Well, have fun then."

It was difficult for Oren to have fun, however, when he'd been directed to do so, and when he was wrestling with (and losing to) that undersize weakling, his conscience. In the end it was easier not even to try. Easier to be the good boy who stays after school and helps out. The teacher's pet. Wasn't that how he'd got to be acting vice principal in the first place? And how did acting vice principals act? They acted busy, very busy. They solicited substitutes, they called back parents, they rescheduled canceled hockey games and organizational meetings, they ordered up materials for the next in-service day, they ran off copy after copy of bureaucratic and unreadable memos on the sluggish photocopier in the outer office. Above all, they worked late, gazing out wistfully at the smudged and darkening sky, the empty, sleet-slickened parking lot, watching their fellow faculty members struggle into *their* coats, get into *their* cars—their exhaust trails vanishing into the gloom—and leave the tedium of *their* jobs behind. At home they had families waiting, hasty dinners, noisy arguments, children to haul back and forth to pottery or basketball or tae kwon do.

More tedium, Oren thought. No one got away free. It was just a matter of exchanging one mess for another. He tried to take some consolation from this thought as he holed up in his office in the evenings, raiding the secretaries' ramen soups and candy bars for nourishment.

During the day of course he rarely thought at all, busy as he was hurtling like a pinball through the school's noisy, lit-up maze, stepping in where needed. It seemed he was needed everywhere. From seventh-grade Social Studies in South Wing, he went directly to Supervised Study in East Wing, to eighth-grade Social Studies in North Wing, to Lunch A in the Cafeteria, Student Council in West Wing, Lunch B back in the Cafeteria, a half hour of administrative duty in the Inner Office, and finally one last detour to North Wing, where he'd pound his head both figuratively and, on one particularly dismal afternoon, literally against the blackboard, trying to encourage Don's defiantly untranscendental Language Arts class to invest themselves in the great works of nineteenth-century American literature.

And mind you that was *during* school. After school he was *really* busy.

On Monday afternoons, filling in for Don, he supervised the yearbook staff, who appeared to be composed of the same cohort of bright, can-do, civic-minded kids Oren had avoided like the plague—or had they avoided him?—in his own school days. On Tuesdays he filled in for Jack Russo, the ponytailed, droopy-eyed music instructor, with his Introductory Guitar group, so Jack could attend couples counseling with Melanie, his soon-to-be third ex-wife. Thursdays he filled in for Teddy Hastings with the chess club, all three of whose members, Oren was gratified to discover, he still had the chops to destroy at will and send home in tears. And on Wednesdays of course he filled in for God. That is, drove to the hospital's sparkling new rehab unit to spend an hour or so in Don's semiprivate room, reading aloud choice excerpts from *Times* op-eds and reporting, to no perceivable purpose and with no perceivable encouragement from Don, any new and/or interesting developments at school. After which—and he assumed his path and God's diverged at this point—he'd head off to the Carthage Y, where he and Gail Hastings would swim laps, then drink coffee and, in a low-key, indirect way, tend to the maintenance and growth of their own small plot of sexual tension.

And Fridays? On Fridays, instead of shooting over to the Lyons' Den after school as on Fridays of yore, to join Jack, Zoe, Renee Daley, Sue Harper, and the other single members of the faculty in their weekly rituals of gossip and exorcism, he now—thanks to Gail, or rather to his own mystifying compulsion to impress or confound her, he wasn't sure which, perhaps both—found himself driving twenty-odd miles of unpaved road to the far reaches of the Carthage valley. Where, in exchange for exactly zero remuneration, he'd pass the week's final hours in a trailer behind the milking barn at the Duquette dairy farm, instructing Emanuel, Carlos, and Demetrio, three Mexican workers of dubious legal status, in the arbitrary workings of his native tongue.

And that wasn't even the noteworthy thing about Fridays. The noteworthy thing was he enjoyed it. Enjoyed it immensely. Which perplexed him. Because so modest were Oren's talents in the ESL area, and so rudimentary were the exercises he'd unearthed from a workbook in the Carthage library, and so vapid and peppy did he sound to his own ears, cheering the three young men on as they worked away at their makeshift desks, that when each session ended and they stood at the door of their drab double-wide and shyly, solemnly, with eyes half-averted, took turns shaking his hand, it was all their new teacher could do not to break into giggles or sobs. What on earth was happening to him? And when would it stop? By what strange alchemy had he been transmuted from the person who receives instruction to the person who gives it? What a joke *that* was! And yet the Mexican fellows weren't laughing. They appeared to take their teacher rather seriously, a good deal more seriously, in truth, than he took himself. Surely his manic pacing around the trailer, commenting on everything he saw, as if he'd never set foot on a working farm before; surely his way of hesitating in the doorway at the hour's end, saying his own shy, formal, almost apologetic good-byes, as if he were no more certain than they of the rules governing his silly and capricious language; surely the haste with which he jumped into his car afterward and backed it down the rutted, ice-slickened road, as if someone were chasing him . . . surely for Emanuel, Carlos, and Demetrio, all this must have fallen, on their own maps of civilized behavior, somewhere to the left of strange.

It seemed that way to Oren, in any case, as he skidded down the driveway in reverse, trying to put it all behind him in the rearview. The frigid trailer; the shitty rabbit-eared television; the two-burner hot plate; the mud-spattered bikes they rode to work in the barns. It was five o'clock in the afternoon. For the twenty minutes it took to drive home, even the smallest, most predictable comforts that waited there—a hot shower, a working phone, a comfortable bed—came to seem fantastical, other-worldly. That was the good side of his little foray into volunteer social work. That and the pleasure of the men's company, their eagerness to learn, their warm, teasing humor. The bad side of course was everything else. Knowing, in a way he had managed not to know before, that the trailer was there all the time, even when he wasn't, which was why people like him could zip over to the store whenever they liked and pay $1.89 for a half gallon of milk. Knowing they had relatives and friends at other farms but no car to go see them, and besides, it was better not to attract attention. *We must be shadows always,* they told him. But the pay was good, and every other Sunday the church brought them dinner, and Senora Hastings had arranged for a dentist to come fix their teeth, and now thanks to Oren, the golden one, they were learning better English, so they would not complain about the small things.

Four thousand miles they'd come to milk other people's cows in the freezing dark, and they would not complain about the small things. Some system.

He wondered, driving away, whether Emanuel, Carlos, and Demetrio thought of him as part of that system or an exception to it, or if they thought of him at all. Did they mention their new teacher in their letters home? Did they make fun of him when he left, for his blond, uncombed hair, his nervous laugh, his *loco* driving, his habit of blushing and apologizing when he corrected their grammar, as if *he* felt sorry for *them?* How absurd. They had come to this place voluntarily; they knew what they were doing, and for whom, and for how long. It was *him,* their teacher, this educated gringo, this native son with his university degrees: *he* was the one who seemed not to know things. All he had were borrowings. He spent his time with another man's wife, did another man's job, took care of another man's house. He was no more at home in this world, no less a shadow, than they were. At least they had a home somewhere else, where they could be themselves. Did the golden one have that?

But the golden one was gone.

And so went the days. If it was Oren's nature to hold himself back, to remain exempt from the suck and swoosh of quotidian life; and if the ground on which he'd planted his feet was now revealed to be sand, hissing away in some tidal undertow he sensed but could not see; and if his resistance was now crumbling, bit by bit, into the fogbank of exhaustion . . . well, too bad. He would not stand watch over himself like a lighthouse, sweeping his beam around. He had neither the time nor the energy. And that was good. That was *great.* Not having the time or the energy to think seemed the most wondrous new accomplishment of all. Or would have, if he'd had the time, and also the energy, to think about it. But he didn't. No, the news came to him only glancingly, in odd, unbidden moments . . . stepping out of the shower stiff-legged in the morning, or driving home through the dusk, the headlights scooping out their small, grudging portions of road . . . that this was *it,* the very thing he'd been seeking all these years, what other people called, with no apparent irony or loathing, *real life.*

And yet nothing had ever felt quite so *un*real. The days peeling off, light and flimsy and blurrily similar, like copies off a mimeograph machine. Then another, then another. How strange it was, how novel and extraordinary, being ordinary. Working hard all day on small, achievable tasks, then spacing out at night in front of the television, then waking the next morning to another set of small, achievable tasks . . . he'd never felt so weighed down by commitments and yet at the same time so weightless, so blank. If this was normality, then he couldn't say he liked it much. On the other hand he didn't dislike it either. He didn't know if it was the numbness of indifference or the serenity of acceptance, but the most he could say about his life that winter was also approximately the least he could say: it was something new.

*   *   *

And then there were the weekends.

On Saturday mornings, like failed rabbis everywhere, he slept late. Or rather tried to. Sleeping late was hardly a new regimen for Oren—he'd slept late for years, even at times he may have passed for awake—yet now that sleeping late was no longer an elective but a requirement, now that he *needed* to catch up on weekends for the rest that had evaded him all week, it began to evade him on weekends too. A cramp in his bladder. A stray branch banging against the window. The leaden rumble of the snowplow, scraping away night's fluffy insulation, baring the raw, gray morning that waited below. An enormous effort was required to ignore all this and go on sleeping, precisely the sort of effort Oren was way too tired these days to pull off.

The latest he managed to sleep anymore was nine thirty, a far cry from the epic slumbers of his youth. Still, nine thirty wasn't so bad. If you were married, say, married with kids, as virtually everyone he knew at this point was, sleeping to nine thirty would be an enchanted dream. No wonder married people with kids complained so much and looked so haggard, so bereft. Though if you were married with kids, there would be other compensations too, he imagined, such as engaging in sexual contact with a more tender and resourceful companion than your own right hand.

Not that he was belittling the pleasure his hand still brought him, with admirable regularity. Not that he was complaining about *that*.

Anyway by the time he'd extricated himself from bed, had showered and shaved and dressed, and downed three or four mugs of coffee while listening to the radio and reading every word of the newspaper, it would be close to eleven, and eleven was within hailing distance of lunch. At which point, between the food to be cooked and the dishes to be cleaned afterward, he was well on his way into afternoon. As for the rest of the day, it was a piece of cake, really, something to be nibbled away with chores and errands, and grading papers, and, when he was feeling particularly outdoorsy, trekking through the woods on a pair of snowshoes Gail Hastings had lent him, either solo or in the company of Gail and her large, clumsy, unintelligent dog. The snowshoes, possibly because they belonged to her husband (he had gone off on a long trip, though she was reluctant to share the details), didn't fit. The bindings were loose, fixed for a wider sole and higher arch; they tended to snap under stress and fall off. But it was good exercise, slogging through the crusty snow, following the tracks of the deer and the birds, and however slowly the hours passed, they did pass, and then they were gone.

But then the Presidents' Day holiday rolled around, and on Friday afternoon Gail and her daughter were headed off to visit relatives, and Zoe and Jack and Renee and his other single friends on the faculty would be off to Boston or Montreal or New York on their hopeful marathon quest to no longer be single, and the radio was forecasting an enormous stalled front of sleeting rain, and he knew that no matter how late he slept and how many errands and movies and cups of coffee he pumped into the fuel tank he'd never get to the end of the vacant seventy-two-hour highway that stretched before him. So he went ahead and volunteered to take over care of Don's house for the weekend, and Gail went ahead and let him.

Don Blackburn lived on Obtuse Hill Drive, a dirt road four miles south of Carthage village. Because the house stood so far back from the road, and the road was such a thin, meandering tributary of another dirt road, Oren might have passed it by were it not for the map Zoe Bender had given him, which was fanatically detailed. Pulling into the ice-slickened driveway, he parked at the low end so as not to get stuck. He looked up at the house, a disheveled-looking Victorian with drooping eaves. It too could use some rehab, he thought. Shutters were falling off their hinges. The chimneys needed pointing; slate tiles had sheared off the roof. The gutters, clotted with frozen leaves, bent and zagged like drinking straws.

Zoe had, in addition to her map with its neat hand-drawn arrows that left nothing to chance, also handed him a set of keys, each one labeled with its own little lime-green Post-it, and a bullet-pointed checklist of tasks to be attended to both inside and outside the house, and in what order. No one would ever accuse Zoe of being inattentive to detail, only of being boring and exasperating and maybe breaking your heart. She was like Jenny Saunders from his eighth-period class, the kind of girl who candy-stripes at the hospital and organizes outings for the youth group at church, and who in the evenings, after the dishes have been cleared and the homework done, the piano scales practiced to perfection, snuggles under the covers and falls asleep under the watchful gaze of a whole menagerie of stuffed animals. But then the world was full of nice, competent girls like Zoe and Jenny; in fact it depended upon them. So why make fun? It wouldn't kill him to be a little more like Zoe and Jenny, Oren thought, and a little less like himself.

Besides, it did make things easier, having Zoe's thorough checklist to guide him as he let himself in through the garage and heard the door wheeze shut behind him.

Immediately he set about executing his instructions. He brought in the mail and sorted it into piles on the dining room table. He watered the plants, fed the fish and the parakeet, measured out the cat food, and filled the water bowls to the decreed level. He went down to the basement to examine the insulation around the water heater for slippage. He ran the taps in the sink for ten minutes so the pipes wouldn't freeze. He checked the oven's pilot light so the house didn't surreptitiously fill with gas fumes and explode. He tested the furnace. He turned off the upstairs-hallway light and then turned on the downstairs-hallway light to confuse any potential burglars. He shoveled and de-iced the steps to provide traction for the postal carriers and Jehovah's Witnesses who came to the front door. Finally, he ran the engine on Don's car to keep the battery alive and the engine lubricated. The old Volvo sedan was a classic of sorts. Oren wouldn't have minded taking it for a little spin himself.

He felt that way about a lot of Don's things, actually. The planky antique farm table. The comfortable leather sofa, the handsome rugs and funky lamps. Don's stereo was first-rate; his shelves were full of nice hardcover books. The burgundy wingbacks that framed the fireplace, the round oak coffee table with its whorls and scars, and the hutch that held the dishes, and the weathered but solid-looking lowboy—all were in surprisingly good taste. A game of chess was under way on the ottoman. No one appeared to be winning, on the other hand no one appeared to be losing either. Even the plants Oren had watered so patiently (maybe *too* patiently: pools were rising in their ceramic undersitters), the coleus and jades, the spider plants and avocado and lemon trees, had a shiny, prosperous air.

He withdrew a bottle of Bushmills from Don's liquor cabinet and took a quick pull. Then another. Then he wandered around the house for a while. Finally he wound up, as he knew all along he would, in Don's bedroom. Among the magazines on Don's night table were the usual Blackburnian suspects: *TLS, The Nation, Harper's,* and so on. None of these would do.

It took a little searching, but in time he found what he was looking for, on the floor below the bed. He lay atop the duvet for a while, reviewing the table of contents. There would doubtless be some important articles he wouldn't want to miss.

When the phone rang, he didn't answer. The machine, however, appeared to be full from all the previous messages it had absorbed—forty-six, according to the digital indicator—and had no appetite left. So at last he was forced to pick up. "Is this the man of the house I'm speaking to?" asked some solicitor or other.

"Actually that's kind of a gray area at the moment."

"I beg your pardon?"

Miss July was a patriot of sorts, a flag-draped brunette with a smoldering gaze and a taste for cherry pie. She was lying across a picnic table on her stomach, her lips, glazed and shiny, pursed into an *o*. Meanwhile the fingers of her right hand, like some shiny and purposeful centipede, busied themselves in the depths of her red-white-and-blue thong. "You'd better call back," Oren said.

All the glib, nasty little judgments he'd directed Don's way over the years darted like mice through the baseboards of his mind. Clearly Don, no less than this house he was the man of, had his doubled facets, his quirks and complexities, his incongruous interiors. Don too presented one face to the world and kept another, more complicated one to himself. Maybe everyone did. Maybe you always wound up choosing where you wore your particular mess, inside or out, like a coat with a reversible lining.

In any case Oren was inside and out of there in an hour and a half, give or take. If you discounted those two sips—okay, *slugs*—of whiskey, and his interrupted pleasures with Miss July, he didn't even steal anything this time.

But later, back in his own kitchen, with the snow slanting against the windows and the radiator clanging like a bell, bucking and shuddering from its pent-up gases, it was difficult to settle down and concentrate on the Manifest Destiny essays to be graded, the lesson plans to be completed for the Civil War and Reconstruction units. Knowing he had plenty of time to accomplish these things, the whole three-day weekend in fact, did and did not help. He put down his red pen and stretched. He'd already discharged his duties at Don's house. The two movies in town were conventional fluff; besides, he'd already seen them. He'd given away the television because it was useless without cable, and he'd canceled the cable because it was too expensive and he was too cheap. His shoulders ached from shoveling Don's steps and walkway. Meanwhile his own steps and walkway needed shoveling. The coffee was tepid, he had hardly any food in the fridge, and—he rubbed his eyes with an ink-stained finger—the number on the answering machine read zero. Those were the facts. He remembered how over at Don's house the machine had been too full of messages to pick up any more. Was his own too empty? He supposed they too had to be lubricated every so often; otherwise they froze up on you.

There was no one he particularly wished to call, however, other than Gail Hastings, who for better or worse—probably the latter—seemed to have morphed these past weeks into his best friend. He punched out her number from memory. Then he remembered she was with her family all weekend, so he hung up, and called Sandy Krause instead.

Sandy, his old friend from film school, taught screenwriting at a small college in Maryland. Five years before, he'd left his wife and two children and hooked up with Janet, a ceramist with three kids herself. Sandy had endured his share of the heart's erratic mood swings all right. It was what made him such a wise, generous friend. Over the years, Sandy had burned Oren countless CDs for which he'd gone unthanked; had talked him through countless lesson plans for which he'd gone uncredited; had advised him on countless bleak nights in his dealings with Sabine for which he'd gone unheeded. So it was not entirely clear why the second the line was engaged, and a child's voice came on, thick-tongued and pliant against the background noise of Sandy's overpopulated kitchen, Oren hung up the phone at once.

Immediately he felt suffused by shame. His eyes burned. The back of his head felt pulpy and swollen, as if he'd sprained it. To ensure that he would put an end to this irritating new habit of calling people and hanging up on them, Oren now set about tearing the phone from its jack. The cord was made of sturdy stuff however; it refused to tear free.

Vengefully he gazed around his rented flat. Next to the ordered comfort of Don's house, the place was an eyesore. He was tempted to take out his red pen again and give it the failing marks it deserved. Scribble *unclear* over the dingy wallpaper, and *awk* across the counter, and *sloppy* on every cheap, listing cabinet, and *try again* over the chocolate-colored drapes, and *is this what you really intended?* over the faded fake-Orientals scattered limply across the floor like so many used Band-Aids. The whole place cried out for a do-over, for some resourceful and industrious person to rebuild from scratch. Oren, God knew, was not that person. Home improvement had never been his style. Though maybe it should have been. He remembered Sabine telling him, back on Avenue B, "There's nothing cool about living in a shit-hole where nothing works. It's not a revolutionary statement or anything. It's just laziness."

Okay, she was right. But then the absent were always right. Their every throwaway opinion lingered in the mind like a proverb, sonorous with truth. It wasn't hard to turn yourself into an oracle of wisdom: all you had to do was leave.

A thought sprang from his brain like from Zeus, fully formed. *He too would leave.* The day—no, the moment—the school year ended in June, he'd get in his car and go.

He saw now, after his day at Don Blackburn's—those cats! That bird! Those gaudy drooping plants that refused to die and refused to blossom!—how easy this would be. How inevitable. He felt the wind's cold breath on his ankles, the hard, unforgiving nudge of the kitchen chair against his spine. To leave a place you've never fully occupied wasn't hard. And he should know. He should know. Ninety minutes in a stranger's house was all it took, it seemed, to estrange a man forever from his own.

The next morning he went back to Obtuse Hill Drive and stayed all day. He did the same on Sunday, and again on Monday. There were just enough tasks to deal with at Chez Blackburn— a fresh layer of snow in the driveway, a leaky faucet in the upstairs bathroom, a rattling knob on the hallway closet—to make this seem less like loitering or trespassing than it did responsible house-sitting.

It would have helped, of course, if he'd known the first thing about fixing faucets and doorknobs. As he poked through the mess in Don's toolbox, the jagged screws, the rusty wrenches, the malevolent-looking pliers, he pictured his own father, that wizard of fixing, turning over and over in his grave like a rotisserie chicken. *You see?* All those evenings Oren had lingered outside the garage, fiddling with the automatic mechanism that opened and closed the sliding door (which was, thanks in part to his fiddling, forever getting jammed) while the old man labored at his workbench, peering through his goggles at some worn, recalcitrant hinge, his curly hair fringed white by the halo of the worklamp. Why had he never gone all the way in? It was as if he'd been waiting for some magic word, some mystical command to release or ensnare him for good. But Solomon Pierce was no word man. If you wanted to graph out your investment strategy or run interference with the IRS, okay; but for the intricacies of filial discourse you looked elsewhere. The bookshelves he sanded and stained, the chairs he refinished, the mahogany birdhouses like geometric puzzles—these *were* his discourse. He was a limited, melancholy person, Solomon Pierce, and Oren had vowed never to be like him, never settle for hobbies and small pastimes, the narrow compensations of the garage life. No, he'd hold out for something better. A visionary and extraordinary life doing something he loved, something he'd never seek to escape from . . .

Just looking? the old man would ask, without glancing up. *Or are you maybe interested in helping?*

I got to go and do some stuff.

Ah.

A tiny filament flicked on, or off, in his father's eyes, registering the reluctance of his only son to pick up the wrench. The hammer. The screwdriver. The torch.

Oh, he'd gone and done stuff, all right. *Lots* of stuff. And now here was the place all his going and doing had left him: back at the toolbox, square one. Even the small chores he undertook on Obtuse Hill Drive had a way of turning into big ones. Just changing a washer, a five-minute operation at most, took a half hour of intense concentration, and left him both sweaty and irritated and also bleeding gingerly from two knuckles as he went back to Don's liquor cabinet, seeking a reward for his labors in that capacious closet.

The well-aged Irish whiskey he found there, along with the muscle memory, pleasantly fading as the daylight waned, of his selfless expenditure of blood, sweat, and tears on the battlefield of home maintenance, provided a nice buzz. He pried his feet out of his boots and put on a pair of Don's slippers. They were light, fleecy things with little bulges at the toes. They fit perfectly. The house was cozy and warm; the parakeet whistled airily in his cage. He chose a book of poetry from Don's shelves and settled into the depths of the cool, plummy sofa, flipping the pages as he half-watched, in the background, a sitcom he'd never seen before on Don's enormous TV. That it was so much more enjoyable to lie around wasting time at Don's place than his own seemed only to confirm what he already knew: house-sitting agreed with him. Its rites and duties, its monastic discipline and sudden sanctifications . . . all this was what he'd been training for, this higher purpose; he would be inscribed in the book of life as a man who devoted himself to others.

Indeed, he'd never felt quite so relaxed and at home as he did at Don's that weekend—shoveling Don's driveway, tending Don's plants, sorting Don's mail, drinking Don's whiskey, watching Don's cable, skimming Don's library (his own books were in storage somewhere; he hadn't seen them in years); leafing through Don's magazines, not all of which were pornographic, though of course he was grateful for those that were; absorbing himself in the various handpicked materials Don had surrounded himself with by way of consolation, Oren supposed, for his loneliness and fatness and loudness. He felt like the curator of the Don Blackburn Museum. With each passing hour, his attitude toward Don's things grew increasingly watchful and proprietary. The interesting thing about the Don Blackburn Museum was that Don himself did not seem entirely essential to it. It was the man's absence that lent these items of his meaning; his presence would only confuse the issue. No, Don's place would just not have been Don's place, in Oren's opinion, if Don were there.

Oren read until his eyes grew heavy, until the light went dull in the windows. The very vacancy of the house seemed full to him, immanent and indivisible, like an echo in a cave. He hoped Don never came home. He'd have liked to remain here forever. But if and when Don did come home, he hoped the two of them might become friends, might drink together and compare notes on their journeys away from and toward this same fine sofa. Yes, Don would understand better than most the art and practice, the higher calling, of the horizontal life.

Come late Monday afternoon, he had the horizontal life going full swing—actually he was sort of dozing—when he heard the knob jiggle on the mudroom door. There was a soft, sucking pop, and then the door swung open on its jamb.

"Honey?"

Oren had napped just long enough, and drunk just enough of Don's whiskey, to wonder if he was dreaming. Not moving seemed the right strategy in any case. Stealthily he sank a little lower in the sofa and drew the plaid comforter up over his head. In the dusk it might be possible to miss him.

Meanwhile he wondered who Honey was.

"Hey, are you here? Come on, baby, the door's unlocked, I know you've got a key."

Oren said nothing. Not moving, and lying low, and remaining quiet: those were the orders from mission control. The footsteps went up the stairs, then across the ceiling over his head. Then they stopped.

He heard a voice say, "Over at Don's. Where are you? I thought—"

And then: "When?"

Unfortunately the next words were muffled by layers of plaster and wood, and by the dense, scratchy weave of the comforter on his face.

"So what did they . . . Okay. Okay. But did you tell Dad? . . . Okay."

Muffled again.

"But we're going to need to tell him. . . . Yeah. When he gets in."

It was getting a little hard to breathe, down there under the comforter. He'd done his best to clean the place, but Don's vacuum cleaner was an old machine; by now all the must and cat hair that had evaded him all weekend were insinuating themselves into his sinuses. It was tempting to just go ahead and stand up like a man and take what came. Only how did men go about standing up exactly? Even the best-case scenario was bound to be unpleasant, entailing a hasty defense of his presence in Don's living room, and the uncapped bottle of Bushmills, as empty as it was full, an arm's reach away.

On the other hand he could always sneak out the back door. That was an option too.

Upstairs the voice had now fallen silent. It might have been the silence of someone tracking a noise in another part of the house. The silence of someone placing a quick whispered call to the authorities. The silence of someone rummaging through a desk drawer for a small-caliber weapon. . . .

Definitely time to get up, Oren thought. Only, between the napping he'd done, the whiskey he'd consumed, the entanglements of the wool comforter, and below it his loosened belt and his pants' current and increasingly habitual residence in the neighborhood of his ankles, getting up was complicated, with some effort and struggle involved. Which may have been why in the end he did not so much get up as get down, thudding face-first onto the floor instead.

The breath whooshed from his lungs. He lay there waiting for it to come back. In an ideal world, of course, whoever was upstairs would not have heard him crash to the floor and would hence have no reason to come down at this moment and find him sprawled on the carpet, gasping like a flounder. And in fact no footsteps were forthcoming. Which meant possibly he hadn't crashed to the floor as hard as he'd thought. In which case he failed to understand why his face hurt so much.

A cell phone rang. It couldn't have been his because he didn't own one, and it couldn't have been Don's, because Don's was in a drawer in the rehab unit, its battery long since gone dead.

He got to his feet and zipped up his pants. He knew whose it was.

He went to the bottom of the stairs and stood there trying to look blasé and preoccupied so that when Gail Hastings came down, she'd be disarmed right away by his nonchalance, his savoir faire, his je ne sais quoi, and not call the police or shoot him or do any of the other things one might well be inspired to do, catching a trespasser drinking and dozing and jerking off in your cousin's house in the middle of a cold, cloudless Presidents' Day afternoon. But Gail did not come down. Only the sun did, sinking gradually behind the mountains, turning down the heat, turning off the lights. The sun went to bed early in cold weather. *Go with it,* Oren told himself. *Just go.*

He took one last look behind him, at the comforter still flung over the arm of the sofa, giving no comfort, and at the warm happy valley in the cushions where his body had lain, the impression of an invisible man.

Then he went up to find her.

She was lying on her back on the king-size bed in the master bedroom, staring calmly at the ceiling, or whatever she could see of it in the sepulchral haze. Her face was white. Her coat and shoes were still on.

"Hey," he said.

"Hey yourself."

"You okay?"

"I was looking for Mimi. I asked her to drop by and check on things. But she wasn't here."

So Mimi was Honey, he thought. Not him.

"Then, I don't know, I felt like putting my feet up all of a sudden. I'm kind of wiped out, to tell the truth."

"I thought you were out of town. I wasn't expecting you to be back so soon."

"I know." She turned to see him better. "What about you?"

"Oh, I just came over to, you know, like, feed the cats and stuff."

"You sound like *you've* been spending, like, way too much time at the middle school."

"Tell me about it," he said. "Anyway it's nice to see you."

"It is?" She put a hand over her eyes, as if holding back a glare. But the little light that remained was watery and gray. "What is it about you easygoing men? You have this way of bringing out my aggressions."

"I'm not so easygoing. I wish I were. Anyway I don't think you're aggressive. I think you're passionate."

"Passionate! Mother of God, I think I'm going to cry." But she didn't. "Listen," she said, "you're very sweet, but you don't know the half of it. I'm incredibly vain. I was one of the pretty girls in high school, and I never got over it. I'm bitchy and ungenerous and narrow as the day is long. I complain all the time. Really, you'd be amazed. It just fills up the day."

"Maybe you have reason to complain."

"Everyone has reasons to complain. But not everyone does."

"Well, maybe everyone should." Then he made his confession. "I heard you before. Talking on the phone."

"So I'm not crazy. I thought somebody was down there. I assumed it was Mimi or one of her friends." She turned to face him. "Why didn't you say something? Why did you hide?"

"I wouldn't call it hiding. It was more like not quite getting it together to announce myself."

"You're a big one for subtle distinctions, aren't you, Oren?"

He shrugged.

"Okay, then let me be subtle too. I think I'd maybe like to be alone for a while. I'm not feeling so well. Danny called," she added gravely, as if that should mean something to him.

"Danny?"

"My daughter Danielle. The one who's gone off backpacking around India and Nepal? Except it turns out she's in Kenya now. Or, no, wait, where's Addis Ababa? Is that Kenya or Ethiopia?"

"I'm not sure. I've never been to Africa. I know it's a hot destination these days."

"I thought Vietnam was hot. I thought Thailand was hot. I thought India and Nepal were hot."

"Oh, India's always hot," he said. "I was there back in the nineties."

"I thought college was hot too. Especially when you've got a merit scholarship you'll lose if you don't go back. But it seems she's found her calling. She's working in this AIDS orphanage, and she wants to stay. She was going to be a great environmental scientist. Now she's Angelina Jolie."

"Sounds pretty admirable to me."

"It would be, if she was doing it for the right reasons. Reasons she came to herself. But all she's doing is following that boyfriend of hers, Gabi. He says Africa, she goes to Africa." Gail yawned and stretched. "See? I told you: bitchy and ungenerous. Probably I'm just jealous. I mean, how great, to just do what you feel like doing and not worry about the consequences. Go anywhere you want. Know that feeling, Oren?"

"Yes. Very well."

"And is it great?"

"I suppose for some people it must be."

"I wouldn't mind trying it out, to tell you the truth. Like tonight. Maybe just shoot up to Montreal on a whim. Throw a few things in a bag, grab the passport, and go. How would that be? Eat someplace expensive by the water, where I can wear pearls and a good dress and speak French to the waiters, and order nothing but hors d'oeuvres. They always turn out to be the best part of the meal anyway, don't you think?"

"We probably go out to different kinds of places. Generally I just get the wings."

"Some brandy too. And something really fancy for dessert, with poached pears and lychee nuts and balsamic reduction. And then maybe just stroll around for a while, look at the lights and shops, see what's hanging in the windows. An hour or two of that would suit me just fine. I wouldn't object to a little making out in the cab on the way back to the hotel, either."

"Should I get my car? What do you say? It's right outside."

She was silent for a moment, examining the cuticle on her thumb. It looked pretty chewed up.

"Other than my husband," she announced, "I've slept with exactly two men in my life. There was Tom, my eleventh-grade boyfriend, who turned out to be bisexual, and there was this good-looking lifeguard at Lake George. We only did it once. He took me to the office behind the refreshment stand, and bango! I could hear the popcorn machine going the whole time."

"Sounds fun."

"The thing is, Tom and I were still together. I never told him. I didn't think he could take it."

"Look, wanting to have sex with someone new doesn't make you a bad person."

"It's not the wanting," she said. "It's the having. That's different. It's especially different when you're married."

"You don't need to keep reminding me you're married."

"It's not you I'm reminding." She wriggled deeper into the mattress, getting more comfortable; she seemed in no particular hurry to get up. "So let's move on. Tell me about your weekend. What did you do all day, other than call me on the cell phone that time and hang up?"

At the sight of his expression she laughed. "Didn't you know?

You can't get away with that sort of thing anymore. The technology's too good. The phone keeps a record. You have to own up to everything you do now. Even the mistakes."

"It wasn't a mistake," he said.

"What, did you miss me? Sit down and tell Mama all about it."

"I would, but there's no room."

"There's plenty of room." She scooted over, making space for him on the bedspread. "Poor boy. You're not very good at this, are you?"

"Apparently not."

"You shouldn't have asked me before if you should get your car. You should have just done it. But maybe you were afraid I was serious, hey? And then where would you be?"

"For what it's worth," he said, "I thought you *were* serious."

"Really? Well for what it's worth, I probably was." She sighed; all this use of the past tense seemed to make her weary. "But then I'm not very good at this either. We've got that in common anyway."

"So that's something." He reached for the hand that was closest to him, her right one, the one without the ring. "Is it worth mentioning that the car's still out there? With a full tank of gas?"

She stiffened. "I'm not a frivolous person, Oren. I don't like to flirt, and I'm generally afraid of new things. That's probably why marriage suits me. You know what they call marriage, don't you? The coward's adventure."

He laughed. "I thought that was adultery."

"Yeah," she said. "That too."

8

Missions

Fiddling with his watch, Teddy tried to calculate the hours he'd gained, or lost, since taking off from Logan. The number escaped him. And he'd always been so good with numbers. But his watch, once gravity's yoke was shed, had developed a will and metabolism of its own. The hands were running fast, wheeling around in fitful, frantic circles, like drunks on a patio, like the legs of the animals in that moronic cartoon. It was always the same story too. A pursuit, a lunge in midair, and then a fall . . .

Once you left the ground, there was only one way to reattain it, he thought. The hard way.

To relieve the congestion in his head he chewed a stick of gum. It didn't help, but it gave his jaws a first-class workout. Unfortunately the rest of his musculature was stuck in coach. The narrow seats had been designed for third-world survivors of scarcity and drought, not thick-waisted Americans with capacious backsides. No matter how he folded or unfolded his limbs, he could not accommodate his lumpy, swollen frame or achieve any comfortable distance between his knees and his face.

He picked up the in-flight magazine and flipped through the pages heedlessly, looking for the flight maps with their hubs and arcs, their arrowed paths radiating across the continents like an enormous web. The world was full of destinations. You could take off from anywhere and land anywhere: the web would bear your weight. For some reason this made Teddy fidget more, not less.

He got to his feet.

"Sorry," he mumbled to the lady in the aisle seat. "I'll try to make this the last time."

Without putting down her book, she retracted her legs, ceding just enough territory for him to pass. He didn't blame her; it was his fourth trip in two hours.

He padded shoeless down the aisle and wedged open the flimsy accordion door to the bathroom. People were burrowed in, reading or watching movies or nestled in sleep. He himself appeared to lack the constitution for long flights. His head thrummed like a tunnel; the membranes in his stomach fizzed and popped. He'd grown delicate over the years, it seemed, had lived a pampered and comfortable life. Now he had to toughen up for the long journey.

Coming back from the lavatory, he felt compelled to apologize to his seatmate again for making her perform yet another tedious do-si-do in the aisle. *"Pfft,"* she said, with an absent wave. "Why should you apologize when clearly you are not well?"

"I'm sure I'll be fine. Just getting my sea legs."

She eyed him worriedly for a moment—sea legs?—then went back to her book. She was not so old as he'd taken her for. In fact she looked roughly his own age, if not younger. Her hands were smooth. Her white hair, rising thickly from her temples, was knotted into a bun. As she read, she fingered a pendant that dangled at the base of her throat, on an all but invisible chain. With her ivory blouse and khaki pants and hoopy, silver, Santa Fe–ish earrings, she might have been one of Gail's friends, one of those handsome, no-nonsense women she volunteered with at the food co-op, filling bins of free trade coffee and spraying mist over the organic vegetables. A serious and committed person. A woman of depth, substance, and discipline. In short, the very last person that he had any desire to converse with at this moment.

Not that she seemed so terribly eager to converse with *him.* Deep in her book, with a pair of rimless half-glasses perched on her nose and a plaid airline blanket draped across her thighs, his seatmate had the settled, self-sufficient aura of a scholar in front of a fire. Meanwhile Teddy squirmed by the window, looking down at the rough, slate-colored sea, all heaving and senseless below.

"Jesus," he said, "will you get a load of this view. Unbelievable."

The vastness, and the transient insubstantiality of the plane's shadow upon it, made him expansive. As did the peripheral sight of the flight attendant bearing trays of food in their direction.

"I don't understand why people complain so much about flying," he went on. "I think it's great, don't you?"

"Perhaps to be up in the air," said his seatmate, "does not agree with some people."

"How about for you?"

"For me?" She peered at him over her reading glasses. "For me it is the best part."

Her voice was reedy and low, with a dusting of some light, transitional accent. Teddy wondered if he sounded that way to her too, vaguely foreign, vaguely exotic. It seemed the best part of being a passenger, this shortcut to strangeness. You could be anyone to anyone.

She received her food without thanking the stewardess, then left it there on the folding tray untouched. He was already halfway through his chicken breast. And what a parched, anorectic old hen *she* must have been, he thought.

"Here," she said, "take mine. You look very hungry, and I ate before."

"Thanks." He picked up her roll and gnawed off a hunk like a dog. "I ate before too, actually. Back in the airport. God knows why I'm so starved."

"You're a large man I think. It must take a lot to fill you up."

"It does. Oh, it does." He chewed the roll with relish. The texture was gluey; it wobbled the old fillings in his molars. But it was nice for a change to have his appetites understood and supported by a woman. "It's nervous energy I guess. The happiest moments in life, they say, are starting on a journey to unknown lands." He paused to swallow, before adding, "That's Richard Burton by the way."

"Yes?"

"The explorer I mean. Not the actor from *Lion in Winter.*"

"But unknown to whom?" she asked. "They are not unknown to the people who live there."

"To me I mean. Unknown to me."

She made a joyless, patronizing nod, as if he'd just betrayed some moral flaw in himself, some selfish, racist, imperialistic attitude for which he should be ashamed. But he couldn't help it if his own feelings were more real to him than other people's. Weren't everyone's? And wasn't it selfish, racist imperialists like Burton who'd mapped out the globe in the first place, for reasons they themselves did not fully understand? *The devil drives . . .* Okay, he thought, maybe the Burtons of the world were products of their time. Okay, maybe that time had passed, and a good thing too. But Teddy wasn't going to apologize for showing up late. At least he was here. At least he was here now.

"Please"—she proffered her tray—"go ahead, take the rest. Otherwise it will be thrown away."

"Well, waste is a sin, right?"

"Yes. One of the worst."

Of course gluttony was a sin too, Teddy recalled, but too late, the damage was done: he'd already eaten everything on her tray but the toxic wedge of lemon cake with its pale gelatinous glaze. Now he ate that as well. His days of holding back were over: he was on his way.

Only afterward, licking his fork clean, did it occur to him that he'd been wrong about *Lion in Winter.* Richard Burton the actor wasn't *in* that film. That was Peter O'Toole. O'Toole was the lion—the great lithe, shaggy hero who roared and burned, who flew across the desert, blue eyes flashing, a pure bright creature of instinct. Burton was the introvert. The head case. Burton played the weak, tortured, vacillating types, the Hamlets, the Antonys, the spy quavering out in the cold, all those sulkers and brooders and tenured professors and defrocked priests.

And Teddy Hastings? What type was he?

He turned back to his seatmate. She had given him her meal; she seemed intent on either sustaining him or diverting him, he couldn't tell which. "So what brings you to this part of the world?" he asked, as men of all types, he imagined, do. "Business or pleasure?"

"Neither one of those quite describes my mission, I'm afraid."

"Mission?"

"Yes, I'm afraid so." She smiled abstractly. "First I must go to Alexandria for our meetings and training sessions. Then after a week we arrive in the Sudan."

"I knew it. You're one of those Doctors Without Borders people."

"Something like this."

"Well, be careful. I hear they're killing people down there."

"Yes, I hear this too. This is why we go."

"It would be just as good a good reason not to go too."

"But there are always good reasons not to go, yes? Always, when you add them up, more of those kind than the other. Surely there are good reasons for you not to go where you go?"

"Oh, absolutely," he said. "A long list."

"So you see."

Eventually she filled him in a bit on her own personal story. She was a retired nurse from Montreal, a widow with three grown children and a flat in Outremont. Nowadays she traveled a great deal. Gaza, Afghanistan, Chiapas. She spoke matter-of-factly of her travels, in a way that made him restless, gloomy. What was it about these people who moved so freely around the globe, while others could not find access to it at all?

"You seem a little young to retire," he commented, wiping his mouth with a heroically soiled napkin.

"But I'm fifty-six. Is that young?"

"Christ, it better be."

"Of course I miss my work at the hospital. But then they merged with another hospital, and I knew they wanted me to go, not bother them anymore with my boring appeals for more outreach to the poor. And then my husband died, *pfft*. So that was the end. I took the early option, and then I did the next thing you do when you retire and your husband dies after thirty years of marriage."

"Oh? What's that?"

"I went on a cruise. To be honest, I thought I would never enjoy such a thing. I had no wish to be trapped on a boat with so many old people, trying to have fun. But I did. I read and swam, and I discovered many interesting cocktails. I even had a shipboard romance. A very nice lawyer from Minnesota. It was his twentieth anniversary with his wife. But he wished to practice his French, he said."

"That sounds like a joke."

"I assure you, it wasn't. This man took me quite seriously, and I him. The trip had cost us both a great deal of money, you see. We felt entitled to the full menu." She smoothed her hair back. Her eyes had a languid light. "One day we were in the Dominican Republic, my friend and I. We took a drive into the mountains. It was a pleasant day, but I must have eaten something not good. I became very ill. It was a small village. There was no doctor. Someone told my friend of two old nuns from Belgium who ran a mission in the next village, so he took me there. When I saw how primitive this place was, I confess I was afraid. I looked at the cross on the wall and I prayed to God, which I had not done since I was a child. I believed I would die there. I felt it so clearly. I thought to myself, 'I will never get back.'"

"Where was your boyfriend? He didn't leave you there alone?"

"His wife was on the ship. He had no choice. And I wasn't alone—the nuns were with me all this time. I was there in bed with them for six days. Long enough to create the world." She

260

smiled sadly, as if this were somehow a joke at her own expense. "Perhaps I think it is still with me a little bit. In the stomach. I will be in my kitchen, slicing a tomato, and I suddenly remember that village with no doctor, how afraid I was." She was silent for a moment. "*Io non mori, e non rimasi vivo.* You understand?"

"Sure," he said, though of course he spoke no Italian and hadn't a clue. His thoughts were pounding ahead on their own tiny treadmill. "About your husband—can I ask what he died of?"

"Why? Are you involved in cancer research? Why do you Americans always feel entitled to know such things?"

"We're optimists I guess. We like to think if we get the facts, we may be able to help somehow."

"Yes, but this help you provide is so often destructive. Perhaps you should try helping less."

"Okay, okay. Point taken." Now that he was officially an American abroad, he would have to get used to this, Teddy thought: being hated and distrusted and called upon to apologize for every last thing—every offer of aid, every minor coup or limited incursion. Did you only become a real American when you *left* America? Exposed your innocence and privilege and your extra-large backside to the kicks and grievances of the world? "I didn't mean any harm."

"He died of lymphoma, my husband. To answer your question. And he was fifty-four, if you are wondering about that."

Teddy grimaced: he *had* been wondering. He was tempted in the spirit of reciprocity to mention Philip, but what good would that do, laying down your dead like so many trumps. Piling up the sympathy points. As if there were any benefit to winning such a game.

He pushed back his tray and stifled a groan. His belly was roiling and tight. Eating most of her meal on top of his own had turned out to be, like most of his ideas these days, a lousy one. When was he going to stop lunging around so clumsily, mistaking appetites for inspirations? His bitter memories, his clenched intestinal tract, the very drift and sway of the plane—all channeled themselves now into one profound, unnameable emotion. He reached across the seat and took the poor woman's fingers in his own big sweat-damp palm. "Is that why you travel so much? Because it's too painful to stay home without him?"

"I told you, I travel on missions. So that someday when my granddaughter asks me what did you do when so many people were dying, I should have an answer." She smiled at him coolly and reclaimed her hand. "Why do you travel so much? To make passes at widows and eat all their food?"

"Hey, I'm just being friendly. I'm a married man, for god's sake."

"Yes, I know about married men." She was, he saw from her face, only teasing; he'd not offended but amused her. He appeared to have lost the ability to give offense. And he used to be so good at it too. "A woman traveling alone meets many married gentlemen along the way. I see what they are like, when they are between destinations."

"What *are* they like?"

"Vulnerable," she said. "So many stories and confessions. Everyone shares their little heartbreaks."

"Want to hear some of mine? I've got enough for a whole book."

"Forgive me, but I think no one wants to read such a book, if I may be honest."

"Oh sure, go ahead. Be as honest as you like."

"Yes? Okay, then also," she said, warming to the task, "that shirt you have? It should not be worn with those pants."

He laughed. Was this to be his new life? Being insulted by people he didn't know on the way to places he hadn't been?

"Doesn't your wife tell you these things? I would never let my husband on a plane in such clothes."

"My wife and I, we weren't quite on the same, uh, wavelength when I left. Not that she disapproves of this trip," he added quickly. "In fact on some level she's probably all for it."

"Probably?"

"She's not the easiest person to read," Teddy conceded. "I'm the transparent one in the family, or so they tell me."

"So this is why you're running away?"

"Hey, I'm not running *away*. I'm running *to*. Can't anyone tell the difference?" People nearby turned his way; it seemed all of a sudden he was shouting. "I'm going over to see my daughter," he explained.

"Ah."

"We're not sure what she's up to these days, but we're worried. She's been gone for a long time. She went on this junior year abroad to China."

"But we are flying to Africa."

"See, that's the thing—her junior year was *last* year." He sighed. It was a chore, talking to new people, making yourself understood. "She's got the travel bug bad. She was supposed to come back after China, but she went to Thailand instead. Then Cambodia. Vietnam. Then Nepal, and India, and on and on. Now Africa. Typical Danielle: even when she fucks off, she finds a way to overachieve. Care for a Tums?"

"No thank you."

"She's off the grid, basically. We e-mail her every week, but it's like shouting in a void." He popped another antacid in his mouth, cracking the hard shell between his molars. "Maybe once a month she drops by an Internet café and writes a few lines. Then the power goes off because of a monsoon or whatever. Just saying hi. And oh, by the way, she's not coming back to school this year after all. Did she ever let them know this down at the Bronx borough president's office to which she'd made a good-faith commitment? No. Did she get in touch with her suitemates at NYU so she has a room to come back to? No. Did she make contact with the administration office or the financial aid people or her academic adviser or anyone whatsoever to let them know her plans? No. Hasn't had time. She's too busy *unwinding*, see. That's her word, *unwinding*. Which turns out to be code, by the way, for getting loaded on ecstasy and tooling around the beach in a sarong, while some horny Israeli guy just out of the army makes you his love slave. Why not just stay in college? It would have been easier and cheaper all around."

"Sometimes a child needs to get lost," his companion observed with irritating serenity. "Otherwise they never learn to find their own way."

"I thought that's what junior year abroad was for. You go to some other country and hang out in strange bars getting drunk with people who speak another language. But you don't go abroad from going abroad. It's like answering a question with a question."

"Maybe your daughter likes being off this grid of yours. Maybe she's found a new grid she likes better."

"Yeah. That's what we're afraid of."

Gloomily he peeled off another Tums, studying his reflection in the black window.

"And Africa?"

"Africa." He shuddered; the word, even now, conjured in him a strangeness. He thought of all the explorers he'd read, all the times he'd lain on the carpet down in his basement gym, gazing up at the map, at that huge, top-heavy continent shaped like a question mark. "Christ knows. We're still piecing it together. My wife thinks it has to do with the boyfriend." He sighed. "She says she misses us. I mean, *that* got us worried, let me tell you."

"Please, take a Kleenex. Your head is perspiring a great deal."

"It is?" He wiped his forehead; sure enough, the tissue came back inlaid with beads of sweat. The pressure gauge in his forehead was oscillating wildly. He eyed the plastic vomit bag in the seatback in front of him with real seriousness of purpose. "I don't know what's wrong with me, I can't seem to digest things anymore."

"You must be careful. You are not someone who should travel by himself, I don't think. Especially outside the capital."

"You're probably right."

"If not your daughter, then I suggest you arrange for a guide.

There are many guides now. You can find them outside all the hotels. So many important people coming to Africa these days for their special and unique experience. One week they tour around, maybe two. Then *pfft*—time to go home and raise awareness."

"That's kind of cynical, isn't it? At least they're over here trying."

"Yes, you Americans like to try, don't you? Trying is good, you say. Trying is almost doing."

"Well, it's better than not trying."

"Is it?" Her gaze turned dry. "In what way?"

"All I mean is, who *doesn't* want a special experience, when they've come so far? I know I do."

"Perhaps you will have one then. But are you in condition for such a thing? You look so white in the face."

"Don't worry about me. I'm fine."

Except was it possible to be perfectly fine and also not fine in the least? For all the reading Teddy had done, he was still new to the practicalities and procedures of the exploration business. Still given to rookie mistakes. He had, for example, according to the guidebook, somehow managed to pack the wrong shoes (loafers), the wrong luggage (suitcase), the wrong soap (Ivory), the wrong money (cash), and, he was increasingly certain, the wrong malaria pills entirely. He knew they were the wrong malaria pills because they appeared to be *giving* him malaria, not protecting him from it. But maybe that was how the pills were supposed to work: inversely, like a vaccine. A little dose of the thing you feared, to ward off the larger one.

For that matter he'd probably got the wrong vaccinations too. He was no doctor. He'd been in a hurry to get out, and the guidelines were ambiguous on the subject.

"Entirely your call," Dr. Wainwright, who *was* a doctor, had told him back in Carthage. "I've checked the CDC guidelines. With the yellow fever, it depends how far out of the city you go."

"I don't know how far out I'll go."

"Then it's difficult to advise you," Wainwright said.

"Tell me, does the shot hurt?"

"A three-inch syringe needle in your arm? Of course it hurts."

"And are there side effects to such a shot?"

"Of course there are side effects."

"Like what?"

Thoughtfully, or with the appearance of thought, Wainwright leaned back in his chair, stroking the clefts of his angular chin. As Teddy himself used to do, chatting with some miscreant student in his office at school. Back when he still *had* an office. Back when he still *had* a school. "Death, principally."

"You're saying death is one of the side effects?"

"No, I'm saying death is the principal side effect."

"And if I don't get the shot—"

"That's entirely your call."

"If I don't get the shot, and I wind up contracting yellow fever over there after all—what are the side effects of that?"

"Death, principally," said that smug and mordant internist. He was beginning to really enjoy himself, no question.

"No others?"

To which Wainwright, his patience now exhausted, said, "How many others do you need?"

Nonetheless, if it was possible to feel nauseated and apprehensive and borderline malarial in a good way, that was Teddy's condition at this moment, hurtling toward the Horn of Africa in a cramped, juddering box. It was more or less how he'd felt in the back of the police cruiser last summer, being carted off to jail in the middle of the night. All messy and new. A raw, bloody hatchling peering through the shards of his shell. At least this time he wasn't going to be locked up when he arrived, he thought. Whether he'd be locked up when he returned was of course another story, a story he preferred not to read.

Meanwhile the seat-belt light had now chimed on. The engines were slowing, the plane banking into a slow, languid turn. His seatmate gathered her books together and stowed them into her carry-on bag. Then she took one last sip of her bottled water and screwed the lid shut.

Light came blasting off the wings. Below, unfolding like a carpet, lay the crescent coastline of Alexandria.

They circled over the bleached sprawl of the city. Tall minarets, spindly and lean, shimmered in the heat. There were fine hotels, citadels, and palaces with enormous gardens. Canals snaked out from the city center, writhing toward the outlying terraces of the suburbs, which were wrapped in a haze of dust. The Mediterranean was slipping away behind them, falling back into the clouds. Europe and all its artifices were fading fast, a dream they'd woken from and forgotten.

Beyond the last houses, the land looked parched, uninhabitable. Dust devils whirled across the hills. The saline in the soil glittered like frost.

He recalled a line from Burton: *the sand softer than a bed of down.* Well, it didn't look soft from up here. But fortunately he didn't want softness. He wanted things hard. And now he would get them. Once he crossed into the interior he'd be on his own, like any other nomad—wandering and exposed, looking for signs. The sands like a blank page unfurled below. You could make all the marks on it you wanted, he thought. Soon they too would be erased.

Now they were descending in earnest. Hydraulics groaned in the plane's big belly. People were pushing up their tray tables, stowing away their trash. The seats shuddered and bucked. Teddy gripped the armrests. His seatmate closed her eyes. "Now this part I can do without," she said.

"Me too."

"It's good we met. I will pray for you. That you have a good and productive journey."

"Oh, you needn't bother," he said. "I'm sure it'll go fine."

"I am sure too. But prayer you see is never a bother."

Some low, ringing note in her voice made Teddy examine her more closely. Then he saw it. The silver cross dangling at her neck, on its slim, immaculate thread.

I'll be damned, he thought.

The plane went on lowering itself through the clouds. Dutifully the runway, a good host, rose up to greet them, to extend its smooth and welcoming services. Palm leaves fluttered in the wind. The ground sat baking in the sun, hot and red like the inside of a kiln. He watched his life scud by in wisps like so much exhaust. Soon they were right in the thick of it, and nothing could be seen through the white glare of the window, at least nothing he could name.

It was true his plans had been conceived in a great rush; many crucial details remained unresolved. For instance, after that one brief, bewildering phone call, he'd never heard back from Danielle. Whether she'd received his e-mails telling her of his plans, whether she'd be waiting for him at the airport, whether she'd be happy to see him, he had no way of knowing. And now it was too late: he was coming anyway.

He wasn't going to apologize either. Did a lion, tromping through the bush to retrieve a missing cub, apologize? No, you heard a cry in the darkness and you went to it at once. That was the natural order of things. How a family—a species—endured. He looked around at his fellow passengers. The handsome and good-humored Egyptians with their shiny complexions, the slender, almond-eyed Ethiopians. Surely *their* children would be waiting for them at the airport. Surely *their* children understood that when you've been in the air a long time, all you wanted was to be greeted at the gate by a loved one who was glad to see you, to absolve you of your weariness and worry. Even if you went on to fight with them a lot later, which you inevitably would.

Danielle, God knew, was no stranger to fighting. She was fierce and taut, high-pitched as an E-string; no feats of shrillness or antagonism were beyond her. Where fighting was concerned, genetics had doubly blessed her, with her mother's rhetorical skill and her father's gross and blundering need.

So there would be plenty of fighting. Fortunately Teddy didn't mind fighting. He didn't even mind losing. It was the intensity he relished, not the winning. Just letting fly.

Well, he was flying now. He had both seats to himself: his seatmate had deplaned in Alexandria, having put together a little medical kit for him before she left, a Baggie stuffed with cipro tablets, multivitamins, and tiny sachets of antibacterial hand soap. Maybe when you're born-again or whatever she was, you no longer required so much in the way of protection yourself. She'd said a quick, impersonal good-bye, and marched off down the aisle in her plain flat shoes, her suitcase rattling behind her on its tiny wheels like a compliant pet. Then she disappeared through the hatch, off to another ruined quadrant of the world.

Teddy looked down at the Nile, a ribbon of blue in its brilliant emerald-green basin—the river of destiny, the Egyptians called it—wending its way through the silted ocher of the Sudan. In Khartoum the great river split in two: the White Nile, gray as nonfat milk, forking south to Uganda, while the Blue Nile, which was in fact blue, bent east toward the Horn. But wait, he thought: that had to be wrong. The Nile tributaries didn't *split* in Khartoum, but *merged* there, became one, and flowed toward the sea.

All the great explorers, Burton and Speke, Stanley and Baker and Grant, had documented this. They'd come ashore in Zanzibar and tracked the river north, following its hidden sources, the inland seas and underground reservoirs where it fed and steeped. He was all turned around, upside down. He couldn't follow in their footsteps: he could only parody them, reverse them. Well, maybe reversal for some people was a kind of progress, he thought.

Anyway what did it matter? The paths had all been laid. The maps were long since full; no new worlds to explore. *There are guides everywhere now.* He had come too late. The age of imperial expansion was over. Now downgrades and deflations were in effect. What had once been a grand, heroic vocation was now a mere vacation, a holiday package wrapped with a bow. Duty-free. All those small, expensive comforts for sale at the airport—the headphones, the neck-rests, the portable game players, the downloadable language discs. Yes, they knew how to package the exotic these days, how to make it circumscribed and safe for people like him. And doubtless there were a lot of such people.

He reached for another Tums and cracked it hard between his jaws. Who was he kidding? He was no demonic romantic hero, no Richard Burton or T. E. Lawrence. He was only another amateur, chubby, middle-aged escapist with a camera around his neck and a virtual ticket.

The light was waning in the windows, the jet banking its way east now, over thorny stubbled mountains and highland plateaus. Not a soul in sight. He could feel the Horn out there like a magnet, drawing him forward by invisible current. Or was it backward? Back to the cradle, the primordial rift. The ancestral home.

Danielle was down there somewhere too. A child who'd chosen to get lost.

He rubbed his eyes. Calcified particles of sleep-stuff flaked out from the corners. How many hours had he been flying? It had begun to feel like one long, biblical day. He looked down at the hands of his watch, revolving in random circles. Useless. He took the thing off and stuck it deep in his pocket with his cell phone and keys and American coins, all those useless personal items he'd need to stash away when he arrived.

"Daddy, you're here! My *God* . . ."

Tears sprang into Teddy's eyes. All at once, with the familiar mass and musk of his daughter against him (her face burrowed in his chest, her hair, thick and unruly and rust-colored like his, tickling his neck), his exhaustion fled, the clenched fist in his stomach relaxed its grip. The whole trip was redeemed. Certified in advance. He clutched her close, inhaling the clean damp scent of her scalp, like some distilled essence of being. His entire life as a father of children clicked snugly into place and whirred away at the center of his chest like a pacemaker. *Daddy's here. My God.*

Oh, you weren't supposed to have favorites, he knew that, but of course everyone did, and this one (he'd never admitted it to himself until this moment; possibly it had never been *true* until this moment) was his. With this one everything came easy. This one was the outgoer, the live wire, the girl whose moods could be read on her face, who did not require a licensed psychotherapist or a Turing machine to decode. Unlike Mimi, she seemed to recognize and approve of him naturally. She had got to him first, known him when he was less uptight, less constrained—she'd adopted what was best in him and let the rest go. He could feel her bones thudding softly against him through the damp, sticky place where their shirts conjoined. Her arms were leaner than he remembered, tougher, more sinewy. Her time abroad for all its mysteries and deferrals had solidified her, rendered down the last of her baby fat. Now she was that most formidable creature, a grown woman. So he held on tight.

Every man who embraces a woman becomes Adam, trembling with gratitude that he's no longer alone. That was how Teddy felt now. Like an exiled king reclaiming his throne. It was a moment to savor, all right. A moment to deposit in the memory bank against future withdrawals. Because really, how long could it last? Love for parents was a raging stream; for children there were dams and pools, and slippery stones, and little frothy resentments that piled up along the banks. Already she was beginning to squirm, take the first halting steps in an away-from-Dad direction. Soon she would break his hold. Soon like all fathers he'd be forced to let go.

"Hey, you're not crying, are you?" She pulled back to get a better look. "Your eyes look a little funny."

"It must be the lights."

"Bright, aren't they? They just redid the terminal. It used to be pretty dreary here they tell me." Above their heads, across the vaulted ceiling, the white girders gleamed. It was an impressive structure, much airier and more modern than he'd expected. He felt obscurely disappointed. "They've been sprucing up the place, you know. For the millennium celebration."

"The millennium? But that was over a long time ago."

"It's a different calendar here," she said. "Technically they're seven years behind us."

"Ah."

Other passengers were surging up behind them, red-eyed and intent, getting on with the arrival business as in any old airport. Unlike any old airport however the duty-free shop was empty, the currency-exchange dark, and there were no benches or chairs arranged in companionable clusters for an overweight, travel-weary person with a frayed meniscus to rest. Just as well: the brigade of lean, smooth-faced boy-soldiers smoking and smirking behind the Passport Control desk did not look tolerant of loiter-ers. Automatic rifles were slung casually at their hips. AK-47s? AK-48s? For all he knew they were Uzis. Well, they had their battles to fight, he supposed, and he had his. A cry had sounded in the darkness. The lion in winter was padding out on his big soft paws, in search of his pride.

And here she was. His honor girl, his A student, his lead singer. She gave him one last squeeze, then broke their embrace for good. "Wait," she said, "why *are* you here?"

"You called, didn't you? It's been so long. Your mother and I were concerned."

"I didn't say you should come though."

"Listen, I needed the trip. Christ but it's wonderful to see you, Danny. I can't tell you how much."

"Well," she said warily, "it's nice to see you too. Let's go get your bag."

Down at the baggage claim, they stood side by side as the first massive suitcases tumbled onto the revolving belt. Danielle, with her mussed hair, peasant blouse, and thin, balloony cargo pants, looked like what she was—a college kid rousted half-willingly from bed. The toes that poked out from her flip-flops were long-nailed, discolored. A smell leaked from her armpits, musky and warm, not entirely pleasant. From the sideways look she kept giving him, she did not seem too impressed by his appearance either. "What?" he said. "What are you looking at?"

"Wow." She rose on tiptoe, cupping his ears in her hands to inspect his shorn scalp. "Mimi wrote me about this. I thought she was kidding."

"The new me. What do you think?"

"You look like a decrepit monk. That's what I think. Plus it's coming in all gray. What on earth were you thinking?"

"It's hard to explain. It's like one day you wake up and you're in a box, and the only way to get out is to punch a hole in yourself. Go to war with yourself. Does that make any sense?"

"No," she said. "But let's face it, you were never big on impulse control, were you?"

She was speaking of him elegiacally, he thought, as if he were dead, a casualty of the oedipal wars, her long struggle to emerge from his shadow. Maybe he was. If so, it would explain this weightless, limbo-like sensation he'd been experiencing since he'd stepped off the plane.

Suitcases came wobbling by. None of them were his. Danielle stood beside him, radiating intermittent warmth. He had to restrain himself from pushing the hair off her cheek, an old habit, and curling it around her ear. He knew she'd flinch and move away. That was an old habit too.

"Well, it'll grow back." He made a point of looking in the direction of the luggage belt when he added, "I'm glad to hear you and Mimi have been writing each other. I didn't know."

"You weren't supposed to. It's none of your business."

"I guess not."

"What's with this fugitive-from-justice stuff? What kind of trouble are you *in* back there anyway? Mimi says you're the big buzz around town."

"You know what small towns are like. People always gossip. It releases tension. Otherwise they'd get bored and have to become fugitives themselves." He scanned the belt for his luggage. "You should hear how they talk about *you.*"

"I'll bet."

"You dropped out of college. You're on drugs in Ladakh. You're pregnant in Burma. You're getting a sex change in Bangkok. You had a psychotic episode on the streets of Mumbai and had to be institutionalized against your will. And those are just the rumors I've spread about you personally."

"I'm not coming back, Daddy," she said, unamused. "Let's get that straight right off."

"Fine, fine. We'll talk about it later."

"No, I want to be clear right now, so there's no misunderstanding. I'm staying. You can't make me go back."

"Settle down, Danny. No one's making anybody do anything."

"You're here, aren't you? It's obvious what you and Mom are thinking."

"Don't be too quick to decide what Mom and I are thinking. We think all kinds of things we never act on."

"Well, not me," she said, pulling herself up straight. "I try to act on the things I believe. Maybe if you guys acted on what you believe, you'd be happier people."

"Spare me the nineteen-year-old profundity, okay? I had a long flight."

"Look, no offense, but no one told you to come. And I'm not nineteen, I'm twenty, remember? I turned twenty this year."

"See, this is what I'm talking about," he said, though in fact he was not sure he'd been talking about this at all. Nor could he have said with any certainty what *this* was. "A tree falls in the forest, and no one hears."

"Plenty of people heard, believe me. We were in Annapurna. We threw this big rave for everyone at the teahouse, and Gabi made this incredible lemon cake with coconut frosting. His mom e-mailed him the recipe. You use rice flour, see, instead of regular."

"The famous Gabi. Where is he, by the way? I'm eager to meet him."

"That must be yours." She pointed to his enormous potbellied suitcase, teetering drunkenly toward them on the revolving belt. She swooped it up before he could stop her. "Oof. How long are you planning on *staying?*"

"You were the one who said go to Costco. I got a hundred and fifty bucks' worth of eyedrops and chewable vitamins in there. I could hardly fit them in the suitcase."

"You should have let Mom deal with it. She'd have known how to pack."

"Yeah, well, Mom was busy. She's famously busy, as you know."

In response to which Danielle's brow crinkled up like foil. The radar of filial loyalty kept sweeping in circles. She may have been his favorite but he was not altogether certain he was hers.

"Here," he said, grabbing at the suitcase, "I'll take that."

"I have it." He marked the first sandpaper rasp of annoyance in her voice. First he'd presumed to appear in her life; now he was trying to take charge. Her dark eyes flashed; her plump lips pouted. Sometimes you had to go to war against your family too, wrestle with your fate like Jacob and the angel. And Danielle was a formidable adversary. She had her parents' height, her mother's shrewd, assertive gaze, and her father's beakish and implausible nose. The rest of her was a combat zone in which his genes and Gail's had skirmished to a draw. All the bone baskets of their ancestors lay sunken in her flesh. He stared at her now as if communing with their spirits, the living and the dead.

"God, Daddy, you're not going to *cry* again, are you?"

"It's just that you're so skinny," he complained. "Where in the world have you gone?"

"Hey, I'm right here." Her voice was gentle but firm; she might have been talking to a child, or a blind man, or an imbecile. "I'm right here, and you're right here with me. So let's get going, what do you say?"

"I've got going. I've been going for a while now."

"Mmm." She patted the suitcase between them. "So I've heard."

Outside the terminal he sniffed the air like a dog, reading it for news. So this was Africa, he thought. He'd readied himself for adverse weather, for blazing sunlight and tropical heat—looked forward to it even—but the sun had gone down hours before, and the air was cool and dry. A mild scent, like the smell of cough drops, floated down from the foothills. He followed Danielle to the curb, where a dumpy blue car waited in idle, belching out smoke.

"Look who I found," she said.

A young man in a windbreaker sat behind the driver's seat, talking on his cell phone. He gave Teddy a cursory glance, then shouldered open the door and got out. He was tall and lean, severe-looking, with a sparse mustache and an even sparser soul patch at the bottom of his jaw. Above his indrawn cheeks the eyes sloped and spread, like the eyes you saw painted on sarcophagi in museums. The phone in his long hand looked like a toy.

Now he snapped it closed and said agreeably to Danielle, "Hello, my mother."

"Dad, Yohannes. Yohannes, Dad."

"Excuse me," Yohannes said, "but I hear of you many times. Mr. Teddy. The schoolmaster."

"Ex-schoolmaster," Teddy said, shaking hands.

"*Ex?*" Danielle looked at him skeptically.

"Long story." He reached for the passenger-side door. "Should we get going?"

"No, no, please," Yohannes said, "you must sit in the back, Mr. Teddy. You are very old."

"The hell I am." Irritated, he ducked into the backseat. He may have been old, but he felt like a child, sitting back there with his legs folded, his knees up close to his face. "Listen, go ahead and call me Teddy, will you? Or Ted. Or Mr. Hastings. That's fine too."

"Yes, of course, I will call you what you wish," Yohannes said, gunning the engine into drive. "So not to disturb your mind."

"Too late for that," Danielle muttered. They careened around the rotary and onto the main road. She turned back to look at her father. "Bravo, by the way."

"What?"

"He's doing us both a favor, picking you up at the airport. And it took you, what, twenty seconds to insult the man three different ways?"

"Don't be ridiculous. He likes me, I can tell."

"Correction. He *respects* you. Because of your age. All he meant was the backseat's more comfortable. But now that you've chewed his head off for no reason, being respected won't be much of a problem."

"Why does everyone keep talking about how old I am? I'm not that old."

"For Africa you are. They don't live as long around here as we do."

"I'm not surprised. Look at this road. Look at this *car.* A Lada!"

"So?"

"So you know how they make these things? They take the worst parts from a Fiat and stick them in the body of a Yugo."

"Please stop shouting, Daddy. You're making everybody nervous."

"Just trying to be heard above the engine noise." Chastened, he looked out the window. Here he'd only just arrived, and already he was getting on her nerves. Family, he thought: what a project. "Why does he call you 'my mother'?"

"Yohannes? Who knows? I guess it's from my work with the babies. He's concluded I have a maternal temperament." She tilted the rearview mirror so she could watch herself fix back her hair with a scrunchie. "Shocked?"

"Not so much."

"Well, I am. The more time I spend here, the more I keep surprising myself. It turns out there are all these sides of me nobody's ever seen. Not even me."

Teddy nodded. He was a little bored by this self-absorption of hers, this new fascination with the twists and turns of her own intrepid consciousness. How tiresome young people were when they started analyzing themselves. How much reassurance they required. Thrilled as he'd been to see her at the airport, he'd almost have preferred to be alone right now, learning his own lessons, making his own mistakes.

The buildings whizzed by. Danielle, giving Yohannes directions, draped her left arm proprietarily over his headrest. She had been a loner in high school, studious, self-propelled, but now she appeared to be accumulating friendships at a prodigious rate. Teddy himself was going the other way. Traveling light. His life was all he had. He was so tired of it, he could hardly keep his eyes open. Through a haze of woodsmoke he looked out at the palm trees, the billboards, the tin-roofed shanties, the unlit signs with obscure messages. It was as if they were moving and he were standing still. Those few streetlights that worked did so dimly; in their pale glow, the mounds of trash heaped on the sidewalks looked shadowy, menacing. Only later, settling into bed at the hotel, would it occur to him that they were human beings.

Meanwhile the car rocked along the cratered streets, its shocks jostling and squealing like accordion tones. "Babies?" he asked dreamily after a while. "What babies?"

"Never mind," Danielle said. "You'll meet them tomorrow. Here's your hotel."

"I'm not staying with you?"

"Oh, God, no." She laughed so immediately and with such bitter amusement it almost spared him from injury. Almost. "Besides, you'll be more comfortable here. It's not the best in the city—that would be the Sheraton—but I thought you might like to stay in an African establishment. Go native, right?"

"Sure," he said without enthusiasm. "Why not?"

"Also it's really cheap. I figured you'd like that too. With your reduced income these days and all."

"Very considerate."

They turned into the narrow alley that led to the hotel. Some boys who'd been lounging invisibly on the sidewalk now sprang to their feet, shouting and running alongside the car, pounding on the hood. Yohannes ignored them. He shot up the driveway and pulled to the curb. "What's that they were yelling?" Teddy asked.

"Farenji," Danielle said. "Basically it means 'white person.' "

"And is that a compliment or an insult?"

"A little of both. Better get used to it, you'll hear it a lot around here."

She paused, waiting for Yohannes to ease himself out of the driver's seat and go around to release the trunk. "I'll walk you in."

"What about the bags? Will Yohannes get them?"

"He's not a servant, Daddy. He's my friend. They'll send a porter for your bags."

The lobby of the hotel was simple and clean. Polished wood, mirrored walls, slate floors. Teddy handed over his gold card and waited for the receipt. Danielle said something in Amharic to the desk clerk; both of them laughed. She'd been living in this country for what, two or three months, and here she was talking the language. But the young were like that, it seemed, freakishly proficient. Their inexperience only emboldened them. Stumbling into a strange room, they entered like lords and made themselves at home. The old of course were another story.

Suddenly, weary as he was, he was reluctant to let the girl go. "Stay with me," he said, "just for tonight. They can bring in a cot."

"No thanks. You snore, and I need my sleep. I'll be back in the morning. We'll have breakfast." She hugged him again, briefly this time, with more air between them. "Night, Dads."

"Night."

"Tomorrow you'll come to my place for dinner. I've turned into a good cook, you know. Mom'll be, like, *shocked.* Hey, let's call her tomorrow, okay? I haven't talked to her in a long time. She's probably pissed, huh?"

"She'll get over it. She's pretty forgiving as a rule. So am I."

"I know."

Oh, he was ready to forgive her everything, he thought, even this silly, transparent need of hers to shock her parents. Let the shocks come. They'd been taking shocks for years. Soon they might deliver a shock or two of their own. "I tried to call her from London, you know. When I changed planes. But no one was home."

"She probably turned the phone off when she went to sleep. Doesn't she do that when you're not around?"

"I don't know," he admitted. "I'm usually around."

But of course Danielle usually wasn't. Not anymore. As if to underscore the point, she was already skipping away, out to the curb, where the car was idling, and where Yohannes was talking on his cell phone again to some insomniac or other, waiting to get home.

9

The Changing Room

"So what do you think?" Oren said. "Getting tired of this yet?"

They sat by the YMCA pool, dangling their legs in the tepid water. Children were splashing nearby; their voices echoed through the vast domed room. Gail's hair was bunched into a swim cap. Between that and her clouded goggles, she looked like an alien. Her feet waved around peaceably, creating their own circular currents. "But I love swimming," she said. "It keeps me sane."

"That's not what I meant."

"What did you mean?"

"I meant hanging out this way. With me." The chlorine was up in his sinuses; his voice had taken a brief detour through his nose. "What's the appeal?"

"But I'm not the one hanging out with you," she said lightly. "You're the one hanging out with me."

"Okay, now who's into subtle distinctions?"

"Anyway, strange as it may sound, I don't subject myself to such questions. I'm not like you, Oren. I don't examine my own motives all the time before or after I do things."

"Well, maybe you should," he said. "Maybe it would be healthy to do that. I bet *they're* examining us." He nodded toward the other swimmers, doing their laps, each in his or her own narrow lane. "I bet they're talking about us too."

Gail smiled tightly, a muscle in her jaw puffing out like a blister. "Do I look like someone who needs the approval of other people? Or lessons in how to think about things in a healthy way?"

"Of course not."

"So what's your point then? I don't understand."

Suddenly they were on the verge of a real argument. Why? Over what? "All I'm saying," he said, "is a little introspection and self-analysis never hurt anyone."

"Now there's a naïve remark."

"Look, all I'm saying is—"

"What? What *are* you saying? Why don't you just come out and say what you mean? *You're* the one who's tired of it."

"That's not what I mean at all," he said, though just saying it made him a little tired, to tell the truth. "You're leaping to conclusions."

"Not that anyone would blame you, an urbane young man like yourself. I'm sure, even in a hick town like this one, there are more interesting ways to pass the time than hanging out with sick people and poor people and the occasional abandoned wife."

"Actually I've checked into that, and there aren't."

She sighed, as if she'd been expecting him to say something along these lines. Her suit was biting into her thighs; the flesh looked goosey and raw. Why she was so angry with him, he didn't know. Why he too was angry, whether for the same reason or some other, or else simply because she was angry with *him,* he didn't know that either. Oh, he *was* tired of it, Oren thought. Meanwhile the children in the pool went on splashing each other cruelly in the face. They treaded water with their bright, inflatable wings, churning things up.

"Look," he said abruptly, "what if one of these days I put the moves on you? What happens then?"

She looked at him uncomprehendingly, as if he had broken into a foreign tongue. Then she gave a queer, inward smile, and launched into the water. He watched her swim the whole length of the pool, then turn around and swim back, perhaps in pursuit of an answer to his question, perhaps as a way of avoiding it. Then she did it again, and again, and again, her stroke as steady and unvarying as a metronome. Oren sat there and watched as if in a trance. He had, it seemed to him, always been sitting here, at the edge of the pool, watching this woman skim back and forth like a figure in a dream. Each lap seemed a kind of pure, clean thought. An argument, a theory, a resolution. People did their best thinking when they were in motion, between things. Sitting still was no good. *The more one sits still, the closer one comes to feeling ill.* Who said that, he wondered—Kierkegaard? Pascal? Maybe it was Nietzsche. What difference did it make? Jump in the pool, he thought. Swim after her!

But it was too late. Gail came bobbing out of the water, wiping her eyes and blinking rapidly, like a sea creature newly born. She padded up the ladder on the balls of her feet. Beneath her sleek blue one-piece, her belly pulsed in and out. Her nipples strained against the fabric. A few dark, wild-looking hairs streamed scraggily from the V of her crotch.

"Mind throwing me that towel?" she asked, breathing hard. "I'm cold."

"Sure."

He could invite her to dinner. Men and women did that sometimes, went out to eat together; it kept the economy going. On the other hand she was married to somebody else, the mother of that other person's children. You could see this in everything she did. Even the brisk, no-nonsense way she dried herself with the towel, as if afterward it would be time for pajamas and story and bed. Soon she would vanish into the changing room and he'd lose all sight of her, he thought.

"You're a hell of a swimmer, by the way. I've been meaning to tell you."

"Thanks." Her lungs were still heaving a little. "You could be too, if you pushed yourself a little harder. You've got the strokes."

"Oh, I bet you say that to all the boys."

She was quiet for a moment.

"It's probably something wrong with me," she said, "but I've never found that sort of humor funny. All the compulsive little quips people make when they're nervous—frankly I don't see the point of them."

"That's too bad." Blood flew through his veins like a train, thronging that hot terminal, his face. "What sort of humor *do* you find funny?"

"I find plenty of things funny, believe me. More and more."

"As long as we're speaking so frankly, let me ask *you* something," he said. "Don't you get bored, doing the crawl all the time?"

She flinched; it was as if he'd struck her. "As a matter of fact, I do. But it happens to be the only long-distance stroke I'm good at." She peeled off her cap and shook out her hair. "And on that note, I better get back now to my narrow, boring little life."

"I'll meet you outside."

"Don't. You haven't even gone in the pool yet."

"I'm not in the mood for swimming. Anyway I was thinking we could go grab a bite." If anything, the transparent lameness of this idea, now that he'd put it into words, increased by a quantum factor. It was five o'clock in the afternoon. What were they going to grab and bite, a bowl of pretzels? "If you want to I mean."

"I better not. There's this preliminary hearing tomorrow, and I'm way behind."

"Maybe I could help. I'm an almost former lawyer, remember? That should be good for something."

"Wow, an almost former lawyer. That *is* impressive." The angle at which her head was inclined, as she toweled water from one ear, only enhanced the natural skepticism of her gaze. "You do like to be useful, don't you? So let me see. How much environmental case law do you remember?"

"Okay, that's a fair question. A very fair question."

284

"Forget it," Gail said. "It's a sweet offer, but no. Even if you *could* help, it's wrong to keep leaning on you every two seconds. It's taking advantage."

"Of whom? By who?"

"Go ahead and get your laps in. Really, you'll see, it'll make you feel good. We'll catch up with each other later in the week."

Which, given her refusal to meet his eyes, and the brisk officious way she strode dripping over the tiles and pushed open the door of the changing room, seemed to mean hail, farewell, and so long. Good. Oren had plenty of uncompleted work of his own waiting for him back on the chrome table in his kitchen. Papers to be graded, reading logs to be annotated, lesson plans to be finalized. So good, he thought. Enough. Every time he took his leave of Gail Hastings, or she took leave of him, these same twinned feelings of regret and relief teetered back and forth on a sliding scale. He could no longer identify one from the other. No longer be bothered even to try.

He went over to the diving board and bounced up and down for a while. There was grit in the paint, it gave the surface texture. Normally Oren disliked diving off the board, but then normally he disliked doing a lot of things he went ahead and did anyway. Because when you disliked doing as many things as he did, it simply wasn't possible, let alone practical, let alone advisable, to not-do them all.

A few days later, he was out doing one of the things he disliked most—standing high atop Don Blackburn's utility ladder, taking one last whack at that recalcitrant shutter—when he heard the hollow *whomp* of a car door, and looked down to find Gail Hastings, small and tousled-looking in her down jacket, squinting up at him from the driveway.

"There's no getting away from you, is there? You're always around."

"I'm good at aroundness," he said. "In all modesty, I believe I have a gift."

"I feel like we're being manipulated somehow. Like there's some higher being out there lurking behind the scenes, and he keeps placing you in my path."

"I thought you didn't believe in higher beings."

"I don't know what I believe." The sinking sun was in her eyes; she peered at him through the flat of her hand. "That ladder doesn't look too stable. Aren't you afraid you might fall?"

"I was at first. But then something happened."

"What's that?"

"I fell." He held up his arm to show her his bruised elbow, purple and swollen below his sweatshirt. Not that she could see beneath his sweatshirt. She was a powerful woman, but not that powerful. "I'm starting to get the hang of it finally."

"Falling?"

"Fixing things."

"Well," she said, "are you almost finished? We need to talk."

We need to talk . . . no other phrase in the language had such a withering, cryogenic effect on a man's testicles. And how poorly they'd all gone, Oren thought, those previous talks women had at some point or other needed to have with him. Reluctantly he climbed down the ladder. The angle of the shutter still seemed off, but perhaps he'd lost perspective. That was what came of working too hard and too long at a fundamentally simple problem.

Inside he found Gail at the kitchen table, sorting through Don's mail with a fixed, absorbed expression, like a person playing solitaire. "I'm making coffee," she said. "Want some?"

"Sure."

He drew up one of Don's ladder-back kitchen chairs and perched himself on it backward, so the slats formed a fence between them. Gail poured out the coffee into two of Don's ridiculous mustache mugs, of which he had an extensive collection, as Don of course would. To Oren she gave the leering one-eyed pirate; the plump Victorian gentleman with muttonchops and bowler she kept for herself.

The coffee tasted bitter and stale. Freezer burn.

Gail took a clementine out of her bag, peeled it expertly in a spiral with her long fingers. "Want a piece?"

He hesitated. He wasn't hungry, but he had a distinct memory of being offered an orange by her husband once and turning it down, and feeling afterward that he'd made a mistake. Why were the Hastings so intent on feeding him citrus? Did he look sick? "Maybe just one," he said.

The juice stung his fingers. His hands were raw, chafed from the cold; every time he stuck them in his pockets he bloodied his knuckles.

"Listen," she began, "I just want to say, none of this is your fault."

Oren nodded, chafing a bit himself now. It was already clear where this was going.

"I've been impossible, I know. I've been bitchy and contrary and I've sent a lot of really mixed signals. I'm not a very brave person, Oren, down deep. I used to think I was but I'm not." She plucked a seed from her mouth and deposited it on her napkin. "Couldn't we just forget all this? And please don't say forget what."

"I wasn't going to."

"Good."

They were silent for a moment.

"Actually," he said, "I *was* going to say forget what. But I restrained myself. I've been restraining myself a lot lately, as you may or may not have noticed."

"Well, now you won't have to restrain yourself anymore. At least not on my account. That's good news, right?"

"Right, yes. Maybe." He took a sip of his coffee, almost relishing the burn. "No."

It seemed he had covered the options all right. But Gail was intent on her own thoughts. "I just don't want to walk away from this thing feeling I've wronged you in some way," she said.

"You haven't wronged me."

287

"Because really, you've been a trouper. You've been generous and patient and kind. If I'm wronging anyone here, it's myself."

"Stop it. You haven't wronged anyone. You've made a decision not to do something that probably you wouldn't have done anyway. Do you hear me trying to talk you out of it?"

"No," she said. "No, I don't."

"It's your call to make, and you're making it. It's that simple. We're forgetting all this. Moving on. Whatever."

He could see from her face that his tone had been harsher than intended. She looked at him with a new, keen interest. Was this all it took to get through to people, acting irritable and snappish? If so he had an impressive future ahead, getting through to people.

"How do you know I wouldn't have done it anyway?" she asked. "How do you even know that?"

"Trust the expert. The more time spent deciding, the less time spent doing."

"No wonder you're so unhappy." She reached for his hand and gave it a brusque squeeze. "You're a romantic, aren't you? You've been hoarding yourself all this time. Waiting." She looked down at her plate, where the vacant clementine peel lay tilted on its side like a toy globe. "But I'm afraid we can't all afford to wait that long."

"Look, I said I was okay with this." Bad enough to be an unhappy person, Oren thought, but to be *told* he was an unhappy person, *accused* of being an unhappy person, and by Gail, who was not just the bearer of this news but the cause, this made him *really* unhappy. "What else do you want from me?"

She lifted her shoulders and let them down again, helplessly, as if the shrug were some vexing new dance step she'd failed to master.

"Look, there's no controversy here," he said. "We're in agreement. We're doing the right thing. It feels good to do the right thing once in a while."

"Yes. It does."

"So good. It's settled."

288

"It's settled." She exhaled audibly. "So you're not going to hate me?"

"You must be joking. Of course I'm going to hate you."

That she smiled at this, however briefly, gave him hope. Perhaps she might still be moved to sleep with him after all, if not by charm than by pity. "No, you're not," she said. "I almost wish you would. But you're not."

"How can you be sure?"

"Because we'd have to love each other first."

Exactly eight seconds ticked off on Don's wall clock before Oren said, "At least you didn't say you still wanted to be friends."

"Should I have?"

"No. . . . So." He rose from his chair. His movements were slow, laconic, an aging cowboy saddling up his horse. His work here was done.

"You don't have to run off you know."

"I'm not. I'm walking off. You're the one—" He stopped. There was no point.

"I'm the one," she agreed quietly. "That's right."

Without further discussion they cleared the dishes and washed and dried them in the sink, like thieves erasing evidence of a break-in. They were nothing if not tidy people. Oren was now desperate to get away; the house felt like a prison. He wanted to be out of there, to return to that other maddening indeterminate business, his life.

So preoccupied was he trying to formulate his exit strategy, he almost failed to register the soft, persistent friction of Gail's body against his, the hairs on his arm levitating toward her wool sweater, his jeans crackling from the whiskery electrostatic shed by her skirt. The dishes were done. The last of the coffee grounds had washed down the drain. The mustache mugs, like two tubby, jovial acrobats, stood upturned in their rack. So why were they still here? Against his hip he felt Gail bump and sway, deferent, gentle, inquisitive, a bumblebee browsing drowsily among flowers. Her cheeks shone in the steam that rose from the faucet. Her eyes had a tranquil, honeyed glaze, like someone humming a favorite song.

Good lord, he thought: she's waiting for me to kiss her. Or was she? He was pretty sure she was.

All things being equal, it should have been up to her of course, the married person, if it were up to anyone, to get the thing started. But there were no rules for this game, clearly. If you were going to get all hung up on rules, Oren thought, you'd never make it in the adultery biz. Besides, it could be argued that by leaning against him this way, she *had* got the thing started, and was now waiting for him to continue it.

Condensed vapor came dripping down the windowpane and puddled on the ledge.

Gail was shorter than he was, and her head was declined at a discouraging angle; this left a considerable expanse of space to negotiate before he finally touched down at the shadowed crater of her mouth. Along the way he rehearsed a number of witty, mood-lightening remarks, the sort of remarks he was known for, liked for; the sort that had always made women want to kiss him in the first place. Gail opened her lips obligingly.

"Please don't," she said.

"Don't kiss you?"

"Don't say anything."

She understood him better than he did himself. And yet the amazing thing was she appeared to still want him to kiss her. Though there was some evidence to the contrary as well. The shaking of her head for instance, no no no. The dryness of her lips. Her skeptical, assessing, open-eyed gaze, as if he were a plumber who'd come to unclog a defective sink. In the end it was all very complicated and inscrutable, very mixed-bag, very adult.

So this is adultery, he thought, kissing her. He'd never committed adultery before, he wasn't sure what constituted it exactly. Hard to go about breaking rules when you weren't clear what they were. So far so good though. No one had slapped him or screamed; no peals of thunder had sounded in the heavens; no stern hand of judgment had descended to smite him. It was no different than all those other commandments he'd broken in the past, stealing and coveting and failing to honor the father and mother and engraving a false idol on his wrist and so on. Gail was wrong: he was no romantic. He believed in nothing. Or rather, in no one thing. At some point you had to choose between an orderly life devoted to absolute values and a messy one swamped by relative ones, between the old prayers and prohibitions and the world as it irreducibly was. And he had. It was hard enough, Oren thought, just to deal with *that*. Just to keep plain, actual, physical existence going, like this kiss for example, without troubling too much over the ethics and morals. After all, he was the one doing most of the work. His tongue was probing her mouth, not vice versa; his was exploring her little caverns, her hidden nature sanctuaries and preserves (the mossy glades, the creviced rims of bone) while hers lounged by the front gate, collecting admissions. Was he living up to her expectations? Was she living up to his? He'd lived so long in a state of expectation, he didn't know where it ended or began, what borders it might share with its tiresome neighbor, reality. He thought of Don Blackburn, drooling feebly onto his pillow. Of Teddy Hastings stumbling through some fetid jungle. *Ever been to a jungle, Oren?* He was in one now. The life of men was a war of attrition. You shot off your gun a few times, and then you were gone.

Nonetheless he continued to kiss her. He kissed her as if he meant it, when in fact he didn't quite; kissed her as if overwhelmed with passion, when in fact he was only whelmed at best; kissed her as if he'd successfully shut out his surroundings, when in fact he remained more or less attuned to them the whole time . . . the hot water trickling in the sink, the window clotting with steam, the sun misting up behind it, whether from sorrow or happiness he didn't know. He kissed her until his mouth went numb, until his heart flopped against his ribs like a trout in a net. Then all at once he felt the net slacken, or tear; a great foamy, tumbling current rushed through, upending him like a raft, and after that whatever had been dammed up inside him began to move, as if space were being cleared for the next thing. And after that he just kissed her. That was what he did. He pressed his weight against her, he poured himself out as if filling a mold, and whatever he'd been doing before was now revealed to be something else, something less. His head was vacant and calm, a dark room. All the usual echoes had ceased.

At last they collapsed against each other in a heap, like two accident victims flung through a windshield.

"Mother of God," Gail groaned, "and I gave that whole speech and everything."

He nodded. He couldn't speak.

"The thing is," she said, "I *do* want to be friends. Is that so bad? I'm entitled to make new friends once in a while." Her nose was red. She clutched his shirtsleeves with both hands, pinching the fabric. "What happened to you back there?"

"What do you mean?" He gazed dully at the door that led to the backyard. The cats had left scratch marks at the bottom.

"Well, something changed. Didn't you feel it? About halfway through. It was like being kissed by two totally different people."

"Only two?" he said.

He led her out of the kitchen and up the stairs—as if they were *his* stairs, as if she were *his* wife—and down the long wainscoted corridor to the master bedroom. Sunlight was pouring through the blinds, striping the bed and Don's black cat, who lay asleep on the quilt. Ties hung from a hook on the back of the door. He watched Gail sit down on the bed, and now she too was striped.

"Okay, Cato," she said. "Scram."

The cat slunk off the bed and onto the floor with a thud. Any half-sentient creature could see Gail wasn't to be trifled with today.

Once she'd laid claim to the bed, the rest followed as a matter of course. Off went the duvet. Off went the throw pillows. Off went the leather clogs, the nubby sweater, the rayon skirt. Of her bra and panties she divested herself with such deft erotic efficiency—her bracelets tinkling like a xylophone as they rode her arms—he began to wonder if she'd done this before. Was she an old hand at this adultery game? Had she been the one putting the moves on him all along?

A draft came rattling through the storm windows and into his bones.

"Second thoughts?" She regarded him from high on the bed, lying cushioned against plumped pillows like a queen. "You look a little nervous."

"Why would I be nervous?"

"Then why don't you go ahead and take off your pants. I'm getting cold."

God help him, he did like a woman who took charge in bed.

The sex itself was touch and go, with an emphasis he supposed on the latter. Gail's movements were deliberate, like someone recovering from an illness; she would not be hurried along. At one point he looked down at her eyes, which were closed, and her jaw, which was clenched, and he wondered whom, if anyone, she was thinking about. He felt reasonably sure it wasn't him. Yet even knowing this did not detract from Oren's pleasure, but in an odd way enhanced it. He was accustomed to solo sex these days; this seemed just another agreeable variation.

Slowly, as they warmed to the act, her breath in his ear grew hoarse, insistent. Her soles gripped the backs of his thighs. He tightened his sphincter, squelching himself back, so as not to come too soon. He knew how to squelch himself back, all right. In the end however he wound up tarrying behind and almost failed to come at all.

Neither of them spoke. They lay side by side, like twins joined at the hip. Okay, he thought, he'd had better sex in his life. He'd had *much* better sex in his life. But it was their first time. He'd endured plenty of first times before; he knew what they were like. Knew too that they didn't always lead to second times necessarily. So he tried to remain philosophical when Gail said, "You were so quiet. I'm not used to that."

For a number of reasons Oren decided to take the observation at face value and try not to see it as the complaint it probably was.

But she wasn't finished. "With Teddy, he huffs and roars, you know right where he is. But you're different. I couldn't tell if you were with me or not."

"I was with you, believe me. I was with you the whole time."

"You don't have to say that, you know. I'm not fishing for compliments. I was just trying to understand."

Too bad there *was* no rule book for adultery, Oren thought, because surely, if there were, to compare your lover's prowess in bed to your husband's—and unfavorably at that—would have to be considered a major infraction by any standard. Just uttering the man's name seemed an act of bad form, bad faith, and bad magic. It conjured him into bed with them. And because that bed, Oren reminded himself, belonged to yet another man, with that other man's books piled on the nightstand and that other man's antiquated and unflattering wardrobe moldering away in the closet, and a triptych photo of that other man's now ex-wife poised atop the dresser, this made four, no *five* people present and accounted for in the bedroom. Plus watchful old Cato, slinking stealthily along the floor, lying low. How did adulterers manage to get any actual *sex* in, Oren wondered, with all these crowds around?

"I'm always quiet," he said, "when I'm trying to concentrate on something."

"You're not supposed to have to try. It's supposed to come naturally."

"You were trying too though, weren't you?"

"A little," Gail conceded.

"So you see. When it comes down to it, we're not so different. We're both . . ."

"Sensitive?"

"That's one word for it, I guess."

"Repressed? Ambivalent? Neurotic?"

"Okay, that's three words for it."

"There's only one problem." She got up on one elbow to look at him. "We can't both be those things. It doesn't work. The energy's all wrong."

"Actually I thought the energy was pretty good there, once we got going."

"Oh, hey, listen, don't get me wrong. I'm not complaining. I enjoyed myself, honest."

"But?"

"No buts." She frowned, as if making an effort to stop herself; then she went ahead and made her admission. "But maybe I thought it would feel different somehow."

To which he very sensibly said nothing.

"Scratch that." She shivered a little, crossing her arms over her breasts either for warmth or protection. "See? I *am* neurotic. That's the truth, my dirty little secret. The only ones who're onto me are my daughters. They see everything. Everyone else thinks I'm the together one. The solid one. Even Teddy. But I'm not, you see. I'm afraid all the time."

"What of?"

"What's anyone afraid of? I'm afraid the best part of my life is already over, and here I am waiting for it to start."

"Maybe it's coming along right now." He ran his hand down her back, along the bumpy ladder of her spine. "Or does that scare you too?"

"You bet it does."

"Why?"

"You're a shortcut, Oren. Nothing good ever comes from shortcuts."

"I disagree. When you want something in a hurry, a shortcut can be just the thing. Anyway, what are we even talking about? I'm losing track."

295

"We're talking about what we always talk about. This affair we're not going to have. All present evidence to the contrary."

"Why not?"

"Isn't it obvious?" She wheeled to face him. "Because people like us are no good at these things."

"Maybe you're worried we'll be *too* good at it."

She mused on this for a second, her lips compressed almost to the vanishing point. "No way. We're amateurs, let's face it. Look, we even forgot to draw the shades."

"I thought you don't care what other people think."

"Look, I have to live in this town, okay? I have a practice here. I do yoga here. I shop at the supermarket here. My daughter on her good days even goes to high school here. It's tough enough at the moment, thank you, without pinning a scarlet letter to my chest."

"You're right," he said, "let's forget it. It isn't practical. We'll be proper New Englanders. Good fences, good neighbors."

"Is that what you want?"

"No, of course it isn't what I want."

"Are you sure you know what you want? You don't sound sure."

"Pay no attention to that man behind the curtain. He never sounds sure."

"Think about it," she said. "A middle-aged woman with menopausal tendencies, not to mention married to someone else. Who happens to be your boss. Talk about a no-win situation."

"I'm not looking to win. I'm happy just to play. Of course in an ideal world," he added, "that finding-out stuff won't happen."

"It's a small town. It might. You're willing to take that chance? Why? I'm not even good in bed. I've been married my whole adult life, and Teddy, bless his heart, has never been one for variety."

"So what?"

"So we've just run through about half my carnal repertoire, that's what. I'm forty-nine years old, my dear. Just getting me lubricated at this point is a half-hour project."

"We'll see about that."

"Oh my." One hand went to her cheek. Had she not blushed, he'd have thought she was making fun of him again. "Let me get this straight. You're saying you actually want to fuck me again, Rabbi Pierce?"

"That's the general idea."

"And specifically. This time you'll let go a little? Maybe even make a little noise?"

"I'll try," he said, though from the level way she continued to regard him, it was as if he hadn't answered. "Wait, you mean right now?"

When she laughed, or cried—and she appeared to be on the verge of one or the other—Gail's face reddened and shrank, like the heating element in a toaster. It was doing so now. Before he understood what she was up to, she'd climbed on top of him and begun to work her hips back and forth, burrowing in, making a place for herself at the center of him. She was a slender woman; her weight wasn't much. And now her breasts, warm and pendulous, came brushing against his face, and the tiny hairs on her calves were prickling against his ribs, putting the flesh there, the flesh everywhere, on high alert. "You'll try?"

He looked up at her through the bars of ocher light that came streaming through the window. The stretch marks on her belly were illuminated, their faded calligraphy gone vivid and flushed, inked in blood. He thought of how she'd looked the other day emerging from the pool, blinking, slinging back her hair. How he had wanted her then! Still, he'd wanted a lot of women in his time, and what did he have to show for it? For Sabine too his desire had proved unreliable, more broad than deep. When it came to wanting, he was destined to be a generalist, he feared, a floater, a free agent. Even now he had to strain to stay on task, to keep his mind on the problem at hand—Gail—and not go straying off into peripheral areas . . . a book he'd meant to reserve at the library, a concert up in Montreal he'd meant to go online and buy tickets to, that new take-out Thai place on Route 17 he was still hoping to try . . . all the many small pleasures dangling like paper lanterns along the side yards of consciousness, smoky and fragrant, lighting up the dark . . .

"Yes," he said. "Hell, yes."

"Golly." She mock-fanned her face with one hand. "An unequivocal yes from Oren Pierce. Be still my heart." Hovering above him, she made an oblique, thoroughly nasty adjustment in the area where their legs conjoined. "So this is what you want?"

"Yes." His breath was shallow, spongy. He could hear a fly buzzing on the window, bumping its head moronically against the pane. "Dammit, yes."

"How do I know which one of you is even talking—that first guy I kissed, or Bachelor Number Two?"

"Take your pick. Whichever you want."

"*Bronnk!* Wrong answer." She lifted herself off him partway. It was a game and it also wasn't. "Try again, please."

"Number Two. Number Two."

"Good." She allowed her weight to descend in slow, moist increments, absorbing him like a sponge. "You could have gotten up anytime, you know. But you just lay there."

"Don't knock lying down. It's a perfectly respectable posi—"

"Okay, shush now." Her hand was on his mouth. "Shush and come here, before you blow it for real."

10

The Burnt Ones

Waking in darkness, he had no idea where he was, who he was, even *that* he was. He'd been deep in night's well; he'd lost hold of the ropes that bound him to the surface. He blinked and stretched. The unshared bed seemed far too large; with all his bulk, he seemed to barely occupy it.

Outside, the drone of a siren. The sound had woken him, he realized. Some kind of alarm or emergency signal. Were they under attack? He remembered the soldiers at the airport. The travel advisories, the embassy postings. Armed conflicts were in progress all around the Horn. Somalia, Eritrea, Sudan. And those were only the ones you heard about. Doubtless there were others.

Slipping from bed, he padded barefoot to the window and drew back the curtains. What he expected to find he wasn't sure—something like Jericho, he supposed. But the view told him nothing. The sky was oatmeal gray, sodden with mist. The ghostly silhouettes of banana trees swayed over the rooftops. Across the street two skeletal office towers leaned precariously against their bamboo scaffolding, listing in the wind. The window shuddered in its frame. The siren wailed on, insistent, like a tape in an endless loop.

Maybe he was dead, Teddy thought, and this noisy droning limbo was his afterlife. If so, it wasn't much of an improvement.

He got down on his hands and knees. No point letting his

body go to seed just because he was halfway around the world, jet-lagged and exhausted and under assault by some great, powerful voice he did not comprehend. But he'd forgotten the altitude. The push-ups left him dizzy, light-headed; the crunches stole his breath. After a while he lay on his back, inhaling whatever ancient dusts resided in the carpet as he waited for his heart to stop juddering in his chest. At last it was quiet. The room, the very world, seemed a vast, expectant place.

He went into the bathroom, showered and shaved, used the last of his mineral water to brush his teeth, and evacuated his bowels explosively. Then he came out in his boxer shorts with his hair still dripping and sat down on the bed to wait. It was not yet six. He heard voices stirring in the other rooms, footsteps thudding across the ceiling. Every separation between himself and other people seemed provisional, arbitrary. He wondered what Gail was doing at this moment. He was so many hours ahead of her now, it seemed impossible to reconcile their schedules.

His first day abroad, and the intrepid explorer was already homesick.

He picked up the remote and turned on the television. There was no signal.

"Oh, that," Danielle said over breakfast. "Yeah, the call to prayer. It's pretty intense."

"Christ, I thought I was going out of my mind. You're telling me you wake up to that every morning?"

She nodded. "The mosques have these huge amplifiers now. State-of-the art. It comes blasting out five times a day. For some reason morning's always the loudest though."

"And no one complains?"

"Only the tourists." She smiled. "You'll get used to it, Daddy. Everyone does. You'd be surprised what you get used to here."

"I'm already surprised."

They were sitting in the hotel dining room, eating cold eggs and toast, pale wedges of melon. The coffee was so good he was happy just for that, just to make contact with the real thing for a change, bitter and strong, close to the source. He drank it down black. Never mind that his stomach was rioting like a cellblock; he motioned to the waitress for more. A solemn-faced woman in traditional dress, she bent toward him shyly with her metal pitcher and smiled, as if nothing gave her greater pleasure than serving breakfast foods to white people from a rolling cart.

"Stop gawking, will you?" Danielle said when she'd gone. "They're not *that* beautiful."

"Come now. They most certainly are."

"Okay, you're right, they are. They're absolutely gorgeous. Especially that one there." Her eyes followed the path of a waitress at the far end of the room. "See that blue tattoo around her throat? She's a Mursi. From the south. Supposedly the Queen of Sheba had a tattoo just like that."

"Very fetching. Maybe you should get one."

"Please," Danielle snapped. "I hate it when people swoop in and start appropriating signifiers like that out of all cultural context. It's so ignorant."

"I was only kidding, Danny." Signifiers, he thought. Good Christ. For a change he was almost glad she'd dropped out of college, or whatever she called this little impromptu sabbatical of hers. "Aren't you eating? This fruit's delicious."

"Not hungry." She was still steaming.

"Fine, I'll have it."

"People are so stupid." He remembered this now, the girl's righteous, ranting streak, her fast burn. Another genetic gift he'd bequeathed her. Once she got started there was no dialing her down. "There was this girl I met in Nepal, she had one of those Chinese-character thingies on her shoulder? Totally hideous. She thought it meant 'dragon.' Except then she actually *went* to China, and guess what? It really meant 'roof.' And it wasn't even Chinese—it was Japanese."

"That's just the sort of thing Mimi would do," he reflected sadly.

"Leave Mimi alone. She'll be fine." Danielle had a way of drawing herself up and baring her neck when she was concentrating, like a bird alert to danger. She was doing so now. "Tell me about this cancer thing. It was just a false alarm, right? I mean you're okay, bottom line. Healthy as a bull and all that."

"Are you asking me or telling me?"

Now they were both annoyed.

"I don't have cancer," he said. "I had what might have turned into cancer, or might not have. Nobody's sure. For all I know it still might. Or might not. In other words I'm about where most people my age are."

"Clueless?"

"In the middle. Somewhere between okay and scared to death. Above all, in no mood to waste any more time."

"Aren't you wasting time right now though? Playing hooky like this in the middle of the school year?"

"Not at all. So far, so good. Being here makes me feel closer."

"Closer to what?"

Sipping his coffee, he hesitated. There seemed a thousand names for it. No one of them successfully made the journey, however, from his mind to his mouth.

"To bottom lines, let's say."

"Dear old Dad." She shook her head and signaled for the check. "Well, if it's bottom lines you want, I can show you some. You may not like them so much as you think."

"So where's this famous Gabi of yours, anyway?" They stood out on the sidewalk in front of the hotel, waiting for Yohannes. The air had a faint blue cast; it smelled of dirt and woodsmoke and diesel fumes. "When am I going to finally meet him?"

"That depends."

"Depends on what?"

"Oh, you know—" Her eyes flickered away; her face went stony. "On how close hell is to freezing over, basically."

Teddy reached for her hand. She conceded it without a fight.

"We were on this train to Asmara," she said. "There was this Italian girl, Giulia? She was sitting across the aisle, all tits and big hair and these really cool sunglasses. She was having some problem she said with the zipper on her backpack. At least she said it was on her backpack."

"Poor Pumpkin."

"You know what's funny? He told me right away he wasn't good at monogamy. And guess what? He was right."

"Oh well, fuck him," Teddy said. "I never liked the sound of the guy anyway."

"I'll tell you what he *is* good at, though. Getting women to be nice to him. He's good at that." She smiled bitterly. "His whole life, women've been cooking his meals and washing his boxers out in the sink and changing their lives around just to be near him and his famous charm and charisma. The gift of Gabi, I call it. Good one, huh?"

"You were always clever with words. All your teachers said so."

"Yeah. Bully for me." She looked down at her shirt with controlled distaste, as if she'd spilled something on it that might not come out. "What is it with guys anyway? Explain it to me. Why does it get old for you so fast?"

"It doesn't get old for everyone, Danny. The thing to remember is, you're still a very young girl. There'll—"

"Don't. I'm *tired* of being told how young I am. It's not interesting. The only people who think it is are people like you, because you're not." Her face suddenly brightened. "Hey, look, here's Yohannes. Right on time."

They watched the little blue car shoot toward them up the driveway.

"See?" Teddy said. "A lot of men are faithful. You can't write them all off."

"His girlfriend kicks him out early in the mornings. Her husband works nights."

"Ah."

"Don't look so disappointed. He's a really great guy. Come on, old-timer, get in. Time for the grand tour."

The streets of Addis, whatever else they might have been good for—begging, pissing, sleeping, herding goats and cattle—were no place to drive. The intersections, choked with cars and blue jitneys, were exercises in gridlock, the lane markings strictly for idealists. Buses wheezed and hissed like burdened beasts, lurching their way toward the curbs. Traffic signals dangled overhead like plastic fruit, ornamental but ignored. Any order to the flow of cars—any *flow* to the flow of cars—seemed accidental, haphazard. People poured out heedless into the streets. Men in cheap suit jackets, holding hands; tall women in bright skirts and heels; children in flip-flops—all took their chances, working their way fastidiously between the car bumpers and then pausing at the median strip, drowsy and impassive, to watch the cars whiz past like so many flies. Nothing disturbed their poise. They were the original people—*the blameless Ethiopians,* in Homer's phrase—the source material for the entire species. They'd waited six million years already. Waited out the Stone Age, the Ice Age, the dynasties and jihads of the Middle Ages; waited out the Jesuits, the Italians, the Chosen One of God, the Emperor Haile Selassie I; waited out his assassin Mengistu and the thuggish Dergue. So a little car traffic wasn't going to fluster them now.

Yohannes honked the horn perfunctorily to warn them off, then gunned the Lada out into the rotaries. He steered the wheel with one finger, like a tycoon in a Cadillac. This was not his real work, he'd let that be known. He was a filmmaker. To support his projects he ran a video store with his cousin Teshome and went on errands for the foreign NGO types who administered the orphanage. Sometimes he took the kids on field trips; that was how he'd met Danny. Mostly though, from what Teddy could see, he talked on the cell phone. He was doing so now.

Teddy turned to Danielle. "Is there always this much traffic?"

"What do you expect? It's a city." She waved a hand toward the windshield. "You remember cities, don't you, Dad? Places that don't have cows and cornfields, where you can actually go out and enjoy yourself?"

"I reckon I heard of them, all right," he drawled drily.

"God, we've got to get you out of that ridiculous town. Really, it's getting kind of pathetic, don't you think? The same little stores, the same little people, everywhere you look. How do you even *breathe?*"

"It can be hard to breathe anywhere." He reminded himself to do so now. It wasn't easy, with the stink of the diesel fumes, and his daughter's smug new habit of wielding her independence over him like a club. Plus he disliked sitting in the backseat. He could hardly see where he was going. "As I recall, you used to like that pathetic little town. You used to talk about getting married and having children and settling down in that pathetic little town, in fact."

"I used to play with Barbies too."

"No you didn't. You never played with dolls. You had no interest in make-believe at all. No fantasy stuff, just facts. Like me."

"God forbid."

They drifted through the slummy, shapeless sprawl. Dusty unpaved alleys wound mazelike behind the shops. Jackhammers pounded at the sidewalks. Half the buildings were going up, the other half, stripped to cinder blocks and rebar skeletons, coming down. From where Teddy sat you could hardly tell the difference. He rubbed his eyes, watching the signs flick past. How mediocre and jerry-rigged it was, this business of human occupancy. Nissan, Mobil, Reebok, Fujifilm. Danielle was right, he thought, cities were cities: everywhere you went, the Esperanto of commerce prevailed.

She was still talking in the front seat, pointing out the sights. The monuments, the museums, the government buildings, the emperor's palace. Endearing, the effort she was putting in, showing him around. If only he were a better tourist. If only he weren't so tired, so crabby. She turned to face him. "Hey, still awake? You're awful quiet back there all of a sudden."

"Just thinking."

"Should we go up to the mountains? There's a nice view of the city from there."

"It's your town. Whatever you say." Maybe it was the altitude, the jet lag. Something was lagging anyway. Ever since he'd woken that morning to the terror and monotony of the muezzin's call, he'd felt sunken in apathy, buried in it like a seed.

They turned off the main road and began the slow laborious climb through the foothills. The air grew cooler. Bark came peeling off the trees in long faded strips. Soon the roads were no longer paved, and instead of sidewalks there were grooves in the earth, narrow drainage trenches that stank of sewage. Deep tire tracks lay etched in the dirt. Mongrel dogs loitered in sullen packs, short-haired and indolent, like skateboarders in front of a convenience store. A young girl came trudging toward them down the mountain, bent double under a staggering load of wood. Danielle pointed her out. "That's what you smelled last night at the airport. Eucalyptus. Acacia too. About eighty pounds of it I'd say."

"But she's just a kid. Why isn't she in school?"

"No reason. It's just this little problem they have that gets in the way. Poverty, it's called." She examined the girl in the rearview mirror. "She'll sell that load downtown on the sidewalk for ten birr a bundle. Then she'll come back up here for more."

"Is that legal?"

"No. But the cops are foxes in a henhouse. If they catch her, they may beat her, or rape her. Or both. Unless they're sober, in which case they may just let her off with a bribe."

"I thought you weren't supposed to burn acacia wood. It's supposed to be sacred."

"Who says?"

"The Bible. And there's the Osiris legend too."

He could see she had no idea what he was talking about. They'd sent the girls to Unitarian Sunday school, ten grand a year, filled their heads at bedtime with the best world mythologies, and neither of them retained a thing.

"Osiris," he said pointedly to Yohannes, "was a great Egyptian king. Until his brother conspired to kill him, unfortunately."

"Is a shame," Yohannes agreed. "Between brothers there must be love."

"Yeah, well, this one had issues. What he did was, he had his best carpenters make a sarcophagus from acacia wood and cover it with rubies. He told his brother the king it was a magic box from the gods. Whoever fit inside it would live forever. The king, being your basic greedy excitable type, climbed right in. Wham! They threw down the lid and tossed him in the Nile."

"Not one of your really *sharp* great Egyptian kings, was he," Danielle said.

"Ha!" Yohannes snorted appreciatively. "Good trick! So this king he then dies?"

"Yes and no. See, Isis, the queen, gets wind of this, and goes down to the river, and there's the sarcophagus, floating against the bank. Lo and behold, an acacia tree's growing out of the wood. Isis takes this as a sign—the king's still alive. So she fishes him out of the river, and then, and I don't remember how this part goes exactly, but she gets herself pregnant somehow, and then the king dies for real, and she buries him way out in the desert where no one can find him, and the gods are so impressed by how well she's handled the whole thing they make Osiris lord over the dead. And from then on, according to the myth, the wood of the acacia tree was supposed to be sacred."

"Yeah, well, it's sacred here too," Danielle said. "They use it for cooking. And it's girls like these who have to haul it around."

"What about the men?"

"Good question." Danielle playfully punched Yohannes on the shoulder. "What *about* the men?"

"Men is too busy."

"See? Patriarchal society," she said, "just like your story. The women do the dirty work and make all the magic, and the guys sit around partying and chewing khat. If the women stop working miracles, this place'll fall apart. And how do the men pay them back? By giving them HIV they get from their girl-friends."

"Not me," Yohannes said. "Safe sex. Safe sex only."

"Yeah, right," she said. "Famous last words."

After lunch, Teddy was hoping to nap for a while and restore his strength. But it seemed Danielle had other business. They drove along the city's western outskirts; to his eyes they were indistin-guishable from the eastern outskirts. The same fetid streets lined with the same corrugated-tin shanties, everything jumbled together like worms in a bait box. People kept turning to look at him as they drove past, as if the paleness of his face were an advertisement for something. He had no idea what.

At last they pulled into the driveway of a square, high-walled compound. To signal their arrival Yohannes honked the horn twice. It appeared to be his favorite mode of expression.

"Where are we?" Teddy asked.

"I thought you'd like to see where your daughter spends her days. Give me a sec, I'll go see what's happening."

She leaped out, slammed the door behind her, and slipped through the blue iron gate. The girl was as impatient with petty delays as he was. Good. He sat there scratching a bug bite on his elbow. Yohannes fiddled with the radio dial, skipping from sta-tion to station. Banana palms fluttered in the invisible breeze, nodding like chess players. Atop the whitewashed walls, shards of colored glass glittered in the sunlight like costume jewelry. You could do some damage to yourself, he thought, trying to force your way in here.

Meanwhile Yohannes had now found his desired music. He drummed on the dash with the flat of his palm. In the rearview mirror his eyes could be seen, bulbous and inquisitive, checking out the Leica around his passenger's neck. "Your camera, Mr. Teddy. How much will it cost?"

"I don't remember. It's just your basic thirty-five millimeter. Here, try it out."

"For me digital is better." Yohannes hefted it in his hands. "Lighter to carry. But this looks quite good also," he added charitably.

"Danielle tells me you're in the movie business."

The driver's eyebrows lifted affirmatively in the mirror. "Yes, I and my brother. We are planning an action film now. Big scale. Good guys against terrorists. Prostitutes with golden hearts."

"Sounds like a hit."

"There will be many impressive explosions, you may be certain of that. In Ethiopia we like these films very much."

"Americans too."

"I like to go to America someday," Yohannes said. "But it is very difficult to get the exit visa. Many people in Ethiopia will like to go to America."

"Well, I'm sure there are many Americans who'd like to come to Ethiopia too."

"So?" Yohannes snorted, incredulous. "I think they must be crazy people. The political situation in our country is very nasty. We are in danger all the time. When we shut our eyes, we are afraid."

"Oh, we're used to that."

"Last year the police arrive, and I am taken from my bed in the night and beaten in the kidneys until I bleed." Yohannes eyed him skeptically in the rearview. "Surely you do not mean in America you are used to this?"

"No, you're right. Our fear is different." The bite on Teddy's elbow was itching miserably. Could he have caught yellow fever already? "But if no one likes this government of yours, how does it manage to stay in power? I thought you guys had a democracy over here."

"Ah. But you must ask yourself this same thing. Who benefits for our government to be so militaristic? Who is the one who gives to our government the billions of dollars in development projects and aid funds? And why? So we will kill Muslims for you."

"But you still want to come."

"Yes, of course." Yohannes sighed; the issue seemed too complex to explain. Then, as if savoring the taste of some fresh inspiration, his heart-shaped lips pursed thoughtfully. "Perhaps you would like to help me and my brother produce our film?"

"Me? I wouldn't know the first thing about it."

"Is not so difficult, I promise you. Actor fees are very low. The camera, the editing machine . . . maybe birr sixty thousand together. Please, I assure you, I will not go beyond your capacity."

"Sounds like a lot." He did a fast conversion in his head. It came out somewhere around $7,000. Roughly the value of his Pfizer stock. "It's not my usual thing. But let me think about it."

"Think, think," Yohannes agreed. "I will wait for your answer. I swear by the names of God."

Names? But then Teddy recalled that the Muslim God had ninety-nine names, every one of them flattering. So maybe Yohannes was a Muslim. He made a mental note to ask about this, to get a fix on exactly who the good guys were in this movie of his, and who the evildoers. Surely it wouldn't do to invest in a propaganda tool for your own destruction. Unless of course part of you *wanted* that destruction. Wanted to burn down your life to its blackened foundations. Wipe the slate clean and start again.

Finally the iron gate, with a grudging squeal, swung open on its hinges. Yohannes gave Teddy back the camera and engaged the gears. No sooner had they entered the compound and parked then there came a tremendous *thunk;* it shook the car's roof like a bomb.

Teddy ducked instinctively. He couldn't help it. All day he'd been fearing an attack of some sort, and now here it was.

"Is okay, Mr. Teddy, is okay." Yohannes was laughing. "It is only a football. No one is shooting you."

"Yeah, well, the day's still young."

They were parked, he saw now, roughly in the center of at least four different games—hopscotch, jump rope, basketball, soccer—going on at once. No one appeared to object to their presence. A few of the children detached themselves and flocked over to greet Yohannes, who was clearly a great favorite. Only after they'd high-fived and chatted for a while did they cup their eyes against the window to check out the big old white guy dusting himself off in the backseat.

"How you doin'?" Teddy said agreeably. At this point he was used to being gawked at. "Good to see you."

The children pressed closer. It was as though they'd been sent to free him from this shoddy, rattling cage in which he'd arrived. Remembering the boys outside the hotel, he reached for his wallet. "No need, Mr. Teddy," Yohannes said. "They only wish to meet you."

"Oh."

"The children have heard that Danny's father will be coming today. A great teacher from America. A very important man."

"Who told them that?"

"I think Danny, must be."

"An important man, eh? How do you like that?" He pushed open the door. No sooner had he extricated himself from the Lada than his hand was seized by a skinny long-faced boy with a shaved head. "And who might you be, son?"

"My name is Mekas," the child said. "And please, what is yours?"

"Call me Mr. Teddy, I guess." This foolish and insipid name seemed as good to him as any other. "At your service."

"Mr. Tony, you must take my picture, so I will find a family in America."

"Teddy."

"You will help me find a family?"

"Okay, sure, no problem. Let me just get the thing focused . . ."

All at once Yohannes hissed fiercely in Amharic. The boy

blanched and went still. His eyes, large and dark, receded into their sockets; his lips swelled up like tires. Then he ran off and disappeared behind an outbuilding at the end of the courtyard.

"What was that for?" Teddy demanded. "I was just taking his picture."

"You are the guest. The childrens have been told this many times. They are not to take advantage of your kindness."

"Well, where I'm from, the guest chooses for himself."

"Yes, you do as you like," Yohannes said, still angry. "This we all know about the Americans. You honor your own ways above others."

Here we go again with the insults, Teddy thought. Indignant, he strode off across the courtyard on his own, determined to make his own mistakes, find his own friends. The children at least were happy to see him. They crowded in close, grabbing at the camera, admiring their reflections in the lens. Their breath ruffled the hairs on his arms; their fingers entwined themselves in his. It had been a long time since children had wanted to touch him, had done so voluntarily. Now he waded through their ranks like a man in a flood. They surged forward, bestowing unto him their odd, complicated names. Mesfin. Abebe. Tamrat. Ruweni. His own name in comparison sounded paltry and bland even to him. Made-up. His face was hot. He felt a pressure in his chest. Birds twitched and twittered in the juniper trees. Danielle, in accordance with her new policy of abandoning him whenever she could, was nowhere in sight. He appeared to have lost Yohannes too. There was no one to mediate or translate for him; no one to steer or instruct him in how to behave. He was happy about this and also a little panicked. He looked down to find two small boys hanging upside down on his pant legs, clinging like pandas to the trunks. "Okay," he roared. "Off."

They giggled and shook their heads. His mock-rage, if that was what it was, delighted them.

"So that's how it is, huh? You want to live dangerously, do you?"

312

He gathered them in his arms and flung them high in the air, spun them like pizzas overhead. Everyone cheered. Why shouldn't they? They were just kids. How natural it felt to play the old roughhouse games with them. The Ogre on the loose again. On some level, he'd never *stopped* being the Ogre, never given up being that shaggy, maniacal monster who bellowed and roared and chased kids around the yard, threw them over his broad shoulders like potato sacks, and dangled them upside down until they whimpered for mercy. Say what you would about the Ogre, for all his faults he wasn't boring. He knew how to put on a show.

"Daddy!"

Another one, he thought. He was accumulating quite a crowd. All these awestruck children begging to be carried away.

"What are you doing?" Danielle said. "Are you out of your freaking mind? Put those children down before someone gets hurt!"

"Now let's not get excited." It seemed an unfair and lamentable trick of fate that his daughter, when appalled by something he'd done, sounded so very much like his wife. "I was just playing around a little."

"Well, stop. These are children. They're not your personal toys."

"Fine." In truth her righteous indignation bored him. What was all her travel for, if she was going to insist on the same old proprieties?

"You think this is why I brought you here? To terrify these poor kids with a sicko game like Ogre? God, I always hated that game too."

"Untrue." He shook his head. "Untrue and unfair." And, he was tempted to add, unkind.

"Okay, maybe not always. But it got old, getting chased around all the time. My friends stopped coming over. Mimi's too. We used to hide in our rooms after dinner sometimes, just to avoid you and that stupid game. Didn't you know that?"

"Now you're being spiteful." The sun swam in his eyes. "You're mad at me now so you're trying to hurt me."

"Face it, Daddy. You were the one who liked that game. Not us."

"Face it, Daddy!" the children jeered. *"Face it, Daddy!"*

The tables had been turned: now it was the Ogre's turn to be rendered vulnerable, to teeter from his great height, a giant encircled by flies, under the assault of all the many things he must face. He looked around the courtyard as if in a dream. His shirt was soaked in sweat, and like any old monster he'd begun to stink. "Okay," he said to the kids on his back, "party's over. Off."

He bent low, like some faltering Atlas, so they could climb down off his shoulders. He couldn't see their faces and so had no way of knowing if it was disappointment, or relief, that impelled them to disperse as quickly as they did.

"Find Yohannes," he heard Danielle say to someone. She was already moving on to other business. She'd taken possession of one of the babies from a staff assistant and was now looking him over worriedly. "And then let's call Doctor Dave."

"What's wrong?"

"Nothing. A touch of fever. No biggie." With casual authority she cradled the baby high on her shoulder. "Listen, Daddy, I'm sorry if I hurt your feelings just now. I know you mean well, but these aren't your children. You have to remember that. You can't just plunge in without thinking and expect everyone to go along." She touched her lips to the baby's forehead, frowning. "Where's Yohannes? We need someone to go on a meds run."

"I'll go."

"You'll never find the place. Let Yohannes do it. Mind fetching him for me? He's probably out back as usual, shooting hoops."

Teddy hurried off, determined to make amends. The kids had gone back to their games. The soccer ball the boys were using was flat. He made a mental note to buy them a new one. The girls were less focused on playing hopscotch, he noticed, than they were on the intricacies of braiding each other's hair. But they could probably use some more chalk. From the kitchen he smelled charcoal fires, some peppery stew. He rushed through the courtyard, looking for Yohannes. The children had to swerve to avoid him. They knew an Ogre when they saw one, all right.

"You must take my picture, Mr. Tony. So you will not forget."

Mekas again. The boy, with his shaved head and his sly listless expression, had arisen before him suddenly like a vision.

"Here, kid," Teddy said, all but forcing the Leica into his hand. "Knock yourself out."

Behind the courtyard, on the laundry lines strung over the alleys, T-shirts dangled like pennants. Every T-shirt on the planet, it seemed, was born in China, emigrated to America for a better life, and then was sent here to Africa to die. America was only a way station, Teddy thought, a middleman. It bought things cheap, then got bored, stuffed them into trash bags, and donated them at church.

He remembered the woman on the plane. *Trying is almost doing.* Then he remembered himself, wasting long afternoons on the sofa, worrying about a disease he didn't have. His fingers idling dreamily on the remote, the world a flat pixelated screen on the other side of the room. Killing time. When really it was the other way around. Yes, death was a contagious disease, he saw that now. Philip had got sick and died. But what he, the survivor, had done with his vigor and capabilities, he who could rewire a radio and program a computer and construct enormous pieces of furniture with his own hands—what was the word for that?

He'd stepped into the coffin like a fool, and the box had refused to sink. His life bobbed up and down on the surface, stubborn and witless as a cork.

"Ah now, Mr. Teddy. You wish to play?"

Yohannes stood at the top of the key, smiling wolfishly, showing off his crossover dribble. Only there *was* no key. The court wasn't much of a court, either. The ball had no tread. The hoop was a bent, rusted, oblong thing nailed on planks against the wall.

"No way."

"Come now, one game. I give you the best guys. What do you say?" A predatory smile flicked across Yohannes's face. There was not much respect for elders in it.

"I just got off a plane. I'd never keep up. Besides, you're wanted in the office."

"One game only."

"Anyway I can't play in these loafers."

"Please now, look here." Yohannes pointed to his own open-heeled sandals. The rest of the boys wore flip-flops, not that it appeared to slow them down any. Slim-hipped and coltish, they flung themselves around the court like kamikazes. At their age—thirteen, fourteen—adoption was less likely. He supposed they had to channel their energies somehow. "You are a strong man I think, Mr. Teddy. I believe you have some game in you yet. Maybe you school me, eh?"

Just what the world needs, he thought, another trash-talker. He stripped down to his T-shirt. The great mound of his belly swelled against the fabric. "Okay," he said. "You're on."

The game itself went as games, in Teddy's experience, often did: he huffed and heaved and threw his weight around in the paint like a bully, and in the end he both enjoyed himself enormously and lost when he might just as well have won. That he was playing against boys half his own height did nothing to restrain either his enthusiasm or his aggressiveness. After all, he too had been hammered on by grown men in his youth. He too had been pushed around the court by a hulking, hairy-backed butcher with love handles and bad breath. That was the male drill, the timeless rite of initiation. To mix it up out in the driveway, in the failing light, with the hot juices flowing, the gnats swarming your hair like a halo, the sneakers squealing and the mowers roaring like big sullen animals down the street . . . to feel an old man's slick, foul-smelling torso grappling against you, hear his harsh grunts in your ear, the sound of a man fighting for breath in a constricted space, as if breath and space were privileges to be earned . . . this was a good thing, he believed, a thing to be craved and pursued like a birthright. So he went all out. It was what he did best.

What he did not do best alas was shoot or pass or dribble. Consistency in these skill areas was not his strength. Yet the boys on his team kept passing him the ball anyway, as if it amused them to watch this fat slob stumbling and cursing around the court, flinging up his wild erratic shots. His lungs were boiling. His glasses had completely fogged over. Eventually he sank a ten-footer from the baseline and the adrenaline began to flow. Then a fifteen-footer, falling away. A finger roll. Yohannes had been lying low, letting his young teammates do all the shooting. Now his eyes flashed, his brows locked together over his fine Abyssinian nose. "You are in the zone, Mr. Teddy."

"Bah." Teddy shrugged. "Law of averages."

"Perhaps the law now will change."

The two of them began going at it for real, throwing forearms and elbows, jostling for position under the basket. Teddy could hear his heart down in his chest, thundering like hooves. It seemed a good sound. He felt jubilant and strong. True, he was going to be sore tomorrow, but it would be a good soreness, the soreness that comes from exerting yourself too much. He knew about the other kind.

Unfortunately Yohannes, sensing introspection under way, chose that moment to pivot hard and drive right. Teddy was caught flat-footed; he had to resort to middle-aged hacker's default mode and grab the guy's shirt. For a moment they stood there locked in a bear hug, in the center of what would have been the paint had the court been painted or had any other features in common with a basketball court. Meanwhile the ball went bounding away down the baseline and across the alley.

Teddy chased after it, joyously, recklessly, in the grip of some heroic delirium. What was it about chasing balls that excited the instincts so? At bottom it seemed he was just another old dog with a pendulous belly, running back and forth for no reason and calling it a life.

Eventually the ball found its way to Yared, one of the boys on Teddy's team, a short, droopy-eyed fellow with a measles-like rash around his mouth. Yared lifted the ball in his hands with a calm, impeccable solemnity, as if Mr. Spalding himself had entrusted him with it. Then he banked in a shot. Tie score.

Yohannes laughed. "What you say, Mr. Teddy? Shall we stop now, or is it joyable for you to finish our game?"

"You must be kidding." To fly six thousand miles across the ocean only to end all tied up on this rutty joke of a basketball court—it would be worse than losing.

"Okay, so." Yohannes took a step back and lazily popped a long-range jumper; it shot through the hoop like a pellet. "The school meets."

"We'll see." Teddy bulled his way down the lane and threw in a hook. Yohannes answered from the baseline. Then each sank a long jumper. It went on that way for a while, back and forth, until Yohannes appeared to tire. He grew casual with his dribble, the ball left exposed. Teddy drew up tight, waiting for an opening. When it came, he lunged. The ball wasn't there. Instantly he knew he'd been snookered, caught out of position far from the basket, overplaying his man. And if in retrospect he should have just conceded the head-fake and easy jumper that followed, this seemed only the latest in a series of bad mental, physical, and temperamental mistakes both on the court and off. Indeed, it seemed only fitting that his shaggy high-domed head—the source of these mistakes—should go on at this point to collide with Yohannes's elbow and suffer a sharp, sickening crunch.

The day went dark. His glasses sailed off onto the asphalt; his eyes, exposed, filled with tears. His last sight before hitting the ground was of Yohannes polishing one final web gem, laying in, with a feathery touch, the winning basket. From somewhere nearby he heard splintering glass. It was a sound he had come to recognize.

"I trust you are not hurt, my friend?" The driver bent over him, looking worried, solicitous.

"Just. A bit. Winded."

"Yes, I am very tired too." In truth Yohannes was not out of breath in the slightest. "Come, we will go see Danny in the office. She will care for you like a mother."

As it happened, when they hobbled into the common room, like soldiers back from a war, Danny was caring for *other* people like a mother—setting out tiny cups of juice and a platter of yellow, tasteless-looking cakes for the youngest children in the orphanage. Of course, it was Teddy who did most of the hobbling. His trousers were torn at the knee, his left leg seeping blood in two different places. He looked around for a place to sit, but all the chairs were tiny. They formed a dense, forbidding clot at the center of the room, like the terminal phase of some protracted Scrabble game. The walls were covered with maps of Europe and the United States. Curiously, there were no maps of Africa. But he supposed the children knew where Africa was.

"Ah," Danielle said, "the prodigals return."

"Sorry, it's my fault," Teddy said. "We were playing ball and the time got away."

"I love it when guys bond. It's so . . . selfish."

"I already said I was sorry. Besides, you wanted us to be friends. Right, partner?"

"Partner?"

She flicked a little glare in Yohannes's direction. He avoided her eyes. "You must tend to your father. He is in need of attention."

"How do you like that?" she said to Teddy. "Known you one day, and he's already got your number."

"Very funny." Wincing, Teddy worked at the geometrical problem of fitting his economy-size self into one of the dwarfish chairs. "I don't suppose you have any Band-Aids around this place."

"You'll have to wait. It's snack time."

"Sure." Blood was leaking through his pants, darkening the fabric. The smell of the juice and the cake reminded him that he'd had no lunch. "A couple of ibuprofen might be nice too."

"I'll see what I can find." She poured out more juice. "So how was the big game?"

"Humiliating."

"Your father is very strong," Yohannes said. "Like Shaq. He is a man with great will."

"Sounds like an epic struggle. Of course we've got a sick baby here desperate for antibiotics, but that can wait, right? The important thing is you two had a fun game." She was silent for a moment, fuming. When she spoke again, she told Yohannes curtly, "You better get going now. Dr. Dave's got a package waiting."

"Okay, my mother."

"Ask him to throw in some anti-inflammatories too. Shaq here looks like he'll need them."

When Yohannes was gone, she blew a sigh toward the empty doorway. "Great, now he's pissed too."

"Nonsense. He reveres you."

"No, he doesn't like the way I spoke to you just now. He thinks a woman should never sound harsh."

"I don't mind a little harsh."

"I know. That's what bothers me. I don't either." She put down the juice pitcher and wiped her hands on her shorts. Her little mouth was all bunched on one side, the lashes of her eyes darkly defined, like grass after a thaw. "I called Mom last night by the way. After I dropped you off. She was kind of in a mood."

"Oh?"

"Imagine how stupid I felt. Here you're like, 'Oh, gee, everything's fine at home, I'm just popping over to see how you're doing.' You guys should get your stories straight."

"We intend to. Soon."

"Meaning what? You're telling me you don't even know if you're still together or not? That's supposed to inspire confidence?"

"Grow up, Danny. There are bigger things involved than your confidence."

She flushed, absorbing this. Now it was his turn to be harsh. With an automatic gesture she tried to toss back her hair, but it didn't move—she'd secured it with a band. "Even so, you could have told me. How was I supposed to know you were getting separated?"

"Look, Danny, nobody's getting separated from anybody. We've been married a long time. We're not going to throw it all away just because of a rough patch."

"A rough patch." She went back to pouring out her little thimble-size cups of juice, like a nurse dispensing medicine. Her face was puffy with meditations and complaints, but her hands on the pitcher were as steady as you could want. Put this girl on a flag, he thought. Engrave her image on the prow of a ship.

"What about you and Yohannes?" he said. "What's up with that?"

"None of your business. We're friends. What's up with *you* and Yohannes? If you're thinking of investing in one of his quote-unquote movies, I should warn you, he has a rotten track record. Like as far as I know he's never made one."

"What about this action thing he's doing? That sounds promising."

"Oh, God, he told you about *that*? He and his brother, they sit around drinking beer all night watching *Godfather* movies and making notes. To give you an idea, they like the third one best." She bent low, inspecting the bruise on his knee. "Hmm, looks like you've got a little gravel in there."

"That's okay. It doesn't hurt."

"I better take a look. This is no place for an infection."

Frowning, she brushed off the fragments of stone and then blew softly on the wound to dry it. Teddy shuddered. After a sharp sting, the pain receded, and a cool, vacant sensation spread down his leg. "Better?"

"Yeah." He looked down at her gratefully, a fairy-tale lion relieved of his thorn. "Much better, actually."

"You know, if you really want to throw your money away, why not throw it away here where it can do some good? I mean, *look* at this mess."

"What's wrong with it?" Admittedly without his glasses everything was kind of softened and vague, a low-resolution affair. But he could see that the walls of the common room were painted a bright semolina yellow, like the petals of a sunflower, the bulletin boards dense with bashful smiling children in Alpine settings, the shelves so heavy with books and puzzles and Disney videos—*Dumbo, Beauty and the Beast, The Jungle Book*— they sagged in the middle, straining their brackets. "I like this place. I think it's great."

"Really?" Her tone was not casual; it wasn't his opinion about the place that she was soliciting. "You're not just saying that to be nice?"

"You know me. I never say anything to be nice."

"True."

"Of course I haven't worked up the courage to check out the bathrooms yet—"

She laughed. "Best not to, I think."

"But the kids seem happy, and that's the main thing."

"I have to say, Daddy, you're blowing my mind here a little. This wasn't what I was expecting. I was sure you'd be all over me about this. I thought you'd say"—here she put on her pinched, derisive Teddy-voice—" 'Hey, listen, Sweetpea, you're wasting your time here. Go home.' "

"Well, the day's still young," he said. "Only I thought you said you were teaching English to these kids. I don't see any classrooms."

"You're sitting in one. This is where we do geography. It's also where we eat, and watch videos, and do art projects, and sing songs. It's got a lot of uses. The other classes meet out there."

"Where?" All he saw was a windowless metal trailer at the end of the courtyard. "That thing? Hell, it looks like a freight car."

"It *is* a freight car. But until we raise funds for a proper building, it has to do. Dr. Dave, he was just in the States. He has this PowerPoint thing he does in churches and synagogues. They eat it up. He says in nine or ten months we'll have enough to break ground."

"Nine months!" It was a toss-up as to which unnerved him more at this moment—the children out in the freight car having to wait that long, or Danielle working here that long, or the thought of his lower back seizing up in spasms before Yohannes returned with the ibuprofen. Already he could feel a belt tightening invisibly at the base of his spine. "Tell you what. I'll write your Dr. Dave a check. Speed things along."

"You're writing a lot of checks all of a sudden." She made it sound like an accusation.

"So what? That's my business."

"Isn't it more like Mom's? Shouldn't you call her first?"

"Don't worry about Mom. Mom'll be fine with this. She's a great one for liberal guilt—half her work these days is pro bono." What the other half was these days he didn't know. But he was touched by the girl's suggestion, her need to keep them in touch with each other, ongoing partners. For all her bravado and independence she was like any other child. Wishing for magic. Trying to coax a green shoot from the old sodden coffin.

"I don't get it. Since when are you such a soft touch?" She yanked up one of her droopy spaghetti straps and hooked it over her shoulder blade. "You're like the cheapest person I've ever met in my life."

"Not anymore. Haven't you heard? I'm a very important man from America. And now," he said, "if you'll excuse me, I think I better go lie down."

11

Self-Inflicted

It was one of those winters that wears down, flattens out, and slips away. Not toward anything in particular (the spring, like a girl getting ready for a prom date, was still primping upstairs and would condescend to arrive in her own sweet time) but just away, away from its own brown, twiggy vistas, its sparse dispensations of light, its fixed and frozen parameters. On the first day of March the temperature climbed into the forties and stayed there. The sky was like dishwater. The snow had long since stopped falling; even the rain couldn't be bothered to get itself together. The ice around the lake receded incrementally, like an old person's gums. Everywhere you walked there was slush and mud, the soft suck-and-wheeze of feet being inhaled by the very medium they counted on for support.

Really unusual weather, said the good people of Carthage. It was, to be fair, what they said about all of their weather.

Not that Oren had ever paid much attention to the good people of Carthage. Not that the things he didn't pay much attention to their talking about—maple sugaring, the price of gas, the college basketball rankings—were any more interesting these days than whatever he hadn't paid much attention to their talking about previously. But at least they were different, he thought. At least they were new.

Newness: he was obsessed with it now. He had come upon the word in an essay by Emerson, and had not let it go. This newness he sought was not some abstract idea or formula you drew up in chalk on a blackboard, but a base, earthly element, something you quarried up with dirt from the ground. Something you discovered, not invented. Something *already there.* The design embedded in the carpet. The scrambled message in the acrostic. The tiny blue egg cradled in straw at the bottom of a nest. A newness that lay latent in its opposite, like oil in rock. All you had to do to get at it, he thought, was break through the crust. Break through the crust, and pump hard, and then the stuff of the future would come spurting out.

Of course breaking through anything was bound to cause a little damage. That *he* might be the one damaged was a possibility Oren preferred not to dwell upon at the moment. If by trading away certain problem areas in his life (celibacy, loneliness, too much time alone), he'd only succeeded in exposing new ones (guilt, performance anxiety, not enough time alone), and if these problem areas too would in time have to be traded for others . . . no, he was in too good a mood this morning to dwell on such things. As he winged down the wooded lanes toward Carthage proper—a route now grown so familiar he could drive it, and often did, with his eyes half-closed—his window rolled down, the breeze fluffing out his still-thickly abundant, still-blondish hair, the head to which that hair was rooted felt far too dreamy and content, his tongue too fuzzy and thick, his belly too bloated, his penis too warm and webby from its nocturnal spelunk in Gail's vaginal grottoes, to indulge in the usual top-down brooding and navel investigation for which he was, in the ever-receding circle of his acquaintances, mildly famous. No more brooding, Oren thought. He was an ex-brooder now. Indeed, he couldn't remember the last time he'd felt so unburdened by bad thoughts, and by bad thoughts' clamorous retinue, the Four Horsemen of His Consciousness: Fear, Worry, Anxiety, Depression.

This, it seemed, was what having regular sex *did* for people: swept the cobwebs and clutter from the mind's garage. Left every tool hanging from its hook. Oren had almost forgotten how it felt, to be at once utterly spent and utterly relaxed, a vessel that emptied and filled and then emptied again, impersonally. No wonder he'd been at loose ends: he hadn't enjoyed regular sex since he'd broken up with Sabine. And regular sex with Sabine had never been all that regular, and frankly not all that sexy or enjoyable either. No, with Sabine it was really the aftermath they savored: the quiet clinging, the soft, attenuating glow. Two high-strung people cuddling under blankets, taking refuge from a perplexing world. He was a bit like a girl in that sense, he supposed. His therapist used to say he had a lot of anima. It had to do with his mother apparently, but then what didn't?

Only here was the bewildering part, and the reason it didn't pay to think too much about these things: it was only now that he'd begun to enjoy regular sex with Gail, that he began to miss, retroactively but intensely, the regular sex he'd long since stopped having with Sabine. He missed it more now, in truth, than he had during all those months of no regular sex, and very little *ir*regular sex to speak of either. Why? Was everyone else as bad at living in the moment as he was? Were other people as subject to these same wayward and regressive fits of nostalgia? Was Sabine, for example, cabbing home at this moment from some Rivington Street rendezvous, thinking about how much she missed *him*?

He looked out at the leaden mist that hung over, or clung to, the flattened fields. Soon the mist would burn off, and fresh patches of green would lie revealed in the snow, like vents for the earth, that underground man, to breathe through. He supposed the alarmists were right: the globe was warming up. The permafrost was not so perma these days, and not so frosty either. Even the baggy gray cushions of the clouds overhead seemed a function of thaw and seepage. He wished he were the sort of firebrand teacher he read about in the newspapers, the kind who inspired students to organize demonstrations and march on the state capital. Global time was so short, and double-bloc classes so long, and the curriculum so dull, and the culture so insular and attention-deficient . . . if the Orens of the world didn't give these kids a crash course in the body politic, who would?

But, no, political activism was generally fueled by rage, and the Orens of the world were not rage people. No, the Orens of the world, thanks he supposed to all this anima of theirs, tended to be conflict-avoiding, simmer-not-burn types, resilient, double-minded, highly adaptable to the prevailing climate. Even when that climate had gone catastrophically awry. Which, given how relaxed and well sexed he was feeling this morning, as he pulled up to the doughnut shop for his morning coffee, and given how despite all the persuasive new data and computer projections, the dissolving ice caps, the polar bears floundering for purchase on eroding shores, it was still cold enough in the Dodge to see clouds of breath huffing dismally out his mouth like steam from a grate, combined to make his outrage over global warming seem rather abstract and hypothetical at the moment, even to him, and in no way a deterrent from leaving the Dodge's gluttonous, inefficient six-cylinder engine idling in the parking lot of the doughnut shop while he ran inside for a cup of their miserable coffee.

"Hi, can I help you?"

Naturally in this age of universal abundance, no place within thirty miles served a decent espresso. Oren had taken to getting a large container of *premium artisan blend* and hoping for the best. "Just the usual," he said, as if apologizing for some obscure failure of imagination. "Large coffee."

"Mmm."

Mornings in a doughnut shop are romantic occasions. The scent of refined sugars wafting from the trays, the rack of crisply folded newspapers by the door, the workingmen reading the sports pages, filling in their pool brackets for March Madness . . . it gave an underdog hope. Perhaps that was why he always felt obliged to flirt with the pretty oval-faced waitress who worked behind the counter on Mondays, Wednesdays, and Fridays.

"Cool earrings today." He smiled privately, like a poker player eyeing a flush. His clothes still reeked of last night's sex, he was pretty certain of that. "What are they, jade?"

"Mm-hmm." She frowned; her left hand flew up to her lobe for reassurance. The lavender blouse she was wearing, with its foreshortened waist, lifted from her tiny, involuted navel, providing the usual soft-core exposure of flesh. "Black, no sugar, right?"

He nodded. It was worth drinking bad coffee sometimes just to be recognized as a regular customer, with all the perks that went with it.

She went over to the doughnut racks. "Glazed old-fashioned?"

"No."

"No doughnut today?"

"No."

Good as it felt to be recognized as a regular customer, it felt bad if not worse to be recognized as some *other* regular customer. Why did so many of his life's transactions come under question? He must give off some vibe of hesitation, he thought, some failure of the acquiring will. "Actually," he said, "I don't eat doughnuts. They're terrible for you."

"I don't like them either."

"It's not that. I do like them. I like them way too much. If I let myself I'd eat five doughnuts at a time. So I make a point of not letting myself, you know?"

The girl behind the counter took this unsolicited confession in stride. She fitted a cardboard cup with a cardboard sleeve and held it carelessly under the percolator. "Coffee's bad for you too," she observed.

"You're right." How nice to meet a kindred spirit, he thought, a fellow featherweight in this land of giants. He tried not to look down at the girl's trim, bare waistline again, or to think about how she spent her Tuesdays and Thursdays; tried not to linger over her flaming-red hair, or the prodigious slope and swell of her body, the lean, elongated, small-breasted torso sweeping up like a stem from the round bulb of her rear. Though why, after two racking and voluble orgasms with Gail the night before, he'd even be *looking* at this girl's body, let alone lusting after it—a girl he didn't know, and who rarely remembered his regular order, and was in fact borderline rude to him pretty much every time he came in—was a mystery to Oren, even if it did not appear to be one to the cashier herself. She turned her back to him now, their business done; she zipped her face shut like someone putting away a cello. The way people do when they're indifferent to your gaze, when you're in no way sexually relevant to them.

Then he saw his face reflected back at him in the glass counter, and he knew why. He was beginning to look his age. And his age was no longer young. His skin was no longer as smooth, his waist no longer as lean, his eyes no longer as bright as those of the guys a girl like this went out with. He was playing for the other team now. The losing team. A terrible thought took shape in his head: *he'd never have sex with a girl like this again.* The leaden gate was closing, squealing shut. Never again would a girl like this lead him by the hand to her one-bedroom apartment over someone's garage, with the candles on the nightstand and the Indian bedspread and the Buddhistic texts; never again would a girl like this massage his bony shoulders with exotic lotions and oils her sister had sent her from Santa Fe, and undertake to reveal to him the slow, unfolding mysteries of the tantra. It was unfair and unjust, but it was the case. And now the case was closed. He could read it in her flat efficient movements as she fitted his cup with a plastic lid. Time to take his to-go cup and go.

Except all of a sudden he really did want a doughnut. In fact he wanted two.

"Hi, can I help you?" the girl said to the next fellow in line, a younger guy in torn jeans and a flannel shirt.

"Hey there, Pammy."

Pammy. The door wheezed closed behind him. Pammy.

It may have been the soft, cheery murmur of that name. It may have been the blast of cold wind that greeted him outside, or the tubercular rattle of the muffler, or the syrupy light dawn was pouring so stingily over the bare flat waffle-colored fields. Or it may have been the lousy coffee, at once weak and astringent, as if the beans' overseas journey in a burlap sack had denuded them of whatever dispensations they'd been granted by their rich homeland soil. Whatever it was, it was giving Oren a headache. To teach for a living was to ensure you'd never outgrow that childhood anxiety dream, running late for school. He had thirty-five minutes until the first bell to shower and shave, eat his breakfast, and review his lesson plans for the day ahead. So he gunned the engine in reverse and got back on the road.

A hawk soared overhead, turning straight lines into question marks. In his hurry to get grounded, it hadn't occurred to Oren how much nostalgia he'd feel for the air, for those fine invisible currents that kept you aloft.

Because the Dodge was a lean, pared-down machine that pre-dated such bourgeois extravagances as cup holders, he was forced to place his coffee delicately between his thighs and try to avoid all the fast turns and frost heaves and speed bumps. It would have been smarter to stop loading up on bad coffee, of course, on his way to work, but that would require him to get more sleep at night, and to drink less wine, and smoke less dope, and have less sex than he was having too. He hadn't done quite so much drinking/dope-smoking/sex-having since college. But Gail Hastings had been a good girl back at college, had failed to get drunk and high and laid as often as she should have, and now she appeared to be making up for lost time.

Below his jeans, tiny blisters were rising. The coffee spurted up in bubbles through the slotted lid.

In bed these days he was no longer so reticent or withheld but giddy and licentious, like a teenager drunk on some absent parent's booze. His throat was an uncorked bottle; the words poured out in glugs. The need to bare himself to her, confess his long history of false starts and premature conclusions, his whole bloated inventory of wishes, lies, and dreams, came tunneling up from his core. Nothing went unsaid. No bad relationship, no botched degree, no shameful act or nonact; not even the highly explicit fantasies to which he'd masturbate sometimes during A-Lunch behind the one stall door in the teachers' lavatory that actually closed, while food was flung and spitballs spat in great wadded bursts a few short yards away . . . fantasies that revolved ecstatically and kaleidoscopically around Gail herself, her red, one-piece bathing suit that showed off her broad back and rippling hamstrings, her long, inquisitive nipples . . . even these fantasies, *especially* these fantasies, he refused to censor or sanitize or in any way repress. Because he wasn't ashamed of who he was. And even if he *was* ashamed of who he was—and come to think of it, he probably should have been—that was okay too, because it meant he was changing, becoming a new man, a man capable of feeling (among other things) shame over the past. And a man capable of feeling shame over the past was not by definition shameful at all. At least Oren hoped he wasn't. At least not in the same way.

Oh, he'd been wary at first, quiet and evasive and irresolute in the sack. But now all that had changed. He was no longer a spectator. He was an accomplished adulterer. A gambler at the big-stakes table. All-in.

"So who do you fantasize about now?" Gail had asked him that morning, in her blunt, not-so-good-at-teasing way.

"What makes you think I've stopped fantasizing about you?"

"It's obvious. People only fantasize about what isn't there." She shook her hair out a little; the curls straightened a moment, then snapped back into place. "And I, as you may have noticed, am here."

"You're saying that married people never fantasize about their spouses?"

"Oh, married people . . ." Her voice trailed off, her eyes gone gelid in their dark pouches. Why had he brought that up?

"I'm not all that interested in fantasies at the moment," he said. "I've had a bellyful. I was starting to worry I'd turn into one of those guys who lives alone with a lot of cats and has all these weird trivial fetishes, like your cousin Don. I like reality better now. I'm starting to think it agrees with me."

Gail smiled placidly but said nothing.

"I'd like to think it agrees with you too," he said.

Again she said nothing. Her jaw was set but her eyes wandered. Was she leaving him already? Plunging back into her own private natatorium? This middle-aged, provincial woman with the messy briefcase and unshaved legs, who'd been out of the country, other than weekend trips to Montreal, all of twice, who'd slept with all of three men in her life, who had no evident or quantifiable sense of humor, who remained either hostile or indifferent to virtually every cultural icon (Dylan, Beckett, Preston Sturges, the Clash) he held dear . . . what was the source of her power over him? How had she reduced him, in a few short months, to this sack of formless putty, waiting only to be taken in her mouth and breathed into life, into definition? The whole thing was unfathomable. He might as well be standing at the ocean, trying to fathom that. He remembered a line from Nietzsche, how in every couple one person looks out the window, and the other looks in. It was the kind of profound insight only a brilliant, syphilitic madman could come up with. And in Oren's case it was true. Typically he began as the one looking out, then somehow by the end wound up the other. He supposed something was wrong with his *way* of looking out, however, some excess or deficit that incited the women in his life to want to look out themselves. It was very disheartening.

At the same time it was also very *heartening,* he thought, to have it matter so much to him who was looking where. So he tried to stay positive on the new-relationship front. Tried not to begrudge Gail her other activities and obligations. Tried not to fret when she was late for a rendezvous, not to pout when she canceled, not to seize on every wistful sigh, truncated phone call, or less than spectacular orgasm like a prosecutor gathering an indictment. What did he expect? He'd got himself involved with a lawyer, a mother, a married woman. No one had imposed these burdens on him; he'd taken them on himself. Deliberately, methodically. And if he'd overshot the target somewhat, if in his panic to nail down some of the looming intangibles of his youth, the job and the house and the woman, the things that rooted you in place, he'd skipped over the best part of his adulthood, gone directly from a (protracted) late adolescence to a (premature) middle age without ever passing Go; if he now discovered himself to be boxed in and trapped at the center of the board, the Chance cards gone, no Get Out of Jail Free, in a game he could already imagine growing tired of someday— well, that was the deal he'd signed up for, and he would accept it and submit to it, as prematurely middle-aged people do. Yes, looking at him now, you'd have almost thought he was growing up, or going mad, or whatever it was you called it when you began deliberately and methodically to cause yourself pain.

12

The Egg, Walking

"What time do you have?" Teddy asked. He shaded his eyes, trying to gauge the sun's position, its temporary arrest, its slow-motion decline. His watch had long since given up the ghost. Without it, the heat, the cloudless sky, the sight of his own big, doughy hand in front of his face, puffy and ridged like a pastry—it all left him feeling a bit alien, unmoored.

"Four fifteen," said Dr. Dave.

"We're not going to make it tonight, are we?"

"It's the hot season. Radiators get cranky when they're hot, just like us."

"What about the train?"

"Last time I took the Djibouti line," the doctor said, "it broke down before we left the station. They wouldn't let us off. The lights weren't working, the windows were wedged shut. Some of the women fainted. They had to be taken off on stretchers."

"Big deal," Teddy said. "You're talking to an Amtrak rider. We're used to that sort of thing."

"There were some Somali soldiers on board on their way back from leave. They'd been drinking all day. They held a pissing competition in the aisle that got fairly heated. Then they started in hassling the passengers." He scratched at the label on his beer bottle with the tip of his thumb. "Naturally, being soldiers, they were drawn to the women first. They had a whole routine they'd worked out. First they'd ask for a cigarette. Then they'd ask for a light. Then, if the girl was especially pretty, they'd ask f—"

"Okay, okay. The train's out."

"That line's been discontinued anyway." The doctor took a sip of his Castel. "Cutbacks." He leaned back on his stool, his fingers laced behind the back of his faded Dartmouth baseball cap, his legs outstretched, like an accountant on his lunch hour. He was a short, stoop-shouldered man in a polo shirt and running shoes. Behind the zealous magnifications of his glasses his blue eyes had a hard, particulate shine. If his temperament were a mineral it would have been quartz.

Teddy had liked him right off. They'd been traveling together for three days now, through the dry plains east and north of Addis, visiting clinics in small villages, delivering medicines. It had been Danielle's idea, and a good one, that he tag along. "You wanted to see the Danakil, right? Like this guy Thesiger you told me about? Okay, here's your chance." She had her back to him as she spoke; nonetheless he could read in the tight line of her shoulders how eager she was to be rid of him already. And why? He'd only just arrived.

Still, she'd been right. It was an opportunity like no other. And after a week in filthy, teeming Addis, it felt good to be out on the road again, a free agent, exploring unknown provinces. And he liked David Fleming, this brisk, intense, no-nonsense little doctor, this renegade Catholic with his choppy haircut and tube socks. The man had energy. Even idle, he jiggled his knees below his chair, fanning his thighs. Like most men of science he assumed he knew more about the things you were curious about than you did about the things he was curious about. Generally this proved true. He had come to East Africa after med school to do research in tuberculosis and other infectious diseases, while he considered which of the dozen top-tier residencies he'd been offered up and down the Eastern seaboard appealed to him. East Africa turned out to be something of a gold mine for infectious diseases. Of course it was generously endowed with noninfectious diseases as well. Diseases as a rule tended to flourish over here in East Africa. And so, it seemed, did Dr. Dave. Now he had an Ethiopian wife, five adopted children, research and consulting gigs from Cairo to Nairobi, and all the infectious diseases you could ever want. Three days a week care packages arrived via FedEx, chemo drugs and retrovirals from Brussels or Houston or Johannesburg. Just to keep track of what came in seemed an enormous task. And what went out—the X-rays, the blood samples, the digital photos of monstrous deformities—that too. Yet here he sat, marooned on the dreary outskirts of Dire Dawa, drinking Castels in the heat of the afternoon and shooting the shit with Teddy Hastings, fugitive and child pornographer at large.

"I don't get it," Teddy said. "How do you get anything done in these dysfunctional conditions? It would drive me nuts."

"You wouldn't be the first," Dave said. "White people have been going crazy in Africa for centuries. It's part of the attraction."

"I don't see *any* attraction."

"You will. You just have to unlearn some stuff first. At bottom you see we're a very primitive, superstitious race."

"Us?"

"Take this idea of ours that things should go on working the way they're supposed to. If the electric is on today, we think, it will come on tomorrow too. If the mail arrives in the afternoon today, it will come tomorrow around the same time."

"What's superstitious about that?"

"Well, it's not very realistic, is it? It's just blind faith in some higher power grid we can't see. Africans are more modern. They don't expect to have everything under control all the time. They don't even *want* to. So the idea of losing that control doesn't paralyze them like it does us."

"Maybe if it did," Teddy said, "they'd work harder to keep it."

"Maybe." The doctor nodded pleasantly, but his voice turned a degree or two colder. "Or maybe neither of us are in any position to lecture these people about how hard they should work."

"Okay, don't get all huffy. We're just talking."

"One thing you learn right away, practicing medicine here. Don't be a stickler. You go for home runs, you'll strike out every time. The thing is to make contact. Remember: the perfect is the enemy of the good."

"We say that at the middle school too. On the other hand, the bad is the enemy of the good too, no? Like that van of yours—what a piece of crap. I thought you people here all drove around in Land Rovers."

"You people?"

"You know what I mean," Teddy said. "Every soccer mom in New England goes zipping off to the mall in one of those big off-road safari vehicles. So why are you poking along in that rattletrap clunker is the question."

Dr. Dave looked down at his running shoes and shrugged philosophically, his eyes hidden below his cap's peaked visor. "It hasn't been a priority. I'm not that well funded."

"Well, we'll have to do something about that," Teddy said.

"We?"

"Somebody." Flies were buzzing his arm like some weedy, overgrown airstrip. He tried to wave them away. "You want to get this school of yours up and running? You need somebody writing grants. Somebody doing assessments, evaluation. Tech support. Building and maintenance. Educational consultants."

"Yes, that would all be very useful, I'm sure."

"Useful? Try the raw minimum. Day one." God, he missed it, being a principal, a main man. Sitting in his big leather chair with a mug of fresh coffee and an oversize muffin, bossing people around. "You have to go about these things professionally. Time is at a premium. You're an expert in your field. What sense does it make, humping all this valuable medicine around, hundreds of people dependent on you, and you lose a whole day to something as trivial as a blown radiator? That's just wrong."

The doctor gave a gnomic smile. "Who's to say what's trivial? The older I get, the less I can tell the difference."

Here we go, Teddy thought: another Buddhist. The harder you pushed the guy to admit to a recognizable emotion—boredom, frustration, rage—the more he receded into the shade of his own private serenity garden. Some people were like that under stress: they shut down. Teddy as it happened was the opposite. Stress opened him up. Pricked by thorns, he blossomed like a cactus flower.

But you could only open up for so long. And by now they'd been marooned here for two and a half hours, waiting for the van to be attended to at the ARCO service garage across the street. It was the only car in the place. Yet, for all the spirited commentary it had inspired among the three lean-faced young mechanics—the tutting laments, the vigorous philosophical forays into diagnostic theory—no one had showed much interest in actually dirtying their hands and *dealing* with the thing. That was an oral culture for you, Teddy thought. Every decision collectively discussed. Like that other feckless and intransigent tribe, the Carthage Union School Board. He was ready at this point to roll up his sleeves and dive under the hood himself. But the inner workings of the motor were strange to him. Anyway it was too hot to be outside.

It was too hot to be inside too, of course, but here he was. The air was stifling. Flies clustered congenially in the ashtrays. The sluggish, rocking revolutions of the ceiling fan did nothing to dislodge them; the cure seemed worse than the disease. Half the blades were missing, the others waved rhetorically at the walls, generating their own hot air, like politicians in a motorcade. Reddish dust flew in through the windows and settled over the tables like a benediction.

They drank some more Castels. As cheap, flat, tepid beer went, it wasn't bad. Teddy had stopped drinking beer after that disastrous night at the Lyons' Den; only now did he remember why. He yawned mightily and scratched his many bug bites. High up on the wall-mounted television, *King Kong*—not the original but the remake, and a low-quality bootleg at that—was suffering the torments of all wild things, being chased around by white people smaller and less powerful than himself.

Teddy's heart gave a squeeze, shuddered in its shell. A dense liquid sensation ran through his chest like a yoke. *Sorry, friend,* he thought, *the world's a bad movie, endlessly remade; there's no getting free.* You fled your native state with the highest of hopes, only to find the things you'd left behind you had run on ahead, were already there waiting when you arrived. He thought of all the used goods he'd seen peddled on the sidewalks of Addis—the cast-off hardware and corrupted software, the tattered jeans, the old T-shirts with runic, fading logos. Africa was where old things wound up when they lost their shape and sheen. One last go-round before they wore out completely.

How lamentable, Teddy thought. To have come so far only to be encased in the same old shit.

Dr. Dave was thumbing through a newspaper someone had left behind. It did not look too current.

"So what's the news?"

"Nothing too exciting. Government crackdowns. Borders on alert. Temporary shortages."

"Crackdowns on what? On alert for what? Shortages of what?"

"Doesn't say."

"Well, pass me the sports section, will you? I want to check the standings."

"You're welcome to try. Keep in mind they're in Amharic."

"Doesn't matter," Teddy said. "Numbers are the same in any language."

They drank another couple of beers each, passing the sections of the newspaper back and forth in silence, like a suburban couple on a Sunday afternoon. Outside the sun sank toward the foothills. Teddy's stomach was rumbling again, secreting dull, miasmic vapors and gases. He was down to his last roll of Tums. Between the heat and the beer and the spicy foods they'd been eating, the rubbery, gray *injera,* the desiccated chicken parts and puddly sheens of clarified butter, he'd been tossing down the

340

antacids like M&M's. He'd enjoyed the food as he ate it of course, but now his inner organs felt crowded, the grease lay on his lips like a clown mask. He sat there belching softly, poring over scores he didn't understand for games he hadn't seen. A small expeditionary guerrilla force of biting insects traipsed through the jungle of his chest hair, hacking a path to his navel. His lids drooped. His neck itched. Below his wrinkled khakis his boxers scratched at his balls; the fabric, saggy and stretched, had long since soaked through. "I think I'm kind of starting to like this place," he said.

"Shh. Listen."

"What?"

"The kids. They're singing. Can you hear them?"

"Now that you mention it, yeah."

High, piping voices floated up from the riverbed, where white-shawled children picked their way barefoot along the banks, herding goats. The doctor scratched one cheek with the backs of his fingers, his eyes tender. "Look, I'm not belittling the problems," he said, "but if they could just catch a break, they've got tremendous resources. Half the population of Africa is under fifteen. Do you have any idea what that means?"

"Yeah. They're going to need a whole shitload of middle schools."

"It means they can solve their own problems, if we just stay out of their way. Look out at those fields. That teff they're growing? It's the most nutritious grain in the world. The people want to work. Why are we giving them eight hundred million dollars in aid and almost nothing in agricultural development, nothing in roads and infrastructure? How does that help? The farmers can't compete with free food: they give up. If we could just level the playing field a little, let them compete equably for a change in the world market—think what they could do here."

The doctor spoke of Africa, Teddy reflected, as if it were some chronically underperforming, small-market baseball team; if you kicked out the old management and built up the farm system, everything would be fine. But maybe he was right. Teddy for his part was ready for a nap. A rift yawned open in his mind, between where he was and his understanding of the forces that had led him here. Some part of him had already detached itself and gone running on ahead to Harar—Harar, the ancient gateway to the east, where he and the doctor, if the gods of ARCO permitted, would arrive tomorrow. He tried to focus on that, on what lay ahead, beyond the arching doorway—the round, thatched-roof huts, the thorn trees silhouetted against the sky, the camels trudging through the haze, silent as an apparition, bearing sacks of salt from the brown hills of Somalia.

"Christ," he blurted, "it is beautiful here, isn't it?"

The doctor paused; he looked almost angry. Apparently he'd still been talking all this time.

"It's beautiful," he agreed, "and it hurts."

"Think the van's ready?"

"No."

"I've lost track of how long we've been sitting here."

"So have they, I'm sure." Dave set down his paper. "There's a saying around here. *Kes be kes inculal bekuro yihedal.* Step by step, the egg starts walking."

"Yeah, well, I'm not a step-by-step person. It's not to my credit, I know. It's just how I'm made."

"You can change how you're made."

"Think so?"

"I know so." Dave thought for a moment. "My predecessor told me a story when I first came. It's about one of your explorers. One of those well-bred young athletic Brits who wants to make a name for himself before he settles down for good on the family estate. So naturally he heads off to Africa. Puts this huge expedition together and goes marching into the bush. Makes fantastic progress too. He finds mountains no one knew about, lakes that aren't on any of the maps, animal species that have no name. He makes notes for the book he'll write, the lectures he'll give at the Royal Geographic Society. Nothing but glory ahead, right?

"Then one day something happens with the porters. They just stop. Stop for no reason. "The explorer isn't abusing them, there's nothing unusual about the weather, it's a day like any other. They just stop. The explorer doesn't know what to do. He doesn't speak the language, he's sent his interpreter on ahead to the next village. So he gets down on his knees and lays out his maps. He talks very reasonably about the schedule he's worked out, the need to avoid the rainy season, the dwindling rations and supplies and so on. The porters just sit there. He starts to panic. He promises them whatever they want—more food, more money, more women. They still won't budge."

"They weren't members of the Teachers Federation by any chance?"

"Okay, so now he's losing it for real. He's waving around the hunting rifle, screaming threats, ready to kill them all. *Exterminate the brutes,* right? Only just then, as luck would have it, his trusted interpreter returns. Right away he sizes up the situation. O great one, he says, put your gun away, your bearers revere you like a god. It is only that your progress has been so glorious, they *must* stop.

"But why? the explorer asks him. What's the problem?

"They must stop, the interpreter says, to wait for their souls to catch up."

"Good one," Teddy said after a moment. "So what was the real reason?"

"What do you mean?"

"Well, obviously the explorer was a boob. He'd buy any dumb story the interpreter sold him."

"But it wasn't a story. The interpreter was telling the truth."

Teddy frowned. Clearly he'd misheard something in the doctor's tale, something crucial and salient, but what? Gail was right, he never listened closely enough when other people talked. Other people's stories, like other people's dreams, they just weren't his forte. "Well, fine, if you say so. But I don't see the relevance."

"The relevance?"

"We're Americans, dammit. We don't *have* souls."

The doctor's brow knotted for a moment; he appeared to be ready to laugh, but didn't.

"Let's go see about that radiator," he said.

The radiator could not be fixed, however, only replaced, and the fellows at the ARCO station had no replacement parts of that size in stock. They had no replacement parts of *any* size in stock. Which raised the question of what they meant by stock, exactly. Their entire inventory, so far as Teddy could determine, consisted of two crates of motor oil, a six-pack of orange soda pop, and some cartons of Dunhills. That, and the enormous mound of threadbare, multiply lacerated tires heaped behind the station.

"Tomorrow maybe will be better," they offered, with no special conviction. "We cannot know for sure."

"Tomorrow *will* be better," Dave said. Beneath his beige surface tones, gravel was in his voice now, the dregs of an unglimpsed bottom. Zen patience and cultural relativism were all well and good, but he had medicine to deliver, patients to see. "Okay? Am I making myself clear?"

"Yes, okay, okay."

A brief, murmured conference in Amharic followed among the mechanics. It was the most animated Teddy had seen them. They came back to present an offer of their own. Then, in a solemn, highly ritualized ceremony, several hundred birr changed hands (the notes so faded the numbers could hardly be read), after which the mechanics went back to whatever it was they'd been doing—i.e., not much—and the two weary, beer-sodden Americans hailed a taxi downtown to the Ras Hotel.

"The best of a bad bunch," Dave said, "accommodations-wise. Let's hope it's only one night."

Indeed, the Ras was not a particularly fresh or presentable-looking hotel. Though the façade was being whitewashed when they arrived, which seemed an encouraging sign, the justification for it, they discovered later—a recent grenade attack—was not. No surprise, a lot of rooms were available, and at a very reasonable price. "What do you think?" Dave turned to Teddy at the front desk. "Go for two singles, or share a double?"

One reason they got along, he and the doctor: they were both cheap. At moments like this Teddy understood how Robinson Crusoe must have felt, tracing those footsteps in the sand: here was the companion he hadn't realized he'd been missing. "Hell, live a little. Make it two doubles. I've seen the beds in this country."

Up in the room, however, he took a pass on the beds, which were bow-shaped, and on the television, which didn't work, and on the shower, which was filthy and cold, and on the bottled water, which had a broken seal, and on the tiny balcony with its view of the kidney-shaped pool in the courtyard, which was slimy and viscous and green, as if someone had mistakenly filled it with motor oil. This left nothing to do but head down to the adjoining restaurant, and wait for the doctor to finish his nap.

He took a seat at a table for two in the back. The menu offered several variations on the theme of spaghetti and toast. Teddy looked it over hopelessly. The room was full of foreigners—Russian businessmen, Chinese bureaucrats, Swedish missionaries, an Elderhostel tour from Holland, three brawny Uruguayan helicopter pilots who worked for UNESCO, and, at the bar, surveying them all with seamless and regal disinterest, two striking young women of local provenance who turned out to be prostitutes. Teddy found this out the hard way: by stopping to chitchat on his way back from the men's room. That got their attention, all right.

The three of them were still chatting warmly at his table, discussing the vagaries of auto mechanics and other twists of fate, when the doctor wandered in, looking no better rested than he had before his nap. His eyes were small and red, blinking rapidly in a flutter. His hair was stiff from his cap; it stuck straight up in patches, like Dennis the Menace. He failed to spot Teddy at first, or maybe he just pretended to.

"Here." Teddy handed him a Castel. "I took the liberty."

"Looks like you've taken more than one liberty here."

"Doc, I want you to meet my new friends, Fruweni and . . . tell me your name again, dear?"

"Adey."

"Adey. That's a pretty name. What does it mean?"

"Mean?"

The doctor said something to the girls in Amharic. Whatever it was seemed to chill the air a bit.

"Okay, so what should we drink to?" Teddy said.

"Let's drink to eating," the doctor said.

"No, I got it. Let's drink to tomorrow. *Tomorrow maybe will be better,* right?"

"Tomorrow."

They all clinked bottles. Tomorrow, they agreed, was an attractive proposition in any culture. Of course as far as the ARCO guys were concerned, so in all likelihood was the day after tomorrow. But they'd deal with that later. They'd deal with that tomorrow.

"You've decided to live dangerously, I see," Dave said, after the girls had excused themselves and gone back to their stations at the bar.

"C'mon, we were just talking. They're a couple of kids. I've got one their age at home."

Dave turned in his chair and studied them thoughtfully. "I have to say, I don't like the looks of that tall one. Did you see that rash on her arm?" His gaze was dry, clinical. "Typhoid. It's progressed too."

"You can tell that from here?"

"Typhoid isn't subtle. She needs some sulfa or ampicillin in her system right away." He glanced down at the menu and scowled. "Looks like pasta night for me. What'll you have?"

"Nothing. Jesus, how can you eat? I'm still sick as a dog from lunch."

"Have some toast. You need to keep up your strength."

"It's not my strength I'm worried about." In fact he *was* worried about his strength, but he was worried about a lot of other things too. "Those drugs you mentioned. You've got those in your bag, don't you? Back up in the room?"

"She'll never take them." Dave was still looking over the menu. "It would be a waste of perfectly good drugs that could go to someone else."

"What happened to *tomorrow maybe will be better*? What happened to *the perfect is the enemy of the good*?"

Dave pursed his mouth in a grudging frown, like a tutor whose slowest student has just bagged a B-plus. "Have another beer."

They gave their order to the waiter. Then they turned back to face each other across the table. Suddenly there was nothing left to say.

The next morning, after cold, dribbling showers from the lime-encrusted tap, they took a cab out to the ARCO station to check on the van. The mechanics had only just begun to straggle in, however, for their long day of lassitude and nonlabor. Clearly it would be a while. "What now?"

"I'm not sure."

"I'm still hungover from yesterday. I can't bear the thought of that café again."

"Tell you what," Dave said. "We're Americans, right? We'll do what Americans do when they're bored and stressed."

"We're going to invade another country?"

"We'll go shopping."

At that hour the downtown Mercado, a huge, rambling, open-air bazaar behind Moorish gates, was already thronged. Women in traditional dresses squatted under their parasols, waving flies off their little piles of produce—peppers, tomatoes, red onions, mangoes and lemons and prickly pears. Dave strolled casually through the stalls, exchanging greetings with the merchants. Teddy hurried along behind him, jugs of oil wobbling in his wake. It wasn't easy negotiating the aisles: the passages were narrow and his hips were lumpy and wide. He caused a little damage in the spice area, where a few reed baskets full of *berbere* and turmeric and fenugreek wound up toppling in the dirt. He tried to atone for this by reaching into his fanny pack and tossing around money indiscriminately, like some visiting dignitary from FEMA. In this way he attracted a following.

"Wait here," Dave said. "I'll be right back. Try not to knock anything else over."

Teddy watched him disappear into the maze of stalls. Through the sagging canopy of burlap sacks the sun blazed down in slanting columns, agitating the dust. Smells of roasting meat came wafting over from the butcher shops. All he had to do was stand there with his hands in his pockets. But the kids kept pestering him, trying to sell him a lot of cheap, plastic, Chinese-made things he had no use for, and thus initiating the tedious daily round of moral self-investigation. There was no escape from it. Surely these kids and their particular cheap, plastic, Chinese-made things were as good and deserving as anyone's. So why not shell out for them all? Meanwhile people were jostling him from behind, trying to get at the goods. They had meals to shop for and families at home to cook for. Why was he in the way?

You had a choice, it seemed, between knocking things over and being knocked over. He could find no neutral ground.

At last the doctor came back with an enormous trash bag slung over his shoulder. "Feel the weight of this baby. Two dozen sneakers. I got a deal."

Teddy hefted it approvingly. "You must do a hell of a lot of running."

"They're for the orphanage. The proprietor likes me. He has a nasty case of gout." He observed Teddy for a moment. "What's the matter? You look antsy. You're not hungry already?"

"Famished."

"You should have eaten a proper dinner last night."

"I was exhausted last night." They were like an old married couple now, scoring petty points at each other's expense. It happened when two people traveled together. For the first time, he felt he was betraying Gail. "Come on, let's get something to eat."

"Very well."

Long sticks of incense were smoldering amid the butcher stalls. To keep away the flies, Dave said. But the flies came anyway. They buzzed giddily around the pigeon corpses, the tufted goat hooves, the sheep skulls with their matted, blood-caked fur . . . all these animals that would never know the secular miracle of refrigeration, and lay piled in heaps or dangled upside down from hooks, bleeding into the dust. Amid all this exotic butchery, a bearded Harari gentleman in a blue-green skullcap stood behind a counter, wielding a shiny, medieval-looking scimitar, hacking away at a haunch of gleaming meat.

"Looks like fun," Teddy said amiably, like someone trawling at a crafts fair. "Mind if I watch?"

In truth he liked nothing better than watching men at their work. Shaping things, making things. Stripping away the flaws and excesses. The butcher's acuity and grace, his no-nonsense authority as he set about flaying the carcass, peeling flabby flesh from blameless bone . . . all this entranced him. Teddy stood there reverent. It was as though some timeless ritual of sanctification were being enacted for his benefit.

Do me next, he almost said. Where the words arose from he didn't know.

The butcher glanced up at him now with calm, milky eyes—the eyes of a blind seer. With the point of his knife he impaled a glob of meat, then proferred it to his visitor encouragingly, like a mother urging her son to eat. Teddy took it in his fingers. He was no fan of shopping but he did like free samples. The meat was slippery and warm and smelled rancid beyond belief.

"What is this? Some kind of lamb or mutton?"

"Camel hump," the doctor said.

"Jesus."

"Our friend there must like you. Camel hump isn't cheap. It's something of a delicacy in these parts."

"Just my luck." The butcher was examining Teddy carefully as he spoke, with a fond, even scholarly attention, as if picturing this stout fat-marbled creature hanging upside down with his ribs fanned out like the white keys of an accordion. The real object of exoticism here, the real tourist attraction, was not the butcher, he realized, but himself. "He's going to be insulted if I don't eat this, isn't he?"

Dave smiled. "Undoubtedly."

"But I shouldn't, right? I mean, all the books say you should never eat meat out on the street that hasn't been refrigerated."

"Or washed." Dave rubbed his chin for a second. "It's true, you could contract a nasty parasite. The older the camel, the higher the ash content. That's the rule of thumb. And this one here, poor thing, looks like he's seen better days."

"Ah well, who hasn't?" Teddy thought of the camels he'd seen the previous afternoon, trekking stoically across the lowlands—their melancholic persistence, their elaborated necks, their sly, lofty, aristocratic expressions. "What the hell. What's a little ash between friends."

"Good for you."

Warily he nibbled at the perimeter fat. God knew he and fat were not strangers. The taste was brackish and rank, phlegmy in the mouth. He tried not to breathe, and if possible not to swallow, clamping the fat in the back of his jaw, but some of it leaked down his throat anyway. He gagged. The butcher's gaze grew weighty, concerned. Clearly, in his eyes, this was not the way a man went about eating camel hump. No, the way you went about eating camel hump (the knowledge arrived in Teddy's head with an invisible jerk, like a strike on a line) was by bolting the

whole sticky, spongy mess down fast with no dithering or fore-
thought, and then afterward if necessary you ducked behind a
fence and vomited discreetly. That was the way a man went about
eating camel hump.

The idea, however, proving, as usual, worse than the reality,
the meat shot down his gullet and sank cleanly into his belly
like a stone into a well. "Not bad," he said.

The doctor smiled tolerantly, but he was already sneaking
looks at his watch. Enough nonsense, you could see him thinking, time to get going.

Before they left, however, the butcher wanted his photo taken
with his new friend. Then he wanted this new friend's e-mail
address, because his nephew worked in a government ministry
and had access to a computer. The doctor explained that they
were on the road all week, heading first to Harar and then up
north to the Afar country, so he should not expect an immediate
reply. The butcher nodded, fingering his beard. Then he made a
remark and spat on the ground.

"What?" Teddy said.

"He says we must avoid the Afar. There's nothing out there,
and the people are heathens. They carry long knives—longer
even than his. They castrate their foes."

"C'mon," Teddy said, "that's just an old myth to scare people
away."

"I wouldn't be too sure."

"But you've been up there lots of times. You've never seen
anything like that, right?"

"Actually, no. I've never been to that area. I told you, I'm not
the explorer type. My work keeps me busy. I may not get there
now, either. I'll know better when we get to Harar."

Beyond the eastern gate they came upon the sprawling exurb
of the Mercado where the household goods were sold. It was a
Sargasso of dented pots, rusting tools, recycled appliances, flat-
tired bicycles with buckled frames. Thousands of used auto parts
lay upended in the dirt, like some luckless decimated army. The

doctor waved his hand at the mess expansively. "Not too pretty, is it? Like a Wal-Mart without the walls."

"Why do I have this weird feeling there's a radiator out there somewhere with our name on it?"

"Wouldn't surprise me," the doctor said. "It's where the last one came from too."

When they left Dire Dawa it was late afternoon. They wound their way slowly up the escarpment and into the mountains. It was a new road, freshly laid by Chinese engineers; nonetheless they were the only vehicle on it. The air smelled of hibiscus, climbing roses. The motor, taxed by the climb, sounded petulant and sluggish, like a teenager woken from a nap. The new radiator made a peculiar, warbling rattle that was suspiciously reminiscent of the old radiator. A light mist rolled in. The higher they ascended, the lower the temperature fell. Junipers and cypresses cast shadows over the pavement. Leafy, bright-berried coffee plants grew on the terraced slopes. It was as if, having left the barren heat of the plains, they had now gained access to a lavish private garden, secreted away out of view.

Ahead lay the walled city of Harar.

The arched gate through which they entered was uncomfortably narrow, a needle's eye. It had never been intended for cars. Around them the walls loomed twelve feet high. They inched through the opening, scraping lightly against the stones. They might have been squeezing their way through a birth canal.

Then all at once they were inside, and the gates were behind them, the local chaos in full swing—honking trucks, squawking chickens, braying donkeys. The local dogs rushed to greet them in what appeared to be the local manner, by lunging at the tires and growling viciously.

"Well, Toto," Dave shouted over the din, "we're not in Kansas anymore."

"Where to first, the clinic or the hotel?"

"Too late for the clinic. The day staff has gone home by now."

"The hotel then."

"Maybe. I want to check something first."

They followed the steep cobbled road to the central square. Twin minarets swayed over the rooftops. The sandstone houses were crumbling; the roofs tilted and buckled like huts in a Chagall. Women hurried by in bright-colored shawls, lugging home produce in raffia baskets, their hair parted down the middle and piled up in buns. The men hung out in outdoor cafés, staring dreamily ahead, jaws working steadily, docile and meditative as herd animals. Beneath their white skullcaps their eyes were red. Every so often they'd reach below the tables and snap off leaves from the saplings piled at their feet.

"That's khat they're chewing," Dave said. "It's pretty big around here. Opiate of the masses and all that."

Wistful, Teddy watched them strip the leaves with their teeth, rolling the stems in their mouths. "I wouldn't mind trying some actually."

"Well, just say the word. There's no shortage. The farmers around here have stopped growing coffee. The khat money's better. You can thank your local Starbucks for that."

"We don't have a local Starbucks. The town's too small. We're lucky to have a McDonald's. Where are we going anyway?"

"You'll see."

Deeper they traveled into the city's stubbled, serpentine labyrinth. Kids ran behind them, pounding their back fenders. *You-you, farenji! You-you, farenji!* Girls were scrubbing floors. Cats were yowling in the alleys. The jumbled shanties, the tilting minarets, the drooping electrical poles, the disintegrating balconies—all went by like a dream. Or were they themselves the dream? The walls of the city loomed like gravestones overhead. The radio was hissing, *Get lossst.* Through the shadowed arches of the mosques he saw men on their knees, heads pressed to the floor. A dark cloud rose up in the rearview in a great, funneling column. As if the men in the mosque had summoned it somehow, generated it by prayer. But, no, it was only the tires of the van spitting up dust.

He pointed the camera out the window, framing two old women in luminous red robes against a splintering doorway. Immediately upon seeing him they began to shriek.

"Christ, they hate us here, don't they?" he said, excited in spite of himself.

"What did you expect, trumpets? You've read the books. Why do you think they built those walls, for fun? This is Xeno-phobia Central. Even your friend Burton didn't know if he was a guest or a prisoner. He came dressed in Arab disguise. Otherwise they'd have torn him apart like the others."

"Yeah, well, the last thing I want is another fight."

"Then put the camera away."

He did as he was told. That was his new style. Kindness and tolerance, bland submission. He was done with fighting. True, he'd had some contentious moments back in Carthage before he left, with Gail, with Mimi, with Bruce Germaine, with Fiona Dunn—with a lot of people, come to think of it—but now he was through with all that, he'd laid down his arms and shields. *No más.*

Even when Danielle had told him what she'd told him, that night in her apartment in Addis, he hadn't fought with her, hadn't raised his voice, had only clucked his tongue and made soft, cooing, pigeonlike noises, the mildest, most understated conscientious objections. Not that this had helped very much. Not that this had kept Danielle from pacing furiously around her tiny living room with its solitary, anemic light fixture, shad-owboxing for all she was worth. You'd have thought she'd *wanted* an argument. Was *counting* on an argument. That this was why she'd brought him to Addis—to argue with her. Argue and win. Twenty-year-old women don't call their parents from half a world away just to chat and say hello. There had to be an agenda, a subtext. The pulse of some tiny, hidden truth . . .

He remembered that quip of hers after breakfast at the hotel. *The gift of Gabi.* Suddenly it was clear. Suddenly he understood.

He was here to send her home.

That was why she'd asked for him, and not Gail. She was in a jam, and there was only one way out. Call in the Ogre. The Tyrant. The Barbarian. The Noble Savage. The Big Bully Who Never Listened, and so couldn't be charmed or persuaded or counted upon for empathy. No, he'd just go ahead and do what he always did—carry her off against her will.

He understood this now, his role in things. If she went home on her own, it would feel like a failure, a betrayal. He had to do it for her. He had to pretend to be strong, and she had to pretend to be weak, and in the end everyone would get what he or she wanted.

Of course it was bad behavior on her part, summoning him here under these false, manipulative premises—it was self-indulgent and irresponsible and surely in the scheme of things an important issue to fight about, unless of course one has renounced fighting, in which case maybe not.

Anyway there was no time to fight. She was already in her third month. Already her belly was softening, her breasts swelling with love's milk. Her eyes, bruised and low-hanging, heavy with unshed tears.

Okay, okay, he'd said. *Come here.* What else could he do? Their bodies, themselves: that was how they were raised. He'd pulled her onto his lap, stroked her bony, tremoring shoulders. Patted the clumps and knots in her hair, dabbed the snot from her nose with the back of his hand, smeared the dewy trails that ran down her cheeks like foul lines marking off the shining diamond of her face. *Okay, okay.* She'd clung to him that night as she had at the airport, with the same feverish intensity, the same flush of discovery and relief. As if each new moment were merely a repetition of an old one, which in the repeating became new.

He was beginning to cry now himself. He slipped his American Express card from his wallet and handed it to her like a passkey.

Go home, he said. *No more orphans in the world. Go home.*

I can't, she kept saying, *I can't.*

But in the end she could. She could and she did. It was something of an astonishment, in fact, how little it had taken to persuade her, how easily she'd slipped herself free. How gracefully she'd packed her things, hugged the children at the orphanage good-bye, exchanged gifts and addresses with the staff. And all the while her eyes remained dry. He admired her for it; at the same time it appalled him. He had reached the point, he thought, or they had, where his children were stronger than he was.

Now he watched her settle into the passenger seat of the Lada. One last trip to the airport. He could see relief in her face. Whatever her reservations, it was good to be a passenger again, in transit to someplace new. She had the travel bug bad. It seemed a sickness for which there was no inoculation. And yet her jawline trembled as she blew the kids kisses through the window.

"Call me when you get home," he said. "No more disappearances. From now on I need to know where you are."

"Look who's talking." She'd stared up at him critically through the open window. "You should come back with me, you know. It's going to be a real shit-storm. Just the kind you like."

"One storm at a time. We don't want to overload your poor mother."

"I wouldn't worry about *her.* Did you know, she's already pulled some strings and got me an appointment up in Northfield. This Friday. She's of the opinion that it's a total no-brainer and I should get it over with right away."

"So you've decided then?"

"I think so. I'm not sure. I guess I need to live with it a few more days." Danielle paused, weighing her words. "She asked about you, by the way."

"What did you tell her?"

"I told her the truth. You've been incredibly weird."

"And what did she say?"

"She said, in a good way or a bad way?"

He nodded. It was the same question he'd have asked. In fact he was tempted to ask it now.

"She says to tell you you're missed," Danielle said. "Especially down at the school. I guess it's not working out too well with that guy you got to fill in for you."

"Filling in is hard," he said. "You've got some school issues to deal with yourself I guess, huh? Bridges to unburn?"

She shook her head. "Sucks, doesn't it? The way anything you do that's the least bit different causes all these logistical hassles. But I guess if I want to go to med school someday I don't have much choice."

"Med school!"

"Don't get excited. It's just an idea."

"It's a *good* idea."

"Yeah, well, maybe. I'd have to take, like, a ton of bio and chem courses, which I'll probably hate. But according to Dave it's pretty common, actually. College kids come here on internships or whatever, it gets under your skin. Pretty soon you want to come back and do more than just pour juice and read uplifting stories."

"No *just* about it. You've done wonderful work here, Sweetpea."

"Oh, bullshit, bullshit, bullshit." Suddenly she was furious, either with him or herself. "Is this what happens when you become a parent? You turn into a liar? We both know I've never done anything for anyone but myself. But just because I haven't doesn't mean someday I won't. I mean, hey, look at you."

"Me? Are you kidding? I'm as selfish as the next person. More so."

"I know. But you're like one of those people who're so selfish, it sort of circles around into the opposite. It's weird, but you're kind of my new role model these days."

"Funny, I was just thinking the same about you."

"Bye, Daddy. Come home soon." And with that she'd tapped Yohannes on the shoulder, and the Lada sped away.

Dusk was falling as they parked the van beyond the Old Town walls. The murmur of evening prayers swelled out from the mosques. They walked a while in silence. Behind them they could hear the motor, no longer employed in the travel business, ticking away like a bomb. "It's not far now," Dave said.

"What's the big mystery? Why won't you tell me where we're going?"

"You'll see. You'll like this. You wanted something outside the comfort zone, you said. Or was that just a lot of talk?"

"That camel hump I ate doesn't count?"

The doctor didn't answer; he'd gone rocketing ahead down the alley in his running shoes. Teddy, back-sore, did his best to keep up. This was what he was now: a shadow. His loafers chuffed the ground, raising dust that seemed to erase his footprints behind him, like a photograph on cheap paper. The moon rose, ripe as a blood orange, pocked with unsightly craters. Its dull glow filtered over the streets like a judgment.

There were almost as many bars as there were mosques. In the reeking open drains that ran along the alleys, every base element of the species—the piss, the blood, the phlegm, the shit—could be seen or smelled or by some other sense detected.

"Sshh. There he is."

Dave pointed through the dimness to a spot just beyond the walls, where an old man in faded robes sat cross-legged in the dirt. His eyes were hooded. Cats circled hungrily around the sack at his feet. Nearby, fragments of broken glass gleamed like stars in the moonlight. Beautiful wreckage.

"Listen," Dave whispered, "he's praying."

"I don't hear anything."

"He's praying that Allah watches over him. That he sees the sun come up in the morning, and the city remains peaceful, and no one carries off the children when they're asleep."

"These Sunnis," Teddy said, "they're kind of paranoid, aren't they?"

"On the contrary. Look."

Now the first of the hyenas came bobbing into view. There was no mistaking them: ugly, haggard, they slunk warily down the hillside, ruby eyes aglow, like a posse of schoolboys on their way to detention. Teddy didn't move. It wasn't fear exactly. The stunted legs and spotted heads, the listless, low-slung gait, the yips and yelps of their harsh, eerie laughter, all seemed instinctually familiar, the sound track to a movie he'd seen but forgotten.

The old man waited in the shadow of the wall. His expression was fixed, remote, his jaw working robotically, like a man eating peanuts at a ball game. Then he reached into his sack, and the hyenas surged forward in a frenzy. Their eyes glittered in the dusk.

"Christ, what's he doing? They're getting all riled up."

"He's feeding them," Dave said. "This is his job. He's out here every night."

"Some job."

"Oh, this goes way back," the doctor said. "There's a long tradition here of feeding the hyenas. The Hararis believe they're almost human. It all dates back to this one emir, you see, with a very beautiful daughter."

"Yeah, daughters are tough."

"Seems every night the suitors would come to the palace and pace around outside, scheming how to get in. With all the noise and worry, the emir couldn't sleep. Finally he got mad and turned them into hyenas."

"Nice," Teddy said.

"Actually the Hararis are right. Hyenas *are* like humans. Their brain structures turn out to be remarkably similar. Their social hierarchies too. The only difference is they're matriarchal—the alpha female rules the kill. She takes as much as she wants."

"Come over to my house," Teddy said. "Same thing."

"Shh, here we go."

The hyena man reached again into his burlap bag, and produced what looked to be the mother of all flank steaks—a raw, glistening, purple-black hunk of meat. The blood did not so much drip as pour out of it and puddle on the ground. The first of the hyenas sidled forward. Her movements were slow and lazy, fake casual—head low, eyes half-averted—like a celebrity entering a restaurant. She was a regular customer; there was no hurry. For a moment she sniffed at the blood with a kind of polite connoisseurship, calculating its freshness and bouquet. Then she lunged.

At first she wrestled with the meat as if it were still a living creature, putting up a fight. But once that lost its novelty, she stopped pretending and slunk off into the shadows at a half-trot, carrying her prize.

After a while, from somewhere off in the darkness, came the sickly crunch and pop of bones.

"Impressive, isn't it?" Dave whispered hotly. "That's your killer in the cave, right there. Your ultimate predator. They're all over the fossil record, these puppies. They could devour a primate in a minute flat. Nothing left but the skull."

"I know all about that. I used to teach eighth-grade math."

"Joke if you want. But they've been out there all this time, since the beginning. They've never gone away. They're in our dreams, like it or not."

Now as if by signal they began to emerge in earnest, phantoms out of the darkness, hot-eyed and snarling. They moved in on the littered yard, chewing up scraps. People were gathering for the show. Tourists, backpackers, extreme travelers with headbands and good sandals, they all stood in a circle, shining flashlights over the mottled fur with its snaggy, bristling spikes. There were no movies in Harar, no theater, no opera; if you were looking for thrills this was where you went.

The saliva unspooled in glistening threads from the hyenas'

mouths. Only now did it occur to Teddy the nature of the glowing fragments he'd seen strewn in the dirt. They weren't glass, they were bones. Teeth.

"You talk about your big cats," the doctor said. "Your sabertooths and leopards and lions. But come *on*. Look at those jaws, that dentition. These guys are *machines*. Imagine what it felt like, trying to sleep, hearing them laugh like that just outside the cave."

"They should have run like hell," Teddy said.

"They'd never have made it. No, probably what they did was build up the fire, and then pass the night telling stories and rubbing up against the females, trying not to think about those beasts out there. Then eventually they'd build a little house in a walled city, and raise some kids. And they'd find themselves a good hyena man too, like our friend over there, just in case they came back." Dave laughed. Like all doctors he appeared to find it drily amusing, the stratagems of laymen in flight from stark truths. "Now get your camera ready. You're going to want to record this."

Again the hyena man reached into his sack, pulling out another long, gristly strip of meat. He placed it between his teeth; it hung from his jaw like a second tongue. Blood dripped on the ground. The hyenas seethed forward in a frenzy, yipping and chattering, breath tearing raggedly in and out of their lungs.

"Enough." Teddy couldn't focus; his hands were shaking. "This is a little sick, even for me."

"Not at all. The man's a healer. A shaman. He's performing a public service."

"By getting himself killed, you mean?"

"By *not* getting himself killed," the doctor said. "By stepping outside the walls, and confronting something wild and scary in the dark. And then again the next night. And the next. Until it's second nature. Until he doesn't get spooked anymore, he doesn't look away. Believe me, you'll want to look away in the leprosarium tomorrow too. Everyone does. But you won't."

"How do you know?"

"Because, it's why you came."

Teddy no longer had any idea, if he ever had, why he'd come. The stubbled moon, the stench of offal and blood, the moronic *heh-heh-heh*s of the hyenas, their noisome ravings . . . the whole night seemed hostile, unpenetrated. Even as the hyenas fed on their suppers, they kept nipping at each other compulsively, unable to hold back, to let each other alone. Letting each other alone was not in their nature.

"You wanted to know what it was like here, you said. Back in the wild old days of Burton and Rimbaud, and for centuries before that? Well," Dave said, "it was like this."

The hyena man stuck another strip of meat in his jaw. The blood ran down his chin in dark strings. He stared directly at Teddy, showing his teeth. He appeared to want to communicate something.

Madness. And yet Teddy could not for the life of him look away.

"Your turn," Dave said.

13

All That Stuff That Comes Later

"I don't care about the movie. It's just good to be out."

"If you call this out," Oren said.

"It's out enough. Look how lovely everything is," Gail said. "What more could you ask for?"

Oren shrugged. It was the question of his life; it had begun to take on, over time, an almost religious weight. Unfortunately the more it weighed, the less prospect there seemed of an answer.

But later for that. It was Saturday night and they were going to the movies like an ordinary couple. Whether there was any such *thing* as an ordinary couple was yet another heavy, semi-religious question, he supposed. According to Heidegger, the ordinary was always extraordinary. But suppose you were one of those people who perpetually longed for the extraordinary; did that mean you really longed for the *ordinary*? Or was longing for the extraordinary the most ordinary longing of all?

Oren was feeling pretty ordinary himself at the moment—extraordinarily so, in fact—and in a good way. Because it *was* lovely out; any fool could see that. The air was warm. The sun, that plump aristocrat, lounged on its chaise of silken clouds, dispensing its golden favors. Fragrant white blossoms sifted down from the trees, feathery and buoyant, like a parody of snowfall; he felt their soft landings in his hair. Up ahead, under the slanted marquee of the Carthage Twin, the other ordinary couples were pulling out their wallets. True, unlike them, he and Gail would not be sitting together, or holding hands, or sharing a box of the Twin's rubbery popcorn, or breaking off hunks of dark chocolate bedded in foil, let alone engaging in the sort of furtive and delirious groping that kept not just theirs but indeed all theaters, and that great thronged projection room the planet itself, in business. No, none of these pleasures would be available to them. Still, just to coexist for a few hours in the intimacy of that darkened dome, watching other peoples' dramas play out for a change—that would be no small thing.

Except when they arrived at the ticket window, the movie they'd hoped to see was sold-out. And the other, to judge by the garish semiotics of the poster, looked not just mildly but offensively stupid.

Stymied, he jammed his hands into his pockets. "What do you think?"

"Oh, I don't care," Gail said. "What do you think?"

"I don't care either."

"You choose." That her voice was still light did not entirely disguise its edge of insistence. "It doesn't matter to me, honestly. Whatever you think."

Oren knew what he thought: he thought he'd have liked to stop standing around running old lines from *Marty* and go in and see a movie, any movie. All he wanted was a couple of hours in cool, anonymous darkness, free of the ethical, moral, and, increasingly, sexual discomforts to which his affair with Gail Hastings had consigned him. But he also knew what Gail thought, or rather how. Knew that for all her apparent blitheness she was less frivolous (i.e., more uptight and humorless) than he was; that she had zero affection for the tropes and traditions (i.e., glibness, fart jokes, gratuitous nudity) of Hollywood comedy; and that as a consequence she'd sit there enduring the thing stoically (i.e., miserably, resentfully) but also checking her watch every so often— the face glowed in the darkness, a blue, flickering, iridescent moon—and sighing audibly, as she did whenever he screened for her something from his repertoire of personal favorites. When it came to movies, it wasn't just the silly comic stuff that bored Gail. They all did. Indeed, the whole elegant narrative arc Oren had labored to master back in Intro to Screenwriting—setup, plot points, complication, resolution—left her sunk deep in the cushions, lips compressed to the vanishing point, gazing at the screen with the lidded resignation of a teenager trapped in a car with her parents. *Nothing new or interesting,* she seemed to be thinking, *could possibly come of this.*

"But you're enjoying it," she'd protest when he reached for the remote. "You don't have to turn it off on my account."

"It's only a movie," he'd say, with a breezy Gallic insouciance that had never come naturally to him, or for that matter unnaturally, though he'd been working on it for years now, ever since his first midnight screening of *Breathless* back on Roger Barstow's sofa in Alphabet City. Of course that was only a movie too. So what? Oren *liked* movies, preferred them in fact to that other passive indoor diversion, his life; and though perhaps someday, when he was Gail's age, say, he too would grow tired of movies and consent to see only the most obscure, plotless, low-budget offerings, with no-name actors who did not speak English and whose faces were grooved in unfamiliar, unshapely, half-ugly ways, he hoped that day did not come soon. Because few such movies came to the Carthage Twin. And even when they did, they did not stay long.

Still, going to a movie was a means, not an end, part of his ongoing campaign to normalize their time together, provide a few shared experiences that weren't strictly sexual. Especially as the strictly sexual wasn't going so well either at the moment. More and more he felt the pressure of some expectation in bed, some act of aggression, some minor savagery, and in response to this pressure his body had begun to register its own protest. It would not be moved. But Gail seemed on a mission these days to satisfy herself by any means necessary, and she had. Even now, an hour later, under the marquee, she glowed a little in victory, her eyes creamy, her lips full and shapely like the spout of a pitcher. People she knew were checking her out surreptitiously from the lobby. She paid no notice. Little kazoos of private pleasure were buzzing inside her. She hung against Oren's arm with her hair rumpled, humming to herself. Where to now?

But there was nowhere to go. Their hours in Don's bed had ruined them. It was as if they'd awoken from an uneasy dream to find the sun gone down, the windows glazed in frost, and themselves helplessly conjoined on the mattress, an ungainly, twin-like creature with multiple limbs and a doubled back. Just getting out of bed was a trial. And what then? Where should they bend their steps? The doors of the prosaic were closed to them. Gail had a daughter at home and loathed his apartment even more than he did. Going out to dinner was a nonstarter. They had no mutual friends. It was too warm outside to swim indoors and too cold in the lake to swim outside. He had no bike or aptitude for tennis, and no power on earth or in heaven would induce him to take up golf.

The only place he could think of to go was Chez Blackburn—their winter palace, their fortress of solitude. But that too was off-limits to them now.

Don had been sent home from rehab. On the surface of course this was a good and hopeful thing, a sign that, after four months, his progress was sufficient in the eyes of the insurance company to recommend discharge. But what it really meant was the opposite. His recovery was no longer statistically probable. The insurance company, unwilling to pay out tens of thousands of dollars in a losing effort, would wipe him off the books and cut their losses. They'd sent Don home with a cane, a part-time Bosnian attendant, some heavy-duty prescriptions, and a sheaf of printouts detailing the various regimens he should follow for his various physical therapies. That tidied up their account sheets and made everyone feel better.

As for Don, and any hopes he may have nurtured for a triumphant restoration to home and hearth, that was another story.

366

For Don it was more like house arrest. He spent his days on the sofa in his terry-cloth robe, unresponsive and immobile, staring out at a gray, tenebrous sky. His eyes were like marbles, bright but opaque; they reflected more than they admitted. Behind them his brain was either busy reorganizing itself—borrowing live neurons from its undamaged hemisphere and swapping out the dead ones—or else it had gone under completely. In the silence of the house there seemed no way to know.

In any case, Don's house was off-limits now. They were in exile, banished from that garden. They had to venture out and take their chances on a Saturday night like everyone else.

Overhead, the gulls made plaintive little half-cries, finding themselves off course as usual, no seas in sight.

"So okay, let's bag the movie," Oren said. "It's pretty out, like you said. Let's just walk."

Gail's eyebrows vaulted northward. "Together?"

"Either way. I'm happy to walk behind you if you like. It'll give me a chance to check out your ass."

"So that's what you do back there. I thought you were just a natural follower."

"That too."

"I don't know about this." She glanced around at the pedestrian traffic; for the first time she seemed to register the extent of their exposure. "Where would we walk to?"

"Who cares? We don't need a destination. We'll just walk."

"I think I need a destination," she said. "I'm a more conventional person than you."

"Fine. How about a drink?"

"We just had a drink."

"Dinner then."

"I'm not hungry, are you? Anyway it's Saturday: there's no place good we could get into without a reservation." She pulled back her hair and affixed it with an elastic band. "What about the bookstore? That might still be open."

"Sure." She'd just been complaining, a few hours earlier, of having too many books at home she hadn't yet read. But he let that go. "Why not?"

"Why not," she repeated carelessly.

But any lingering doubts soon dissipated into the plush and amiable quiet that held sway over the street. Okay, it wasn't a movie, but the evening cinematography had a beauty all its own. The maples and spruces that lined the sidewalk, dormant just the week before, were now splitting themselves open, sprouting buds, spilling out shoots. And here was Gail, humming beside him, her linen jacket brushing the hairs on his forearm (they rose obediently to her touch), the beads on her necklace ticking like a watch. They paused on the bridge and gazed down at the river, murmuring placidly below. The surface was glassy, as if in denial of its own lower currents, which were intent on the falls. Or at peace with them, he thought.

What was it, this harmonic force that came blasting through the twilight like a pipe organ and made Carthage seem in that moment no longer precious and insular in a bad way but in a *good* way, rare and cherishable and (for he knew his existence here was only a passing experiment) poignant, like chamber music in a village church, or a fairgrounds glimpsed from an airplane? Here was the human community that he'd sought and avoided for so long. Retired men in fishing hats hitting tennis balls in the park. Kids selling candy to raise money for the lacrosse team. Young families out biking after dinner, the parents peeking over their shoulders, the kids in their absurd helmets and training wheels tootling along behind them. The rituals and protections of family life. Would he ever join in?

Through the open doorway of the bookshop they could hear the bland acoustic music its owners preferred, guitars and banjos twanging in a minor key. Gail strolled right in and was warmly greeted, like the regular she was. Oren lingered outside. It was a small shop and it seemed politic to maintain some distance, so he pretended to be absorbed in the window displays while he in fact checked out his hair. It looked windblown, displaced; he tried to pat it down where it was lopsided. Inside, Gail was scanning the bookshelves, her head cocked, her weight poised adroitly on one leg, like a ravenous bird greedy for crumbs. What was she looking for now? No wonder her husband had run off—the intensity of her search was boundless, prodigious; he too would be broken and lost in it. Overwhelmed.

She glanced up. *Well?* she seemed to ask. *Coming in?*

But he had given himself to this woman, however grudgingly, however incompletely; there would be no getting himself back now. He pushed the door open. Despite the bell's loud jingle no one looked up. The owner was on the phone, the clerk was boxing up an order. And now Gail was talking to the sole other customer, a fellow in a black sweater. He looked, Oren thought, with his scarf, his serious dark-pored face, and his mass of inky backswept hair, like some visiting lecturer or chamber musician, someone who smoked unfiltered cigarettes and stayed up late talking to colleagues in Berlin or Milan. Behind him were the stacks of new memoirs. Everyone had a story.

Gail laughed, curling a hand at her throat. Clearly no matter how long Oren stood there waiting to be introduced, the results were bound to be awkward. So he went and browsed the CDs and DVDs instead.

Lately, and he wasn't proud of this, it was his habit in bookstores to ignore the books. He'd had it with books. Had it with hoarding himself alone in a room, lost in intangible spheres. Fortunately ignoring books was easy to do these days, especially in bookstores, where, with all the CDs and DVDs for sale, the calendars and diaries, the espresso drinks and cookies and scones and so on, you could hardly *find* the books.

Though to be fair, the Carthage bookstore didn't sell cookies or espresso drinks. For that matter it didn't sell many books. Like most independent establishments in the area it barely held on. And Oren wasn't helping. Because in the end, which was not so far from the beginning—they'd been out on the town, if you could call it that, for less than an hour—Gail bought three paperbacks and a hardcover at full list price, and he bought nothing at all.

"Here," she said, when they'd arrived back at her house. "I got you a present."

"You didn't have to do that."

"Oddly enough, I did. I find myself wanting to treat you to things. It's this bizarre compulsion I have to put my stamp on your life."

"Thanks." She makes me sound like an envelope, he thought. "Should I open it now or later?"

"I'm afraid you'll have to decide that for yourself."

"You really didn't have to." He slipped the bag with the book down below the seat. He was unaccustomed to receiving presents for no reason. "So?"

"So what?"

"You know so what. The guy in the bookstore. With the Italian shoes."

"Richard? I told you about Richard."

"I'm more or less sure that you didn't, actually."

"I met him in yoga. He just moved here. He bought that frame shop over on Essex. Don't you remember, they had that article about him in the *Carthage Courier*?"

"And reading the *Courier* would interest me why?"

"I don't know. Me, I live in this town. I like to know who's getting born, who got married, who just died. I guess I'm old-fashioned that way." She squinted out into the dusk; two squirrels were chasing each other across the lawn. "Richard's a dear man. You'd like him. He's from New York. He reads, he meditates. I think he might even be Jewish."

"Great. That makes, what, three of us now? In another ten years we'll have a minyan."

It didn't bother Oren that he was no longer the newest, youngest, most New York Jewish guy in town. If anything it was a relief. The torch of the Law had been passed; he could reclaim his hand.

"Let's go in." Gail's hand was poised on the door handle. "I'll make tea."

"Won't your daughter be home?"

"Mimi? On a Saturday night?" Gail looked incredulous, amused. Never mind that the two of *them* were now home on a Saturday night. "No chance. Her boyfriend's in the senior play, and there'll be the party afterward. You'll have to find a better excuse."

"What play?"

"Ibsen. *A Doll's House.*"

"Isn't Ibsen sort of depressing for high school? Whatever happened to *Bye Bye Birdie? South Pacific?*"

"They do those every year. The director wanted a change. Unfortunately I made the tactical mistake of encouraging Mimi to try out. Talk about your kiss of death."

"Some people would rather watch plays than be in them," Oren said.

"Some people get too used to watching. They need to be pushed." Gail's breath billowed up against the windshield. "Look, if you don't want to come in, you don't have to come in."

"Of course I'll come in." But he didn't want to. For some reason—the bad sex earlier, the missed movie, his low blood sugar, the good-looking guy in the bookstore—all he wanted was to go home, pour himself a drink, heat up some leftover chili, and settle in front of the television with a magazine . . . all the great new habits he'd acquired in that winter of house-sitting. Granted, it did not feel quite the same, indulging such habits in his own house—it felt just a wee bit pathetic in fact—so as they got out of the car, he said, by way of apology, "Who's he playing? Mimi's boyfriend I mean."

"The husband. What's his name. Torvald."

"Poor guy. Well, if nothing else it's good practice."

"For what?"

"You know," Oren said, "life. The misery, the mediocrity, the humiliation—all that stuff that comes later."

Her hand shot out as if to slap him. But she was only smoothing back a stray curl loitering over his forehead. The gesture was at least as maternal as it was romantic. "You don't have much faith in people, do you?" she said. "We don't all leave you know."

Why not? he wondered, following her into the house, as he had followed her over the bridge earlier and into the bookshop, as he'd been following her into rehab facilities and swimming pools and other people's bedrooms for weeks, for months. Everywhere they went was Gail's domain; he was only a visitor, a passenger.

In the kitchen, she kicked off her boots, slung her purse and bag over a chair, took note of and ignored the blinking light on the phone machine, and commandeered the stove. A calendar of painted Mexican doorways was thumbtacked to the wall. The white grid of days was thick with penciled-in appointments. There were photos on the fridge, laughing friends in colorful ski clothes, laid out every which way like a puzzle. "Who are all these people?"

"Those are mine," she said, pointing out two of the girls, "and that's my niece Olivia. That tall woman with the big boobs? That's Sonya, her mother. And that's her new boyfriend, Jack, with his kids from his first marriage. Evan and Emily."

"Nice." How would he ever learn all these names, Oren was thinking, let alone their gossipy little backstories, the idiosyncratic vectors and tangents that bound them together?

"We only have herbal. . . . Oh, wait, that's right, you prefer coffee, don't you?"

How do you like that? he thought. Finally someone remembers.

Roused by their voices, the family dog got up from his bed in the laundry room and sauntered sleepily and dutifully toward the visitor, his nails clicking across the floorboards.

"He's starting to like me," Oren said. "Check it out, he didn't even bark this time when I came in."

"Poor old Bruno. He's not much of a guard dog these days. No bark, no bite. Getting towards the end, aren't you, baby?" Gail crouched on her heels, scruffing the old dog's belly. "He's only got three teeth left. At least he's not in pain. There's nothing worse than an animal in pain. I'd kill him first."

"You mean have him put to sleep."

"Of course." She stood, brushing off her hands. "What did you think I meant?"

She yanked open the freezer. Her face fell. Any illusions of order she may have harbored for herself lay impacted, it seemed, in that cave of glacial frost. Gamely she rummaged around amid the broken burritos and petrified pizzas, her head wreathed by vapor clouds, her fingers scrabbling at the stippled ice.

"Voilà." She brandished a lumpy paper bag, wrested from the depths. "Success. Danielle sent us these Ethiopian beans. The best in the world, she says."

She held down the lid of the grinder with the flat of her hand, like a shield. He could hear the beans jumping around, decimating into shards. "I never know how long to do this," she complained.

"I tend to just go by ear."

"*Quelle surprise.*" She poured the grounds into a cone-shaped filter, shaking her head. "Honestly, I don't understand this whole fetish with coffee and food. The best this, the best that. Where it comes from. Who grows it. What it does in its spare time. Who cares?"

For a moment she seemed almost angry; then that moment passed. She turned on the radio and hummed mindlessly along to the classical station, content to be back at the counter of her messy, lived-in kitchen, with the hanging pots and pans, the unpaid bills in their jumble on the counter, the tendrils of the spider plants aspiring toward the window, the golden tufts of dog hair blowing across the floor. Her feet were bare. Lemons ripened on the counter, avocados dangled from the ceiling in an aluminum cage. From a shelf in the pantry she took down a box of cookies and laid them out in a fan-shaped pattern on a ceramic plate. Her expression was languid. The crisp skin of efficiency, of minor surface tension, had peeled back from her face. What lay below was some quality Oren hadn't seen before, something runny and mutable and sweet. Could it be she was content with *him*? He remembered how she'd hovered over him in bed earlier, sightless as a statue, concentrating on some private image she had conjured or imposed. He'd almost come to prefer it that way, to be unseen on the bottom, solid and supporting, like the base of a fulcrum, a hinge. His fingers on her hips, tracing the braille hieroglyphs imprinted there by her panties. The breeze puffing out the curtains, then drawing them back in to rub indolently against the screens. Her breasts bobbing against his face like apples in a bucket. And then her legs had begun to jerk. He'd looked up at her, bound up in a chain of her own combustions. He had to work like hell just to hold on.

"Oh, maybe I *do* love you," she'd said.

It had come out all in one breath, like a balloon collapsing. She sounded, he thought, a little vexed. As if she'd just lost an argument.

"That's it?" She'd gone up on one elbow to examine him. "That's your response? I bare my heart and you lie there and say nothing?"

"I love you too."

"*Bronnk,* sorry. Time has expired. Thanks for playing though." She punched him on the arm, hard enough to hurt. "Couldn't you at least be gallant enough to pretend you're surprised? *I'm* surprised. Why aren't you?"

"The only surprising part is the stuff about me. The rest I know."

"What does that even mean?"

"It means you love. That's who you are. You're the kind of person who loves."

"Bullshit. Everyone's that kind of person." She trailed a finger over his wrist, the veins and bones, the barbed fence of his tattoo. "Even you."

"I'm not sure what kind I am."

"Hey, show a little class. You'd think someone getting laid as much as you are would spend a little less time feeling sorry for himself. But it works for you, doesn't it, Oren? It gets you off the hook."

He was about to ask, what hook? But she was already reaching for her panties.

"We should go," she said. "You want to see that movie, remember? And I'd like a glass of wine on the porch first. Maybe two. I'm feeling kind of daring tonight. Kind of wild."

"Two glasses. That *is* wild."

"I know. Let's make tonight the night we do whatever we feel like, how's that sound? Tonight's the night where everybody gets what they want."

And indeed, after they'd showered and dressed and driven into town, her mood remained so tranquil, so affectionate, it was easy to believe that *he* was what she wanted. Because ultimately there was only one way to love, Oren thought. And Gail still had the capacity for it, he could see that; nothing had been lost or used up in her marriage. If anything marriage had preserved it, kept it alive and intact, floating in its amber. He had sensed it there in her all evening, that vastness. It was there in the aftermath of their lovemaking, in their quiet little happy hour on the porch; there in the car as they'd whooshed up and down the shadowed streets; in the tender solicitude of her gaze when they parked downtown and lingered for a while, smoking a joint in the front seat of the Dodge. Just before they got out, she'd cradled his head in her palms, like a blind person committing him to memory. The heart was just a muscle like any other, he thought. You had to use it and use it and use it.

"Poor thing," she'd said. "And you're losing your hair too."

*   *   *

He was still puzzling over that *too* hours later, as Gail took down the mugs and arranged the spoons with all the care and deliberation of a girl playing house. "I've had some news from Danny," she said.

"Oh?" For weeks the name of her older daughter, so musical and boyish, had floated in the margins of his attention, unaffixed. But now it settled heavily at the center. "What kind of news?"

"It seems she might be coming home soon after all."

"I thought she'd decided to stay in Africa through the summer."

"Well, her plans have changed. She's flying in Monday actually. She gets into Logan at six."

"Wait, *this* Monday?"

"Mmm." She opened up the refrigerator, her back to him. "You take milk, right? I'm afraid we only have skim."

She poured the milk into a tiny enamel pitcher shaped like a cow and brought it over to the table. As if the kitsch quotient weren't high enough, she now wore over her shoulders a cardigan sweater. What a fine mess he'd got himself into, up here in the pastures of plenty. All this mediocre clutter, the scarred breakfast table, the threadbare seat cushions, the smelly doggy bed in the corner. Even the cookies she'd put out looked doughy and dense, the kind you bought in a health-food store and kept around for months, not eating.

"Are you all right?" Gail's mouth was twist-tied at the corners. "You look a bit shell-shocked."

"Not at all. I'm just trying to wrap my mind around what this will mean."

"It means I'll have my baby home, that's what it means. It means for the first time in months I won't lie awake half the night worrying and feeling lonely."

Actually he'd been wondering what this would mean for *him.* But he supposed that went without saying. "And her father?"

"Her father." Gail blew away some steam. "Apparently her father's on the road at the moment and can't be reached. At least not by me." Whether this was a good thing or a bad thing her tone did nothing to clarify. "It seems he's made a new friend over there."

"Oh?"

"Some American doctor, Danny says. An Albert Schweitzer type. The two of them are thick as thieves, apparently. They're traveling out in the countryside together. There's some talk of them building a school." She set down the mug again. "For heaven's sake, stop gawking at the cookies and go ahead and have one already. That's why I put them out."

"I'd think that would be quite a commitment, building a school. Wouldn't that take some time?"

"What can you do? The guy likes to build things. It's how he gets his kicks." Her expression grew almost fond. "You should have seen him when he took over the middle school. What a project *that* was. This young, headstrong guy who'd shot up through the ranks—he figured he could do anything he wanted. Did you know, the first year he got rid of about a quarter of the faculty, all the deadweight, in one swoop? The union went batshit. He hadn't even finished setting up his office and they were already trying to fire him. Then once he pushed through that bond for the new wing, he couldn't find an architect he liked, so he wound up drawing the plans himself. And then redrawing them, and redrawing them, until we were *all* batshit. I've never seen the guy so happy. Honestly, I don't think he *wanted* to finish the building. I think he wanted to keep hanging out at the construction site in his hard hat, bossing people around." She expelled a little air through her nose—part laugh, part sigh. "So you see, it's not like I didn't see this coming. He's been wanting to break out of here for a long time. That little photography escapade was just the nail in the coffin."

"Going to jail must be a real downer, though."

"Oh, he enjoyed *that.* It wasn't jail that bothered him. It was coming home." She waved her hand around the kitchen, at the toaster, the dish rack, the fruit bowl, the fat, dog-eared cookbooks with their multiply broken spines. "If you want to know, I'm glad he's gone. Really, I feel like I can finally breathe. No more worrying, is Teddy in a mood? Is he fighting with people? Which of our friends has he alienated now? Let him get out his yah-yahs over there, on safari with that doctor. He *needs* a doctor. Somebody to tell him he's not about to die, and that that's okay, that's just fine. I can't do it anymore. I have my own stuff to deal with. My daughter's coming home—that's plenty for me to deal with right there."

"What about that Israeli guy she was traveling with?"

"The Great Gabi? He's gone too, thank God. Though he left his mark it seems. His own little slime trail . . ." She shivered under her sweater. "However, I can't think about that right now. I've got to focus on Monday. Getting Danny. It's a miracle she got a ticket—her father bullied the airline into giving her his return. If you're forceful enough they give in, you know. And Teddy can be *very* forceful."

"I know."

"He told them it was a health emergency. 'Life in the balance'—that was the phrase he used."

"I'll have to remember that one." He would too. He'd been forced to change a lot of tickets in his life. He'd thought he was through changing tickets, but it was beginning to look as if maybe he wasn't.

"Yes, well, the thing is, it's true. She's pregnant, poor thing."

The news affected Oren strangely. He'd slept with the mother and now the daughter was pregnant. By some weird trick of logic he felt almost responsible, complicit.

"And you've known about this how long?" he said.

"Not long."

"How long is not long? Just out of curiosity."

"You know, Oren, you sound a little aggressive all of a sudden. I wonder what that's about."

"I'm just trying to wrap my mind around the chronology here. Sometimes when people say 'not long' they mean a couple of days, sometimes they mean a week or a month. So how long is 'not long' for you?"

"Not long." She shrugged. "A few days."

He allowed this admission to hang in the air a moment unmolested, though he'd have liked to bash it like a shuttlecock with some hard retort. If he did that, however, he would lose the moral advantage. And it was important to hold on to the moral advantage when all the other, better advantages lay on the far side of the net.

"You were going to tell me though, right? You weren't going to just spring it on me."

"Hello? Do we have a bad connection here? I just *did* tell you."

"You waited though. Until the last minute. You were afraid I'd react badly."

"I wasn't afraid of that at all." She was beginning to react pretty badly herself now, her eyes flashing darkly, her jaw setting tight. "I've been busy making calls and faxing people all week. I haven't had a minute to myself. You and your precious little reaction have been way down the list."

"How far down? Just out of curiosity. Did I make, say, the top twenty?"

"Why are you being like this, Oren? It has nothing to do with you, so there's nothing to be done, is there? Anyway I thought you *liked* keeping things loose. I thought that was the Oren Pierce style. Well, consider me a convert. I'm about as loose these days as they come."

"No you're not. I don't mean that as an insult, mind you. But you're not."

"Please," she said, taking his hand between hers, "it's been so nice with you this last week. So relaxed. Like the end of a really great vacation. The truth is I didn't want to spoil it. Can you understand that?"

"It hasn't been a vacation for me. It's been just the opposite in fact."

"Poor Oren." She searched his eyes a moment; apparently she expected to find something there. "I'm not trying to hurt you. But it's so sweet to see you this way."

What way did she mean? The presence of her hand on his cheek, which was mysteriously hot, made everything worse. How bizarre: Gail seemed to be laboring under the misapprehension that he was on the verge of tears. Him! Oren Pierce! Who hadn't cried for any reason, other than intense physical pain of course, since he was eleven years old, when his guinea pig, Miss Whiskers, escaped from her cage for no reason and vanished into the woods across the street. And he hadn't cried then either, not really. Okay, a little heat behind the eyes. A little mist, a little throb. "I'm just taken by surprise, that's all."

"Yes, I can see that."

"I thought you were feeling good about *us* tonight. But obviously your mind was somewhere else the whole time."

"Oh, grow up," she said. "You and your tender feelings. You think you're the only one who's tattooed for life? Try having a child someday. You may not think about them all the time, you may not like them all the time, but they're there in your skin and they don't go away. Can't you see that?"

In Oren's experience, when a woman told you to grow up, she rarely intended or expected you to grow up right then and there. She meant do it somewhere else, sometime else. So he rose, put his cup in the sink, and began the long march to the foyer.

A car door slammed outside. The dreaded neighbors, probably.

"And they're off," she called after him. "Go. It's what you're good at, right? Flying away. I swear, you've got the constitution of a hummingbird. What is it with you? You hover and hover, but when do you ever *land*?"

"I'm giving you space. I thought that was what you wanted." Now the dog was whining too, his tail slapping the floor. "You've got all those calls and arrangements to make, remember?"

"Tell me, why is it that when a man runs away, he always makes it sound like he's being extra-considerate? You come on all cocky, then at the first sign of a problem, it's 'I'll stay out of your way, I'll give you some space.' Well, I've got news for you, buddy: Things are messy around here. People get sick. People get pregnant. People freak out and calm down and then freak out again. It's a busy and confusing little world, and it would probably behoove you to learn to deal with it. What do you think? Can you wrap your mind around that?"

At which point, as if to illustrate her theory, the door swung open, effectively blocking his exit before he could achieve it, and Mimi Hastings walked in.

She wore torn jeans and a belly-baring tank top; her hair was all over her face. She dumped her backpack by the door like a soldier on leave and cruised past the counter. "Hey, Mr. P.," she said, as if his presence in her kitchen on a Saturday night were only to be expected. "How's it going?"

"I was just leaving," he said more or less automatically.

"Mr. Pierce came over to pick our brains a little." Gail's voice was bright. She was no actress herself, but she happened to be talking to a sullen, self-absorbed teenager, so not much acting was required. "He's subbing in for Dad this year at school."

"Yeah, I heard." She turned to Oren. "You poor man. We pity you. You must have terrible karma."

"It's not so bad."

"Yeah, right. I wasted like three years of my life in that dump. And I learned, oh, let's see . . . nothing?" The dog came up and trailed worshipfully behind her. She ignored him. She plucked a banana from the fruit bowl, then immediately put it back. "You used to be so cool too. My friends all had these huge crushes."

"Were you in my class? I can't remember."

"You had my friend Julie, the year you came. I had Gromlich, the evil troll. Julie said you were nice. At least you had a pulse, not like the others. She said you'd never last out the year though."

"I wasn't so sure myself." He snuck a look at Gail, who was

examining her daughter with the pursed, preoccupied expression of a tailor. "In fact I've been thinking I might take a little time off one of these days."

"Oh?" Gail asked coolly, her eyes still fixed on her daughter. "Is that a fact?"

"This might be my last school year for a while, in fact. I've got some irons in the fire. Various options I'm exploring. We'll have to see." He willed himself not to use the words *in fact* again, or ever. He too made a point of addressing himself to Mimi now. "So how was the play?"

"Sucked. I left at intermission."

"And how was Jeremy?" her mother asked.

Mimi rolled her eyes.

"Have something real to eat. You must be starving. And why are you going out without a jacket?"

"I'm fine."

"Honey, you know—"

"I'm *fine.*"

Bruno, having given up on soliciting any demonstrations of affection from this particular gathering, settled on the floor with a sigh.

"Okay, well, maybe I'll see you guys later," Oren said. "Thanks for everything."

No answer. It would have been easy to despise himself at this moment, but instead he chose to believe that neither of the Hastings women had heard him, occupied as they were with glaring at each other from opposite sides of the counter. The clench of their jaws, the angle at which their necks rode their shoulders, made them seem like one irritable woman arguing with her own reflection, from which there was no possibility of escape.

Oren, all one of him, slipped out the back door unattended. *Isolato.*

The night sky was busy, full of the comings and goings of fugitive stars. He walked around the house and then down the driveway to his car. His feelings were a mystery to him. Sometimes there seemed no distinction between preserving your feelings and not having them, between spreading yourself thin and erasing yourself completely.

As he pulled away, he saw Bruno standing at the front door, his bad breath fogging up the glass. The dog, he recalled, was half-blind with cataracts, so no doubt he couldn't see Oren very well, and that was why he never barked out a good-bye.

14

Afar

So here he was: no-man's-land.

All morning they'd hoofed it around Lake Afrera, through the funnel of the Rift, and then descended single file into the inferno of the depression. It was among the lowest places on earth. Teddy's mule, stumbling over the rocks, made high squealing noises of excitement or complaint. The ground was cratered and dark; it seemed never to have known trees. The sun bore down like an anvil. A hot wind from Aden, like a dog with a chew toy, worked over his face.

With the grit in his mouth Teddy looked out over this moonscape of lumps and stones—the volcanoes towering in the west, top-heavy and jagged; the dry rubbled chasms that ran between the peaks like the ghosts of old rivers; the buzzards picking over their suppers, tearing off strips of leathery flesh from mummified carcasses of dik-diks and goats (the withered, shrunken heads grinned eerily in rictus, as if they'd died laughing). Well, he thought, if this was not an absolute then nothing was. *A nakedness too harsh for volunteers . . .*

Out here only the dead things seemed alive. The obsidian rocks that flew through the air. The dirt devils that staggered drunkenly across the plains. The canyons, gashed and scored by ancient floods, that yawned open hotly, like the ravaged throat-linings of primordial beasts. His mule plodded along in his own shadow, scrabbling over cacti and the egg-shaped stones they came upon everywhere, marked by fine, scalloped impressions that might have been fossils. The geologists loved it out here in the Rift: all the discoveries were right on the surface.

Teddy loved it too. Though the feelings were not unmixed. For one thing he was delirious. He'd come down with a fever their second day out. His face itched, his butt was riddled with suppurating sores, the blood blisters on his palms were puffy and pliant as whoopee cushions, and with every pitch and roll of his mule the meniscus in his knees crinkled up like tinfoil. Not that he was complaining. Heat and glare, sand in his mouth, sulfurous gases that came hissing up from the bowels of the earth—all this was what he'd come for. Even the fever. At first he'd tried to manage the fever with pills, but it kept flaring up again, a flame fed by an unseen draft. Now he submitted to it. He let it have its way. That was what you did out in the desert, he thought. You submitted.

Dr. Dave had been called back to Addis . . . how many days ago now? Four? Five? He remembered watching him zip up the medical bag—the instruments bulging against the leather—in his cramped office at the leprosarium. Here was a man with real battles to fight, against real enemies; why waste any more time squiring around this idle, doughy tourist, accommodating his personal whims?

Teddy too was sick of the personal. Sick *from* the personal. He longed to get beyond the self, beyond all selves, as Philip had. Maybe it was unintelligent to model your behavior on that of a corpse. But you had to start somewhere. And surely the dead should not be exempted from the only sphere still theirs to travel.

His brother's invisibility had long since become his own. He could conceive no separation from it. He understood that this was what had driven him to the desert. This twitch in the blood. This infected wound.

The doctor's clinical radar must have registered this as well, for he'd gone ahead and arranged passage for Teddy with one of the salt caravans headed to Afar. A jeep would take him from

Awash to Serdo; from there he'd travel the rest of the way in the traditional style, by camel and mule. "I should warn you," Dave said, shaking hands by the leprosarium gate, "the Danakil isn't for everyone. It's a pretty extreme environment."

"Come now. It can't be any more extreme than what you showed me yesterday."

"Yesterday?"

"Those kids we saw, with their necks all swollen up like beach balls? Jesus, you've spent so much time in that godforsaken clinic of yours, they don't even register anymore."

"Oh, they register, believe me. And you're right, they're forsaken. But I doubt the nuns would agree with you that He's the one to blame."

"And you?" Teddy said. "Who do you blame? The government? The poverty? The ignorance?"

"I don't have time for blame. I've got a two-year-old girl down at Mother Teresa's I need to go see tomorrow, she's got a choroidal tumor that's metastasized. In other words, her eyeball's exploding." He sounded, as he always did speaking of the worst cases, almost chipper; like an athlete facing a nasty opponent, it lifted his game. "Anyway it's not your problem. You're off on your own adventure, right?"

"Right." But Teddy thought he could hear below the words a soft gong of indictment.

"Just be careful. You're looking at about a week of hard mule travel back and forth. And the Danakil isn't set up for tourists. Very few amenities, even by desert standards."

"Listen, I've had plenty of amenities. More than my share. I can make do without."

"Famous last words," the doctor said drily. It was his version of a joke. He turned to Idris. "What do you think, my friend? Will you two be all right on your own?"

Idris was Dave's third-in-command at the leper clinic, a bald, hollow-cheeked Harari with a scrubby beard and an expression at once mournful and put-upon, like Job's. He puffed away at a hand-rolled cigarette from a discreet distance, waiting for them to conclude their business. To the doctor's question he gave no reply. An educated man, with twelve years of training, he was a former burn nurse in the one good hospital in Addis. If he resented in any way being assigned to chauffeur and babysit this antic, overgrown white person, he kept it to himself.

"You'll want to watch out for earthquakes too, naturally. There's a lot of geothermic activity up there. They say the Rift is sinking. Bottoming out. It should be pretty interesting. It's not every day you get to see a new ocean being born."

"I wish you could come with me," Teddy said. "You're like the only friend I've got." In response to which naked declaration, the doctor looked down at his running shoes uncomfortably. "But, hey, I understand. You're needed elsewhere, God knows."

"And you think you're not?"

"Honestly, Doc, I can hardly remember at this point."

"Well, maybe it will come back to you up there."

"Yeah. Maybe."

They shook hands impersonally. Teddy was hoping for a big, manly, backslapping embrace—his eyes in a sudden access of emotion had misted up like storm windows—but they had both reached the age where good-byes were difficult. The world of men was a lonely place. Idris looked on without expression. He was accustomed to visitors breaking down in Africa. Why else would they come?

"You'll want to watch out for the soldiers and the bandits. Djibouti's a mess these days. Eritrea's worse. Somalia of course is off the charts. Not such a great time to go wandering by yourself, even with an American passport. *Especially* with an American passport. Right, my friend?"

Idris sniffed aristocratically, elevating his eyebrows to indicate agreement.

"Stay close to Idris. He's not very chatty, but he gets along with the nomads and he knows the territory. I'd hate to have to call Danny and tell her that her father's lost out in the desert somewhere. *Ishi?*" The doctor had addressed this last remark to Idris. Now he turned to Teddy. "She thinks you're serious, you know."

"About what?"

"About that school you told her you're going to build. She believes you."

"And you don't?"

Dave gave a noncommittal shrug. "Me, I've seen a lot of people come over here and get all fired up to do things. What actually gets done in the end is another story."

"Listen, it's a done deal. Take my word. You just put me in touch with the donors, I'll take care of the rest. I've got it all planned out in my head." Teddy scratched some bug bites through his shirt, trying not to tear off the scabs—his shirts were streaky with dried blood as it was. "By the way, how do you feel about solar panels? I'm thinking with this infrastructure, renewables may be the way to go."

"Just some pencils and paper would be fine. Books. Blackboards. Teachers. Best to start simple. *Farenjis* have this way of always aiming too high. Then when things go wrong, they blame the Africans and go home." Dave smiled absently, patting his pockets to find his car keys. "One last thing? I'd hide that camera when the Danakil are around. They can be touchy, and they already think Allah's angry with them as it is. The ground's shaking below their feet. Even if that whole testicle-around-the-neck business *is* just a myth, it makes sense to be wary."

Teddy nodded agreeably, cinching up his bag and then hefting it over his shoulder. "Hang on. What testicle-around-the-neck business?"

"Traditionally, a Danakil warrior will cut off the genitals of his enemy and hang them around his neck. Otherwise he's thought to be an unsuitable husband."

"Funny how they left that out of the guidebooks."

"Not to worry. The Afaris are mostly just salt traders and farmers now. It's sad in a way. They've been nomadic since the birth of Christ. Right, Idris?"

Idris nodded sleepily. He'd guided enough foreign visitors around over the years, all those NGO people and Midwestern donors with their fanny packs and water bottles and endless questions, to keep his answers brief. "Heathens," he said, and spat on the ground.

"It's the way of things now," Dave said. "The kids either go radical religious or they go start up IT companies. Either way the real action's in the cities."

"Yeah, how you gonna keep them down on the farm. We get that where I live too," Teddy said. "Anyway, no worries. I'll keep a low profile, I promise. I'm done with antagonizing people. I'm done with even *noticing* people."

But apparently he wasn't. Because even as he stepped forward and, the hell with it, caught the little guy in a bear hug after all—and they did both smell pretty beasty at this point, pretty far gone—his gaze floated up like a weather balloon over the doctor's shoulder, where the lepers had gathered, their faces unreadable behind the half-closed shutters, looking down. Teddy waved and smiled. A rush of air went through his mouth. He must have been gritting his teeth: the crown over his molar had splintered at last, and given way for good.

So far, thank God, they'd met zero bandits. And only a handful of soldiers, peacekeepers actually, in a blue-and-white UN van, jouncing and swerving down the atrocious road from Didhay. As it rattled past with its salt-crusted chassis, the soldiers in back nodded somnolently. They were the first white people Teddy had seen in days, and the sight was not encouraging. Their faces were like masks, waxen and gluey in the heat. He was glad to see them go. He'd begun to feel oddly protective of the caravan, its quiet ways and monotonous rhythms. The hollow thump of hooves, the wind whistling through mountain passes, the musical chitchat of the nomads: these were now the sound track of his days.

The nomads of course ignored him. They were lean, proud men with long noses and abysmal teeth. Every so often their leader, Zelalem, would pivot in his saddle and level a cold, hawk-like gaze over his shoulder, confirming that the stranger was still sweatily slumping at the back of the line on his wheezy hard-backed mule. Then he'd kick up the pace. Teddy's presence among them had been bought and paid for; nonetheless he knew himself to be a source of embarrassment. Idris rarely spoke to him, preoccupied as he was with his own afflictions. The poor man was allergic to his mule. He pulled his headdress high on his face, covering everything but his eyes, the pupils, black as berries, stranded behind the red chicken-wire of the veins.

Teddy's own face lay bare. Below his patchy beard his cheeks were burnt, the skin flaking off his lips. On the good side how-ever his love handles were gone. The flesh in his thighs no longer wobbled; great slabs of fat had dropped from his hips. He was down to a subsistence diet: one flat disk of bread, a few dates and almonds, some charred stringy slivers of barbecued goat. This desert regimen agreed with him. But then so had most regimens in his life—his job, his marriage, his exercise workouts . . . he was a regimental type. He'd have made a good legionnaire. High atop his mule, his shoulders burnished bronze, his faded denim shirt wrapped on his head like a burka, tracing an unmarked path through the sand and the dust, he felt like Han-nibal on his elephant, like Lawrence on his camel—the last of a noble lineage of lonely and intrepid men.

He thought of stoic Ishmael, banished to the wilderness, and for what? A little roughhouse with his kid brother. But then all the old patriarchs were capricious fathers, as capricious as God himself. Stony, half-blind, they bestowed their blessings on the younger, weaker, cannier siblings—the Isaacs, the Jacobs, the Josephs, the Philips—and sent off the big boys to fend for them-selves.

But these were old grievances; why dwell on them now? His parents were gone; his kid brother was gone. Arguably he too was gone—off the rails, off the charts, off the grid. Out here the sun burnt the past off your shoulders; it blistered and flaked away.

All the manufactured materials of his life—his house, his car, his insulated basement with its treadmill and weights—seemed petty and unreal to him now, discardable, like the used household goods at the Dire Dawa Mercado. That too was a desert, that labyrinth of junk. He'd been wandering it for years without even knowing. Looking for a way out. But he wasn't out yet.

There were only two ways out of the desert, he thought. One of course was death. The other he didn't know.

His map was bleached and torn, frayed along the folds. His watch was lost. He had no radio. There was no one to talk to but Idris, and Idris did not like to talk. Hence he felt obligated to live through his senses. It seemed punishment and blessing both. For all the hardships, or else because of them, his body tingled and thrummed. The desert had sharpened his nerve endings, filed them down to fine points, as the bedouins did their teeth. Every loss seemed a gain, every deprivation an enhancement. The narrower the funnel, the more precious and distilled what dripped through it. The taste of fresh water at the end of the day; the brilliance of the stars; the cool, dewy dawns; the scent of tamarisk and wormwood on an invisible breeze.

His mind, bored, had silently unhitched itself; it floated off to watch from a distance, jotting occasional notes in an invisible book. There was too much in the desert to process. Too much or too little. Even the low things he came to savor, the ugly things. The odors of the working animals, their infested manes, their steaming ropes of piss, the nonchalant and untroubled way they rid themselves of waste as they plodded mechanically across the sand.

It was as if a window had shattered; the world in all its particularity rushed in. For too long he'd lived locked up inside himself like a ship in a bottle. All those hours buried in the basement, groaning over dumbbells, running nowhere on the treadmill. Why? He was an outdoor person—a mover, a builder, a Land Rover. That was his nature. *Best to start simple* was the doctor's prescription. What could be more simple than this? Plodding on dumbly like an animal. Onward was his only direction. So he rode on. That was what you did out here in the middle of fucking nowhere. You rode on.

All day the caravan traveled north through the miasmic heat, into the heart of the Rift. As if they were daring the sun to turn them too to salt.

The *gara,* or fire-wind, was against them; their progress through the lowlands was slow. Teddy and Idris rode their mules quietly in the rear, calling as little attention to themselves as possible. They were only hangers-on; the animal necessities drove things forward. The camels were the real talent of the operation. Every few hours they had to be attended to, rested, watered, fed, and fussed over like prima donnas, their bindings drawn tight. When they came to a well, or some sparse but hardy cacti, they'd draw to a halt, and the camels would drink and graze on the crowned fruit. Then the fires would be lit, bread and dates passed among the men, tea brewed from mint leaves, cardamom. When water was short, they drank the thin, bitter camel milk for refreshment. Between that, the hump meat he'd eaten back in Dire Dawa, and his odd new way of chewing on one side of his jaw to preserve the cracked crown over his molar—to say nothing of his multiple layers of fur and dirt and body odor—Teddy was beginning to feel, at this point, more camel than human. A lumpy, comical beast of burden. A conveyor of liquids and salts. He'd drink his fill of the milk, drape his shirt over his head, and lie down by the fire to rest.

He slept like a dead man, flat on his back, hands propped on his chest to avoid the scorpions. Often he dreamed of Gail and woke anxious and startled, caught between worlds. Idris would softly be singing beside him, accompanying himself on a single-stringed instrument he held between his knees.

"That's a pretty song."

"Is pretty, yes."

"What's it about?"

"The song say, death is a horse. It rides to us, but let us, please God, it say, let us eat and drink and keep it away."

"I thought death in your songs was always a lion."

"There are many, many songs," Idris said. "There is a song I am singing while you sleep. The song say, please God, we travel in the desert, far like clouds, make sure we do not perish, help us find our way."

"Find our way where? To what?"

The question seemed to take Idris aback. "To home."

"It's funny, I thought we'd see tons of lions out here. But we haven't seen a single one."

"Is better I think."

"Yeah, I guess so." He waited for Idris to finish blowing his nose. Twin strings of snot flew onto the dirt. "Where are we, anyway? Think we're getting close?"

"Only God knows." As if to research the matter, Idris laid down his instrument and picked up his Bible. These were his twin pillars; they held up the whole structure.

"Do me a favor, go talk to Zelalem. He's in charge. He'll know."

"Zelalem is a heathen."

"Don't be silly. This is his livelihood—he does this route once a month. He'll know exactly where we are."

"You do not want to know this," Idris said. "The answer will bring too much pains."

"I thought you liked it out here in the desert."

"I don't like, no. I miss my wife and childs."

It was the closest thing to an autobiographical disclosure Idris had made. Even he seemed mortified by it; he frowned and looked away. "My wife say, stay home. This place was created by God, she say, when his mood was very bad."

"So why did you come then?"

"Dr. Dave, he say, here is a man who needs you. He gives me birr one hundred for each day. So you do not get lost and die."

"Tell you what, I'll double what he's paying if you turn

around and go home right now. Just go home, and forget the whole business. How's that for a deal?"

"Go home you say?"

"Sure. I'll even cover the days you aren't with me. Here." He reached into his fanny pack for his sheaf of bills. They were worn and limp, in faded pastel colors. "Stuff these babies in your pocket. They're all yours."

Idris frowned and looked away into the soft blues and golds of the twilight. He seemed wary, resistant, as if he suspected he was being tricked or manipulated somehow. Or maybe the idea of returning to his wife wasn't quite so appealing as he'd made out. "No. Dr. Dave will be angry."

"He won't even know. Anyway I'll square it with him when I get back to Addis."

"I will think about what you say." Instead of thinking, however, Idris spat on the ground. "When we come to Dallol, I will think then."

"When will that be?"

"Only God knows."

"I bet Zelalem knows too. Why don't you go ask him?"

"Zelalem is a heathen."

"So what? So am I." They were going in circles now. "That doesn't mean we can't be friends, does it?"

In the face of such questions, Idris had a way of looking not just blank but loftily and imperiously so. They had been traveling together for three days; only now did it occur to Teddy that Idris did not like him very much.

"All right, fine. Go ahead and take the birr anyway. You've earned it. It's just weighing me down."

But now Idris wouldn't even look at him. "Is your money, not mine."

Blue skies, brown mountains, black sands . . .

They came to the Sabba River, in the Upper Danakil. Hippos sunned along the banks. Oryx and bushbuck were drinking in the weeds. Bustards and bee-eaters hovered over the water. The ground was like talc. Eventually the river sank away into the basalt and vanished into the salt pans around Lake Assal.

To the north stretched the lava fields, black as pitch. Limbs of petrified wood lay strewn in the gulleys. The ground was broken, pockmarked; the camels whimpered as it cut their feet.

The fever was with him all the time now. He could no longer distinguish what was fever and what was not. Idris kept urging him to drink, but the water went right through him. Everything did. He'd become a hollow vessel through which all things must pass.

His body plodded along mechanically, driven by some stubborn unreasoning engine that churned away at its core. He no longer cared how it worked, what made it run.

Vaguely he understood that they had descended far below sea level, into some sprawling and inhospitable suburb of hell. The heat was stupefying. The air stank of salt. Black ash rings and volcanic cones littered the plains. Termite mounds rose up through the brush, higher than a man's head. *A land of death,* Thesiger called it. And indeed, the whistle of the wind through the canyons sounded to Teddy like the cry of ghosts.

Occasionally in the midst of this desolation they'd happen upon a watering hole with a few round, *tukul*-shaped huts made from reeds and mud and woven palm. They looked sturdy and tough, like armadillo shells. Idris told him they could quickly be collapsed if the need arose and carried away on a man's back.

"Let's get a closer look, what do you say? I'd like to see how they're put together."

"I do not think the people would like, no."

"Too bad. But maybe if I talked to them they'd change their minds. We're all brothers, right? We all came from the same ancestor. I saw her at the museum."

"Who you saw?"

"You know. Lucy." The poor kid, he'd seen her little skeleton laid out in pieces in the basement of the National Museum, like a puzzle not yet complete. Oh, she'd had it good for a while, back in the day, roaming around her verdant valley with its savannas and harboring grasses. But then the mantle had shifted, the climate had changed, and now she and everyone she knew lay entombed beneath the crust. Sad. But then they didn't call this place a depression for nothing.

"The Afar does not wish to meet you in his house. His house is very small, unlike the American house. The American house is very big. Very grand."

"It's true," Teddy said, "we're way out of scale. You should see *my* village. The square footage, the cathedral ceilings—the fixtures alone would blow your mind." For all the distance he'd achieved, Carthage and its discontents still boiled in his blood. "We could learn a thing or two from these guys about downsizing."

Idris thought for a moment. "What is fixtures?"

"Never mind. It's hard to explain."

Idris seemed to take offense at this. A muscle twitched in his jaw. He was a complicated person, more so in many ways than Teddy himself. But he seemed incapable of understanding how a too-big house could be something to complain about, let alone unlearn.

Then all at once they were there. The salt pans of Dallol.

At the sight of that blackened plain quavering woozily in the heat, he almost laughed. Here it was: the bottom of the world. The ground rumbled and tossed. The crust was molten, fissured, like the hide of an elephant, like a shattered pot. Great clouds of ash spumed high in the air, dimming the sun. When he wiped his brow with the back of his wrist it came back dry. He felt in the grip of some terminal hallucination. True, he'd wished to carry himself to the end of things—the beginning of things—the place where ends and beginnings were one. But he'd never expected to find it. Now he scanned the horizon through his telephoto lens, fighting off a small, buglike flutter of disappointment. From here on out there would be nowhere else to look.

"Well, Idris, what do you think? Not in Kansas anymore, huh?"

Idris spat on the ground with no particular emphasis, unimpressed. "Is too hot I think."

"How old are you, Idris? I'm just curious."

"I am thirty-four years."

"Thirty-four!" Teddy roared. "Are you joking? I thought you were older than I was. But you're just a kid. You're just getting *started.*"

Idris looked at him as if he were insane. Maybe he was, Teddy thought. The skin on his hands was like paper; he could see right through to the veins. It was inconceivable: he was an old man. Not just in African terms. In *any* terms.

Idris, having now discharged the last of his responsibilities where the visitor was concerned, turned his mule around and, without a word, commenced the long trudge back to Hamed Ela. There the caravan would be resting at the watering hole, the camels grazing, the nomads sitting cross-legged in a crescent of shade. They'd chew khat and drink mint tea and exchange ritualized hand kisses with men from other caravans, sharing the news—*dagu,* they called it—about weather and trail conditions, political alliances, weddings and funerals, all the information a nomad required to move through the desert and get his business done.

Teddy watched him go with a kind of dreadful elation. He was alone in the desert at last.

He looked out over the shimmering salt flats, the parched mountains, the sunken, shuddering ground. Beyond the hills, the Red Sea was waiting, biding its time. It had been gone for 40 million years, but it was coming back now, reclaiming its old home. Below the restless crust, great plates were in motion, sliding along their transform faults, magma surging up through the Rift even as it sank. The earth dredging and remaking itself, tearing things up and then starting again. And now a new ocean was being born, or rather the old ocean returning from its exile underground. Soon it would arrive en masse. And then all the maps would have to be thrown away, Teddy thought, or else redrawn from scratch, because Africa's Horn, cut off at the root, would break free at last of its mournful, dangling head and go floating off on its own adventure, untethered, unbound. Yes, geologically speaking, it would all happen soon. And then the flood would come and fill this barren valley with its nutrients and organisms, and all the withered fossils would come back to life.

Approaching the camp, he heard a terrible shrieking. The nomads were huddled around the firepit, clucking their tongues, their faces long and sorrowful with worry.

"What's wrong?" he asked Idris. The guide crouched by his mule, reading his Bible by the last of the light. "What's happened?"

"Is one of the camels, he is hurt."

"How bad?"

Idris shrugged.

"Well, let's not hang back here. Let's go see if they need help."

But Idris was absorbed in his Scriptures, or pretending to be; he would not move. So Teddy strode down to the firepit alone.

He found the men gathered in a ragged ring, stroking their beards, looking down at the camel writhing on the ground. Froth was around its mouth. Its neck thrashed blindly back and forth; its eyes rolled up in their sockets. Zelalem crouched beside the camel in the dirt, somberly inspecting its foreleg. It appeared to be broken. He lifted the limb and tested it, twice, then eased it down gently. He put his ear to the creature's heaving flank. Like an old friend, he patted it with his palm and kissed it. Then he murmured a brief prayer. Then from beneath his robes he unsheathed a long, curved dagger and cut the camel's throat.

Something flew up onto Teddy's glasses. By the time he'd wiped them clean, the creature was dead.

Zelalem rose stiffly. His eyes were glittering, his robes spattered with blood. He pushed his way angrily through the men and, covering his face with one hand, strode off into the thorn trees, alone.

Idris was still reading his Bible when Teddy returned from the firepit. They said nothing to each other. Their time together seemed at an end.

Teddy lay on the ground, staring up at the sky's black skin and the stars that prickled its surface like a rash. His tongue probed a vacancy at the back of his mouth. The crown was gone. He'd never felt so lonely, so bereft. What was he doing here? When he closed his eyes, he saw the little covered wood bridge on Montcalm Road, which from a distance always looked like a coffin. But now it looked like what it was: a bridge. The further into blackness he traveled, the more homebound grew his thoughts. His wife, his daughters, his neighbors, even poor old indolent Bruno . . . they were all with him now, tagging along in their own phantom caravan, their features etched over the lava, over the scrubby formations of the hills. He'd thought the empty space would liberate his imagination, had hoped by his adventures to wipe the slates clean. But every erasure left its own prints, own trails, every darkness broken by small, familiar lights.

What a drag, Teddy thought. What a bore. The stars just hung there in their usual arrangements, submitting to the same old hand-drawn stencils and designs. They too had followed him here, to the ends of the earth. He supposed they always would. He'd read about Johanson's discoveries back in the National Museum in Addis; how, years after digging up the Lucy skeleton, they'd found another collection of bones from the same period, two adults and three children, nearby. Family. There was no getting away from it. The codes of the helix were determined to be passed along.

So fine. He knew when he was beaten. It was nearly spring, it was time to go home. Let the stars go on hovering up there, let their lights fall over him like a net. He'd been floundering in nets all his life; he didn't even want to get out from under them any longer. Only to go deeper in, and deeper still, until the borders of the net were no longer visible, no longer borders.

Even out here, it seemed, at the farthest reaches, you still carried your house on your back. And the hell of it was, there was no other shelter.

About the Author

Robert Cohen is the author of three previous novels, *The Organ Builder, The Here and Now,* and *Inspired Sleep,* and a collection of short stories, *The Varieties of Romantic Experience.* His honors include a Guggenheim Fellowship, a Lila Acheson Wallace–*Reader's Digest* Writer's Award, the Ribalow Prize, the Pushcart Prize, and a Whiting Award. He teaches at Middlebury College in Vermont.